D is for Death

D is for Death

Harriet F. Townson

**HODDER &
STOUGHTON**

First published in Great Britain in 2024 by Hodder & Stoughton Limited
An Hachette UK company

1

Copyright © Venetia Books Limited 2024

The right of Harriet F. Townson to be identified as the Author of the Work has been asserted
by her in accordance with the Copyright, Designs and Patents Act 1988.

A CIP catalogue record for this title is available from the British Library

Hardback ISBN 978 1 399 73147 8
Trade Paperback ISBN 978 1 399 73148 5
ebook ISBN 978 1 399 73149 2

Typeset in Sabon MT by Manipal Technologies Limited

Printed and bound in Great Britain by Clays Ltd, Elcograf S.p.A.

Hodder & Stoughton policy is to use papers that are natural, renewable
and recyclable products and made from wood grown in sustainable forests.
The logging and manufacturing processes are expected to conform
to the environmental regulations of the country of origin.

Hodder & Stoughton Limited
Carmelite House
50 Victoria Embankment
London EC4Y 0DZ

www.hodder.co.uk

For Cora and Martha
And for all the giraffes

'How often have I said to you that when you have eliminated the impossible, whatever remains, however improbable, must be the truth?'

Arthur Conan Doyle, *The Sign of the Four*

'I am half sick of shadows,' said the Lady of Shalott.

Alfred, Lord Tennyson, *The Lady of Shalott*

I

The contents of a clergyman's suitcase

London 1935

> *'I am no bird; and no net ensnares me: I am a free human being with an independent will.'*

Dora Wildwood never intended to cause trouble.

Yet trouble seemed to find her, ensnaring her in a net, and it was not until she reached the advanced age of twenty-one that she realised it was high time one threw the net off.

One golden, misty October morning, a train from the West Country arrived in London. Dora Wildwood, lost in her favourite novel, happened to glance up out of the window. Though it was several years since she had been in town, she knew instantly that they were on the final approach to Paddington Station; hurriedly she closed *Jane Eyre* and stood up, removing her cape from the luggage rack so energetically she jabbed an elderly cleric in the chest with her elbow, leaving him wheezing against the carriage door, clutching his heart, hat askew.

'Please, do forgive me – I am most dreadfully sorry,' said Dora, helpfully lifting down his suitcase, and inadvertently flicking open the catch. The lid flew open, and the clergyman's possessions tumbled through the air as if in slow motion, depositing tattered undergarments, long stockings, some rather odd-looking novels with pictures in French, and an orange onto the floor of the carriage.

'Oh my word,' said Dora, removing a sock from her shoulder and handing it to him. 'Sir – once again – I am so *very* sorry.'

Next to her, a respectably upholstered matron gave a low, scandalised moan, and covered her eyes. The cleric, still unable to speak, gave her a beseeching look. *Please*, the look said, *stay away from me*. Dora was used to that look. With a regretful yet polite smile she moved carefully towards the door of the carriage so she might enjoy the last few hundred yards of her arrival into London, hopefully without incident.

She leaned against the cool wood panelling, and watched the city pass by, biting her lip. There was almost too much to see – a manicured green park hemmed with a ribbon of black railings, a tall, Gothic church, a knot of men, unloading barrels from a cart outside a pub. The leaves on the rowan trees lining the white stucco terraces were like coral and yellow flames on black branches against a silver-white sky: just as dramatic, more so in a way, as the rust and mist that crept over the wooded valley below Wildwood House every autumn.

Dora pulled her navy beret down over her shining chestnut hair, buttoned up her tweed cape (lined with teal silk, a twenty-first birthday present from her father), and gathered herself, her knapsack, and her small suitcase. She stood with one trembling hand on the smooth brass handle of the carriage, waiting.

Steam engulfed the train; porters scurried along the platform; passengers emerged, rearranging fur coats and tugging down trilbies, shivering in the sudden chill of an autumn morning. The milk carriage was opened, then came the clink and echo of heavy metal churns from Cornwall and Devon, lifted out onto carts to be taken into town. Through the open window the smell of the city assailed her – heavy, metallic, alive – coal smoke and wood smoke and cigarettes and heavy, spiced perfume.

Carefully she opened the heavy door, and stepped onto the platform.

'Well,' Dora said to herself, looking up at the great arch of the station. Her heart was thumping: all of a sudden, she didn't feel brave and excited, just scared and sad. She couldn't remember at all why she was here, other than that she had always wanted to visit a

Lyons Corner House and see a giraffe and neither of these seemed like much of a reason. She hesitated, and turned back to the carriage door, half minded to get back on. Had she made a dreadful mistake?

Already, the memory of her departure was as though from another life: gathering scant possessions hurriedly into a knapsack, nabbing a lift to the station with dear Albert, huddling in the waiting room until the milk train shuddered through the soft night mist into view, she clambering unsteadily aboard unnoticed by anyone but George Fish, porter, one of many people, little though she knew it, who was On Dora's Side.

'I say!' As she passed First Class now there was a knock on the window, and Dora jumped. 'You! Dora Wildwood! Hi? *Dora Wildwood!* Is that you?'

The speaker, a brilliantine-haired gentleman in his late fifties of florid complexion and suit of rough tweed, peered out of the open window into the swirl of passengers, newspaper boys, and smoke. 'Dash it,' he said to his companion, a listless young woman. 'She's gorn. I'd have sworn that was Furlong's girl, Dora. You know, the one who wrestled the Green Man to the ground last May Day . . . heard she'd eaten the wrong kind of mushroom, what?'

'*Who?*'

'Dora. Wildwood. You know the Wildwoods? Oh – course not. Next village from us. One of the oldest families in the county. All very odd. She's the only child. Mother died, rather strange circs. The daughter is –' he popped a mint into his mouth, crunching it furiously – '*mysterious*. That's the word. Never quite sure if she's a genius or a cretin.'

'Jimmy, I'm *bored*,' said the listless young woman, pulling a fluffy white mink coat around her. 'Let's go. I want to go to Boodles before Quag's. You promised.'

'Let me just see where she's orf to . . .' He stared along the platform. 'Yup, gorn. Funny girl; they say she's run wild. What my aunt Augusta would call a regular hoyden – here, don't frown, my dear. We're in London. Hop out, and I'll take you for a gin cocktail at the Ritz before Boodles *then* lunch, what? Hah! That's more like it.'

The faint mist was lifting: morning sunlight shone through the great steel and glass arch, illuminating the last tattered remains of a piece of bunting left over from the Jubilee. No one saw Dora Wildwood leave the concourse. She had a trick of vanishing even those who knew her could never quite explain; Dora liked it that way. As a child she'd believed life was bright and exciting, there for the taking, but more recently events had taught her when trouble came that it was best to stay at the edges, able to disappear if need be.

'Well, hey ho,' she said, once she was clear of the platform. 'You're here now. Best get on with it.'

She took a crumpled piece of paper out of her pocket.

Dear Dora
I am sorry to hear of your situation. How very unpleasant. It is
best you come to London at once. My maid, Maria, will meet
you at the station and take your bags back to the house. Given
the situation in which you find yourself, I should advise giving
her a password: Fun and games. Do be careful upon arrival for
PIGEONS.
With very great affection
Your godmother Dreda

Dora looked up and around her.

'Well,' she said. 'Here I am.' She ignored the prickling feeling of danger, squared her shoulders and took a deep breath, then jumped, violently, as someone tapped her on the arm.

'Afternoon, miss. Busy?'

Dora turned around, to find a young man in a loud tweed suit smiling at her.

'I'm meeting a friend,' she said. 'Is that you?'

He bared his yellowing teeth in a rictus grin, and said:

'No my dear. But I could be if you want me to be. Fancy a walk?'

'Oh good God,' said Dora. 'Do scram, there's a dear.'

'Hard to get, eh?' said the persistent suitor. 'I say, be friendly.'

'And I say, do leave off—'

'Miss Wildwood?'

Dora spun round. 'Thank goodness,' she said. 'Are you Maria?'

'Be off with you,' said the dark-eyed girl, in front of her. She shook her umbrella at the strange gentleman. 'Here! I'll call the police, I will. Get away.'

'Just a bit of fun, my dear,' said the tweed-suited miscreant. 'A bit of fun.' And he raised his hat, flashed his teeth at her again, and melted away into the crowd.

'Thank you,' said Dora, after he'd gone.

'My pleasure, miss.' There was a slight pause as both women stared at each other.

'Oh! Yes. What's the password?' said Dora and the girl in blue at the same time, and then they smiled at each other. 'Fun and games,' they chorused.

'I'm Maria, Miss, Lady Dreda's maid,' said the girl, holding out her hand. She was dressed neatly in a beautifully cut navy coat and skirt.

'Well, you're the first person I've met in London,' Dora said. 'Apart, of course, from the clergyman and that rather noxious specimen in the tweed suit and a ghastly bore who goes hunting with my father who once shot his groom in the foot. You're the first *nice* person I've met in London.'

'Thank you, Miss,' said Maria. 'Lady Dreda sent me to fetch your bags. She wasn't sure how much luggage you would have been able to bring with you, if you'll excuse me.'

Dora held out the small suitcase and gestured to the knapsack. 'I don't have much. It's awfully kind of you to come and meet me, but there was no need.'

'Lady Dreda sees danger everywhere,' said Maria without expression, 'and she was worrying about you travelling on your own from Somerset, and in such haste, that she thought it would be wise to make sure you reached us safely.'

There was something about the use of the word 'us' that made Dora stop, and blink. Maria took the suitcase from her, and they walked towards the exit. 'I hope your journey to town was comfortable?'

'Very,' said Dora. 'Trains are so exciting, aren't they? I was foolish, however, and didn't realise the one I caught stopped to pick up the milk and the mail and then deposit it, too. We spent an awfully long time offloading milk churns in Middlesex. I leapt off to help at one point, actually.' She gestured at her slightly sodden navy twill skirt. 'I'm sorry if you've been waiting.'

Maria inclined her head politely. 'It couldn't matter less.'

'Thank you. It's almost eleven however; I could have stayed in bed a little longer and got a later train. I do hope—' She narrowed her eyes as they emerged onto Praed Street, taking in the white stucco buildings, the trundling bright red buses that seemed to hurtle out of the smog. 'I know it sounds awfully childish, but you can't imagine how exciting it is to be here.'

Maria smiled. She had not minded waiting; her cousin worked in a patisserie within sight of the station, and she had sat in the window, sketching dress ideas and eating free cakes for two hours. Each time they announced another train was coming into the station she'd hop up to go and see if it was the one she wanted. 'Dora's an unusual girl, but she's not one to make a fuss,' Lady Dreda had told Maria. 'If she says she needs to come and stay, mark my words, Furlong will have done something utterly idiotic again. Or – something else. Her mother, you know . . .' And she had trailed off, biting her lip, and Maria knew not to ask any more questions when she got that look in her eye.

'Look at that conductor in the peaked cap, ringing the bell. Don't you love buses?' Dora was saying.

'I do, Miss.' Maria said, nodding, and she gave a small, secret smile. 'My most favourite thing about them is if I'm quick enough I can nab the single seat on the top deck, right at the back, next to the stairs. It's like being in a little cabin.'

'I'll try that,' said Dora, smiling at her. 'Thanks.'

'You haven't been to London before?'

'My mother and I used to come and stay with Dreda – but that was an awfully long time ago,' said Dora. 'There was the time Albert – that's my greatest friend back at home in Combe Curry, Albert Jubby – and I ran away to London to see a giraffe, because we simply didn't believe it, but we only got as far as Ealing. Very interesting place, Ealing.'

'Really?' said Maria, who had been born within the sound of Bow bells, rather doubtfully.

'Oh yes. The suburbs, all those lovely new houses. Quite marvellous. But Albert's toe started playing up – his big toe,' she clarified, as if Maria might have prior knowledge of other, problematic toes belonging to Albert Jubby. 'It got run over by a mower and it's entirely flat, the cartilage was destroyed and he can roll it up, like – like a brandy snap, you see? It's a marvellous trick, he rolls it out every year at the village fete and the children scream and it makes heaps of money for the Deserving Poor, but it's enormously painful when it's about to rain. Of course something *that* entertaining must come at a price. Don't you agree?'

'No, of course, yes,' said Maria, utterly lost but completely fascinated.

'Anyway, there was no point after that and so I never saw a giraffe, and I still don't really know if they're real or not – I know they are, but sometimes you have to see things with your own eyes.' Dora nodded. 'Forgive me. I have a dreadful habit of rabbiting on. Father sent me to boarding school to cure me of it, and it only made it much worse. I'm most awfully grateful to you for coming to meet me.'

Maria said gently, 'Well, Miss, Lady Dreda's glad you've come to stay. We'll be back home in no time and you can have breakfast and then unpack and decide what you're going to do.'

'Oh, I know what I'm going to do,' said Dora. 'I'm here to find out who murdered my mother.'

'I – see,' Maria said, after a pause. A throng had gathered by the road, waiting for a traffic policeman to signal it was safe to cross. 'But I thought—'

7

'I ran away because I couldn't stay and go through with it, the business at home.' Maria had to strain to hear what Dora was saying. 'But really, you know, I have to discover what happened to Muzz. I feel her near me all the time, she's restless. She wants me to get to the truth. Don't worry, Lady Dreda won't find out, I'll be ever so discreet.' She turned and gave Maria a brief, sweet smile. 'I sound crackers, I am aware of that, and maybe I am. And – oh!' She broke off.

'The bus,' said Maria brightly. 'I know!'

Dora screamed again; and this time the sound made Maria turn around. 'Miss Wildwood'

A long arm, clad in black cloth, had extended itself into the crowd and grabbed Dora's wrist in a vice-like grip. The other hand clamped itself over her mouth: the knuckles gleamed white in the dark melee of bodies, and coats. Pedestrians swelled around them on the pavement, rushing across the road: Maria lost Dora for a second, then the crowd parted for a moment, and she saw her, biting the hand pressed against her face, yanking herself desperately away.

'Oh hell!' she shouted. 'Maria, I'm most dreadfully sorry about this—'

'Here!' Maria yelled. 'Let her go!'

Dora wriggled through the knot of people, working her way to the edge of the group.

'Dora!' a man's voice shouted from behind them. 'I say! Dora! Come back, damn you!'

'Miss Wildwood!' Maria called, a catch in her voice. 'Dora! I say! You! Leave her be!' And in a frenzy, she pushed back at the man trying to shove her out of the way.

'Who the blazes are *you*?' he said, fury twisting his handsome face. 'Get out of my way. She's coming back home with me. Now.'

And he pushed Maria viciously again, knocking her against a surprised, well-upholstered matron who hooked the man with her umbrella and started to give him a piece of her mind about young gentlemen on the streets of London. Maria saw Dora, eyes darting round, looking for escape and whilst the stranger was apologising and untangling himself, she broke free of his hold on her wrist.

'Don't go!' said Maria impulsively. 'Stay with me and I'll see you to Lady Dreda's and—'

Dora smiled. 'Awfully sorry. Can't risk it. Got to take off—'

'Take these sandwiches, at the very least!' Maria said. She fumbled in her pockets. She wanted to cry. 'You must be—' She took something out of the right pocket, and pressed it into Dora's hand. Dora looked down at it in surprise. 'Odd sandwiches,' she said with a smile, but she tucked the package into a pocket and Maria watched as she made her escape down London Street.

The stranger, having now raised his hat to the angry old matron, turned back. He was a young man in a dark suit, trilby on his head, black hair. He shouted after Dora. 'Help!' he said, looking round wildly. 'A girl in a beret has just run orf! She's mad! Very dangerous! Help me catch her!'

'That way!' a balding, barrel-chested man said, pointing south. 'There, you see her, sir?'

Maria, pushing her way through the crowd onto the road. She could just make out Dora, her long legs flying, beret jammed tightly on her head, knapsack on her back, with the tall, dark-haired man in hot pursuit.

The policeman signalled; the pedestrians crossed the road.

For a moment, no traffic went past. Maria could hear a bird singing in a nearby birch tree. She blinked, took a deep breath, and stuffed one hand into her pocket. And then she froze.

'Oh no,' she said, as her fingers closed over a small, soft package, and she drew out a waxed parcel of egg and cress sandwiches. 'I've given her – oh no,' she said.

She looked ahead, blood draining from her face. There was no sign of either of them. 'Oh . . . dear.'

For instead of giving her the sandwiches Lady Dreda had asked her to make up for her – 'She'll be famished, poor girl, I've never known anyone with an appetite like Dora's' – she had handed over the pistol Lady Dreda had asked her to dispose of – 'I've no idea how it came to be in the spare room, Maria dearest, but it absolutely *can't* be in the house. Wrap it in paper and drop it in the nearest canal, but let that be an end to the matter.'

Dora Wildwood had got off the train but, almost immediately, had disappeared, pursued by a vengeful stranger, having accidentally acquired a gun instead of a packet of egg and cress sandwiches.

Slowly, Maria made her way to the bus stop. She realised her mouth was completely dry. Looking down, she saw she still had Dora's suitcase. It had been less than ten minutes since Dora had arrived in London.

2

Lady Dreda's breakfast is disturbed

'Vanished? What do you *mean*, vanished?'

'I mean, my lady, she just disappeared, and a tall, dark man was chasing her. I searched everywhere for her. I'm dreadfully sorry –' Maria stood in the breakfast room, panting, and then mopped her face – 'There wasn't time to ask her where she was going to go. I don't think she knew.'

A dollop of marmalade fell from the spoon in Lady Dreda Uglow's hand onto her plate.

'Oh dear,' she said, shaking her head. 'I knew she'd cause trouble. I simply *knew* it.'

An hour ago Lady Dreda had been sitting in the yellow and black little breakfast room overlooking Lloyd Square in Clerkenwell, idly finalising the seating plan for her intimate dinner *soirée* that evening, and flicking through the *Illustrated London News*, marvelling at Vivien Leigh's gun-metal grey silk evening dress and matching bolero jacket with the darling pageboy collar, at the shock of reading about Wallis Simpson dining at the Savoy in a group with the Prince of Wales, tutting sympathetically at the unemployment figures, a picture of some barefoot children in rags in South London, picking over litter. The scent of polished wood, of fresh coffee, of lingering warmth and spice in the air from the window, opened just a little on this crisp, beautiful morning.

A gloomy person by nature, Lady Dreda very much enjoyed autumn: every year at about this time she reread *Childe Harold*, *Mariana*, *Goblin Market*, and any other appropriately Gothic poems featuring innocence ravished, death, decay, and leaf mould. She had looked out *The Lady of Shalott* to peruse on this day in hopes the east wind might pick up, necessitating a day indoors, and had just helped herself to a fourth piece of toast when the front door had slammed so ferociously and Maria had burst into the room so dramatically that Lady Dreda had dropped it, butter-side down.

Lady Dreda had not seen Maria with a hair out of place in the five years she had worked for her but now her hat was askew, her face flushed. She regarded her with surprise, then horror, as Maria told her the dreadful news: that Dora had vanished.

'A tall dark man chased her away? You – you did *meet* her though, Maria? You gave the password?'

'Yes, my lady.' Maria's eyes were huge; Lady Dreda slid a half pint of Guinness, which she normally drank with her toast, over towards her. Maria gulped it down, gratefully.

'Did she say why she was coming to London?'

'Thank you. No, my lady.'

'Nothing at all?'

Maria appeared to be struggling with what Dora had told her. 'Well, she said something about having to get away, and how she'd always wanted to see some giraffes—'

'Some giraffes? What are you talking about?'

'Oh, and her friend,' said Maria desperately. 'The one with the toe that rolls up—'

'Maria,' said Dreda sharply. 'My dear girl, you're babbling. Did you give her the sandwiches?'

'Oh, Your Ladyship –' Maria, normally so calm and collected, so grave, so sensible, let out a panicked howl – 'I'm so awfully sorry. I – I gave her the gun, by mistake,' she said.

'Instead of the sandwiches?'

'Instead of the sandwiches.'

Lady Dreda contemplated the magazine, the ruined breakfast, the cosy fire. She closed her eyes briefly.

'I'll – I'll go without pay, my lady, I'll—'

'Now, then, dear Maria. Calm down,' Lady Dreda said firmly. 'Don't panic. Really. We've no idea why the gun was under the floorboards in the spare bedroom. We only decided to get rid of it. I think – well, it's one of those things, isn't it? Nothing to be done about it. And well, Dora is a sensible girl.' She said this confidently, but could not quite meet Maria's eye. 'No, she is. Don't worry.'

Maria took a deep breath, and pressed her hands to her cheeks. 'She was awfully interesting. I've never met anyone like her.'

'No,' said Lady Dreda thoughtfully. 'No, you're probably right. I haven't seen her for a while, but you're right. Her mother was the same. Fascinated by everything.'

Lady Dreda still remembered with a shudder her final Saturday-to-Monday at Wildwood House with her dear friend Elizabeth, Dora's mother – it must be the last time she'd seen Dora, when she thought about it. The whole thing was something of a blur – she could recall with any clarity only a house so glacial in temperature she had worn her fur to bed. And a bird that had flown into the conservatory and spoiled Dreda's new delicious peacock kimono. And Mrs Lah Lah – yes, that was really what they called her – the woman was a housekeeper yet was *most* forward, making utterly inappropriate jokes about the family dog and its relationship with a dining chair, which Lady Dreda, who liked to think of herself as broadminded, had found beyond the pale.

Other memories came back. The cream was fresh, but there was dung in it. And poor dear Elizabeth, swathed in ancient knitwear, her hair actually fastened with a *pencil*, laughing and finding the whole situation hilarious. (She had seemed happy, truly happy. What on earth had gone wrong there?) And in the midst of it all, a small, determined child with curly brown hair who kept a pet kitten in one of her large pockets, a supply of peppermint creams in the other, and kept reading pages aloud from *Jane Eyre* whilst an extraordinarily dirty young boy from the farm down the lane, unbelievably, had sat next to Dreda, counting out small pine cones into a sort of bowl that appeared to be fashioned from mud. He had glared at her whenever she glanced at Dora, over whom he clearly felt protective. On Sunday night, after this juvenile guardsman had been persuaded to return home, Dora had somehow climbed into the attic, become entangled in a bedsheet and fallen half out of the hatch, and when the dreadful Mrs Lah Lah found her, dangling upside down, utterly encased in Irish linen but for her rather long nose poking out, her shoulder dislocated, Dora had said she was practising at being Tutankhamun. And of all things Elizabeth had simply *laughed*, wrenched the shoulder back into place, and given her small daughter a brandy. Dreda was appalled, and left as soon as possible after breakfast (she would have gone before, but as we have seen breakfast was her favourite meal of the day, and Elizabeth's forward housekeeper's devilled kidneys were *particularly* good, the bacon from the despised farm down the road, and Lady Dreda was at that time trying something called a Bacon and Offal cure which entailed eating only those two and the broth derived from them).

But Elizabeth was dead now these four years and her daughter motherless and alone, her hopeless father off with that dreadful French woman, and Combe Curry still as strange and unsuitable a place as ever, particularly for a young woman wishing to acquire a patina of maturity and sophistication. All because Elizabeth had gone on a walking holiday.

So Lady Dreda had not believed her goddaughter when she asked to impose herself on her but confidently asserted there would be no trouble, even though the tenor of the letter had given her pause.

Dear Dreda
Please may I come and stay with you? I should like to visit London again, and very much want to see the giraffes at the zoo. And I find myself in a situation re: marriage from which I should be glad to disentangle myself. There will be no trouble, I promise, but I am quite alone aside from you, and Muzz left me a note which said that were I to need help I should go to you. I am not able to say more at this time. I am quite desperate.

With love
Your goddaughter
Dora Wildwood

Dreda disliked trouble. However, she had stood at the font of St Cyprian's church in Combe Curry all those years ago and promised to protect her godchild against any manner of sin and the devil and she would never be accused of shirking her duty.

(Reading up on the ancient, tiny church later, she had discovered St Cyprian was the patron saint of occultists and the panels around the church which she took to be of Christians conquering the devil were in fact of an orgy during Roman times. Various scenes, including one of a man with a bowl of figs and a lady devil, she supposed one would call her, kept coming back to Lady Dreda for months, whenever she closed her eyes.)

Lady Dreda sighed. She looked hopefully at the piece of toast, but found her appetite had quite gone.

'My lady, what should I do?' Maria had removed her coat, folded it, and stood, awaiting a decision.

'Do?' snapped her mistress. 'I've absolutely no idea. It's like looking for a needle in a haystack. I suppose we have to wait for her to turn up again. And hope in the meantime she comes to no harm.' They looked at each other, each unwilling to say what she thought. Lady Dreda slumped a little in her chair, and Maria nodded and turned to go, but as she reached the door Mrs Bundle, the housekeeper, appeared, waving a telegram.

'My lady, a telegram for you.' She gave Maria a covert glance. The glance said: *more trouble. Have extra toast on standby.*

Lady Dreda gave a small moan, like the Lady of Shalott, as Mrs Bundle bustled forwards, slapping the thin paper down on the breakfast table. 'Well, as I expected,' Lady Dreda said, scanning it. 'It's from her father. Hopeless.'

Maria leaned over and stared at the paper.

TO: UGLOW
FROM: WILDWOOD
IS DORA WITH YOU STOP SHE HAS VANISHED STOP
LEFT A NOTE SAYING COULDN'T GO THROUGH WITH
IT STOP ONLY CLUE AS TO WHEREABOUTS SHE TOLD
LOCAL IDIOT WHO STYLES HIMSELF DRUID SHE WAS
GOING TO LONDON RE GIRAFFES STOP SINCE YOU
ARE ONLY LONDON ACQUAINTANCE BE GRATEFUL
INFORM IMMEDIATELY IF SHE IS THERE STOP SHE
MUST RETURN IN TIME FOR WEDDING STOP FURLONG
WILDWOOD

'What wedding?' Lady Dreda demanded. 'I mean it's all a terrible mystery. Oh, I hate mysteries. Did she mention a wedding to you?'

'My lady, it was only a few minutes,' said Maria. 'Barely enough time to say anything. Apart from the giraffes, of course. And her friend with the – well, he has a flat toe, he can roll it up . . .'

'Do not,' said Lady Dreda, 'mention the friend with the flat toe again, if you please.'

'Yes, my lady. She didn't say anything about a wedding, though,' said Maria. Even after the Guinness her mouth was still dry, and she couldn't have explained why, only that there was something so very appealing about Dora Wildwood she was quite distressed to think of that strange man hunting her down.

Lady Dreda, despite appearances, was an intensely practical woman. 'Whenever Elizabeth went to London she headed straight for the library,' she said, folding up the telegram and putting it in the pocket of her kimono. 'We must hope Dora does the same. Gracious, it's nearly lunchtime. If we've not heard from her by this evening, I'll telephone the police. But perhaps for now, given . . . everything –' again they stared at each other – 'we must hope she is safe. Maria, my dear girl, thank you for your assistance. You are my mainstay and I am so grateful. Will you make sure her room is ready? No – ah, other surprises there? We'll have salmon mousse for supper. Nice and light.'

Maria nodded gratefully, and withdrew. Lady Dreda picked up the marmalade jar and placed a fresh, glistening orange dollop on her toast. She stared out of the window, chewing, quite lost in thought until Mrs Bundle brought in some more buttered toast and set it before her. Lady Dreda nodded her thanks. She had very little appetite, but after the shock of this morning perhaps she might have just one more slice.

3

Strides short and fast, girls

Dora had run through the garden squares of Bayswater, out onto the Edgware Road, with no clear idea of where she was other than that she must head south, towards Piccadilly. She always knew where north and south were, it was a quirk of hers to be certain of the direction she was travelling even if she didn't know the destination. Halfway down the Edgware Road, hoping she had thrown off her pursuer, a 23 bus appeared. She thought of the single seat at the top Maria had told her about.

'Might as well,' she said to herself, and climbed aboard, leaping upstairs and finding, to her pleasure, the single seat unoccupied.

As the bus barrelled around Marble Arch and down Park Lane, Dora sat with her face pressed to the window, staring at the grand hotels, the beautifully tailored doormen trimmed with gleaming gold braid stationed outside each one, the sleek cars shimmering silver, post-box red or powder blue. Women in velvet, furs and cream silk, with glittering jewels and their shining, waved hair. Dora's stepmother, Carine, had despaired of making her gawky new daughter care about hair, face and clothes. It enraged her that Dora could throw on an old pullover, tweed slacks, and a woollen hat and look as though she'd just been hired as a model for a Burberry photographic shoot. Her eyelashes particularly infuriated her: thick, black, long, straight, they fringed her dark brown, watchful eyes, which so often brimmed with laughter but which, very few people could have told you, never stopped looking, and noticing.

The bus lurched around into Piccadilly, and she saw the sloping vista of Green Park which gave way to Buckingham Palace and St James's and the great buildings of state in Whitehall. The King was at home; the Union Flag was fluttering in the dull breeze. Dora picked her knapsack up. She opened it up, to check the little notebook she'd brought was still with her. There were two peppermint creams wrapped in foil. She would save them for later.

'Oh, I do love the top of the bus,' she said to herself.

It seemed almost impossible that it was only six hours ago she had got up in the dark, ridden in the cart with Albert down the long lane to the station, shivering in the sharp autumn cold that had not yet quite arrived in the capital. It was another lifetime. And now she was here, in London, and she was never going back, not if they dragged her.

At the stop opposite the Ritz, Dora hopped off, waving to the driver. As she clutched the shoulder straps of her knapsack she blinked, getting her bearings. A black cab drew up beside her, and she knew what would happen before it did. A door flung open; someone gripped her arm in a painful hold.

'That's her, driver. Thank you.' The man turned to her. 'Dora, you fool. At last. For God's sake, we're to be married in three weeks, dammit. What do you mean by all this?'

Dora stared up into the face of her pursuer. 'Charles,' she said wearily. 'Hullo. I'm sorry about everything. The wedding, and so forth. But I can't marry you, and that's all there is to it.'

The young man ground his teeth. 'Good God,' he said, shaking her, and wiping his brow with his forearm. 'Do you have any idea how much trouble you've caused?' He gave her a half-dismissive, half-contemptuous flick on the cheek with a finger. 'You really are a silly girl. You're just tired. Come along,' he said, as if to a recalcitrant dog.

'I'm not a girl any more—' she attempted to say but he talked over her. He was always talking over her.

'Here's what I want to know. Why'd you agree to marry me, then?' He rocked up onto his toes, triumphantly. 'See? You did, you know.'

Dora gazed at him steadily. 'I don't love you, Charles. People often say they'll do things they don't really want to. Or don't really think through. I am awfully sorry.'

'You can't simply say "I am awfully sorry", Dora.'

'I am, nonetheless,' said Dora. She shook herself free from Charles's frenzied grip, and gently brushed something invisible from the cloth on her jacket. 'Charles, dear, you must accept my apologies—'

'A hundred chickens, Dora. The Silk-Butters silver cruet, brought up out of the vault and polished by Weatherby for five bally days so we can see our faces in it. All the tapestries of the Great Awakening of Denis Silk-Butters specially cleaned and hung in the church. And now Mother's old complaint has flared up and she's saying after the trouble you've caused she never wants to see you again.'

'Well, if she insists . . .' Dora said slowly.

'You can't just hare off on a whim. You have obligations.'

'Very maligned animal, the hare,' Dora said thoughtfully. 'They're not pushy and cocky at all. They don't peck, not like hens. Shy. Very fast, of course. But not swaggerers. If you look at the average hare—'

'Good God,' said Charles furiously, his face darkening. 'I've had enough of this nonsense. Now, come on.' His hands gripped her arms above the elbows, tightening their hold, and she gave a small gasp.

'Charles,' said Dora, with one last effort. 'I really don't want to go back to Combe Curry. At least – not with y— oh, please, Charles, don't do that. It hurts. It really—'

A shop girl, hurrying past, paused to adjust a seam, and looked up at them both, quietly questioning. Her eyes met Dora's. *Are you all right*, her expression said.

But what could she do? There was nothing she could do. Dora blinked, and nodded, and the girl carried on.

'You don't really have a choice, Dora. Your father says he'll cut you off if you don't come. Harwood Hall needs a mistress, I need

a wife, and there's the chickens. Mother won't do it and someone has to. The magnetic forces are extremely strong around the
chicken coop, and it gives her a headache every time she goes near.
Plus her damned dog keeps eating them.'

'Awfully romantic,' Dora said under her breath.

Charles gave her behind a small, tight squeeze. 'Don't be like
that, old girl. Romance is fine for the pictures. It's fine. But it's
not real. You always knew,' said Charles, then he patted his
suit pockets for his wallet and his hipflask, as he did about ten
times a day. 'You knew we were to be married, it's been made
very clear to you since you were a girl – I know your mother
put ideas in your head, but she's not here now, is she? What else
will you do?' At the mention of her mother, Dora's eyes had
widened, and she froze in his arms. Charles took this as some
kind of assent. 'There we go. Now, we can get the Bakerloo line
to Padders and be back at home for supper. Whole business forgotten. And I'm sure once you've whelped, Mother will forgive
you – she's always saying she was the same, hated it at first.
What do you say?'

Dora looked up, at him, at the square in the distance, at the
white sky. She closed her eyes briefly, still breathing hard.

'Yes,' she said meekly, after a moment.

'Really?' His surprise showed in Charles's voice.

'Yes, really. I suppose I panicked. Too daunting, getting married,
you know.' She met his gaze frankly. 'I'm awfully sorry, Charles.'

'Well,' said Charles. His grip relaxed on her, and she sank back
down, and moved away from him, just a little. 'Right then. Not at
all. I suppose you wanted an adventure, didn't you?'

'I did rather. Gets a bit stale, hanging about at home. You know
I love the countryside, but since Daddy went off and my particular friends were all married it's been terribly dull.' And slowly she
slid her arm through his. He patted her fingers as they strolled
towards the Tube.

'You're shaking,' he said. 'Suppose I gave you rather a fright.
Darling Dora.'

'Oh,' she said, leaning against him. 'A little. But it's marvellous to think you cared enough to come down and rescue me.'

Charles gave a low grunt of approval. 'Well, you've had a good day out. And I don't really mind that, you know, it's not a prison. Plenty of time for days out in London after we're married. No time for that now, however, ought to get you back home.' His hand rested lightly on her rear end again, half invasive, half pushing her along the road.

'Rather,' Dora agreed. 'Oh Charles. I do dislike London. It's so busy. Far too many people.'

'It's a hell hole. Full of dreadful people. Had to move some hag with a sob story about a dead miner husband out of the way at the station. Listen, we'll have time for a drink in the restaurant car if we hurry, what?'

A heavy fog had fallen over Piccadilly, wreathing everything in wispy mist. From a brazier by the entrance to the Tube came the sweet, burnt-butter smell of roasting chestnuts. Dora wrinkled her nose. The sound of the *Evening Standard* seller and the man with a mouth organ and the puttering of cars filled the air.

A long, low Daimler, the colour of winter mist in the gathering gloom, purred slowly past them.

A woman stared out, catching Dora's eye. Her face was perfect, sculptured cheekbones giving way to silver-blond hair set in soft cascading waves, a starburst of diamonds at each ear. She gave a small gasp as she looked at Dora, scanning her up and down, assessing her figure: rather like, Dora thought with a flash, the lingerie-fitter at Jordan & Wright in Bath assessed one, as though she was reading Dora, top to bottom, like a scroll. She assessed Charles, who did not notice her, absorbed as he was by some mauve-and-fuschia diamond-panelled shooting stockings in the window of a gentleman's outfitters.

Then the woman sank back into her dark mink fur stole, closing her eyes, so that her long black eyelashes, dark against the pale face, fluttered against her creamy skin.

There was something so elegant, so languorous, so independent about her, about the way she spread herself out across the seats as if it was her due. Like a Snow Queen.

I know her, thought Dora. But why do I know her?

A long-ago memory was pushing to the surface of her subconscious. Running across the lawn at home . . . But it was gone.

'Jolly nice shooting stockings those,' said Charles. 'Wedding present, what?'

'What?' said Dora absently. Then she recalled herself, staring at the shooting stockings. 'Those? Oh, when we get married, Charles, I promise I'll buy them for you.'

'Hawf.' Charles laughed, pleased with himself.

They had arrived at the top of the steps that descended into Piccadilly Tube station, and a warm, golden light rippled out towards them. Dora gave a deep breath.

'It was a glorious day, Charles, you're right.'

'Yarp,' said Charles, looking idly at his wristwatch.

'But it's time we both faced the future. Went home.' She pinched his arm as they went down the steps into the station and then put her hand in her pocket, and felt the small object Maria had pressed into her hand. It had been wrapped in waxed paper and tied with string, which had fallen off. It was heavy, cold, metallic, beautiful. She had forgotten all about it. Dora gripped it in her hand.

'Marvellous,' he said. 'Silly thing.' And he flicked her cheek again.

Dora stopped on the fourth step up from the bottom, lifting the hand in her pocket. 'But – oh Charles?'

'Yes, old thing?'

Dora had moved two steps further up. She removed her hand. She was holding a tiny, mother-of-pearl pistol. She pointed it at Charles, mimicking something she had seen in an American film about a gangster.

'Here!' he said, in surprise. 'What the devil have you got there!'

In response Dora pressed the gun to his chest, very lightly.

'You didn't listen to me. I don't want to marry you. I don't care about your mother's damned cruet or her awful rash. I'm never, ever buying you those disgusting stockings. I'm not marrying you or any of that or having your children and I'm not looking after your horrible chickens. In fact I hope the chickens peck your eyes out whilst you sleep. Don't grab me like that again. Me or anyone, in fact.'

She dropped the gun back into her pocket and as she did Charles lunged for her. 'Give that here!' he said, and without thinking, with a light, balletic kick, Dora jabbed him in the stomach, sending him ricocheting backwards, so that he slid slowly along the brass railings down to the floor, becoming entangled with a small Jack Russell, its lead, and its angry owner, who hit him with her umbrella.

Charles howled, and started shouting her name again, but by the time he'd scrambled to his feet, dealt with the angry dog and owner, brushed himself off, and darted back up the steps, of course, Dora had vanished.

'Damn it,' he said to himself, his face twisted with ugly rage. 'Damn her to hell.' But he went after her, lumbering up the stairs, pushing commuters out of the way, the greyhound chasing the hare.

*   *   *

Upstairs, back on the street, Dora started running again. 'Too tiresome,' she said to the newspaper boy selling the evening edition. She ran down the street again towards the square she'd seen before, muttering to herself under her breath. 'Buck up, old girl. Keep going.'

She wondered why Maria had given her a gun: it seemed such a *strange* thing to do, and she wondered too whether Lady Dreda was as she remembered her, or had she transitioned since their last meeting into a ruthless backstreet gangster? It would be rather out of character, but Dora knew people were capable of very great change. 'Well, well,' she said, patting the gun, though truthfully she wished she didn't have it, and it was another problem she had to solve. In short, her spirits were daunted, and that was unlike her. She was tired, not having slept, and not having eaten lunch. Peppermint creams were not enough to fill one up. She needed a stroke of luck.

The stroke of luck strangely enough was that, as she ran through the garden square, she tripped on a stone and tumbled over, onto the pavement, where she landed with a thud and lay, slightly dazed, wondering if she was dreaming.

Thoroughly dispirited by now, she crawled out of the square and found her way to the building at the corner of St James's Square, where she collapsed onto its steps, wanting to laugh, for it all seemed so ridiculous now, or cry, because it was all a bit much. She wasn't sure.

After a little while a voice behind her said, 'I say, I don't want to disturb you but . . . Are you all right?'

'Yes, I'm perfectly fine,' Dora said rather sharply, because she thought it was a silly question.

'Could you move out of the way then?'

'Oh. I do apologise.' Dora shuffled along and looked behind her. It was a curious building, she saw now. It had six long low steps up to a wooden door. Through the large windows she could see the ground floor was wooden – wooden shelves, desks, hooks – and as she looked up she could just make out the first floor, which was a series of thin, tall windows. Warm golden orbs of light shone in the gathering mist. She had been in London for hours, and it felt as if she hadn't had a moment's safety. 'There,' she said shortly.

The man behind her had come back down the steps. He tapped her on the shoulder, and held out his hand. She flinched at his touch, but let him gently help her up.

'Why don't you come inside?'

He was tall but slight, his face hidden behind tortoiseshell spectacles. A short lock of light brown hair fell into his face as he hauled her to her feet, his thin hands surprisingly strong.

'It's jolly cold,' he said awkwardly. 'And I see you've hurt yourself.'

'Well, I know that,' said Dora, feeling rather murderous towards him, representing as he did in that moment All Men.

'I am being a dope. I mean, come in and have a cup of tea.' Dora looked up at the thin, softly lit building. 'This is a library, you know.'

'The London Library,' said Dora slowly. 'It is, isn't it? I think I was trying to make my way here.'

He gave her a quick look. 'Ah.'

'You don't understand. Without realising it I knew the way here.'

'I do understand,' he said with a quick smile. He shrugged. 'I did too, a couple of years ago. It's an excellent idea, you know. You can sit in the warmth and read a book until you've decided what you want to do next. What do you say?'

'What do I say?' Dora said. 'Yes please. Only – could you hurry, do you think? I'm trying to avoid my fiancé. Ex-fiancé, rather. I'd rather he didn't spot me. I know it sounds rather odd.'

'Not at all,' said the young man. He watched her, head on one side. 'I say, do come inside and get out of this smog. It's come out of nowhere and it does trip one up, I find. And you'll be safe. From the sounds of it, whoever's after you isn't a great one for libraries.'

Dora laughed. 'I should say so. No, you're right. Thank you.' She held out her hand, smiling frankly up at him from the steps. 'I'm Dora, by the way. Dora Wildwood.'

The young man bent over, and they shook hands.

'Good afternoon, Miss Wildwood. I'm Rutherford. Aha! No. Stark.'

'What?'

'Ben Stark. Is my name.'

'You just said your name was Rutherford Stark.'

He hesitated. 'Oh, well I didn't. You must have misheard.'

'I jolly well didn't.' Dora stared at him. 'I say, I think you might have some sort of issue with – oh, one's inner voice, does one call it that? If you think that's what you said.'

'I assure you that is not the case, Miss Wildwood,' said Ben Stark crossly. 'It's Ben. Definitely Ben. Ben Stark. Thank you. Now do come inside. Perhaps refrain from mentioning the dangerous deranged fiancé to anyone, will you? Just try to be . . . normal.'

'Is that advice? How extraordinary. Saucy pedantic wretch, go chide someone else.'

'Don't quote Donne at me,' said Ben Stark, blinking down at her as if she were an octopus that had suddenly slid out of a tank at the zoo and started talking to him.

'I jolly well will if I want,' said Dora. She looked up. 'Chewing your knuckles is awfully bad for them, you know. Decays the joints. At home—' She stopped. 'Well, never mind. You shouldn't do it because you're unhappy, that's all.'

'How do you—' Ben Stark stopped. 'It's been rather a gruesome day in the library, that's all.'

'I should have thought all days in the library were marvellous,' Dora said.

'Sometimes,' he said, 'they are not. Some days are simply bad days. Forgive me speaking to you like this, Miss Wildwood. And for – saying you should be normal.'

'I won't give it another thought.'

'After all, one of the blessings of attaining one's majority is discovering those people one cares most about don't bother much about normal.'

'That is very true,' said Dora. 'In fact the older I get the more I see how often the good bits of life are in the abnormal. I never had to be normal, though,' she added sadly, 'not until quite recently. It's awfully hard. Let's go in.' The wind shivered through the trees in the square, as Ben Stark opened the door to the library.

'I notice your cape is rather muddied, where you fell,' he said, tentatively. 'Would you like to—'

'Your jacket has a tear in the seam, right shoulder, back,' said Dora, not looking at him. 'And some paint on the cuff. Would you like to—?'

'How did you notice that?' said Mr Stark, glancing down at his cuff, then craning his neck to see behind him, but Dora had gone ahead of him, and did not appear to have heard.

*   *   *

Charles Silk-Butters rounded the corner, calling her name, as the door to the London Library closed behind Dora and her new companion. He didn't notice the tall thin building, the one that had 'Library' on its frontage in nice gold paint. He'd never really been one for books. Made his eyes glaze over. Which was just as well.

Someone tapped him on the shoulder. 'I say, old boy. Everything all right?'

'Yes,' he said crossly. 'Mind your own business. Just looking for a young woman, that's all. I say. . . you haven't seen her, have you?'

And he pulled out a black-and-white photograph of Dora, taken on her twenty-first birthday a month ago, and showed it to the stranger, whose expression changed so imperceptibly Charles did not notice.

'What awfully bad luck, losing someone. I'm killing time, you might say. Come this way, why don't you?'

*   *   *

But Dora knew none of this. Within the hour she was browsing the Fiction section of the London Library, R–Z, her knee bound up in a handkerchief and throbbing only slightly, her slender fingers running along the spines of books, eyes darting ahead. She had made it to a library, and she knew all would be well, for the moment at least, for nothing bad *ever* happened in libraries, or bookshops, and that was simply fact.

28

4

Bookish people

Disappointingly, a quick glance at his engraved nameplate on the Issue Desk confirmed to Dora that Ben Stark was indeed the name of the young man who'd rescued her outside. He was an assistant librarian.

'Why don't you sign in here and I'll show you around,' he'd said, as they stood in the high-ceilinged, wood-panelled Issue Hall. 'I'll take your bag; I'm not saying you'll knock over the First Folio but they are rather strict about that sort of thing,' and gently he took her knapsack.

Dora looked around her, taking it all in, her breathing still slightly ragged. The ground floor was one huge hall, lined with wooden panelling. It was warm and welcoming, and smelled of all one's favourite things: books, beeswax polish, wood smoke. Light flooded the hall from the windows at the front and at the back, where there was a courtyard, behind which she could just make out a secondary building, through whose narrow long windows one could see only books – stacks and stacks of them, from ground floor to sky. As she had done before she breathed in deeply, then out, and this time she truly felt something leave her, something dark and heavy. She was safe here.

Ben Stark cleared his throat, and she recalled herself. To her right was the welcome desk, from behind which a smartly dressed, thin-faced young clerk nodded at her, his starched collar so high it almost reached his ears. To the left, where Ben's nameplate was, a long mahogany counter, behind which sat a line of men and women, carefully stamping books or writing in large ledgers.

'That's Mikey Clark,' said Ben, gesturing to the young man. 'He's the junior clerk. I suggest you stay here for the afternoon, or until you're quite sure the coast is clear, and then I'll see you onto a bus.'

'You don't need to do that. When do you close?'

'Six p.m.,' he said. 'I'd like to if you don't mind, just to make sure that chap isn't hanging around, and your knee isn't giving you too much pain.'

'That's awfully kind.'

'Don't mention it.' And from his pocket he produced a large clean cotton handkerchief. 'Here,' he said. Gently efficient, he tied it over her knee, over her torn woollen tights. 'You'll need to wash it clean when you return home tonight,' he said, and then, perfectly calm, he patted the knee and stood up. Dora opened her mouth to thank him but he forestalled her: 'There. Now, Mikey – could you—' But he broke off as, from behind a closed door on the other side of the hall came the sound of shouting and something crashing to the ground. Dora saw Ben stiffen, flinching slightly. Mikey rolled his eyes, but even he turned slightly pale.

'What was that?' said Dora.

'Sir Edwin Mountjoy. Chief Librarian. He's furious about something. Most probably our resident mystery.' The shouts grew louder. 'I should go and attend to him.' Ben Stark removed his round tortoiseshell glasses and polished them briefly, before putting them back on his nose, enough time for Dora to notice his high cheekbones, dark eyes, the stern brows, the glasses softening and hardening his appearance at the same time. 'Mikey will look after you, Miss Wildwood, do excuse me.'

'Of course,' said Dora, nodding emphatically to show she didn't care if he stayed or not, that he wasn't the only kind person she'd met in London, the brief encouter with Maria aside, that she was absolutely fine. 'Do go, Mr Stark.'

The London Library was a subscription library, and there was some difficulty with Mikey about her entrance, happily solved when Dora remembered she was a life member, a gift purchased for her at her birth by her mother.

'Elizabeth Wildwood. Dawkins was her maiden name.'

The records, however, were not to be located – they were in the basement, someone would be sent to get them – if she had any other form of identification, any papers . . .

Dora had to explain that no, she had nothing with her. She could telephone her godmother, Lady Dreda Uglow, who had been married to a Cabinet minister, if that would suffice?

'It's rather irregular, Miss,' said the young man behind the desk, not without glee. 'I'm not sure—'

'Oh please. I need to just stay for an hour or so, the shortest time, just to—'

'Miss, library rules and regulations—'

'Mikey, don't be a beast,' said a voice behind her. 'Let her in, for goodness' sake, she's trying to shake off a dreadful young man. Did I hear you say Elizabeth Wildwood's name? Now, how do I know you? Because I'm certain I do. And I want to write about you. You're simply charming.'

Dora turned. An older woman was standing behind her, the very same vision of beauty she had seen minutes earlier in the Daimler. Draped around her neck and shoulders was a mink stole, its dark brown fading to violet. Under it she wore a plush velvet evening coat like a loose shrug, lined with oyster silk, and her slender figure was encased in coffee silk, darling oyster-pink silk shoes with the thinnest straps like ribbons studded with diamonds at the button.

'It's you!' Dora recalled her manners, and held out her hand. 'I'm Dora Wildwood,' she said. 'How do you do?'

The woman inhaled, and took Dora's hand in hers. Her skin was softer than the finest face powder and she smelled of roses in a garden on a summer's evening. 'My goodness, how strange,' she said, staring into Dora's face, looking intently at her. 'Yes of course, but you won't remember me. Elizabeth's daughter. I knew it.' She shook her head, quite taken aback. 'Goodness, goodness. Darling Dora. You've no idea how marvellous it is to see you. Because I've wondered about you, so much. Elizabeth told me once that I was hopeless at remembering what was important, and she was right.'

Dora nodded. 'Oh, yes. I'm so sorry, do forgive me – but who are you?'

'Goodness, what must you think of me. I'm Venetia!' She touched her chest, beaming at Dora.

Behind them, Mikey Clark slammed a drawer shut loudly, and made a clicking noise under his tongue as if to say *what a country bumpkin.*

'Do you know Mikey? He's saved my bacon on more occasions than I care to remember. Staunched a nosebleed for me once, didn't you, you darling boy?'

'I'm happy to say I did.' The clerk flinched slightly. 'Very kind of you, Miss Strallen.'

'Strallen?' said Dora, her eyes widening. 'You're – Venetia – *Strallen?*'

'Yes, darling,' said the tall, blonde vision in silk, clasping Dora's fingers in her hand. 'That's me.'

'Venetia Strallen!' Dora flushed with pleasure. 'Of course! Muzz was so proud of you.' She took a step back, drinking this information fully in. 'Why, I – I adore your books! I've read everything you've written! *Death in Beach Pyjamas* is my absolute favourite! And *Whisky, Soda and Arsenic!*' She pumped Venetia Strallen's arm up and down, as a slow smile crept across the woman's face. 'I'm sure I'm about the millionth person to tell you this but *Lady, Be Good!* is the best whodunnit I've ever read. Gosh, how did you think of that twist? You must be so awfully clever. Muzz always said you were the cleverest person she knew.'

Venetia shrugged her slim shoulders expressively and gave a small laugh. 'Hardly. Most of it's smoke and mirrors, you know.' Her eyes darted nervously around; Dora wondered why she seemed so on edge. 'Forgive me, darling Dora. Writers don't like talking about how they write.'

'You're hugely popular in Combe Curry, because of my mother. She bought your books for everyone. Even Mrs Gritten, and she thinks detective fiction is the work of the devil.' Dora stopped. 'She talks to him, you see. Regularly. Well, so she claims. Anyway, she burned your last book. She said there was evil in it.'

'Gosh,' said Venetia. 'How grim, darling. Well, it's a sold copy, isn't it?'

Dora laughed. 'I say, it is lovely to meet you – honestly, I owe you so many happy hours these past few years, when I've most needed them – thank you.'

'You are delightful.' Venetia smiled, and the world seemed warmer, bathed in golden light. 'Thank you so much.'

'Are you writing another book?'

A pained expression passed across the other woman's face. 'Yes, yes I am. In fact I'd been having tea with my fiancé, and I dropped into the library to collect my notebook which I'd left here. I telephoned—' She took it from Mikey, who held it out to her. 'Thank you, darling. Disaster to have forgotten it, it has *everything* in it.'

'How frightful,' Dora said. 'I say, I read the most dreadful book a few weeks ago. Have you read Paul Fredericks? *Death Comes A-Calling?*' Dora paused, for Venetia's smile had frozen: she looked down, adjusting her fur stole and Dora realised she had put her foot in it.

'I don't read old mysteries, though I'm sure they're wonderful, I'm afraid there's simply no time. Now, I must tell you, Dora dear: I thought I recognised you in the car, just now. That's why I was staring so rudely.' Her lovely face peered at Dora, the dark eyes searching hers. 'You're very like her, aren't you?'

Dora took a quick, stabbing breath and stepped back. 'I thought I recognised you,' she heard herself say. 'I used to think I was. Like her, I mean, but I'm not sure now.'

'You're nothing like Furlong, thankfully,' said Venetia. Her beautiful eyes filled with tears. 'Oh my dear, I do miss her.' Her breath caught in her throat. She leaned in close, and squeezed Dora's arm, her delicious scent intoxicating.

'I do too.' Dora shrugged, her eyes bright. 'But she was a free spirit.' She smiled politely at Venetia Strallen, as another member brushed past them, raising his hat to Venetia and nodding at Mikey, behind the desk. 'I mustn't hold you up,' she said.

'Everything is all right now.' Venetia slid the notebook into her pocket, and carelessly tossed her mink stole over her shoulder. Her evening coat opened to reveal a slim, glittering belt around her dress. It shone white-silver, a mass of tiny, sparkling dia-manté, winking in the cosy warmth of the library. Dora stared at it. She, having never thought of herself previously as being a great one for clothes, realised in that moment she would do anything to own that belt, whether it be committing murder or walking a tightrope. 'And what will you do now?'

'I thought I might look for something to read.'

'Well, I never,' said Mikey, who was listening to all this. 'Find-ing something to read in a library, what are the odds?' He glanced at Venetia Strallen, clearly hoping to make her laugh, but she was staring into the distance, watching the closed door at the corner of the Issue Hall.

Dora gave Mikey a pitying look. 'I mean – I wondered if the new batch of green Penguins was in yet. I so enjoyed the first ones. I've read them all, Dorothy Sayers and Eric Linklater were my favourites. What about you, Miss Strallen?'

'Oh,' said Venetia faintly. 'As I said to you before I'm afraid I don't ever read. I'm always working. Working, working. Besides, I can't stand Dorothy Sayers.' Dora gave a small shriek. 'Oh, not like that. She's too good. Reminds me how talentless I am . . . Lis-ten, Dora dear, I'm so late, I must go – are you staying at Dreda's?'

'Yes,' said Dora, as a door banged open and she turned to see Ben Stark emerging from the corner office, his face pale, his eyes dark with anger.

'*You damned fool!*' someone was shouting, as the door closed behind him. '*In God's name, why must I be the one to point these things out!*'

'Why on earth must he *shout*?' said Dora to Venetia, who was smoothing her gloves out on her palm, very slowly. Mikey leaned forwards.

'Miss Strallen, I have to leave my post to go and give Sir Edwin a message. Anything else you need?'

'Gosh no, thank you, Mikey dear,' said Venetia. 'Goodbye, Dora darling. It's wonderful to bump into you; you've no idea how wonderful. I hope I'll see you later on, at Dreda's. *Au revoir*, dear.'

Dora was not exaggerating when she said she loved Venetia Strallen's novels. She adored them, every one, and especially the rakish detective Edgar Dunnett, a taciturn war hero from the Borders who had a chiselled chin, smoked a pipe and spoke in riddles.

She watched her go. She has a notebook, she thought to herself. Of course she does. What a lot I'll have to write down in my own notebook. And it's not even teatime.

Dora looked at her watch. It was a quarter to four. She could not yet be quite sure Charles was gone. A woman in a tweed suit with an umbrella under her arm stopped to ask something of one of the librarians, ranged along the wooden desks that ran on the left side of the Issue Hall.

'That's Gertrude Jephson, the historian,' Mikey said. 'She's just written a piece for *The Tatler* saying Hitler is a bad lot. Now, along at the next desk, that's Lord Rochford. He's a very nice gentleman. Equerry to Her Majesty, you know. And that's Lady Violet Tabor. Ever so grand, writes biographies of all the stiffs.'

'Of course.' Dora's eye ranged past Miss Jephson in her long coat, mustard stockings and broken umbrella, and Lady Violet, resplendent in maroon velvet. She gazed up at the wooden shelves above the Issue Desk, where row upon row of books stretched to the ceiling; at the piles of books on trolleys, waiting to be reshelved; at the men and women walking with purpose in and out of this slim, secret, glorious building, this world full of books. One of the piles looked as if it might fall over. 'What a place,' she said dreamily.

'We keep losing people,' Mikey said, under his breath. 'Sir Edwin takes against them and shouts at them and they won't stay. It's a nice job for whoever wants to do it, but very few as will put up with him.' A noise started in the far corner again and she saw his face twist, blank and sad, like a child witnessing something it doesn't understand.

'*It's the fourth time!*' She heard someone shouting, the same voice as before, louder than ever. 'I damned well won't stand for it! I've warned them—'

Mikey leaned forwards. 'Oh dear. He's coming out now. There he is.' He pointed at a small, squat gentleman in morning dress and tails, who appeared to be in the middle of some episode rendering him almost mute with rage. 'That's him. That's Sir Edwin Mountjoy. Chief Librarian,' said Mikey. He swallowed. 'Always in a terrible mood, but it's worse than ever today.'

'Gout,' said Dora decisively, looking over Sir Edwin, whose face was the colour of an aubergine. 'My grandfather had it. The pain drove him quite mad. We went to the circus once and he tried to strangle a seal . . . it was very awkward.'

Indeed, Sir Edwin Mountjoy was hissing at one of the librarians, his domed shirt-front rising and falling at an alarming rate.

'Listen, you stupid girl. I've *told you*, Miss Amani! Look here!' In his hand he was waving a book whose centre had been torn out, all that remained a ruffle of missing pages. 'Again! What kind of show are we running, that some madman can simply waltz in here and—'

He stopped, apparently running out of steam, and flapped the empty book together.

'Yes, Sir Edwin,' replied the librarian, a young Black woman. She smoothed her hair, which she wore back from her head contained by a beautiful gold leaf hair band, in an unconscious gesture of anxiety. She wore a red shirt with huge voluminous sleeves, and a neat navy tie with a gold tie-pin of a little bird. 'Would you like me to send the book to the restoration team, Sir Edwin—'

'You fool.' Sir Edwin's white frontage strained so hard, his face turning from red to purple, that Dora really worried that he'd explode. She'd never seen anyone so angry before. His face was shining and puffed up, his eyeballs were almost as red as his skin.

'How do we restore this? The centre of the damned book's missing! Someone's *cut it out*! Fool. Dear God, spare me these imbeciles . . .' He glared at the young woman, and at Ben. 'This is the last time, I tell you . . . the last time . . .'

'Go in,' said Mikey quietly, all bravado gone. 'I'll find your membership card, don't worry. I'll make a new one if not.'

'Is he always like that?'

He nodded, and pulled at his collars. 'I don't like it. I don't like shouting.'

Dora understood. She placed the tips of her gloved fingers on the reception desk. 'I don't like it either. Thank you so much,' she said, slipping past him and hurrying past the red-faced Chief Librarian. Their eyes met for a moment – she stared into his, and saw such anger, such rage, that she almost recoiled.

Dora climbed a short flight of stairs, pushed open a green door, which banged behind her and suddenly, to her delight, there was quiet, and warmth, and a strange humming hush: the sound of books.

5

An examination of the rule that nothing bad ever happens in a library

The back of the London Library housed almost a million books in metal stacks that rose behind the original building, six storeys high. The floors were metal grids: you could look from the top and see, through the gaps in the Stacks, down several floors and thousands of subjects: Architecture, Philology, Nubia, Folklore, Garden Design, the Hittites, Bee Keeping.

The walls were a pale mustard; the books were worn, dark red and green and blue, tooled in gold. It was very warm. Dora could not hear anything beyond the faint rustle of pages, the occasional footsteps of other library members and a door, opening and closing.

Gingerly, minding her bandaged knee, she sat down on a wooden stool next to Topography: Yorkshire, her chin in her hands. She looked around, touching the shelves, and pulled *Haworth: A Reminiscence of that Blessed Spot and Surrounding Area* by A Lady of Yorkshire off the shelves.

'It's pretty quiet here, old girl,' she said to herself, gazing at the lithograph of the Brontë parsonage with unalloyed pleasure. 'You'll hear someone if they're coming.'

For the first time in she did not know how long, she felt at peace.

*   *   *

Her father had made it very clear she was not being forced to marry Charles Silk-Butters. Oh no, not at all. It was for Dora to choose a husband, and she was about to turn twenty-one, and the money her mother left her – a not inconsiderable amount, she had been led to expect – would come to her then.

'Time for you to fly the nest though,' Furlong Wildwood had told his daughter. 'No point in you staying here.'

'I'll get a job, Daddy. Only please don't make me marry him.'

'A *job*? What would you do, dearest?'

'Teacher! Or secretary . . . don't look like that. I can learn shorthand, if you'll only pay for a course I'll repay you. Or – or . . .'

But her father had refused to entertain the idea. He was, like most patrician family men, terrified his daughter might be molested, meaning she should be ideally locked up out of sight until she came of age, but he was also terrified she might be left like a book on the shelf. That he'd have to pay for her board and lodgings when she could easily be someone else's charge, to feed and water. Furlong was very fond of Dora, she was his only child and they had at various points, especially after Elizabeth's death, and before the appearance of Carine, been extremely close, but this was the thing in a nutshell.

Lady Dreda had persuaded him and his beloved Elizabeth that Dora should go to school – 'the poor girl must have some education before she's to inherit, my dears, and you don't want her around the house, chanting spells and her only actual job being blocking the lane outside so the toads can cross in safety every spring, now do you?'

So off to Babington House School for Girls Dora went, and she appeared to be happy there. Furlong had worried about her making the wrong friends, and saying things like 'mirror' and 'pardon'. His fears were assuaged when he heard she had palled up with an earl's daughter, Natalie something, but then almost immediately the earl's daughter was sent away for a crime so dreadful Dora was not allowed to speak of it.

After Elizabeth died Furlong had taken her to school himself in his new car, and at the sight of all these girls pouring out of cars and coaches he had had to steel himself. Some of them looked like proper hoydens. One or two of them disconcertingly reminded him of something you'd find in a revue in Soho. 'Is Lady Natalie back? Is Lansdowne here?' he'd said, to soothe himself, hopeful of catching sight of the earl, whom he'd known when they were young bucks in 90s London.

'No idea,' Dora had said. 'Oh look though, there's Laney! I say! Here!' she'd called loudly, and flung herself out of the car. 'I'll be fine here, Daddy,' she'd said gently, leaning in through the window so that the springs bounced, and she had kissed him on the cheek. 'Please don't worry about me. I'll be alright. You can go now.'

It seemed that, ever since, her father had taken that instruction literally. The following week she'd had a letter from him: he had taken up residence in Paris and did not know when he would next return.

That summer, however, he *had* returned and, greatly to Dora's surprise, with a new wife, a silent little French girl called Carine, who did not speak except to say '*non*' and '*oui*' and who shivered all day in the chilly house. She slid from room to room listlessly, picking up items, examining them, putting them down again. She did not like *les moutons*, or *les nuages,* or *les paysannes,* and she certainly did not like *les Anglais*. And there was Dora, who had come back to Wildwood after her final year at Babington House School, back to her old life of sitting on gates with Albert Jubby listening to crickets, and wandering round the churchyard picking yew berries. This annoyed Carine, who was correct in everything she did – her mother was a Montmorency, descended from a line of ducs who had been at Versailles and who had been important enough to be guillotined, lots of them, on the same tumbril. Her great, great, great, great grandmother had worn the family diamonds as the blade removed her head from her body, which was only correct. Carine said correct a lot. She ate myrtille jam delivered by Harrods on paper-thin slices of brown toast, only wore silk underthings, never touched her face with her hands unless washing it, to avoid blemishes, and went to Paris twice a year to visit Worth and Molyneux for her wardrobe and to eat ortolan, which she did correctly, with the napkin draped over the head so the only clue one was eating whole, tiny birds was the sound of crunching bones. As well as all the other things she did not like she did not appear to like Dora's father very much. She certainly did not like Dora.

Charles Silk-Butters was the local squire, descended from those who had marked the same traditions in Combe Curry for centuries: the Boar's Head Procession through the village, the Guy on Bonfire Night, wassailing in January, tying a maiden to a maypole and throwing mud at her on May Day. He led the hunt, was a local JP, handed out alms on Maundy Thursday, and prided himself on never having finished a book in his life. The Wildwoods were the older family, but a previous Silk-Butters had made a fortune with an elixir called Mother's Tonic, had his portrait painted by Millais, built a vast Gothic pile – Harwood Hall, the name out of a magazine story a previous Mrs Silk-Butters had enjoyed – and had gradually bought up most of the land thereabouts. They had now a baronetcy. His mother was famous for her Buff Orpingtons.

He was ten years older than Dora and, having had his eye on her since she was fourteen, and having had permission from her father when she was nineteen, proposed to her five times. On the sixth time, she had accepted.

'I told you I'd wear you down, Dora,' he'd said with satisfaction, as they stood in the hall of Wildwood House, after family drinks. 'Jolly good, what, jolly good,' and he'd kissed her.

She didn't like being kissed by him, though she knew she liked kissing, having been kissed by Natty Lansdowne at school once, and she and Albert having tried it several summers ago. She'd followed up on this with some practice at a dance given by the Coxcombes over at Wroxcombe last Christmas for their son Herbert's coming of age. Dora's birthday present to Herbert had been a kiss in the billiards room, from which both of them had emerged rather flustered. Yes, she liked kissing. But she didn't like how wet Charles's mouth was, saliva pooling on her tongue, his meaty, gritty taste, the smell of cigars. What Dora loathed most of all was how he gripped the back of her neck with one large hand, as if she was an apple he wanted to take a bite out of.

Back at Harwood Hall, the details of what marriage would entail – 'Getting down to business now so the wedding night's not a surprise, Dora,' Charles had said, advancing towards her one afternoon after clumsily manoeuvring her upstairs to the Blue Bedroom, flinging open his paisley dressing gown with gusto like a child opening a pair of curtains on Christmas morning and pinning her down on the bed whilst he grunted over her and she lay there so surprised, not to mention uncomfortable, that she didn't actually speak – were too dreary to relate. 'There. M'father always said best to break them in first, make sure they understand.'

Dora knew this was not true, and knew for most girls virginity was sacrosanct before a wedding. She knew Charles was trying to bind her to him, that he knew she had never loved him. She knew it too. She loved her mother, reading, school, the countryside around Wildwood House, and writing copious notes in lined notebooks that solved mysteries, like what had happened to the butter dish, why champagne made you deliciously happy for a while, and what became of butterflies after they died, not in that order. Moreover she didn't simply not like Charles; after the business in the Blue Bedroom she found herself unable to sleep for worry about it, and the sight of him caused her to perspire. She had quite liked kissing Natty Lansdowne, she had definitely liked kissing Albert, and she had very much enjoyed kissing Herbert Coxcombe, and she liked imagining kissing Clark Gable, like Claudette Colbert in *It Happened One Night*. But if this is what kissing was like then something was very wrong with her, for she could not let Charles do that to her again.

The 'business' was not repeated for a while, and she wondered if she'd got something wrong. Charles's pop-eyed mother continued her constant stream of instructions on running the house, looking after her flock of chickens, collecting and selling the eggs, all of which Dora found either repulsive or dreary, to her shame, having previously thought of herself as someone who liked all animals. It turned out she quite detested chickens. Wedding preparations carried on apace too, and Dora was measured for a flowing, medieval-style gown, greatly to Carine's horror, and the younger sisters of Bryony Fulcher – her horse-mad neighbour and childhood acquaintance whom Dora always thought should have married Charles instead – were fitted for dear little bridesmaids dresses of organdie with powder-blue sashes. And perhaps, perhaps she might have gone ahead with it, but it was when Charles appeared in September, two months before the wedding and said soon it would be time to up the getting-down-to-business to three times a week, so she could whelp by the end of next year, that Dora knew the marriage was doomed, as far as she was concerned, and that she would have to run away.

Once her mind was made up it did not change, though it presented her with a seemingly insurmountable problem. No one Dora knew, once married, left their husband. It was as though a heavy metal door slammed down on the wedding day, the lock turned, the bolts slid across, and one could see and hear everyone from an upstairs window, but one had no chance of passing over the threshold back out into the world again. Dora did not see how she could get away, for what would she do, where would she go?

Without realising it, she sank into a depression. The day after her twenty-first birthday, however, a stroke of luck fell into her lap, a window opening and a sunbeam falling into a darkened room: a crisis occurred in her father's marriage.

Carine, after two years, decided to leave Furlong Wildwood and head back to Paris, to the apartment near the Champs-Élysées, to the fitting rooms and the ortolans she missed so much. When Furlong remonstrated with her that leaving your husband was not at all correct in this country Carine replied that she was French, and did not care for convention, which seemed to Dora somewhat hypocritical. Furlong, in the mistaken belief he could bring his wife to heel, followed her to Paris, where he camped out at the Embassy, annoying everyone by crying loudly and making passes at the chambermaids. He had not greatly added to the attempts to rein in Herr Hitler two years previously, and so was not especially welcome.

He had sent Dora to stay at Harwood Hall, and after a week had cabled his daughter to say the task at hand would take some time, and to ask Dora to remain permanently with Charles, in his mother's wing. The wedding was merely six weeks away and it would not be frowned upon too much, and was surely preferable, he wrote to Charles's mother, than having the poor girl remain on her own at Wildwood, a large, Jacobean manor house whose rambling layout and sloping roofs made it an ideal place for hide-and-seek but not a suitable location for a young woman to live alone.

Dora disagreed – she loved Wildwood House, far more than her father, who was always trying to leave, it seemed. It was where her mother had been, where the inside and outside, living and dead, seemed to co-mingle. Her father had written to ask Dora to go back to the house and once again lay off the servants bar Mrs Lah Lah, so that he didn't have to pay them through the winter; also to put various items in the safe; and also to post him his lucky cufflinks, which were dancing hares. And to look at the bramble, which had appeared at some point in late summer in the drawing room through the floorboards, and appeared to be slowly colonising the house.

At Wildwood, Dora moved from room to room. She had often found silence told her what she needed to hear. She liked the bramble, though it was alarmingly large and threatened to engulf the hallway and the front door from the inside, but since she had always entered the house via the study window this did not concern her.

She saw how much she disliked Charles, that she wasn't indifferent to him: she hated him. His black nose-hair. How he grunted and chewed with his mouth open, and produced far too much saliva whilst masticating. How boorish he was, taking pride in it as if it were a family characteristic one should be proud of. How much he loved the sound of his own voice, and admired his own reflection in a mirror, liked pawing at her whenever she passed by. True, he was seen as a handsome man to some – dark, saturnine, broad-shouldered – but to Dora the idea of his child in her womb made her feel alive for once, with horror, and she saw she could not go back there.

She telephoned to say she would need to spend a couple of nights alone at the house, as she had been detained by several matters which she had to resolve. She wrote to her godmother asking to come and stay, packed a bag of her remaining things, took some money from her father's desk and made her only mistake which was, on the eve of her departure, to write to Charles to tell him what she was doing. At six a.m. the following day, she locked up carefully, and simply hitched a lift to the station with Albert.

'I need your help,' she'd said when she'd turned up at Deepdale Farm, just down the track from Wildwood House, in the darkness. 'I'm catching the first train to London. Will you take me to the station? I have to get away.'

'Of course I will,' he'd said simply, draining his tea and turning back towards the warm farmhouse for his wrench and his coat. 'I think you do, Dora.'

The train was a minute late leaving; Dora, who never lost her composure, found for once she was shaking. But eventually it pulled away, wheezing out of the station, Mr Fish the porter touching his cap as she passed, before she shut the window and sank back into the scratchy seats, breathing heavily. She knew, simply knew what she had understood obscurely all her life: that to be married and stuck in the countryside with the wrong person would be a kind of hell, from the like of which she could never escape. One of her friends from school, a sweet girl named Kitty Nairne, had been married at seventeen, to an old landowning neighbour of her father's, and had died only the previous summer giving birth to her second child in two years, aged nineteen – the doctor, a West London surgeon of great renown, had said she had 'simply given up'.

Dora would not, could not, be like poor sweet Kitty Nairne, or like Charles's terrifying mother Audrey Silk-Butters, who couldn't look humans in the eye but seemed to be in some kind of romantic entanglement with one of her dogs, and most of all she would not be like her mother, the best mother for a small child but a brilliant biologist who should have gone to a university, mouldering away in the countryside having given up her dreams of lepidoptery.

Her mother, who had taught her algebra, played her Dido's Lament and Tchaikovsky, read her *Jane Eyre*, *The Railway Children* and *As You Like It*, who in 1928 had put a copy of the edition of *The Times* reporting the successful campaign for universal suffrage in Dora's room, hiding it ('Your father is a dinosaur,' she had said, 'and dinosaurs' brains tell their tail to wag but it takes a few days for the message to reach the tail, darling'). Elizabeth Wildwood had done what she could for her daughter before she died, but most of all she had impressed upon her that Dora was a person who deserved to live, not to live for others. She had watched her small, curly-haired child move from certainty, through adolescent insecurity, to the cusp of becoming the delightfully intriguing, curious, open-minded, determined young woman she now was, but she had missed that final flowering.

Whatever happened next, she told herself on that cold train journey, when it became apparent she had caught the slowest train possible, one that wouldn't reach London till late morning, she promised herself she would never regret taking this step. She could not be a wife. She had to become herself first. The only trouble was she wasn't quite sure who that was.

*   *   *

Now, in the warm light of one solitary bulb in the depths of the Stacks, hemmed in on either side by books, Dora hugged herself, feeling the warmth of her fingers, the velvet of her collar soft against her cheek.

'Right,' she said, in a soft voice, pulling out her notebook, along with a tiny silver pencil. 'One ought to make some sort of plan. What information does one have? Let's see.' She peered down at the list she had made on the train.

'*Call it off with Charles.* Oh, I do hope he's got the message this time. I do think he must have.' She drew a line through his name, chewing the stub thoughtfully, then looked down again.

'*Money.* Well, I'm supposed to have money, but I've never seen any of it. Is that because it's vulgar to talk about money? I feel rather that people who have money like keeping it so they don't talk about it. Whenever I've asked Daddy about it he's gone extremely quiet, and one wonders if there's any money at all. In fact I think one knows the answer to that, sadly. Well, I'll make a note: <u>To be investigated</u>. Next?

'*Accommodation*: well, I must immediately telephone Dreda and apologise. I do hope she's not worrying. She did seem to be the sort to worry from what I remember . . . Muzz was always so funny about her and Venetia at school . . . Venetia believing she could make everyone fall in love with her and Dreda convinced she was unbelievably hairy and her ankles were too thick and she'd never find love . . . I shall throw myself on her mercy and ask if I can stay for a week, perhaps two . . . I wonder if she knows any-one who needs a companion? A lady who embroiders and carries lorgnettes and talks to the servants, that sort of thing?' Inspira-tion struck her – she raised a finger in the gloom. 'Aha! Venetia Strallen. She said she was awfully busy. Perhaps I could help her.'

A picture came to mind: Dora as a calm, unflappable helpmeet in a stylish new tank top and kilt, round tortoiseshell glasses like Ben Stark's, and shiny brogues, sitting in an office making appointments for Venetia, who wafted in in a silk dressing gown, clasped Dora to her bosom, and said things like 'You have saved me, darling Dora', and dedicated her next novel to her – *For Dora, who taught me what joy is once again*, or something like that – and ultimately pressed upon her the diamanté sparkling belt as a token of appreciation. Dora did not stop to wonder whether she might actually enjoy life as a skivvy for someone else: she had always been extremely enthusiastic at the prospect of any role-play. Had she not, many Christmases ago, shone as both the ox *and* ass in the Wildwood village Nativity, wearing an ingenious two-sided costume of her own creation, a brown horsehair rug on one side, with a taxonomically inaccurate horn Albert Jubby had produced out of his coat pocket for her ('Don't ask where I got it, Dora. It's best you don't know'), and a terrifying ass's head, relic of the Wildwood Drama Society's production of *A Midsummer Night's Dream*, which she had sawn in half. These halves were sewn together and worn around her head with a camel-coloured gabardine draped over her back belonging to her father, who had been extremely angry about the whole thing.

She wrote down on the piece of paper: *Dreda. Then Venetia? Then flat of one's own?* Next:

'*Employment*: well, I think I've answered that. All is solved if Venetia hires me, and it would be super if she did.' The sound of footsteps echoed from somewhere; she sat up, looking around. The feet were two, three floors above, thudding along as if some-one was in a hurry. A voice inside her head said:

What if Venetia doesn't *want me?*

'Oh, come now, Dora,' she said aloud. 'Of course she will. But if she doesn't – ahm,' she said, in a quieter voice. 'I could do the jolly old investigating. That's a good idea. In fact, isn't that what I'd like to do more than anything?' She jutted out her chin, eyes narrowed, and listened again. The footsteps had gone.

'An investigator,' she said to herself, one hand stealing to her pocket as if to remove a magnifying glass, or a pipe – she wasn't sure what. 'Yeeees. I could definitely do that.'

Dora had won the Aurelia Wonkham-Strong Prize at Babing-ton House School for Most Intrepid Girl of the Year, greatly to the amusement of her friend Tommy, a Mohammedan from Rajputana who had gone back to her palace on the edge of the desert after school and whom Dora missed very much. Tommy had a touching faith in Dora's abilities and dreamt of a career for her friend, knowing that she herself was heading back to marry her second cousin Arvind, who had his own palace, in Udaipur, and was a Maharaja, but who sucked his teeth and had never slept on his own because of nightmares. Tommy had spent a lot of time working out what Dora should do:

'How about being a Member of Parliament, Dora?'

'Gosh no. All that listening to men with large moustaches drone. The self-importance.'

'What about headmistress then? You'd be a wonderful teacher.'

'I'm finished with school, Tommy. Aren't you?'

'All right then. Go to Paris, and have an adventure.'

'I can't. My father's there already, having one of his own.'

'Well, be a detective then, just like you wanted. You'd be marvellous at it. You're interested in everyone, you let people talk, and you're extremely eccentric, like – oh, the French one with the moustaches.'

'M Poirot is Belgian,' said Dora, gently.

She saw herself in an office like the ones she had passed on the bus on her way to the Haymarket, employing a gaggle of assiduous young women, a glass door with gold writing on it, distraught fiancés seeking runaway brides, old army majors with scores to settle – a call coming in – 'It's Whitehall, Miss Wildwood. They need you.' And herself, with maybe one of the young women by her side, walking down a long, white-stucco'd corridor in the Foreign Office, frescoes of great deeds of men lining the walls, the stone of the Cenotaph gleaming in the sun on Whitehall. 'A very delicate matter . . . requiring someone operating with the utmost discretion and diplomacy . . . the King of the Netherlands has asked personally for you, following on from the excellent work you did for His Majesty locating his missing diamonds . . .'

The following day, her report, verbally given, crisp and discreet: 'The misunderstanding arises from the King's Dutch accent and hatred of fermented dairy. When he said it was foul, unhealthy, repulsive, putrid and of a slimy consistency he was talking about Laud yoghurt, not Lord Oakheart.'

'Miss Wildwood – we are so grateful. Lord Oakheart responded in an intemperate fashion, thinking he was under attack. He will apologise to the King immediately. Such subtlety – how can we reward you?'

'Ah,' Dora would say, one hand on the door, smiling brightly at them. 'There is no reward for me but greater equality and societal cohesion.'

Something scuttled below her, and she remembered where she was, and that soon, kind Ben Stark had offered to see her onto a bus. She looked at the list again.

1. *Call it off with Charles – DONE*
2. *Money – Will write to Father about inheritance*
3. *Accommodation – Stay at Dreda's; look for somewhere else to live*
4. *Employment – Become a lady's companion / helpmeet to lady novelists*
5. *After that: become a detective.*
6. *Solve Muzz's murder.*

And then, underneath, because she'd forgotten them till now:

7. *Go to Fortnum's for more peppermint creams.*

She stared at the list, and chewed her pencil again. She had begun, and there was no going back. She shut the notebook, marking the place with her bus ticket.

And it was then that she started to notice she could hear something, had heard it for a few minutes now. It was a dripping, shifting, creaking sound, somewhere above her, high up in the depths of the velvety dark floors. Once – just once, she heard a juddering sigh, as if someone was gargling with water, and then it stopped, and there was silence again, but it was not the good kind of silence.

Dora froze. And then a drop fell from up above, close to her shoulder, and landed on the metal floor. She looked down.

It was saliva.

Dora got up slowly, moving towards the staircase. There was a sign on the wall, the shape of a pointing finger. 'Science and Nature A–G / This Way'. Dora followed it, telling herself it was nothing, that she was going up there merely to take a book out to keep her company on the bus ride back to Dreda's. Something comforting: a novel about crossed wires and women buying new hats.

It was very dark in the centre of the stacks, so dark she could barely see where she was going. In the gloom she fumbled for a light switch, but she couldn't find one. She stepped on something, the knee she'd fallen on pulsing with a sharp twinge, the ankle turning underneath her, and heard, as if in a dream, her own voice giving out a cry of pain. Whatever it was twisted and crumpled under her foot – she stared down and saw with horror that she had stepped on a book.

Her eyes adjusting, she noticed almost with detachment that its pages were untidily torn out, the jagged edges flapping gently in the breeze from the floors below. It was so surprising, here in this temple of books, offensive somehow, like a dead, mutilated ewe in a field of gambolling sweet lambs. She peered down at the cover.

'That's odd,' she said to herself. 'Why that book?'

She wasn't sure why her heart was hammering in her throat. She felt in her pocket for the little pistol.

It was gone.

Dora patted herself down, wondering when she might have dropped it. 'Drat,' she said to herself, for she was afraid now, and then she bent down, and her foot hit something, a heavy bulk. She steadied herself on a bookshelf, and looked down. It was a dark, warm shape, soft yet unyielding.

The metal grille floor gleamed, and something caught her eye. A figure, in the darkness on the floor below, moving off, swift as a bird in the night. Dora called out:

'I say! Who's that?'

The bulk in front of her shifted against the pressure of her foot, like sand. She reached down and as the sacklike form sank she felt human hair, brushing against her knuckles, her skin, the cloth of her trousers. Hair, and a human head.

Dora stepped back and scanned the shelves, then pulled on the light switch, torn pages rustling under her feet. When she looked down, bile rising in her throat, she saw a body, one leg splayed out, a foot still twisted round the low stool on which it had been sitting, one arm flung up against the shelves.

As she stared, the head rolled back, eyes open, glistening white, surprised, in the dark. It was Sir Edwin Mountjoy, Chief Librarian. His pale blue bloodshot eyes stared up at her. His mouth was open: a huge, meaty tongue, dark like liver, slopping out at one corner, saliva drooling in long glistening threads through the grilles onto the next floor. Someone was screaming. Dora dropped her hat, her pencil, her books. Something white fluttered past the dead man into the darkness below. It took a moment before she realised the person screaming was, of course, her.

6

Trip hazard

'A body? What do you mean, a body?'

'I mean a dead person.'

'Oh come now, Miss Wildwood. Don't be . . . ridiculous.'

'I'm not being ridiculous. Would you like to leave him there for someone else to trip over?'

'But—' said Ben Stark, turning pale. 'That's impossible. Not again.'

'"Not again"? What do you mean, "Not again"?' Dora said.

'Oh,' said Ben Stark, and he swallowed. 'Someone collapsed. Er – in the stacks, a while ago. It was – ah – it was rather hazardous. That was – what I meant. Forgive me – are you *sure*?'

'I regret to say I've never been surer about anything,' Dora said. Heads were beginning to turn towards them. 'Do listen to me. There is a dead body in the Stacks, and I'm certain it's Sir Edwin Mountjoy.'

'Mr Dryden?' said Ben Stark. 'Could you come, please?'

'Shhh!' The young Black woman next to Ben Stark on the Issue Desk raised her finger to her lips, censoriously. 'I say, Ben!' she hissed. 'Stop shouting!'

'Zewditu,' Ben Stark said, running his hands through his hair so it stuck up on end. 'I assure you this is the one and only time it's all right to shout in a library.'

'I assure *you*, Mr Stark, there is never a good time to shout in a library,' Zewditu Amani replied.

'Zewditu, this is Miss Wildwood. Dora Wildwood. She says she has – ah – found a body. Miss Wildwood . . . Miss Zewditu Amani.' He smiled at Zewditu. 'Zewditu lives in Mayfair. Her father is a diplomat with the Ethiopian delegation to London.

53

She has a pet dachshund. The main thing about Zewditu is that she's read more than anyone else in this place. Put together.'

'It is a pleasure to meet you,' said Miss Amani, nodding politely. 'You must come and meet Bertie. He would like you.'

'She's talking about the dachshund,' said Ben under his breath. 'He does tricks for very small pieces of chicken.'

'Don't we all,' said Dora, wondering once again if she were in a dream, but Ben Stark seemed to recall himself to his senses.

'Mr Dryden!' he said, his gentle voice surprisingly powerful, carrying across the hall. 'Would you come here, most urgently? Mr Clark, would you assist me in keeping members away from the back Stacks? Thank you.' He clambered down from his stool, and removed his jacket. 'Thank you sir; if you'd like to follow me. I think something terrible has happened.'

*　　*　　*

'He's dead all right,' Mikey opined, over Dora's shoulder. He had left his station and followed the gaggle up to the third floor of the Stacks.

The worst part was climbing the stairs again, up to where the body was lying there in the darkness, turning on the lights, and seeing the dead man's face pressed to the metal grille of the floor, visible from below. Dora knew she would never forget that livid red face, the frozen pale blue eye, jammed against the slatted floor, utterly motionless. She could see his mouth, and a string of saliva dangling down into the darkness of the floor below.

She stared at it curiously. 'That's odd,' she said.

Sir Edwin Mountjoy had clearly been sitting on a wooden stool between the shelves when he had died, slumping forwards and to the side, the bulk of his body falling to the ground like a sack.

The dead man's large hands were purple, seams straining on his black evening jacket. His short hair was bristly, flecked with dandruff. Dora's quick eyes scanned the corpse, then turned away, blinking.

She turned to look at Mr Dryden, the Deputy Librarian, but he was silent, almost frozen with horror, staring at the body.

'Let's move him,' said Mikey. 'So he's not in the way—'

'We can't move him, Mikey,' said Ben Stark. 'We have to leave him like that I'm afraid. The police will want to work out how he died, why he was like that.' He stepped back. 'Mr Dryden, should I telephone the police?'

'I have already asked Miss Bunce to do so.' Mr Dryden spoke up now. His soft voice wavered with shock. 'Ben, my boy, go and stand guard here. Make sure no one comes in. Miss Amani my dear, you stand there at the back, be especially careful Miss Jephson doesn't get wind of it, the woman has a mole at every newspaper and we want to keep this quiet for as long as possible. And Miss – er—'

'Wildwood. Dora Wildwood.'

Mr Dryden fumbled with thin, shaking fingers in his waistcoat and took out a pocket watch. 'Four thirty-six p.m. Remember that, would you?'

'Yes, of course. In fact it was four seventeen p.m. when I found him,' Dora said. 'I made a note of it at the time.'

'Bit odd,' said Mikey, behind her.

Mr Dryden shushed him. 'Mikey, go away. I'm very grateful to you, Miss Wildwood. This is a bad business,' he muttered, shaking his head, looking down at the body. 'Dear me. A bad business indeed.'

Dora looked at him. 'It must be a terrible shock,' she said. He was dreadfully pale, even in the dim light of the Stacks.

'You're the one who found him,' Ben Stark said. 'Are you all right, Miss Wildwood?'

'Thank you, I am.' Nevertheless she felt her head swim, as if the metal floor were melting away. 'It's rather strange, actually. This is the second dead body I've seen and it's just as ghastly. My mother always said I never meant to cause trouble, yet I somehow do. Wherever I go.'

'Perhaps your mother is right,' he said with the ghost of a smile.

'Was,' said Dora. 'She was right.'

'Do forgive me.'

'It's absolutely fine. I shouldn't have mentioned it only – given the circumstances—' She shook her head. 'I'm babbling. Have you known someone who died before they should have?'

'Yes,' he said, in a strange voice. 'Yes, I have. This summer. And it was not like this. But that's – that's neither here nor there. Mr Dryden,' he said, his gaze shifting. 'What do you need?'

Mr Dryden was staring at the body, licking his dry lips, tugging at his collar. 'Water,' he whispered. 'I'm dreadfully thirsty.'

Ben Stark said: 'Come to the Chief Librarian's office and sit down, sir. You too, Miss Wildwood. Or would you prefer a cigarette?'

'Thank you, no. Some water would be lovely.' Dora rubbed her eyes. 'I can't leave him, not until the police are here. I'm sorry.'

'Mr Stark,' said Michael Dryden, pulling himself together. 'Before the police arrive, make sure the Issue Hall is cleared. Ask the members to leave. I fear we must close the library.'

'Yes, Mr Dryden,' Ben Stark said briefly, and vanished. The Deputy Librarian went back to staring at the dead body.

'We'll wait together, Miss Wildwood.' He could not seem to tear his eyes away from the slumped, undignified form in front of him. 'Forgive me, my dear.' He shook himself, almost a shudder. 'I'm just making quite sure he's dead.'

'I'd say there's no doubt about it,' Dora told him. 'I am sorry.'

And Mr Dryden leaned over, as low as he could go towards the form on the floor. 'Good riddance,' he said softly, into the dead man's ear, and then he stood up, supporting himself as if dizzy. 'Excuse me,' he said to Dora. 'Don't – don't leave, will you?'

'Of course not,' said Dora. She held out her arm and he took it.

'What brought you to the library today? Any particular book you wanted to find?'

'Oh, it's a long story, and it doesn't matter at the moment,' said Dora. 'Here, Mr Dryden. Lean against that shelf. They'll be here soon.'

*   *   *

They stood in the oppressive gloom, both watching the dead man, rather as if he might leap up suddenly and jump away, like a hare. And Dora thought of the hares on the lawn at Wildwood House, how they came off the fields every spring, when the morning light had blue and golden yellow sun in it, and the earth was wet and black, and everywhere you looked life was springing up. How you could not explain hares boxing to someone who had not seen it in real life. It was so . . . funny, and scary at the same time. Funny, because they looked like the time Albert and his brother Joseph had got into a fight when they were younger, flim-flamming at each other with flapping hands, and young Dora had stood on the sidelines, yelling encouragement like a boxing coach, urging them to greater violence, which they had ignored. Scary, because sometimes one hare would land a real punch on the other, sending it reeling, staggering backwards, dazed, and one was reminded how random violence was, how destiny came tumbling towards one with no way of avoiding it.

Her bandaged knee had started to throb again, but her mind lingered on the boxing hares, fighting for survival. How glorious it was, how they did it every year, how some things never changed.

'You must think my outburst rather odd,' Mr Dryden was saying into the dull silence. 'You see . . .' But he trailed off.

'Mr Dryden, we all say rather odd things in the heat of the moment,' said Dora. 'When my father arrived at school to tell me my mother had died I asked him if he'd like a cup of tea and some madeira cake. Which was very odd, because there was no madeira cake, but it was my mother's favourite, and I think it must have got caught, in my mind, you know.'

57

'Yes,' said Mr Dryden. 'You know, of course, that moments of high drama bring out the fight or flight response of the amygdala – the portion of the brain that controls fear, and panic, and those parts of our nervous system that one tries to keep under wraps.'

'I didn't know that. How fascinating.'

'Well, there you have it.' He shifted slightly. 'Of course, it may be that talk of your mother with your father reminded you of earlier happier times, and perhaps a madeira cake was there during those times. Round a roaring fire . . . a pot of tea . . .' He looked wistful.

'Perhaps,' said Dora. 'We weren't ever really a family for doing things together, you know. Rather it was me and my mother. She loved tea. Assam. She used to make it for me with lots of milk in it, even when I was very little. Milky tea and a spoonful of sugar.'

'Well,' said Mr Dryden gently. 'There you have it.'

'Yes,' Dora smiled at him. 'Once I'd seen it I found it rather hard to drink tea again but I did, and I do. One carries on, you know.' She hesitated, and bit her lip. 'May I ask you why you didn't care for Sir Edwin?'

'He was evil,' said Mr Dryden. He pressed his fingers to his mouth briefly. 'We shouldn't speak of him like this, and if it was anyone else, Miss Wildwood . . . But he was quite the worst man I've met. And he told me once, when he was out in Bloemfontein, guarding the internment camps, the women and children used to cry out for water. Just some water. They were dying in their thousands. He told me he liked watching them die, for something as simple as some water.' He took a deep, juddering breath, his head turned away from the dead body. 'Oh dear – oh dear. And in the last few months –' he put his fist against his mouth and shook his head – 'he made my life most unpleasant, over various historical matters . . .' He shook his bowed head.

Dora watched him for a few moments.

'Isn't it strange how bad people live in full view of everyone,' she said softly. 'Yet no one does anything about them until it's too late. There was a landlord like that in the village. A simply awful man, beat his wife and children, and everyone knew it, and my father took no action. And in the end it was something very simple that sealed his fate.'

Mr Dryden looked up. 'What was that?'

'Bullies are always, always very unhappy, in my experience,' said Dora. 'And their unhappiness leads them to make mistakes. And with Thomas Dexter, it was his unhappiness that did for him. But by then it was too late. His eight-year-old daughter took matters into her own hands.'

'What was too late?' said a deep voice, breaking the silence, and they both jumped. A man in a suit and hat, and a Burberry to which damp rain still clung, loomed forwards in the gloom, bringing in fresh air, and the scent of outside.

'Detective Inspector Fox, Scotland Yard,' he announced in booming tones. He looked around, and shook Mr Dryden's hand. 'Sergeant Crispin and the forensic analyst will be here soon. I certainly hope you haven't touched anything.'

Saying this, Detective Inspector Fox pulled off his large coat, sending raindrops flying everywhere, over the books, the metal floors, and onto the body, pock-marking the dull black of the evening jacket.

'*We* haven't,' said Dora pointedly.

'Good.' The detective inspector peered forwards and stared first at Dora then, apparently finding nothing of interest to detain him, at Mr Dryden. 'Well then. I assume you are Michael Dryden, Acting Chief Librarian?'

'I am the Deputy Librarian,' said Mr Dryden. 'It has not yet been agreed that I am Acting Chief.' His eyes were huge in his hollow face.

'My apologies.' Detective Inspector Fox flexed his giant hands, then clasped them together. Dora found herself staring at them, wondering if he could crush a walnut between his palms like Mr

Lah Lah, husband of their housekeeper, who had abruptly gone to America in mysterious circumstances a few years ago. 'Let us proceed.' He gazed down at the body, and Dora stared at him. He had a beard – she had not really seen a young man with a beard before. It was neat, and pointed: in the darkness it made him look rather like a devil.

'It's Sir Edwin Mountjoy, as you may already have been informed,' said Mr Dryden. 'This young lady, Dora Wildwood, can fill you in as to the discovery of the body.' He shuffled down between the shelves to make room for Dora, who stepped forwards as if they were in a music hall act.

'I see. First, we need to secure the area,' said the detective inspector, glancing coolly at the pair of them. 'Is there an office I could use? Private?'

'Sir Edwin's is the office with a door,' said Mr Dryden. 'But you'll want to search that too presumably.'

'You presume too much, Mr Dryden,' said Detective Inspector Fox, and Mr Dryden shrank back as if he'd been slapped.

'Of course. Why don't you set up shop there, Inspector—'

'*Detective* Inspector,' the detective inspector said. 'Detective Inspector Fox.'

'Oh, but surely you won't want to interfere with—' Dora began, but she stopped. Detective Inspector Fox did not appear to notice she had spoken.

'Right, then. Miss Wildwood, Mr Dryden, why don't you go and wait for me there. I'll try not to keep you too long.'

One of the constables was on his haunches, looking at the pieces of paper scattered around like confetti. Someone began taking photographs, huge flashes of light, and Dora was blinded for a second. When she looked back at the slumped figure it seemed to rise up, heavy dangling arms swinging towards her, purple face drawn into a rictus of horror. She flinched, stepping back out of the light, blinking hard. A voice behind her said:

'I say, steady on, old girl.'

And a hand rested on her shoulder blade, preventing her from falling backwards. There was something so kind, so low-key in their tone, Dora smiled. 'Is that you, Mr Stark? I'm sorry. Keep seeing things that aren't there.'

'I'm sure you are,' he said, and his low voice was kindness, and sympathy. 'It's horrible. Look here, your teeth are chattering. Why don't you come this way.'

'I'm cold,' said Dora, accepting his arm, gratefully. 'Aren't you cold?'

'No, it's actually rather warm in here,' he said. 'I say, Mr Dryden, do we have any brandy?'

'Sir Edwin did . . . But I'm not sure we should be using anything from his office. In case . . .' Mr Dryden trailed off.

'I have a bottle of rather fine Armagnac,' Ben Stark said, unexpectedly. 'Gift from a grateful member. I helped her track down an obscure manuscript.'

'Oh,' said Mr Dryden, rather uncertainly.

'S-sounds good,' said Dora, trying to remember what Armagnac was.

The men behind them were calling out measurements. Someone dropped a yardstick onto the metal with a clattering sound, and Dora jumped. As if someone had thrown the dice down again, like Albert throwing the bones into the square on summer nights.

'Oh,' she said. 'Something's gone.'

'Miss Wildwood?' said Ben. 'What did you say?'

'I'm fine,' said Dora, now unable to stop her teeth shaking, her shoulders juddering. 'It's the shock, that's all really. Let's go to the office.'

With superhuman effort she stopped herself from passing out, driving her fingernails into her palms and staring down at the pages on the metal floor. As they descended the wide, carpeted stairs, lined with portraits of Tennyson and Carlyle, the sweet scent of beeswax and wood smoke in the air, Dora saw the staff and the members of the library assembled in the Issue Hall.

Everyone silent, watching as she, Ben Stark and Mr Dryden made their way towards the office. No one said anything. Once again, she got the feeling that no one minded that the man in the Stacks was dead.

7

Strong drink, awfully nice forearms

'He must have simply dropped dead,' said Mr Dryden, pacing up and down. 'A heart attack. He was quick to anger, and anger is not at all good for you. Not at all.'

'Perhaps,' said Dora. She cradled the second glass of Armagnac, watching the viscous toffee-coloured liquid slip from side to side, inhaling the fumes rolling off it and feeling slightly light-headed. It was remarkable really how strong drink, taken in the right way, could revive one. 'But I don't think so. He looked simply furious. Outraged. And I don't think that's how you'd look if . . .' She trailed off.

'What will I tell his sister?' Mr Dryden was pulling at his collars and his moustaches alternately, whilst pacing. 'Miss Mountjoy kept house for him and when he became engaged she was devastated, you know. I must telephone her. What will she think? ' He glanced at his watch. 'And I promised my dear wife I'd be back by six. She will be waiting for me. The rissoles . . . Oh dear. And a young lady like you must need to be somewhere about now, I'd say.'

Dora thought about six o clock at Harwood Hall. The gins so stiff you could hardly walk afterwards. The guests, more and more languorous or more and more lively. She, bored, almost always silent, except whenever Charles's mother's dog chose to hump her leg or Charles's deaf great-aunt Letty came to stay and people shouted over her, about her and her money and where it might go. On the first night of her last stay, when Dora had shown her to her room after supper she had clutched Dora's arm tightly as they reached the sharp corner up to her tiny bedroom, where she had slept as a girl.

'I hate this corridor,' she'd said. 'Ghosts everywhere.'

Dora had forgotten Great-Aunt Letty was supposed to be deaf as a post and had said: 'Oh, don't worry. I think that too. I think they're friendly ones, though. I talk to them.'

'Friendly? Letty had replied scornfully. 'Not Dubois, dear girl. He betrayed his own mother to the Girondins. Escaped to England. Dreadful man. How he bothered me.'

'He – really?' Dora had begun, before breaking off and staring at her in astonishment.

'They make assumptions, those men,' Great-Aunt Letty had said. 'And my dear, often they're wrong.' She paused in the doorway, her dark small eyes alight with mischief. 'I like secrets, don't you? Let's share a secret, just you and me.'

'All right,' Dora had said, not without some trepidation. 'You first.'

'No, you, dear.'

'Well—' Dora had taken a deep breath. 'I don't think P.G. Wodehouse is all that funny. There. I've said it. Your turn.'

'Marvellous! Now let me think. Ah! I gave away my baby, out in India. I loved her father, but it was no good, we weren't allowed, you know. You have nice hair. Short. Are they making you marry Charles?'

*   *   *

Now, Dora took another sip of the Armagnac, watching Mr Dryden pace. 'I know it's very distressing, but I'm sure the police will have some news for us soon,' she said, in what she hoped was a comforting voice. 'Perhaps he did just have a heart attack.'

'The police! Hah!' said Mr Dryden, his voice suddenly harsh. 'They don't know what they're about, half the time. That inspector fellow. Thinks he's thruppence ha'penny to a shilling, well, I could see through him.'

'They're doing their best, I think,' said Dora soothingly, thinking of PC Whitlow in Combe Curry, who had a bicycle, planted bulbs outside the police station, had patted Albert kindly on the back after his cousin had been killed, and hadn't been quite the same since he'd fallen out of a tree and banged his head trying to rescue a cat.

There was a knock on the door. Ben Stark stuck his head in.

'I do apologise for bothering you again,' he said, glancing at the Armagnac bottle. 'I wondered if you were both all right. Miss Wildwood, do you need anything?'

'Come in, sir! Come in!' Mr Dryden said, beckoning him in. 'This is Ben Stark, my dear – he's our most able librarian – a quite remarkable young man, aren't you, Ben?'

'Er . . .'

'He likes owls, Miss Wildwood. Knows everything there is to know about them,' said Mr Dryden, forgetting his troubles for a moment. 'Isn't that something?'

'Um – yes?' said Dora. 'Tell me something about owls, Mr Stark. Take our minds off our current predicament.'

'Oh. Well, half of all owlets will die in their first year,' said Ben Stark, thinking for a moment. 'Usually malnutrition.'

'Thank you,' said Dora. 'How interesting and also horrifying.' She stared into the glass.

Ben Stark screwed his face up. 'Oh hell,' he said. 'Forgive me. This inspector from Scotland Yard,' he said, advancing into the room. 'He will have some news for us soon I'm sure.' He rubbed his forehead with his hand, sending his hair up into a quiff. 'One must put one's faith in the police.'

'I envy you both your unsullied opinions,' said Mr Dryden, suddenly. He turned to Dora. 'My dear, forgive me, but I've seen them beat a boy to death. Lived next door to us, he was trouble, his dad was a wrong'un. But he didn't deserve that. They pinned a robbery on him, stitched him up good and proper. I saw it.'

Ben Stark clapped his hand onto Mr Dryden's shoulder, squeezing it gently. 'I say, sir, don't fret. Anyone can see you're nothing to do with this foul business, no matter how worried you might be. And we don't know it's murder yet, in any case. Do take heart.'

'Oh – dear Mr Stark,' Mr Dryden exclaimed. 'Such kindness. But we have lived rather different lives, and I have a realistic approach to this, as you shall see.'

Dora remembered the torn pages, the look on the dead man's face. Swimming to the front of her mind was an image she could not quite see, it was not clear enough. She wondered if she could go back, have a look, see if it would come to her again.

'But Mr Dryden, I am sorry to say I think he was murdered.'

'You do?' said Mr Stark, turning to her.

She nodded. 'Something I saw on the body.' She shook her head. 'I won't say more for now.'

'You're as bright as a button,' Mr Dryden said gloomily. 'I wish you could help me. This is bad for the library, and I'm sorry to say it looks bad for me especially.'

'What do you mean?'

Mr Dryden glanced towards the door, running his tongue quickly between his lips. 'Mr Stark is being kind. But everyone knew – *out there* – that Sir Edwin Mountjoy and I were not on good terms. In fact you might say relations between us had completely broken down. I expected any moment to be let go.'

'Why?'

He passed a shaking hand over his brow. 'It's so unpleasant, all of this. Talking about a man like this when he's still warm! This is a library, Miss Wildwood! Not a hardened drinking den in Soho or a footpad-bestrewn wasteland like – like Hounslow Heath.' From this Dora deduced Mr Dryden was getting his facts about murders exclusively from hardboiled detective novels or poems about Dick Turpin. 'There, *there* you'd expect to find a body. Not in the Science: Butterflies section between Carey and Casey.' He groaned, clutching his stomach, and twisting the points of his waistcoat with his long anxious fingers. 'Poor woman . . . What will I *tell* her?'

'You aren't responsible for this,' said Dora, hoping she was right.

'But in part I am!' He rubbed his face in agony. 'The sin of – of omission, Miss Wildwood!'

'That's not a crime, Mr Dryden.'

'Perhaps not . . . but I should have stepped in. I should have decried him to the world. To the world! Revealed him for the tartar, the imposter he was!' Ben Stark had perched himself on the edge of the desk, arms folded tight around himself, watching Mr Dryden with an unreadable expression. 'Oh he knew everyone, Sir Edwin did. Very well connected. But he was a fool. He didn't *even like books*.' Mr Dryden spluttered so much spittle flew across the room, landing on two of the portraits of previous librarians. 'I ask you! I asked him once who his favourite character in *Middlemarch* was and do you know what he said?'

'Who?' said Dora, to whom this was an ideal way of spending the time. 'I mean, whom?'

Mr Dryden said slowly: 'Casaubon.'

'Dear God,' Ben Stark said. Dora gave a gulp of laughter, and drained her glass. She felt completely hysterical, all of a sudden.

The door flew open and Detective Inspector Fox stood in the doorway, his vast shoulders almost touching the frame. 'Thank you for waiting,' he said, glancing at Dora and Mr Dryden, and whipping off his coat again, which once again showered them both with a few remaining raindrops. He nodded briefly at Ben Stark. 'Have we met?' he said. 'You look familiar.'

'We have,' said Ben Stark, but he did not elaborate and Fox did not press him. Something passed between them, it seemed to Dora, watching them both. Then Ben Stark said: 'I'll leave you now. Miss Wildwood, I hope your knee isn't causing you too much discomfort. Do let me know if you'd like me to see you into a taxicab.'

'Thank you,' she said, suddenly wishing he could stay. Fox nodded, as Ben Stark closed the door behind him. He turned to Dora and Mr Dryden.

'I'd like, if you please, to interview you both formally tomorrow,' he said, walking around the office, wiping his fingers on various surfaces. He spun round suddenly, as if he wanted to catch them in the act of doing something, rather like Grandmother's

Footsteps, Dora found herself thinking. 'But for now if you could just tell me briefly: what happened this afternoon?'

Dora laughed. She wondered if perhaps she'd had too much brandy. 'I mean I don't really know what's happened, so I can't tell you very much.'

'Very well.' Fox stroked his beard. 'What *do* you know, Miss Wildwood?'

'Ah. Well, let me see,' said Dora. She screwed up her eyes, focusing on him, wishing her head didn't spin so much. 'I know your full name, for starters. You're Detective Inspector Stephen Mavis Fox,' she said, slowly.

The detective inspector froze. 'What did you say?'

'Stephen Mavis Fox. That's your name, isn't it?'

'Well – yes. But how did you know that?' he said, hoarsely.

'I was going past the police station today,' said Dora. 'Rather fast. I heard a woman, about your age, shouting at you. She was calling you Stephen. Stephen Mavis, in fact.' She looked down into her drink, gathering herself. 'She was in a black dress, white collar. Looked rather like she might be a waitress. She said you were—'

Mr Fox opened and closed his mouth. 'Thank you, Miss Wildwood,' he said. He gave her a strange look and she breathed out, glad not to have been detected, for the moment. 'Now, the library employees at the main desk – their names again?'

'Mr Stark, Miss Amani, and Mr Clark, you mean?'

'Don't you have a notebook?' Dora heard herself asking, but she was ignored.

'I can summon them, if you wish.' Mr Dryden indicated a bell on his desk. Dora noticed his hands were shaking.

'No,' Stephen Fox said. 'What I have to say should remain as private as possible for the moment. In fact . . .' He shut the door quietly. 'I wanted to inform both of you that it is extremely unlikely the deceased died of natural causes.'

'Oh dear,' said Mr Dryden, pressing his hands to his face. 'Go on.'

'Mr Dryden, for heaven's sake pull yourself together,' said Dora, looking at Detective Inspector Fox's huge, muscly arms with appreciation. 'Let the man finish.'

'Thank you, Miss Wildwood,' said Fox, looking uncertainly at her. He cleared his throat. 'Here are the facts. Sir Edwin arrived back from luncheon at three p.m. and went to his office. Miss – the secretary – brought him a cup of coffee.'

'Miss Bunce,' Dora murmured. 'A notebook is so helpful, sometimes, don't you think?'

Fox ignored her. 'Sir Edwin was seen in the Issue Hall of the library at three forty p.m. He was distressed, shouting about something to one of the librarians, but from what I understand that was not an unusual state for him. He went into his office, then came out again a few minutes after four p.m. He went into the area of the library known as the Stacks.'

'Yes,' said Dora. 'I heard someone come in. It must have been just after four. That would fit. I was two floors below him, I think.'

'Excellent,' Fox nodded. 'Thank you, Miss Wildwood.' Dora returned his curious gaze, she hoped politely at him from under her eyelashes, then shook her head. He may have been rather full of bluster but there was no denying he did have extremely nice forearms.

'To continue,' said Detective Inspector Fox. 'This is the possible sequence of events. Some time after five minutes past four, Sir Edwin died. You discovered the body at around four fifteen p.m. Sir James Lubbock is performing an autopsy, and the contents of the stomach will have to be analysed after that, at which point we will have more information, but for the moment that is what we have to go on.' He stroked his chin ruminatively.

'That sounds very good,' said Dora. 'Except there's two problems, which of course, Inspector Fox, I'm sure you've seen for yourself.'

Detective Inspector Fox stopped stroking his chin. 'What?'

'Well,' said Dora, standing up and looking around for her cape. 'There was no murderer there.'

'Come now, Miss Wildwood,' Fox said. 'I think you misunderstand.'

'No,' said Dora gently, and he blinked. 'Mr Fox, I think you do. You see, he had already been poisoned – I'm fairly certain that that will be what they discover at the autopsy. There were faint traces of white powder around his mouth, especially in the corners, one could see them through the metal grille of the floor.' She gestured around the room; his eyes followed her swift fingers, pointing here and there. 'Sir Edwin had a sweet tooth, as evidenced by the boxes of chocolates and Turkish delight secreted around this office which I'm sure you would have unearthed, in due course.'

'Well—'

'What else? Oh yes. And whoever killed him returned to the body after we'd gone.'

'What do you mean?'

'Oh dear,' said Dora, because it had been an awfully long day and she suddenly very much wanted to go back to Lady Dreda's and have a lie-down. 'The floors are metal and have gaps in them. You can see and hear anything and anyone. I was two floors below. I heard one other person. But they weren't on his floor. They were above him.'

'Did you hear them leave?' Dora shook her head.

'I knew they were there. I can't explain it. A feeling.'

'A feeling,' Fox said.

'You must know what I mean. I couldn't see them. They must have kept themselves very still, and quiet. But I say again: Whoever or whatever killed Sir Edwin was either lying in wait above to make sure he died because . . . the act of murder had *already taken place*.' She put on her cape. 'And I can promise you, it wasn't me.'

'Then how did they do it?' said Mr Dryden, his voice a whisper.

'As I say, perhaps they were there already, hiding somehow. But I think that most unlikely, don't you?'

'Well—' Fox began. Then he stopped. 'I don't know.'

'Yes, very good,' said Dora. She drained her glass. 'It's probable someone had poisoned him in some way before he entered the Stacks. Or perhaps something in those books killed him,' Dora said slowly. 'Because you ought to know I *did* hear someone leaving. Several minutes after I'd found him, two floors above.' She shivered, pulling the cape around her. 'I think perhaps they waited until I'd found him. But whoever they were they weren't close enough to have done the deed itself without me noticing. Most likely they'd done it already, waiting for me to raise the alarm and leave; and that brings me to the second piece of evidence I have.'

Fox looked taken aback. 'The second piece? There's more?'

'Someone – I assume the murderer – returned to the body whilst I was getting help,' Dora said. 'There was a book on the floor – I tripped over it in the darkness, and trampled on it. I remember the sound, the feeling of the spine breaking under my foot. Awful.'

'You poor girl,' said Mr Dryden, with feeling. 'How horrible.'

Dora turned to him eagerly. 'You understand, don't you, Mr Dryden? Nothing worse than the sound of a book's spine being cracked.'

'Like bones,' he said with a shudder. 'Ghastly.'

'Oh, that's exactly it. I do think—'

'Horror of the vandalism of books aside, could we get back,' said Detective Inspector Fox repressively, 'to the matter in hand?'

'I am so sorry.' Dora paused, then noticed Fox was leaning against the desk, arms folded, waiting for her to speak. 'When we came back, that is I, Mr Stark and Mr Dryden and the others, the book was gone, you see. Someone had taken it.'

'What was the book?'

'That's just it,' Dora said, clicking her tongue in annoyance. 'For the life of me I can't remember. So foolish. I remember everything, too. Perhaps I will recall, later. I'm quite tired.' She opened her eyes wide, then closed them, rubbing the lids. 'I don't think I can be much more help to you this evening, I'm most dreadfully sorry to say,' she said, apologetically. 'I seem to see stars everywhere, wherever I look. Is it the Armagnac? Is it fatigue? Is it the exigencies –' she paused, not sure if this was the right word, but carried on – 'of the day? Who knows.'

'I do think we should allow Miss Wildwood to go home whilst you continue your enquiries, Sergeant Fox.'

'I—' Detective Inspector Fox began, but he was interrupted by Dora putting on her gloves and saying:

'Our vicar has the middle name Leonora, but that is because his mother died when he was only a day old, and it has always seemed quite appropriate. It was her name, I should clarify.' She added, after a moment's pause. 'Mavis. How interesting.'

'Miss Wildwood, do allow me to escort you to a taxi cab,' said Mr Dryden warmly.

'You're ever so kind. Thank you. I think Mr Stark had offered to see me—'

'I'll explain to him. You're exhausted, I shall see you into a tax-icab forthwith my dear. He's a very good young man, Ben Stark,' cried Mr Dryden, jabbing his finger in the air. 'A remarkable young man. Most interesting family, and we're lucky to have him – but that's enough of that. Come with me, my dear.'

'You will be required to come in for an interview and—' Detective Inspector Fox began, after clearing his throat. 'Scotland Yard is—'

'Wonderful. Chief Inspector, I'm staying at my godmother's, Lady Dreda Uglow, and her address is 4, Lloyd Square. Shall I return to the library tomorrow, or will you call upon me at her house?'

'The library tomorrow at ten a.m. would be most convenient. Th-thank you, Miss Wildwood,' said Fox. 'And if you could try to remember the book—'

'Of course,' she said, rubbing the patch between her eyebrows hard, pressing it as if it were a button. 'I can't think why I don't see it. Anyway, good evening, Inspector Fox.'

'It's Detective – never mind. Good evening,' Fox said, through clenched teeth. He stood up and held the door open. Dora passed by, glancing up at him, and nodded.

She walked out with her arm through Mr Dryden's, having embarked, apparently with some context which was the most bewildering bit of it all, upon a story about her friend Albert's Jack Russell, Trilby, who'd won first prize in the Somerset Jack Russell Society summer show for eating the most sausages.

'He died the next week, *very* sadly, but honestly, the smile he had on his face – he was thirteen, and I think it's a pretty wonder-ful last few days on earth, don't you, Mr Dryden? Yes, of course you do too,' Fox heard her say, as they passed into the Issue Hall again and out of earshot.

Detective Inspector Fox, alone in the office, suddenly wondered how it was he'd let his main witness sail out of the interview without so much as a by-your-leave.

*   *   *

'Well, Miss Wildwood,' said Mr Dryden, as they stood on the curved corner of the pavement, watching out for a cab in the smoggy, wispy darkness of the square. 'It was a great pleasure to meet you. Even if the circumstances were somewhat—'

'Exactly,' said Dora. 'How funny. Here's an idea.'

'What?'

'Nothing. It's silly.' Her heart was racing. 'It can't be true.'

'Is this about the murderer?'

'Forget it. Mr Dryden – can you tell me something?'

'Of course.' He held out his hand, and summoned a taxi.

'Do you like peppermint creams?'

'I adore them.'

'I'm so glad,' she said. 'They're my favourite. Look, here is a taxi, right away. Don't lose heart Mr Dryden. And don't fall into a depression. Knowing a person who has died and having to organise things after their death are two very separate issues. People conflate them and it's a terrible mistake.'

'Yes, you're quite right.' Mr Dryden looked at her thoughtfully. 'I do hope we meet again.'

'Oh we will,' said Dora. 'This is the most wonderful place I've ever been in in my life and I shall come back every day now I've found it.' She smiled at him as he opened the cab door, and climbed in. 'And in the meantime, be very careful. Don't go anywhere alone, will you? Your life is in grave danger as of this moment, as is mine.'

Mr Dryden paused, looking around him. 'Miss Wildwood, please don't make me anxious. What makes you say that?'

Dora wound down the window and leaned out. 'A desperate person killed Sir Edwin Mountjoy,' she said quietly. 'Someone who was very afraid. One could feel it. Someone who hated him – yes,

73

loathed him with a passion I don't think I've ever come across.' She gave him a small smile. 'What does someone do to make themselves hated so violently? And what makes someone so full of hatred, or fear, that they have to kill? That's the question.' She turned towards the taxi driver. 'Lloyd Square, please. Thank you so much.'

'Goodnight, my dear,' said Mr Dryden, his voice rather faint.

'Goodnight. And do take care. I'll send you some peppermint creams. So cheering and the peppermint is so good for the digestive system.'

'How did you —'

'Ah, I see more than other people, some times,' she said, half gravely, but her eyes were twinkling. 'Good night, Mr Dryden.'

And with that the taxi cab rattled away, out of the spooling circle of golden gaslight.

*　*　*

Once Dora was in the cab, she leaned back against the hard seat, blinking quietly, watching London at dusk flash by. The theatres, starting to light up in the autumn gloom. The grand restaurants, polished brass on doors and handles glinting in the light from the streetlamps. A gaggle of young people, the women in chiffon and headdresses, the men in white tie, fell out of a doorway of a restaurant and stood on the street, chattering. Dora looked at them, as the cab stopped to let an old man pass. They were so carefree. She stared hungrily at the girls' dresses, their carefully waved hair. One of them had a diamond clip and matching diamond shoes. I would like to be a girl with a diamond clip in my hair and diamond shoes, she thought.

One of the other girls, shrugging herself into a fluffy white mink coat, slid her arm through a young man's arm and they were on their way. She watched as a doorman opened a door off Leicester Square and they piled in. 'What's that?' Dora asked, peering at the door, the glimpse of a staircase descending down, black and gold décor, the vanishing group chattering as the door closed behind them.

'That's the Café de Paris,' said the taxi driver. 'The centre of the world, it is. Huge staircase, like something out of a palace, gold it might be, curves all the way down into the basement. They get through more champagne there than any other club in London. Anyone who's anyone ends up there. Only the best musicians, best of everything.'

'Oh it sounds marvellous. I wish I could go.'

'I had to go inside once, help a young lady into a cab. She was a little the worse for wear.' He gave a chuckle as if this was the highlight of his life. 'Oh I say! Had to carry her into the cab. Gentleman had vanished, stuck me with the lady.' He wrinkled his nose. 'Don't you go getting yourself into trouble like that, Miss.'

'I wouldn't,' said Dora cheerfully. 'I don't ever relax, not really.'

'Sounds very sensible,' said the driver. 'Do you know what I likes? I likes a crime novel.'

'Well, how delicious,' said Dora. 'Me too. And some peppermint creams.'

'I'm more of a nougat fan myself, Miss. But a square of nougat and a fire and a new murder – that's me, happy as you like. Have you read *The Speckled Band*? Ah, that's a good'un. I tell you, that's a story and a half. Dies of fright, she does. Dies of fright.'

Dora thought of Sir Edwin's face, the ghastly rictus of it, his red neck, his warm body. She shivered.

'Let's not talk about it. Tell me how long you've kept homing pigeons. I die for them.'

The cab driver actually turned his head around, whilst driving up Shaftesbury Avenue. 'Miss. How in God's name do you know that?'

Dora shrugged. 'If I told you, you'd never believe me.'

There was an awkward silence after that. She had gone too far, shown her hand. And it was good, good to sit quietly, not to perform for once. Merely to simply exist, for a few minutes.

8

Lady Dreda is further disturbed

'Well *there* you are, Miss Wildwood,' said Maria, when she opened the door of number 4, Lloyd Square. 'Lady Dreda *will* be glad.'

'Oh dear,' said Dora, plucking her beret from her head and leaning briefly against the bannisters. 'Has she been wanting me?'

'I should say,' said Maria frankly. 'She had a telegram from your father. And I know you said not to trouble anyone, but she was about to call the police.'

'I'm dreadfully sorry to have put *you* to the trouble, Maria.' Dora smiled at her frankly, then pressed a forefinger to a spot between her eyebrows. 'I got it wrong,' Maria heard her mutter to herself. 'Didn't want to cause a fuss. Remember that next time old girl.'

'What, Miss?'

'Charles. My fiancé, the one you saw at the station. Just having a word with myself Maria. Dreda would have been right to call them. I'll go and see her—'

Maria put her hand out as if to pat her, then withdrew it. 'Bless you, but she's just fallen asleep. Come and I'll get you unpacked. I'm glad to see you're back in one piece. *I* was worried, never mind Lady Dreda.'

'That's jolly kind of you,' said Dora.

'Not kind at all,' said Maria stoutly. 'I should have stepped in and I'm kicking myself I didn't. I will, next time. Come this way, Miss. When we're finished we can wake Her Ladyship up and you can have tea and an early night. Because if you don't mind me saying, you look done in.'

*   *   *

'Miss—' Maria said, when they were upstairs a few minutes later. She gestured to the clothes she had laid on the eiderdown in the small, dark blue bedroom with dark wooden floorboards, a cheery Turkish rug and a small fireplace with a bright, warm fire that actually gave out some heat. 'Is this all you brought with you? I don't seem to be able to find anything else.' She paused for a moment, then said again, 'Miss Dora?'

Dora was curled up like a cat, looking out over the square, knees under her chin, arms wrapped round her legs, gripping herself so tightly the knuckles on her hands were quite white. She did not hear Maria.

'Miss Dora?' Maria said more loudly, and Dora jumped.

'I'm so sorry. What was it?' She looked down. 'Oh,' she said sadly. 'Those are all my things. I know, it's a sack of rags. I apologise.'

Maria looked down at the patchwork bedspread, where lay the following: a copy of *The Case-Book of Sherlock Holmes*, a pair of binoculars, a Fair Isle tank top, a dark blue skirt with voluminous pockets, some trousers – still rather daring – in a rather stylish coral, blue and green tweed, one white silk shirt, crumpled into a ball, some stockings and striped knitted socks in blue and coral, a tattered and creased nightdress in brushed cotton, some undergarments – not many, and very worn, one camisole with a torn strap and a teal-coloured tea dress trimmed with lace, which Maria judged by its musty smell and dropped waist had last been worn during Mr Baldwin's first premiership.

'I packed in rather a hurry.'

Maria snapped the case shut smartly, and stowed it under the bed. 'It doesn't matter. We'll get you some new things, Miss, don't you worry. I'll press that silk shirt and trousers, and mend that strap, and – all the rest.'

'How lovely,' Dora said absently. 'Maria, can I ask you a question?'

'Yes, Miss?'

'Where do you live, Maria?'

'Me? Miss, I live on the top floor.'

'Oh! Of course. I mean, where's your family?'

'My family's out in Bow, Miss.' Maria folded up the nightgown with a magic hand that seemed to press it smooth, and put it in an embroidered silk pillowcase.

'Have you got brothers and sisters? If you don't mind telling me.'

'I don't mind.' Maria hesitated. 'It's just my mum. It's grand I've got this job. So she don't worry about me, and I can send some money home.'

Dora got up and went around the room, picking up ornaments, putting things away. Maria noticed how deftly she moved, how at odds her physical grace was with her rather chaotic manner.

'Is she on her own?'

Maria nodded. 'She is. She was a seamstress for years, ever so clever with her fingers, she taught me how to – you know, make yourself smart, stylish . . .' her eyes ran over Dora's clothes: the mustard-coloured short-sleeved cardigan worn over the white silk shirt. 'You're ever so pretty, Miss, and you've got a lovely sense of what goes with what. Lady Dreda likes lending things, she's always pressing clothes and suchlike on me and I don't have any-where to wear them. She'll lend you anything. She's got this dress in her wardrobe, silver sequins like water rippling and it's not even really a dress . . .' Maria breathed in deeply. 'It's a blouse on top and trousers underneath, wide-legged, you know like beach pyjamas. An all-in-one called a jumpsuit, by Schiaparelli – it's beautiful, Miss Dora, the cut is exquisite—' She stopped. 'Sorry. I do run on. My mum says I ought to get my own shop and then I can talk clothes all day.'

'She must be awfully proud of you. Why don't you have your own shop?' Maria looked at her, faintly amused, and Dora blushed. 'How silly of me. I don't expect it's easy.'

'That'd be ever so nice one day, Miss, but I'll have to work here a bit longer first. Save up. I'm lucky to have this job.'

'Of course. Is Lady Dreda good to you? Actually, don't worry, you can't tell me, I know.'

'She's wonderful.' Maria nodded firmly. 'Really. She's a lovely kind lady. And so's Mrs Bundle.'

'Mrs Bundle – yes of course, the housekeeper. She let me in.'

Maria nodded, her mouth tightly shut. Mrs Bundle had looked out for her when she'd arrived, aged sixteen, so small and under-nourished that she'd fainted carrying a heavy pail of hot water up the stairs. Things had been bad at Mum's then, Dad had died, and Mum had lost her job at the atelier in Mayfair making repairs for rich ladies because her eyes got bad, and she couldn't find work – it was 1931, and no one could find work, not then, and no one was buying new things, and there was no money, and it was very bad that winter. Maria had had to go out to work, else they'd have starved, but it was wretched, being away from her mum. She couldn't ever get warm, and on the second night, when she'd been sobbing in her narrow bed, Mrs Bundle had brought her in a hot-water bottle, a glass of warm milk with honey, and a slice of bread-and-butter. 'No point in crying, ducks. You drink that and get back to sleep so you're nice and fresh in the morning. And I'll make sure there's a big bowl of porridge for you, with cream and sugar.' She had stroked her hair, kindly but firmly. 'Lady Dreda won't want to keep you on if you spill that water everywhere. You've every other Sunday afternoon off to go and see your mum, remember. And I've a postcard and stamp you can have tomorrow. Write and tell her you're all settled. That's it, well done. Eat up.'

That was five years ago, and lately Mrs Bundle was having funny turns, and kept forgetting where she was, but Maria wouldn't ever let anyone know. Not after what she'd done for her. 'I wouldn't leave Mrs Bundle, that's all,' she managed to say.

Dora was leaning against the wall by the bed, head on one side, watching Maria, and Maria had the oddest sensation that Dora understood. 'Do you ever go home?'

'Oh yes.' Maria shrugged. 'Every other week. Sometimes Mum comes to see me, and waves in at the window, and I wave back.'

'Is your mother still on her own?' said Dora, staring around the small room that looked out over the rooftops of London, and blinking.

'Yes, just her. My father's dead. It weren't entirely a bad thing,' she added. 'Regular dark horse, he was, always in trouble, but oh he made me and Mum laugh.'

'My father had a dark horse,' said Dora. 'An actual one. It kicked him in the head when he was examining its fetlock. He was never the same again.'

Maria laughed, without meaning to, then covered her mouth.

'Oh don't worry. My mother's dead too. It's awful.' Dora pulled on her cardigan. 'No one wants to talk about her. And I don't know about you but I want to talk about her all the time, to say how much I miss her, and what happened to her, but I have to carry on pretending.'

'That's it,' said Maria, who wanted to tell her about the time her father found a pound note someone had dropped in the gutter, and the happiness it had bought them for a week, a week of enough food and a scuttle of coal and a tiny bunch of forget-me-nots for her mother. But she didn't, because she couldn't talk about her dad without feelings coming up, and moreover, she didn't think she ought to be having this conversation. 'Now, Miss. Why don't we go and wake Her Ladyship up, and you can have supper.'

'Thank you so much, Maria.' Dora stood up. 'By the way, do you know where to get peppermint creams?'

'I beg your pardon, Miss?'

'Peppermint creams. They're my great weakness.'

'Oh! Well, any one of those smart shops on Piccadilly, really. Fortnum & Mason or the Burlington Arcade.'

A voice came from downstairs.

'*Maria!* Is she here?'

'I think that's Her Ladyship, awake now.'

'Thank you so much, Maria. For everything,' said Dora, running down the stairs so fast the bannisters and chandeliers shook.

'Good evening,' she said, flinging open the folding doors which gave out from the hallway onto the drawing room. 'I'm here, darling Dreda, awfully sorry to be so late. I can explain—'

'Dora, *thank God*,' said Lady Dreda, passing a hand over her forehead. She was lying on the chaise longue, an empty box of chocolates on the floor beside her, and a detective story on her chest. She closed it and sat up. 'I was on the verge of calling the police.' She flapped a thin sheet of paper, covered with capital letters, at her. 'The verge, I tell you.' She blinked, still half asleep, as Dora bent down and kissed her. 'Your father sent a telegram, darling, looking for you. It says you're as good as *married*, Dora, and that you should go back home. And something about a boy from the village who's a druid – oh dear, I don't understand.' Dreda said slightly crossly, 'Who was this man, chasing you?'

'Charles – Charles Silk-Butters.'

'That dreadful man with the villainous moustache, the one who lives in Harwood Hall?'

'Yes,' said Dora.

'What on earth is he doing in London?'

'He seems to think I should go back home and marry him.'

'*Charles Silk-Butters* is your fiancé?' Lady Dreda almost shrieked. 'Dear me, what a farrago. Oh Dora.' She brushed some cocoa dusting from her kimono. 'Dearest, why on earth? Oh dear girl, how I have neglected my responsibilities to you, what would Elizabeth say. That is – do you love him?' she amended hastily.

'No, not at all. I've no idea why I said I'd marry him. He wore me down.' Dora slipped her hands into her pockets, and slid onto the sofa. The brandy, and the day's events, were giving her a curious out-of-body experience, as if she were watching herself on a cinema screen, the reel speeded up.

Lady Dreda stroked her cheek. 'Well it's wonderful to see you, whatever the reason. You're awfully grown up. And you look—'

She stopped. 'I look what?' said Dora, amused.

'You are very lovely,' said Lady Dreda. 'That's all. Something about your eyes, you know, always was. Utterly frank and bewitching. Your mother used to say you'd be good in the mountains, you'd know when an avalanche was coming minutes before anyone else – don't frown, darling, lines. Anyway, Charles. I *can't* understand why your father allowed it to happen.'

'It's not his fault. Really. Charles is one of those people who thinks he's born to take what he wants.'

'Well, that's as maybe, but he's *very* odd. I remember sitting next to him at your father's fiftieth celebrations, darling. He spent the whole time talking about magnetic forces.'

'Yes,' said Dora, thinking of the magnets secreted around Harwood Hall, under the table, sewn into curtains, under the bed. 'Anyway,' she said, turning away from her godmother and speaking rather fast, 'I had to run away, I'm rather afraid of him. Dreda darling – don't be cross – I pushed him down the stairs and threatened him with a gun—'

Dreda moaned, and covered her face with her hands.

'We meant to give you sandwiches, Dora dear, I'm so very sorry. Maria gave you the wrong package. What did you do with it?'

Dora said awkwardly: 'I lost it. I'm most dreadfully sorry. I waved it at Charles and it was still in my pocket when I ran off – it's very small, sweet, but I didn't like having it. And when I was in the library later on I realised it must have slipped out. I do apologise. Was it – was it yours?'

To Dora's surprise, Lady Dreda hugged herself, and gave a cheerful shout of laughter. 'No! It wasn't. Maria found it under a loose floorboard, clearing out the spare room for you. We think it must have been left there by someone, when I don't know. Don't give it another thought. I detest mysteries. Oh, I am relieved. So relieved. Dreadful, thinking one had to dispose of it somehow and now you've lost it and all's well.' She smiled at Dora. 'There we are. We're having salmon mousse, Dora dear—'

But Dora interrupted gently. 'Still, that wasn't the strangest part of the day.'

'Oh. It wasn't?'

'No . . . I ran into the library – the London Library, you know, to escape Charles. And I'm late because I was rather held up with the police inspector, or whatever he is.' She turned, still rubbing her slender hands together. 'His middle name's Mavis, he's dreadfully pompous but he has lovely forearms. I'm not at all sure he knows what he's doing and one is supposed to trust the police, isn't one? Anyway—'

'Sorry?' said Lady Dreda weakly. 'Who is called Mavis?'

'The policeman. You see someone was murdered, and I found them. It was rather horrible really. All in all it was rather an unusual day, given that the same Tuesday last week all I did was well, stare out of the window wishing I wasn't here, and ask the shepherd to wring a chicken's neck after she'd got some dreadful infection.' She looked up, and saw her godmother's face.

'Dora darling,' said Dreda, blinking fast. 'Someone – was – *murdered*?'

'At the library, yes. I met your friend Venetia Strallen – she's awfully lovely, Dreda, we had a good talk. But then yes, I'm sorry to say someone killed the librarian.' She stopped. 'It sounds so inadequate when you put it like that.'

'My God,' Dreda said. 'Edwin Mountjoy? *Killed*? He wasn't . . . *shot*, was he?'

'No, poison,' said Dora simply. 'I found him. There was rather a hullaballoo, and that's why I was late.'

'How? When was he killed?' Dora shrugged. Dreda swallowed. 'But Dora my dear. One's known Mountjoy for years. You know who he was, don't you?'

'The Chief Librarian, yes.'

'Oh dear. Oh dear.' She stared at Dora reproachfully, as if she knew Dora to be responsible for Sir Edwin's murder. 'I must get hold of Venetia.' She stood up.

'Why?'

'Oh dear,' said Dreda again, fumbling for the bell, and for her spectacles. 'Poor Venetia. What will she do? So soon after the business with that dreadful Esmé Johnson, too.'

'Who?'

'Oh, a jumped-up little tart – forgive me, dear,' said Dreda crossly. 'And she's anything but little, too. Looks like a giraffe.'

'I love giraffes,' said Dora dreamily. 'There were two awful girls at school who used to tease me, call me Giraffe, because I was tall, and gangly. And I never minded, though I'm sure they were doing it to be rotten. Giraffes are beautiful, don't you think? I came to London to see one.'

'Well, you'll see *her* before too long, I'm sure,' said Dreda darkly. 'Gets everywhere. Utter sewer. She's a novelist, dear. Venetia took her under her wing, gave her her start in the literary world. Well, she treated Venetia incredibly badly. Stole ideas off her, undermined her . . . Poor dear Venetia. You know she never complains, but I thought she'd never manage to carry on. Yet she did.'

Shouting came from the hallway, the sound of a man's voice. Dora, who wanted to ask several questions, tore her mind away from this to the sounds outside. 'I rather fear that's Charles,' she said calmly. She stood at the door and looked out through the keyhole. 'Oh, I say, Maria's telling him he can't come in. Isn't she magnificent.'

'Maria *is* magnificent, yes,' said Dreda. They listened, as Maria's voice rose above the man's thunderous, furious rumbling tones. Dora rubbed her arms, then scratched her face. 'I do rather want to avoid him, Dreda, if I can – I wonder if – oh, dear God. Excuse me.'

There was a loud thudding sound and then unmistakably the sound of a door slamming shut. Outside, someone started to yell, as Maria appeared in the doorway, almost knocking Dora out of the way. Her cap was slightly askew and her cheeks were flushed.

'Your Ladyship, I'm most awfully sorry. Someone's delivered a note for you, most urgent, from Venetia Strallen. And that man appeared on the steps, very rude he was, very aggressive. He tried to barge in here and – well, I couldn't see why I should let him in, and I was—' Her eyes were huge, as if she knew the trouble she was in. 'I didn't realise he was Miss Dora's intended. I slammed the door shut on him.' She started to shake. 'He said – he's out-side now, making ever such a row.'

Dora looked out of the window. Charles Silk-Butters was indeed outside, banging on the railings with some kind of metal cane, fist raised up to the first floor in utter fury.

'I say! You! Give her back to me!' he shouted, his jowls trembling against his starched collar. 'Here! She's mine, I tell you! Get her down here now, you absolute blackguard!'

Dora got up from her chair and went to the window. Pulling it open, she leaned out. 'Charles! Do go away. You're making a frightful din—'

'I know!' bellowed Charles Silk-Butters, his face gleaming with malicious pleasure. 'And I intend to carry on doing so until you talk to me!'

'You didn't let me finish,' said Dora calmly. 'And you're embarrassing yourself, too. Think of the Silk-Butters name, Charles.' Charles looked, for a moment, rather chastened. 'You said you were going home. What on earth made you change your mind?'

'Shan't!' Charles called triumphantly. 'Shan't clear orf! So there!' And then he glanced around shiftily. 'I met an old – an old friend. They persuaded me to stay on for a bit. Said I should bally well fight to win you over. And they're quite right! But I'm losing . . .' He blinked, as if he'd forgotten his lines. 'I'm losing my patience.'

'An old friend?' Dora frowned. 'But – you don't *have* any friends, Charles.'

'I! I have no friends? Hah! What of Dornish?'

'He's your gamekeeper.'

'Good Lord, that man does go on,' said Dreda from the sofa, as Maria brought in the tea tray and laid it on the side table. Dora, recalled to the present, gazed at it appreciatively: scones, jam, cream, a small plate of chocolate biscuits, two perfect fondant fancies, elegant piped bows on each. The crackling, jolly log fire.

'Listen!' Charles was shouting. 'We'd sent out the invitation cards. This girl here is as good as my wife and I—'

'Oh honestly,' said Lady Dreda, impatiently, standing up. 'I simply can't bear bullies. My sister was a bully. Ankles thicker than an elephant's and she never let me borrow the family tiara. Come here, dear. Stand up straight.' Dora walked towards her, and Dreda pulled the tousled, mop-headed yellow chrysanthemums out of the two black glass vases that stood at either end of the mantelpiece. She handed them, dripping wet, to Dora.

'Do go *away*,' she called loudly. 'I've no idea who persuaded you to stay on in town, but they're no friend to you. Firstly, Dora doesn't want to marry you. Secondly, you're making a fool of yourself, and you're forgetting something,' Lady Dreda bellowed as he tried to speak again. 'I don't give a *fig* what anyone thinks of me, and I never damn well have. Go back to Somerset and those dreary magnets of yours, and leave us alone, you poltroon.'

And she emptied the contents of the first, then the second vase out of the window. There was a strangled cry of outrage, and a howling, gurgling sound.

'Dora!' Charles shouted, before dissolving into a coughing fit. 'They said—' he began, but before Dora could hear more Lady Dreda had pulled the window firmly shut, drawn the curtains, and turned to face her goddaughter.

'What a tiring day,' she said, patting her sleek, dark hair and padding back over to the sofa, where she collapsed with a sigh. '*You* are tiring, Dora dear. I knew it would be so.'

She picked up the note that Maria had dropped onto the side table and read it. 'Well, at least Venetia's not coming for supper any more. I must call round tomorrow and see how she is.'

'She's not coming?' said Dora, disappointed.

'My dear no. Prostrate with grief. Can't move. Doctor's with her.'

'Why?'

'The business at the library, of course.'

'Did she know Sir Edwin?' said Dora, surprised at this reaction.

'Know him? He was her fiancé. They were getting married at Christmas. She was absolutely devoted to him.' Dreda shook her head. 'Poor Venetia.' She clinked her ringed fingers against her tea cup. 'I don't know another person alive who cared for the man, but she was giving up writing for him. Her! Well, that's love for you, my dear girl. That's why I'd rather do without it.'

9

The books keep their secrets

In the middle of the night Dora sat up in bed with a gasp. She didn't know where she was for a moment. Darkness covered her like a blanket. She stood up, stumbling towards the wall, and fumbled at the thick brocade curtains that blocked out most of the light from the street. Where was she? Why couldn't she remember? As the curtains parted, she saw a golden circle pooling below a wrought-iron streetlamp, and, on the other side of a garden square, a lone figure walking slowly up and down. A policeman. She blinked. She was at Dreda's, she was in London.

Dora sat down on the edge of the bed. From the confusion of her half-asleep state, thoughts swam in front of her eyes, jostling to form themselves. What had woken her up? Something, some half-remembered detail.

Then she saw it, struggling to rise to the surface, and closed her eyes to capture it.

The book. The pages beside Sir Edwin's body. Mutilated, scrappy, like the paperchases at school, packs of hungry girls scrambling after each other to get to the next hill, over the next stile. But she remembered it.

The title page, there on the floor, in black and white, the author's name, the neat little colophon of a magpie, and the publishers' name:

Morpeth, Neild & Steyn Publishers Ltd
43 Bedford Square, WC1

Dora wrapped Dreda's husband's ancient paisley dressing gown around her and got back into bed. She was shivering, though the room was warm. Closing her eyes again she could see the words on the page, the stumpy edges of the torn paper.

'That is very strange,' she said to herself.

With the clarity of night she saw the events of the previous day with some relief. Her early morning flight – the bus ride – Charles's hard, jabbing fingers, pulling her down to oblivion – Ben Stark's kind voice, like sinking into a warm bath after the rain – the library, and the scent of musty, silent books, yards and yards of them – Venetia Strallen's lovely smile, the glint of her diamond belt – Edwin Mountjoy's red, furious face. The open book on the metal grille floor, the thousands of books below it. His face in death, still red, his pale blue eyes just as furious. Suddenly she understood now his expression: surprise. Not fear, or rage. Utterly surprised that this should be the ending. And she wondered again about her mother, last seen setting off alone from the tiny hut perched on the side of the mountain, wildflowers fringing her walk, butterfly net over her shoulder, and whether she had known that was the day she was going to die.

*   *   *

The library looked quite different in the crisp morning sunshine. Late October light bathed the stern silver stone with flickering shadows. Dora was neatly dressed in her newly pressed silk shirt and a soft navy cashmere jumper, and her cape and beret and, rather daringly, in the new wide-legged tweed trousers she had ordered in Bath with the postal order her father had sent her for her birthday. She had hardly worn trousers before, except to help Albert with haymaking. No woman in Combe Curry really did, apart from Bryony Fulcher, and she usually mounted her horse by springing up onto it from the ground so it made sense, but London was full of young women – some older women too – in trousers. Why shouldn't she? She clenched her slim, kid-gloved hands and trotted up the library steps, waving hello to Mikey, who was dealing with an elderly member who wanted to express his outrage that the library had failed to prevent someone being murdered there.

'Good morning, Miss Amani,' Dora said to the young woman behind the issue desk.

Miss Amani was tightening the scarf round her neck. 'Good morning. How may I help you?' Her eyes, raised to Dora's, were weary and slightly puffy, as if she hadn't slept, but they widened when she saw who it was. 'Oh. It's Miss Wildwood, isn't it? You're the one who found him.'

'I did.' Dora said.

'Ben Stark said you were awfully brave.'

'I don't know about that.' Dora leaned on the counter. 'I heard Sir Edwin shouting at you yesterday afternoon, didn't I? '

'Not really.'

'Something about books—'

'It's a library,' said Miss Amani drily.

Dora looked at her. 'Oh, but you know what I mean.'

Miss Amani nodded. 'I do. I do.' She gave a polite smile. 'Well—'

'There's something I don't understand,' said Dora. 'I woke up this morning with the image of a defaced and mutilated book in my mind. And then I realised I'd seen it next to the body. Has it happened before? Is that why he was shouting at you?'

Zewditu Amani looked quickly around the large, quiet room then at Dora, as if assessing whether she could trust her. 'We have had this trouble for the past few months. Someone is slicing or tearing large sections out of books, then simply putting them back on the shelves. At first we would not have noticed if it had not been for one of the authors complaining to us.'

'Who?'

'A detective novelist called E.L. Palmer. He comes in to check whether his books have been borrowed. He does this every week,' said Miss Amani without expression. 'Someone had torn the middle section of *The Riviera Mystery* out. Then we found a few others. And thought that was an end to it, though Sir Edwin was very angry. Then it happened the week after, we had a complaint from a member that a copy of *Last Train to Samarkand* by Dorothea Manning was missing most of its second half. They'd cut it out, so carefully, and put it back on the shelf. They must use a knife.'

There was something about someone carefully slicing out sections of books in the dark of the Stacks that made Dora shiver. 'How many more?'

'We don't know. But it seems to be only detective novels, crime, mystery. There could be others, but perhaps they are not so –' she hesitated, clearly thinking of the best way to tactfully say it – 'in demand, so we haven't noticed yet.'

Miss Amani looked over; a reporter had come in, asking for information, and Mikey was briskly dispatching him.

'The police will be here soon, sir,' he was saying. 'Most of the library is still closed to members, let alone reporters. It's a crime scene.'

'It is curious, don't you think?' said Dora slowly. 'Why now? These books have been on the shelves, some of them there for fifty years. It reminds me of something . . .' She trailed off thoughtfully.

'If you love books as much as I do,' said Miss Amani gravely, 'it is very upsetting. My father used to bring them home for me from the Embassy. All the English stories. I grew up on them. That's how I learned English. When my father went back to Addis Ababa and I stayed on, books were my friends. I could not do without them.'

'So there could easily be more books back there that a person unknown has sliced sections out of,' Dora said, turning away from watching Mikey back to Miss Amani. 'On a shelf, looking like all the other books, hoping not to be spotted.'

'Most likely, I would say.' Zewditu Amani began briskly stamping title pages again.

'It's rather horrible.'

'I had a Sherlock Holmes last week, it fell to pieces in my hand. They'd sliced out five or six stories . . . and then just put it back. When I opened it again the binding tore and the whole book fell apart. Sir Edwin was furious about it. Somehow more furious than I thought he'd be. I didn't really—' she stopped.

'You were going to say you didn't think of him as someone who particularly cared about books.'

'Yes, that's it, exactly.'

'Why did you hesitate?'

'Well, it sounds so strange. He was the Chief Librarian, after all.'

'Did you like him?'

'Like? That is a strange word to use for a man like him. He did not want to be liked.'

'What do you mean?'

'He reminded me of the mutilated books,' said Zewditu Amani. 'The frontage is present and correct, but there is nothing inside. He wanted to be important. To be displayed on the shelf. And I am a girl, and I am a coloured girl, so he had no use for me, at all, and he could not have made that clearer. He said, quite often, that I should go to Addis to be with my father's family. But I told him several times, I have lived here since I was five. The last time he told me this was three days ago. I told him Mussolini has invaded Abyssinia. The fascists have entered Addis Ababa. Our Emperor has gone into exile. I have no family that I know, my home is here. I cannot go back. But –' she raised her candid, sparkling eyes to Dora – 'he did not seem to care. He was that kind of man. So no, I did not like him.'

Dora nodded. She moved her hand and, very briefly, placed it on the other woman's, which rested on an open book. 'Thank you,' she said. 'I am sorry.'

'I am an exile too,' said Miss Amani. 'It is strange, living some-where that is your home, but constantly thinking about somewhere else that you don't really know. Thank you so much. Now tell me how I can help you.'

'Miss Amani. Do you have a list of the mutilated books, by any chance?'

'I started keeping one,' said Zewditu Amani. 'I wanted to see if there was a pattern. But there doesn't seem to be one. I'm not sure the list is complete . . . I mentioned it to Sir Edwin, but he told me I was fussing. I did not think it was fussing.'

'Did he take an interest in the fact someone was defacing books?'

'Yes and no. He did not want it to exist, to be a problem.'

'My father is the same,' said Dora. 'He thinks if he can pretend something isn't true, then it will cease to exist.'

Zewditu nodded. 'He'd been furious for a while now, several weeks, even by his standards it was becoming much worse, however. He was red-faced, angry, kept saying he had to leave work early—'

'That's very interesting,' said Dora. 'We need that list, Miss Amani. Could you be very kind and update it so it has as much information as possible?'

'I can double-check the titles with Mr Dryden. He was trying to keep track of them, too.'

Dora nodded her thanks. 'One final thing: have you heard of a book called *The Killing Jar*? I think it's by Cora Carson. It's the same sort of thing. It's awfully popular, isn't it?'

Zewditu Amani narrowed her eyes. 'It rings a bell. But it's not a detective mystery . . .' She stared into the middle distance. 'What is it? Cora Carson . . .' She snapped her fingers. 'No. It is in Science and Nature: Butterflies. Back stacks, second floor. Collins, 1931.'

Dora raised her eyebrows. 'Do you know every book in the library?'

'No. But many of them just stick. I like . . . having a place for things. Knowing where they belong.'

Dora was struck by the way she said this, the idea that there was a place on a shelf somewhere for any and every book. 'Stacked just between Carey, A., and Casey, J. . . .' Zewditu nodded calmly.

'A very interesting woman, Cora Carson. First female botanist to take a degree from the University of London in 1889, if I remember rightly.'

Dora wrote this down, in a hurry. 'And – oh. Isn't that where—'

'Yes,' Miss Amani said. 'That is where the body was found.'

'Thank you so much, Miss Amani. Is Detective Inspector Fox in yet?'

'He's in Sir Edwin's office,' said Miss Amani. 'He has knocked over a vase. He is a giant, that man.'

'Bull in a china shop, more like,' said Dora, and she nodded her thanks again.

*   *   *

They had reopened the bottom floor only of the Stacks, and a few members were idly browsing. A stooped man with huge walrus moustaches was grunting to himself as he thumbed through a book on stoats; a well-upholstered lady of uncertain age in mulberry-coloured velvet, was leaning against the shelves, arms folded, discussing something with a man whose back was to Dora. They were both whispering, but as she approached they stopped. The lady stared at her, so hard that Dora smiled politely and said: 'Oh! Do I have spinach?' She rubbed at her front teeth.

'That's *her*—' Dora heard the woman hiss as she passed by.

Dora knew where she was going. She spent a few happy minutes searching for the title she wanted, then wandered slowly back, stopping here and there. She had just got to 'Topography: Somerset and was staring at the shelves, finger running along the titles. She pulled out *Myths, Scenes and Worthies of Somerset* (Mrs Edmund Boger, 1887) and opened it at a random page.

'On the night before Shrove Tuesday, if a back door be left open of a parsonage or any farm house it is quietly opened and a whole sack of dead rabbits shall be shot into that place before anyone can notice. A very curious custom, of the nature of a practical joke.

'Ah, Old George Thumb's trick,' Dora murmured to herself. 'To think it's made it into a book. He'd be delighted, if they hadn't shot him dead.' She turned a page, fascinated. '*The Evil Eye in Somerset* – ah. *One old woman, called upon to resolve a dispute between a land agent and his carter, asked for payment of a live grass snake, a human tooth, 3 jars of cider and a small mound of* – good grief, how disgusting.' She closed the book sharply. 'I wonder,' she said. 'Does it say anything about magnetic – ahh!'

Someone tapped her rapidly and firmly on the shoulder and Dora jumped, letting out a little scream.

'Well *hello*!' said a woman's deep, luscious voice. 'Are you Dora? Dora Wildwood? Oh *do* say you are. *Do*. I saw you come in and I just had to pootle over and say hello!'

Dora turned towards the woman behind her, and gave an involutary hiss.

She had short white-blond hair, curls plastered to her skull like a flapper, though she was still young – Dora thought only a few years older than her. Beneath the fine curls, her skull was pink. She was tall: about six foot, slim, rangy, with pale skin and dark green eyes. She loomed over Dora, hands in the pockets of her silk slacks, smiling: Dora was reminded of the anaconda she'd seen once at Bristol Zoo.

All Dora had ever wanted to do was see a giraffe. For her tenth birthday her mother had taken her, as a birthday treat, to the zoo with Barbara Silk-Butters, Charles's young cousin, a companion thought suitable by her mother by dint of her family and the fact that prior to the trip to Bristol Zoo she had never been heard to utter a word in public. A quiet, polite girl, people said of her. Her parents lived in the gatehouse of Harwood Hall, having lost all their money in some bubble after the Boer War. Barbara Silk-Butters had remained silent until they arrived at the zoo, continued to remain silent when presented with the sight of a wild Bactrian camel, the zoo's famous elephant Delphine, and the new aquarium.

However the moment she entered the live mammals enclosure and saw Alfred, the famous lowland gorilla who was one of the stars of the show, some deep primaeval desire to connect with an ancestral being had overcome her, she had become completely feral and utterly insensible to human pleas, scaled the gorilla enclosure, hugged a surprised Alfred, and when forcibly removed by a zoo keeper had bitten his finger so hard that he had to be taken to hospital and afterwards contacted Barbara's parents about the loss of his fingernail, demanding reimbursement. This request Barbara's father had forwarded to Elizabeth Wildwood with an icy note asking she respond to the zoo keeper herself. 'Reimburse him with what?' Dora's mother had asked crossly, extremely sensitive about the disastrous results of her carefully planned little birthday outing. 'Does he want me to *remove* one of my *own nails* and send it to him in the post? Or pay for him to have a new one constructed out of enamel? Like a Fabergé egg? Honestly.'

But what had stuck in Dora's mind was not the elephant, or the beautiful grounds of the zoo, perched high on the city edge near to the miraculous Clifton Suspension Bridge spanning the precipitous Avon Gorge, or the glittering angel fish in the crystal-blue aquarium or the thin legs of the flamingos, like pink sticks of rock. What had stayed with her was the huge anaconda, sliding across the floor of its cage in an S-shape without apparently moving, slick-slack, slick-slack, till it was in front of her, swaying from side to side, watching without expression, and she had clutched her mother's hand, more scared then than she had been of anything in her young life.

And this woman in front of her was exactly like a snake, only she was talking to her.

'I'm Esmé,' she was saying, holding out her hand with that wide smile in a most friendly manner. 'I say, are you all right? You look as if you've seen a ghost.'

'I don't like snakes,' said Dora obscurely.

'Oh! I don't think there are any here, you know. Hah! Well, apart from the critic of *Time and Tide,* that is. He's an absolute viper. Hah! Hah!' She threw her head back, and Dora saw, to her mounting horror, she had slightly pointed incisors. *She's a real snake, a serpent, like* The Lair of the White Worm. *I shall be murdered and eaten by her.* (Aged thirteen, she had been gravely ill with measles, and *The Lair of the White Worm* had been the only book in the room whilst she was in quarantine. That, and the trip to Bristol Zoo, had made a deep impression on her.)

She shook herself into the present. *This woman is not a snake. Do concentrate.*

'Of course. I'm Dora Wildwood, but you knew that, it seems.'

The woman shook her hand again warmly. 'Esmé Johnson. And *do forgive* me for being so forward: I've heard *all* about you from Venetia.'

'How lovely,' said Dora politely. She racked her brains. She knew the name Esmé Johnson. She did.

'So, I hear you're the one who found the body. How *crushing*.' Esmé leaned sympathetically against the books, head cocked on one side, and folded her arms. 'I can't imagine anything more awful and of course I've had my Barnard suffer far worse! I think it must be something to do with being a writer and having a *very* overactive imagination. But of course,' she said, nodding her head and winking, 'my Barnard can cope.'

'Your Barnard?'

'Yes! My Barnard Castle – my hero!' said Esmé Johnson, still smiling.

'Barnard Castle?'

'What dear?' said Esmé Johnson, with a broad grin.

'The town in the North of England? With a castle. Barnard Castle.'

'I don't know what you're talking about.'

'It was besieged by Mary Queen of Scots,' said Dora, wondering if she was going mad.

'My dear, no . . . My Barnard's a detective. Really rather popular, you know. He's awfully handsome. Very troubled past. Scion of an ancient family! Lovely cheekbones.'

'It's a town,' Dora said softly, almost to herself. 'There's a museum with a mechanical swan. I'm not mad.'

Esmé touched her nose lightly. 'Silly girl!'

Dora rubbed her eyes. 'So – you're a writer, then, too?'

Esmé laughed and then, seeing that Dora wasn't joking, peered forwards. 'Oh! I see! Yes, I am. Just a few books but I've been so *very* lucky and had a *tiny* bit of success – the public has really taken me to their hearts. Have you read any of mine?'

'We're miles from a library,' said Dora apologetically. 'My father doesn't really read anything new, not unless you count the coverage of the Test Match in *The Times*. I've got everything by Venetia Strallen of course; hasn't everyone?'

Miss Johnson's smile became even more fixed. 'Yes, of course they have! Aren't you funny?'

And suddenly Dora remembered Dreda saying something about Esmé Johnson now; she couldn't quite recall it. Instead she said: 'I must read one of yours, I see.'

'I'll have my editor, Michael, drop one over to you – do give me your address my dear. Michael Steyn, at Morpeth, Neild & Steyn,' she said, emphasising every word. 'You know, they're Venetia's publishers, too. He's always saying I'm too modest and ought to send copies out far and wide to my friends and family.' Esmé gave Dora another wide grin, affording her the opportunity to spot something was trapped in one of her back molars. 'It's called *The Guilty Fiancé*, and oh! –' she paused, her eyes alight – 'I do have to get used to releasing my birds into the wild and it's hard to talk about them, but talk I must! I *must*.' She widened her eyes, and said in a booming, spooky undertone: 'Two intrepid friends go mountaineering, and it ends in death—' She pressed her finger to her mouth. 'Well, that's all I'll say. How funny to meet you, Dora! Where are you staying, my dear?'

'I'm staying with my godmother for a fortnight.'

'Oh what fun!' Esmé said.

'So you worked for Venetia Strallen, for a while, is that right?' said Dora, suddenly recalling her conversation with Dreda.

'I was her helper, let's say. She was so very generous to me. So kind,' Esmé Johnson said with a curling smile. 'Well, I was *utterly* astonished when *Ding Dong Death* came out, you know. *Utterly* astonished. *Utter* shock. People saying it was better than Venetia, and then how unpleasant it all became, and I don't blame Venetia,' she said sombrely, putting her hand on Dora's arm. 'But it was *awful.*'

'I'm afraid I don't have any idea about any of that,' said Dora, as politely as she could. She wished she was better at making excuses. 'I don't know Venetia Strallen at all, beyond meeting her yesterday and then once when I was a . . . anyway,' she finished. 'I have to go back to reading about the Evil Eye in Somerset, if you'll forgive me—'

'Yes, of course. Awfully sorry,' said Esmé Johnson, unabashed. She clicked, and put her head on one side. 'How dreadful for Venetia, especially since he was going to be her way out, you know. One felt she rather wanted to step off the carousel. And poor you, finding him, darling. Do you remember where it took place?'

Dora pointed. 'Up there.'

Esmé Johnson leaned forwards. 'Which – which floor, darling?'

Dora stared at her, her lanky, sprawling frame, the whites of her curiously dead eyes, the pink scalp visible between the short curls. She felt a strange revulsion. 'I don't recall. I really must go now. Do excuse me.'

'Yes, yes of course,' said Esmé Johnson, remarkably unperturbed. 'See you soon, darling. Let's go dancing at the Café de Paris.' She flashed her a large, unfriendly smile. 'Do give my love to Venetia. *So* crushing. And of course, my deepest sympathies to her re: Sir Edwin.'

As Dora wondered what could be so crushing it was worse than the death of one's fiancé, Esmé turned and left, clambering up the dark stairs to the Fiction section at the top of the Stacks, a large, long-legged white spider. She was singing 'You're the Top' to herself. Dora could have sworn she was singing 'I'm the top'. The notes died away as she turned the corner and vanished.

Dora went back out into the wood-panelled Issue Hall, warm with sunlight, and knocked on the Chief Librarian's office door in the furthest corner of the building.

'Mr Fox?' There was no answer. 'Mr Fox?' she called again, and opened the door.

10

Detective Inspector Stephen Mavis Fox

The door swung open faster than she'd been expecting and Dora found herself face to face with Detective Inspector Fox, who was leaning over the desk, transferring some scraps of paper from one hand to the other. They fluttered to the floor.

'Good morning, Miss Wildwood. To what do I owe the pleasure?'

'What were those for?' Dora said, picking up the paper scraps. 'DW. MD. EM. Dora Wildwood, Michael Dryden, Edwin Mountjoy?'

He stared at her as if she had told him the location of Tutankhamun's tomb. 'Yes, that's it. How did you . . .'

'All suspects, I assume.'

'You were the one who said there was no murderer, Miss Wildwood.'

'I didn't quite say that,' said Dora. She shut the door behind her. 'May I talk to you, Inspector? It's important.'

'I'm Detective Inspector Fox.'

Dora looked confused for a moment. 'Dora Wildwood,' she said. 'Listen, Mr Fox – I've remembered the name of the book.'

'Forgive me. I'm Detective Inspector Fox,' Fox repeated. His face was turning slightly red.

Bewildered, Dora glanced around her. 'Oh I say, Are we – are we in a play?'

Fox's nose twitched. 'I mean, my title is Detective Inspector. Not Inspector, not Sergeant.' He ran a finger around his collar. 'It's just you keep getting it wrong.'

'How so?'

'Well, you keep calling me either Sergeant Fox or Chief Inspector or Inspector Fox and I'm none – I'm none of those things. I'm a detective inspector, you see. Actually, I'm in charge of all the detectives at the Yard, Miss Wildwood.'

'Are you really?' Dora said curiously. 'I'm so very sorry. How rude of me,' she said, removing her beret and shaking out her hair. 'Now, Mr – sorry, Detective Inspector Fox. I wondered if you wanted me to help with your enquiries.'

'Oh you did.' Fox gathered up the scraps of paper and put them in the pocket of his tweed jacket.

'Yes,' said Dora, assessing him, head on one side. 'I had an interesting chat with Miss Amani this morning. And Miss Johnson. Yes, most interesting.'

'You want to help,' said Stephen Fox. He stuck his tongue in one cheek, willing himself not to be impatient. He'd spent too long making allowances for the vagaries of madcap young women and here in front of him was his main witness, a perfect specimen of the species he most despised. Last month he'd wasted an inordinate amount of time on a runaway heiress who'd gone missing after a night out at the Embassy Club. She was found on the Embankment, swinging from a lamppost, wearing only one shoe and carrying a policeman's helmet. When pressed, she'd said her best friend had been murdered by a sinister undercover gang, that she was getting married to a lord at Christmas and that she wanted to die. That her husband-to-be was decent enough, but she didn't like men, not one bit. Her best friend was the one she loved and she was dead. Then she'd slipped from his grip and fallen into the Thames.

It had taken two frogmen and six constables an hour to rescue her, and Fox was extremely grateful to the careless boatman who had failed to properly secure his boat at Blackfriars, for it was that which had capsized and it was that to which Lady Natalie – that was her name, Natalie – had clung, until such time as she could be pulled from the river, the colour from her fuschia-pink silk dress running in rivulets down her arms and legs, her too-thin body blue with cold.

There were workers rioting at factories near Deptford, someone who liked killing cats in East Dulwich, the ongoing problems of murder, wife-beating, fights, and rape, all usually caused by the Needy Poor in the slums – having climbed out of them himself, Fox was strangely unsympathetic to the Needy Poor left behind in said slums – and he and most of Scotland Yard had spent the best part of a week searching for a society beauty who turned out to be half a mile away, high as a kite on cocaine and champagne and didn't even say 'thank you' or 'sorry' when they had delivered her, wrapped in a standard-issue Scotland Yard blanket (which she'd complained about, said was scratchier than the ones she'd had at boarding school) to Eaton Square back into the arms of her welcoming family. In fact, the family hadn't seemed that welcoming – an unsmiling, thin-lipped father, Lord Lansdowne, rigid with fury, and her mother, pale as the moon and hollow-eyed, not with concern for her daughter but the scandal she might cause.

Fox despised Lady Natalie Lansdowne and her conspiracies about underground societies and her tight-lipped reticence to talk about herself when families were starving in the streets. He especially despised her parents, who'd kept the whole business out of the papers, and who'd had Fox taken off the case when it had looked like it might be getting interesting.

He was from the East End. He had grown up on Hanbury Street without a father, in a row of houses that never got the sun, where women regularly died in childbirth, where drink really was the ruin of many a poor soul, where there was very little hope and where he, as the baby of the family, had been spoiled something rotten. He'd had some of his mum's attention, more than the others, and had gone to school, and had a teacher who liked him, who shoved him up to the Columbia Road Boxing Club, and they'd got him to go in for the police, and now he was Detective Inspector Fox and no one knew now that he'd been a ragged, dirty kid who had no shoes but hosted veritable cohorts of lice, a child on the edge of starvation, who usually ate once a day. No one except his dear old mum, Sarah, and his sisters, Susan and

Sally. He lived now to work hard and do well so he'd make his mother's life better. To take her out of Hanbury Street, to a nice house up in Clissold Park or something. But she wouldn't move. And instead of a bit of gratitude, his sisters hated him for it. Susan, especially – she said he'd abandoned his mother, his family, to better himself, that he was a snob, a fly-by-night, no sense of fun . . . above himself, he was.

Him! Above himself. The man who the other coppers called The Monk. 'Lighten up a bit, sonny.' 'Shh now, put away the cigarette cards, The Monk's here, boys.'

Yesterday he'd seen a young wife beaten so hard her eyeball had blown, like a lightbulb, two tiny kids huddled in the corner, all eyes, not speaking, waiting for whoever he was to come back and do it again. No, he had not much patience for long-limbed young women with hair like dark toffee, in some lights, not in others when it was more like copper, or even – anyway, those young women who thought they were helping.

'So let me get this straight.' Fox turned away, shuffling his scraps of paper. 'You want to play detective.'

'Well,' she said, and she gazed at him curiously. 'Call it playing if you wish. I want to solve the whole mystery, because it is never just the murder, the murder is the end point, isn't it?' said Dora. 'How it came to this, the many different factors that led there. The hundreds of people involved, all tell you something.'

'Well, if you look at it like that—'

'I do.' Dora removed her cape and took off her jumper, neatly rearranging her collar and hair, then pulled out a chair, and sank into it. 'It's very cold out there, but very warm in here. I find London confusing for that. In the country, one is cold all the time.'

Detective Inspector Fox watched her, arms folded. 'Miss Wildwood, excuse me. Could we move on?'

She looked at him. 'Oh, of course you must be extremely busy. I merely wanted to clear something up about how the murder was committed. Well, I said yesterday that Sir Edwin wasn't murdered in the Stacks, but I think you misunderstood me. Someone is responsible for his death. So there is a murderer. Whoever killed him did so with his help. And then they came back, after I'd gone for help, to remove the clues.'

'I don't see how—'

'Think about it.' Dora leaned forwards. 'I was sitting two floors below him. I heard him come in, I'm fairly sure, and one other person somewhere above him. But other than that I did not hear a single person come and go on his floor, or my floor. I didn't even notice him die.' She swallowed. 'And he must have done, whilst I was reading. It's the perfect crime, really, killing someone in full sight of someone else, in a building with books in, and floors through which you can see everyone come and go.'

Fox walked to the desk. He said politely, but not really troubling to keep the sarcasm out of his voice:

'So what do you suggest?'

'What does the autopsy say?'

Detective Inspector Fox sat behind the desk heavily, and moved some of Sir Edwin's papers out of the way. 'I meant to ask you this yesterday. How does a young lady like you know about autopsies?'

'I have a gruesome inner life,' said Dora frankly. 'And I attended one, once.'

'Tell me.'

'No,' she said seriously. 'I don't want to.'

Fox inclined his head. 'Well, the autopsy took place this morning. It is . . . inconclusive,' he said. 'The liver indicates evidence of arsenic poisoning. Sir James is conducting further tests, the results of which we will have in a couple of days. But that's all. His stomach was empty, apart from breakfast and some kind of sweet item: sugar, cornflower, and so forth. His heart simply stopped. They are testing for poison as we speak.'

'The empty stomach is unusual, in a man as corpulent,' said Dora. 'He must have wanted lunch. There must have been a reason he *didn't* have lunch. Perhaps he wasn't feeling well already. A heart attack?'

'No sign of diseased arteries. He was overweight, but Sir James Lubbock does not believe that was the cause, at this moment in time – look here,' said Stephen Fox, scratching his moustache in frustration. 'This is all confidential, you understand. It's a damn mystery. Do excuse me.'

He'd had the Head of Scotland Yard on the telephone that morning. 'Don't mess this up, Fox, you understand?' he'd barked, in his too-loud voice. 'I've already had a Cabinet minister ask me how something like this could have happened. Friend of the family, he was. Don't get it wrong.'

Fox did not quite understand how it was his responsibility to prevent murders of librarians in dark corners. But they always, always found ways to let him know he wasn't one of them. And that was fine. One day he'd be the Head himself.

'Oh, I know, because it should be so simple,' said Dora. She leaned forward, propping her elbows on the table. 'Everyone disliked Sir Edwin. Well, almost everyone. The more I find out about him the more something bothers me about it. That's why I wanted to come and see you. Ask if you could share information with me, and I could – help.'

'This is official police business, Miss Wildwood. I can't simply *give* information away to anyone who turns up asking for it,' Fox said, in cutting tones, waving his arms to and fro above his head in a way clearly meant to indicate a hysterical person, probably female.

Dora's mouth twisted. She smiled. 'We had a chap lodge at the village pub once, he used to do breathing every morning, on the village green. Always raised his arms above his head, waved them around. He ate a lot of ginger, too, it prevents inflammation.' She looked him over. 'You should try it.'

'Ginger?' Detective Inspector Fox said, almost in a daze.

Dora sat up in her chair, and clasped her hands together. 'I really can help you, you know, once you choose to see me.' She stood up and put her jumper back on, adjusting her collar. 'But I quite understand why you'd say no.'

Detective Inspector Fox laughed. He slapped his large palms down on the mahogany desk so hard they echoed round the dull, airless room.

'Murder is a complex business, Miss Wildwood. That is why I use these.' He took out the little squares of paper, and spread them on the desk. 'To take a human life, to be driven to it, requires a number of factors. To know why a person should hate someone, should be so desperate that they wish to cut life short with physical violence, requires supreme intelligence and understanding of the human condition.'

Fox was proud of this speech. He looked up at this young, tall, slender woman with her dark, unreadable eyes, the cape festooned around her slim shoulders, her eager face watching him, utterly still for once.

There was a short pause.

'You don't know me, you think you do. I see everything,' Dora said calmly. 'I know you do, too. But I see things and people don't understand me. I can see when a widow is too tired to go any further, when a bus driver will draw off without noticing a child has clambered aboard, when a fellow pretends he's all right but he hasn't had a meal for three days, when a girl has a broken heart, utterly smashed into pieces, but she puts her face on and pretends everything's jolly. I see it all, and it's exhausting.'

She put her hands on the varnished wood of the desk, and slid them up and down. He watched the crescent shapes in her nails move, up down. Neither of them spoke.

'Edwin Mountjoy was engaged to Venetia Strallen,' she said.

'I knew that,' Detective Inspector Fox said.

'She was afraid of him. They all were. He was a horrible man.'

'Yes. In what way was she afraid, Miss Wildwood?'

In answer, Dora held up a book in her gloved hands. 'I couldn't remember the book with the broken spine on the floor by the body. When we came back afterwards it had gone. Last night I woke up and I'd remembered what it was called. I went to look for it today. Someone had put it back on the shelf, but so cleverly you'd never have known what they'd done – well, look.'

She slid it out from under her cape, onto the desk. It fell open, the pages slumping to the sides. Half of the centre was torn out.

Jagged, ugly tears, not neat cuts. Carefully she turned the book over.

'*The Killing Jar: An Examination of Extinction Methods for Diurnal and Nocturnal Lepidoptera* by Cora Carson, MA, Cantab.'

'Have you read it?'

'No, and I don't know what's in it. Here's why.'

Almost all of the book had been torn away from the glue and string binding it to the cloth boards. And in its place a smaller, thinner book nestled, not fastened in, simply loose. Fox, when she slid it towards him, lifted it and the text fell out, onto the table. The title page faced up.

'*The Guilty Fiancé* by Esmé Johnson,' Fox read aloud. '"*Best friends, the natural world, and a mystery at altitude for dashing detective Mr Barnard Castle!*"

'Esmé Johnson,' said Fox, looking at the book. 'Her again.'

'You know her?'

'I met her over the summer. I was involved in an investigation at her publishers, Morpeth, Neild & Steyn,' he said.

'Really?'

'Yes,' he said, carefully taking the book from Dora. 'A domestic tragedy, nothing more. But I had occasion to spend time in the office, in Bedford Square. The word around literary London is Esmé Johnson was Miss Strallen's secretary, and she left to write her own crime novels, and I've heard some of the plots went with her. I've heard too,' he said, portentously, 'that Miss Johnson did not behave particularly well. But, Miss Wildwood, what does it mean? Why tear an innocuous book about butterflies out and shove this one in instead?' said Detective Inspector Fox, reaching forward to touch the jagged, desecrated book and its succubus-like interloper. He shook his head. 'I'll be honest, I don't know.'

Stephen Fox had never knowingly admitted he wasn't sure about something before. His mother, he thought, would have a field day, were she to see this, not to mention Susan. He rubbed his eyes and thought of what Susan had said yesterday afternoon. 'Where was I?'

'The books in the library. Miss Amani is compiling a list,' said Dora. 'I do like a list. Perhaps we shall learn more when we've seen it. In the meantime, I thought you should have the book. And did you want to hear what I had to tell you?'

By way of a reply Fox nodded. 'Let me wrap this book in something—' He pulled open the middle drawer of Sir Edwin's desk. 'My God,' he said, peering in. 'I've never seen anything quite like it before.'

'What?'

Gently Detective Inspector Fox pulled the drawer out of the desk, and laid it on top.

'Sir Edwin had a sweet tooth, it seems.'

The drawer was stuffed to the brim. Chocolate wrappers, Fortnum's labels. Empty Fortnum's boxes. Sugared almonds, cherries in kirsch. 'He must have sat here sticking his hand into the drawer and munching on them. Why –' Fox peered in, his face crinkling in distaste, and a gentle film of icing sugar blew across the surface of the desk – 'there's a chocolate fingerprint here.'

'He had the appearance of a man who enjoyed the finer things,' said Dora. 'A bit of a pig.' She clicked her fingers. 'Of course. May I?' She took a handkerchief from her pocket, held it over the edge of the drawer, then lifted it up to feel underneath it.

'It's – ah, here. I wondered. Caught underneath the drawer, must have got stuck to it.' Gently, she dropped a small cardboard square, edged in gold, onto the desk. Fox flipped it over with a penknife. On the front was written:

To make your Tuesday sweeter. From an Admirer.

They stared at each other across the desk.

Dora sat down, moving away. 'If I were you, I'd have the contents of this drawer analysed. Don't touch the icing sugar. And really, Mr Fox, I know the science of forensics is relatively untried, but it is a most interesting area. I don't think you should let anyone else in here until this office has been searched and dusted for fingerprints.'

'Yes, I was going to do that,' said Fox reluctantly. He fumbled in his pocket, dropped the card and the mutilated hybrid book into a handkerchief of his own and tied them up. 'Ah. I ought to thank you, Miss Wildwood,' he said, in a slightly strangled voice.

'We must find that book,' she said. 'The original, I mean. Who knows why the detective stories were being defaced. At least, one can make assumptions. But it is very strange that they would remove the second half of an obscure book on butterflies.'

'I can contact the British Library,' Fox said, pulling a scrap of paper towards him. 'They will have a copy – '

'I should think it best not to involve anyone else connected with libraries, for the moment,' Dora said. 'What if someone here, someone who doesn't want us to read that book, finds out the request for that book has been made at the British Library and attempts to prevent it reaching us and something happens again?' They glanced at each other.

'I see,' said Fox.

'Yes. So if you don't mind, and you do want my help, then leave it with me.'

'Really?'

'Yes,' she said. Fox nodded.

'Very well, Miss Wildwood.'

'I don't like this,' Dora said into the silence. She stared up at him.

'Whoever did this knew him well,' Fox said. 'They were in the library.'

'I think the library is the key to the mystery,' said Dora. 'What is it they say? "Once you've understood everything you can about the life of the deceased, then you will understand their death."'

'Oh,' said Fox. 'Yes, I do believe that's true.' Their eyes met. He pulled himself together. 'Listen,' he said, with a small cough. 'Perhaps it might be useful to have a mole on the ground. Nothing official, mind you.'

'I quite understand,' said Dora.

'Did – did I hear right yesterday? You're looking for paid employment?' Dora nodded. 'Might I suggest, if you're serious about wanting to investigate further, that you enquire as to the position vacant here? They need a shelf-stacker.'

'Do they?'

'Yes,' he said absently, thinking of the dreaded phrase situations vacant, of his mother, tramping from shop to shop with him, asking for work. 'When I interviewed Miss Bunce earlier she was drawing up the advertisement to go in Situations Vacant in *The Times* today.'

She held his gaze. 'That's awfully kind of you. I could be helpful to you here, couldn't I? I'll enquire today. And please don't get cross again, but I wonder if you've considered buying yourself a notebook, to jot things down? So helpful, and better than tearing up pieces of scrap paper to write names on as if this is a parlour game. You'll need an office – if you have this place dusted over and properly searched you can be back in here by tomorrow, Mr Fox.'

Fox nodded, feeling rather numb. He watched her drape the cape around her shoulders and fluff out her hair, cram the beret back on her head. 'Well, I must be off. Thank you, Inspector.'

Weakly he called after her: 'Detective Inspector—'

II

The joy of bookshops and elevenses

On her way out of the library, having asked Mr Dryden about the position, and having received word that it was hers if she wanted it, Dora paused to check her appearance in the reflection of the door, and as she was adjusting her beret someone cleared their throat behind her.

'Miss Wildwood,' they said. 'I hoped I'd see you. How is your knee?.'

'How do you do? It's very much better Mr Stark,' she said, moving aside on the steps. 'Thank you so much for your help yesterday.'

Ben Stark nodded. 'I was very little help. I trust that particular gentleman hasn't caused you any more trouble.' He cleared his throat nervously.

'None at all,' said Dora. 'Other gentlemen, however . . .'

'Ah. Well, of course. Indeed. Aah – do excuse me, I'm rather late,' said Ben Stark absently. 'I slept in. My alarm clock didn't go off.' He had been rather elegantly dressed yesterday afternoon; his suit was well cut and his waistcoat lined with a delightful teal colour, but today, she noticed only how dishevelled he seemed, shirt collar wilted and creased, his mackintosh crumpled and dirty. His briefcase was clamped tightly under his arm as if he were afraid to let go of it. His eyes were bloodshot; he looked, she thought, dreadful.

'But perhaps you needed to sleep,' she said.

He did not respond to this. 'Have you seen the police here today?'

'Oh yes. In Technicolor,' said Dora. 'Most extraordinary, to be so certain of oneself. But he does have lovely—' she stopped herself. 'Never mind - oh!'

For suddenly Ben Stark let his briefcase slide to the floor, and covered his face with his hands. 'What's the matter? Mr Stark? Ben?'

'All is well, but I need some coffee, I think,' Ben said, he cleared his throat, and rubbed his face vigorously, as if he were willing himself back into existence. As he bent down to retrieve his brief-case something fell out of his pocket. Dora reached down to pick it up. It was a piece of paper, crumpled into a ball and covered with print. He snatched at it before she could reach it, then stood up straight.

'Good day, Miss Wildwood. Thank you. Good day.' He paused, hand on the door, as if he might say something else. 'Ah, excuse me. I . . .' He trailed off.

'I say,' Dora said. 'Would you like to have tea today?' Her mouth was dry as she stared him, wishing he would not go. 'You were so kind—'

'I'm afraid matters at home detain me,' said Ben Stark. 'Another time, perhaps.'

Dora spread her arms wide, in a gesture of friendly acceptance, and hit someone coming up the steps behind her, an elderly man with a top hat under his arm. Her knuckles struck him exactly in the face, and he let out a loud yowl of shock and pain.

'Oh! I do apologise,' Dora said. She reached out and clutched his hand, misjudging the squeeze she gave him so that he winced in pain again, staggering backwards. 'I am so very sorry, sir—'

'Madam!' The elderly gentleman cowered against the bannis-ter, hands covering his bare head. 'Please!'

'I'm most dreadfully sorry, there you are, here you go,' said Dora, opening the door for him, and ushering him briskly out of the way, but when she looked round, Ben Stark had disappeared. She looked inside and saw him, greeting Miss Amani, removing his hat, putting his satchel down. All the while, she noticed, his hands were shaking.

*   *   *

In Hatchards, on Piccadilly, Dora wandered, apparently aimlessly scanning the shelves but if you knew her, you saw the watchful brown eyes darting here and there, hungrily taking in what they could, picking up books in awe and flicking through the pages, her slim fingers running over the black-and-white photographs: Gertrude Bell standing by a ziggurat in Iraq, Virginia Woolf gazing austerely into the middle ground, Dodie Smith's new play, with the author in a jaunty hat smiling merrily into the camera . . . And over there, on the wall next to the great bow window piled high with new releases, was a whole shelf devoted to Agatha Christie, and another for the new green Penguins: they were utterly delicious. Dora picked one up and fingered it, astonished at how satisfying the smooth paper cover, the bright, heavy green was. Her eyes scanned the open pages, drinking in what she could. Ideas, images, theories, actions. Women (and men of course) *doing*, being, stretching their legs, running towards the light. Women on camels, at typewriters, in boats.

A girl from Babington School, Muriel Youngman, had gone up to Somerville, the first girl from their school to go to university. It was, of course, the fashion to do her down; to say her radical Hampstead parents, who knew Beatrice Webb, were forcing their child along the same rackety path as them. But Muriel had graduated the previous summer, with a First; had accepted a job at the British Museum and now lived in a flat in Bloomsbury, and had her own bicycle. Dora had had a letter from her in September.

It's fearful fun at the BM, she had written. *Yesterday I held a pharoah's toe. It looked like one of Mrs Dornish's dumplings. Do look me up there if you are ever in London. I hope you are keeping well, Dora.*

Dora, usually a placid person, had found this kind, chatty letter enraged her, and she wasn't sure why. She hadn't even been particular friends with Muriel. She told herself it was an imposition; that she didn't care about Muriel's stupid job; that she was a busy person.

Thinking now about Muriel Youngman, Dora stared at a display of Loeb's Greek Classics so intently that a foppish young man next to her, observing the way she glared at Xenophon's

Histories, then ground her teeth, glanced at the book in alarm, wondering what its author had done to elicit such an extreme reaction from this charming young filly next to him.

'I say, my dear—' he began, but Dora had turned, and strode past him, clenching, unclenching her fists, and he melted away. She looked rather terrifying, and that would never do.

Dora was thinking that a library was fine; a library was safe, alive with ideas from the past: old classics and new discoveries. A bookshop was different, though. It smelled of new things, of promise. After a while she felt almost dizzy with the words, the cheery colours of the type, the smell of new paper and cloth. Glancing up, she caught sight a shelf of Venetia Strallens. She went towards it, scanned it with her finger, to make sure she'd got all her books.

'Oh, Venetia Strallen?' a young woman behind her said. 'Not sure I'll buy *Lady, Be Good!* you know. She's gorn orf the boil *horribly*.'

'Absolute staggers,' said another voice. 'I didn't enjoy her last two. Like chewing cardboard, especially *Death in Damask*, but *Lady, Be Good!* is absolutely tip-top. Never read anything quite like it. Honestly, there's a twist at the end that made me drop the darned book in shock!' She gasped at the memory. Dora, itching to turn around and discuss it with her, stayed still.

'Oh marvellous. Because you know I really didn't like *Death in Damask*. For starters, I wasn't really sure what Damask was. I thought it was in Austria. Frightfully disappointing it's just a mouldy old fabric.'

'Letty, you are dim.'

'I jolly well am not.'

'I heard the girl in Boots saying *Lady, Be Good!* was her best-selling book so far. Absolute return to form, which is good.' The speaker carelessly, cruelly, dropped the book next to Dora back onto the table and Dora saw the cover. It featured a horrified-looking maiden, hands outstretched, imploring an impassive young gentleman holding a torn length of material in his appalled hands to do something, something, Dora supposed, murderous to do with damask. 'Still think I rather fancy a change. Ah! Esmé Johnson, Letty – have you read her? Oh, I say. *Ding Dong Death* – couldn't put it down. Mummy said I was utterly useless for the whole week in St Moritz and she might as well have taken Dotty. That's her pug. I nearly skied into a vat of fondue. Imagine?'

'Gosh, Annabel. What bliss.'

'Then Mummy read it in one day and she said it was the best book she'd ever read!'

'She's awfully striking, Esmé Johnson,' Letty said. 'So chic. She was in the *London Illustrated News* this week, shaking hands with Agatha Christie, because she's joined the Detection Club. There was a fearful hoo hah about it, Venetia Strallen hasn't been let in and people *say* she's absolutely furious about it. Usurped, and all that.'

'What's usurped?'

'Oh Annabel, don't be dim.'

'I'm jolly well not dim, Letty. You're the dim one. Here's her latest. *Barnard Castle investigates*. Oh, he's her detective. He's awfully dashing.'

They passed behind Dora, giggling about the imaginary Barnard Castle. Dora felt a sudden loyalty to Venetia Strallen. She too had, in fact, thought a couple of her most recent books had not been nearly so good, but she felt indignation towards bumptious Esmé Johnson, coming in and waltzing off with the limelight. She snatched up *The Guilty Fiancé*, and made her way to the till, at the front. She stared out of the bow window as the bookseller, a prim-looking woman with round glasses, immaculate waved hair done 'up', and a large garnet brooch at her neck, rang the book through the till.

'That will be eight shillings and six pence, please,' she said, grimly. 'Thank you.'

She held out two slim fingers and snatched the ten-bob note from Dora's hand, as though she might catch something from her.

'Jolly good, isn't she?' Dora said, nodding at Venetia Strallen.

'Hm,' said the bookseller. 'Crime fiction is not may sort of thing, Miss. Ay thenkyou.'

'What do you like reading, then?'

'Me?' The woman stopped, astonished to be asked. 'I like Chesterton. J.B. Priestley. Great men, truth thinkers.'

She dropped the book into a paper bag and slid it across the counter.

'That poor woman,' she said, after a moment's silence, then she leaned forwards and said, eyes bulging: 'Her fiancé, murdered in the library yesterday. I don't expect you've heard about it.'

'Vaguely,' said Dora. A carriage went past, an increasing rarity in those days, and Dora stopped to look at it. A man in the doorway, catching her eye, lifted his top hat to her, and bowed. She clutched the book, shivering for a moment, remembering Charles.

'Oh yes,' said the bookseller. '*Ay* heard from someone who was there. He was sprawled out dead in the book stacks, like an upturned crab.' Her eyes gleamed. 'He had a knife in his heart. Right in his heart. *Quayte* awful.'

'Yes,' said Dora. 'Quite awful. You're right. I say . . . Did you know him? Edwin Mountjoy?'

'A little,' said the bookseller. 'He'd come in here sometimes, to buy a gift or two. And of course he bought all *her* books. Bought 'em by the truckload.'

'Really? How strange.'

'He didn't want her to worry, you see, that they weren't selling. He was potty about *her*. I saw them once, on their way to the Proms. Some say he was a difficult gentleman but Ay always thought she rather liked it.' She twitched her lips. 'Some women like the trouble a man gives them, you know. Used to come in here on her own, *quayte* charming. An older lady doesn't want to be on her own, does she? And she was very beautiful, and very correct, you kneighow.' She managed to get several syllables out of the last word. 'She was looking forward to giving it all up and retiring to be a good wife to him.' She folded her arms. 'Now she never will. *What* a tragedy.'

*   *   *

Dora wandered along Piccadilly. To an observer it might have seemed her direction was aimless, but she was thinking hard. She realised she was extremely thirsty, looked about her, and discovered she was standing outside a Lyons Corner House.

Dora was an enthusiast about many things, but at the top of any list of things she was enthusiastic about would have been afternoon tea. Her mother had loved tea-time, and so there was that, but something also about the delicacy of the crockery, the artistry of the cakes, the order and structure of the ceremony of having high tea appealed to her and she adored the idea of Lyons, which she had seen on a Pathé news reel, in an item about the girls who worked there taking fencing lessons on the roof of this very Corner House in Piccadilly.

She opened the door. A rush of heat and the scent of coffee hit her. The carpet was soft, and a pianist was playing 'Isn't This a Lovely Day?' To her amazement she could see the room was peppered with the famous Nippies, the Lyons' waitresses, so called because it was said they nipped around so fast. One of them looked up and caught her eye. 'Sit there, love. I'll be over presently.'

Dora sank into a booth and slipped off her cape, hat and gloves. She rubbed her face with her hands, feeling the sharp cold from outside on her skin, and picked up a menu. But instead of scanning it she simply stared into space, a little numb.

She was here. She had got away. She was in London, in a Lyons, about to order some tea.

And a man was dead, and she had found him and someone, somewhere, knew how he had died. It was very strange. She wasn't scared, not at all, but that wasn't to say it wasn't . . . how did one put it? It wasn't normal.

118

So many things in London were not normal, though. The silver Rolls-Royces that glided like bullet-coloured palaces through town; all the traffic in fact, how terrifyingly fast it was; the phone boxes on every corner, the smart little shops selling smart little kid gloves and glistening marzipan fruits, the policemen with truncheons – she had seen one this morning from the bus, hitting a man quite casually, as if the truncheon were made of feathers, like Mrs Bundle, Lady Dreda's housekeeper's vast ostrich-feather duster, which she had used to tickle a cat off the front steps of 4, Lloyd Square. The policeman, however, had brought it down on a young man, with the same playful force, as if he were a child, and the young man had simply crumpled up in two. And no one had done anything.

She ordered a pot of tea, and a fondant fancy. When they arrived she accepted them with a smile from the waitress, who watched her for a moment.

'What's it they say, Miss? "*Don't look so solemn, Percy, nothing's happened yet. Why worry about tomorrow, it ain't here yet!*"'

Dora nodded and clapped her hands. 'Well, it's quite true,' she said again. 'I say, thanks awfully for trying to cheer me up.'

'Well, there you go,' said the waitress. 'We girls have to stick together, don't we?'

'I suppose so,' said Dora. 'Courage calls to courage everywhere, isn't that what she said?'

'Who?'

'Millicent Fawcett. She was a suffragette.'

'I know who Millicent Fawcett is,' said the waitress sharply. 'But there's no suppose about it, if you ask me. Didn't they gather in here before they marched for the votes, all them suffragettes, some of them so weak from the hunger strikes they couldn't stand?' She picked up the tray and slapped the bill down smartly on the formica table. 'And here we are, and aren't we lucky? Lucky to be earning and standing on our own two feet. Shame some people don't seem to have caught up with that idea.' She glanced above Dora, out of the window. 'Some people don't see what's right in front of them. Now, you take your time, dearie, and let me know if you want some more hot water.'

Dora recognised this girl, as she often did. She knew from the way she walked that she had had hip problems as a child, that she was proud, that her shoes needed re-heeling, that she loved to dance, that she had marched for workers' rights. She knew her, and sometimes it was like that. Left in silence, Dora let her simmering brain quieten, and stared blankly at the tea again. She pulled out the crumpled, folded piece of paper from her cape pocket. The list. She would do the list.

*   *   *

'*Call it off with Charles:* Well, that's done,' she said to herself. 'At least I think. I don't know who's told him he should stay or whether he's just making it up, but really, if he doesn't get the message one can't help it. I've been clear enough. He'll get bored and go back to Harwood Hall soon.

'*Money* – yes well. I should like Father to explain when I'm to inherit. So, to sum up, I won't spend money I don't have but I jolly well should have it. To be continued.

'*Accommodation.* Well, I did see Dreda looking at me with horror this morning at breakfast, and I love her very dearly, but she is obviously not imminently about to open a boarding house for indigent goddaughters. Poor Dreda. I'm too much for her. She needs to read *The Times* in peace in her lovely kimono and goodness knows she's earned the right after the trouble that dreadful husband gave her. When I'm fifty-five I'll be the same, no doubt. I must start looking for somewhere else to live.

'*Employment.*' She took a sip of tea. 'Well, it would be awfully good to get the job stacking shelves at the library, so I can keep an eye on the place and get on my feet.' She bit gingerly into the fondant fancy. 'The more I find out about Venetia Strallen the more I feel she needs someone on her side. I shall persevere. Yes.' She pictured Esmé Johnson cramming her lanky frame behind a small armoire, smiling at Venetia typing furiously away, to pay her wages and in the meantime writing her own novel, waiting for the time when she would stab her kind employer in the back . . . Dora shuddered. Murderous metaphors had never concerned her before. Then, at the bottom of the increasingly tattered piece of paper she wrote:

Who hated Sir Edwin, enough to murder him?

*　　*　　*

She chewed the silver pencil, before remembering the reason she had a silver pencil was so she wouldn't chew it. She had been hospitalised with a splinter in the throat at Babington House and her dear friend Lady Natalie Lansdowne had fed her soup for two weeks afterwards, which was basically an excuse for the two of them to bunk off meals and sit in their dorm chatting, and ranking the mistresses in order of ankle thickness.

Natty was tremendous fun, wild, angry at the world, the child of two uncaring parents and a stiff English upbringing. She had a best friend, Diana, whom she adored, and to whom she used to write long long letters every night, which she would read out to Dora – most parts, anyway. Diana was bookish, like Dora, and refused to do the season. She had been sent to finishing school and had learned to type. Natty said her friend Diana would be getting a job, and that they would share a flat together, somewhere in Chelsea, but Dora found this hard to believe. Young women like them didn't get jobs.

The memory reminded her she missed Natalie. She'd last heard from her when she'd delayed the season for a year because of meningitis. That was another thing she should do – look Natty up. She knew that her family lived in Eaton Square – Dora wondered where that was in relation to Piccadilly.

When she was better, her mother had sent her the silver pencil and notebook. *Darling, please don't endanger yourself like that again. I rather like you and besides it'd be too embarrassing to have to explain I lost my only child because she chewed a pencil xx*

It was the last letter she'd had from her. Dora shook herself. She screwed up her face. She had never yet managed to open the notebook, write in it. Now she was ready. Drawing the slender volume from her cape, on the blank page, she copied out the line she had just written on her tattered to-do list.

Who hated Sir Edwin, enough to murder him?

Mr Dryden – Mountjoy was obviously threatening him – what? A secret?

Zewditu Amani was afraid of him – was he actively trying to drive her out of the country?

The truth about Ben Stark and the torn page; he is hiding some-thing. He is nervous and on edge.

Venetia Strallen? Murderer is usually the wife or husband; she was his fiancée; investigate their relationship?

Esmé Johnson – she would clearly stop at nothing to be the queen of crime – but does that include murder? Did Mountjoy have somehing on her? What is her secret? She has a secret, of that I'm sure.

Finally: the mystery of Detective Inspector Fox, his dreadful temperament and middle name but how very strange it is that he—

The detail of the story of Edwin Mountjoy and the Bloemfontein internment camps came back to her. *He told me he liked laughing at them. Watching them die.*

How galling to have such a man in charge of the library. Some-one who didn't love talking about reading and authors, didn't love the smell of books, the feel of them. She thought of Ben Stark, his angry face when he spoke of him. But was that a strong enough reason to kill someone, not liking books? Seemed a bit rich. Kill-ing someone required darkness, a crack in the soul, a kind of rupture from reality most people could never comprehend.

Dora understood this, for she had known one other murder. A young woman in the village, found strangled in the lane: she'd been Albert Jubby's cousin Lily Jubby. She'd been engaged to the blacksmith but had thrown him over for his brother. The blacksmith had seen red. He'd lain in wait for her, walking back across the fields from meeting his brother, one high summer's evening, and strangled her with rope, before doing unmentionable things to her young, pale body.

Dora had seen her, laid out in the morgue in Trowbridge just before the autopsy, so Albert could identify her. Whilst Albert was being interviewed by police he'd asked her to stay with Lily, and Dora had sat through the dissection of the young woman's body. She remembered the parts of her, lifted out and put back in, like sections, not like a human. She would never forget it.

She had helped Albert's aunt May lay Lily out in the Jubby farmhouse, before her funeral. Furlong Wildwood had been furious with his daughter for going – 'It's the villagers' affair; leave 'em to it, Dora,' but Albert had loved Lil and Dora loved Albert and knew she had to see it.

They'd tried Will Torden, the blacksmith, and found him guilty. He'd been sent to prison for three years. The judge had said he had 'provocation'.

'Shame,' Albert had yelled out, leaping up in court. 'Shame on you! A life for a life! She was eighteen!'

They had taken Albert down, locking him up for the night to cool his head. Will Torden was already out, and romancing the barmaid at the Oak, and no one mentioned he'd murdered and raped a woman two years previously. Lily Jubby lay in the churchyard at Combe Curry, and some summer nights Albert lay next to her grave, in his druid clothes.

'She hated the dark, you see. I don't like thinking about her terrified. Reckon if I'm there just once in a while I can keep her company.'

The busy, warm café receded as Dora thought about Will Torden. He was lean, and full of deep, hard energy, face weatherbeaten, never seen without a whippet with a curled tail. He stood, arms folded, when you talked to him. He was the kind of man you wouldn't be able to push out of the way, not like Albert. But he had lost it with Lily. Lost control, torn that part of himself that had at best been fragile anyway. What had made him kill was rage, anger, and fear. Fear most of all: Dora knew it, along with the other things she couldn't explain.

Whoever killed Sir Edwin was very afraid.

She thought of Ben Stark, scrabbling to pick up the scrunched-up papers, the terror in his eyes.

The jagged edges of the pages of the book. The rage with which they'd been torn out.

Mr Dryden's quiet desperation, his hatred of his own boss.

Esmé Johnson's smiling, smiling face.

Dora cupped her chin in her hands, recalling herself to the present. She looked at the old list on the piece of paper again.

I'll write to Charles again, she thought, setting out quite firmly the reasons I don't want to marry him. I will tell him I'm in contact with the police.

Charles Silk-Butters loved authority and loathed any suggestion of leftist nonsense. He hated Ramsay MacDonald with a fervour that was almost dangerous. She had once seen him throw a piece of coal at a footman who asked for a pay rise. 'Workers' rights?' he'd screamed, picking up the black lump and hurling it, like a cricket ball, towards the surprised man, who dodged and then gasped as it shattered a stained-glass window that gave out onto the croquet lawn. And any threat to the Empire, the Crown, the beloved country, must be quashed, like an insect caught between a man's finger and thumb. Charles loved dispatching insects. He kept a vast spider he'd killed in a glass jar on his desk. It made her want to laugh, it was so obvious, so utterly without nuance. He might as well have scrawled 'I am a villain' across his forehead.

Her father had liked Charles, and perhaps that was what hurt most about the whole affair. She knew her father, knew him to be profligate and silly, selfish and idle, but also knew his immense charm and strength, his kindness, his memory for obscure facts and small acts. It was he who picked violets every January for her mother, placing them in an empty crystal Lalique perfume bottle on her cream kidney-shaped dressing table. It was he who remembered their housekeeper Mrs Lah Lah's sciatica and bought her arnica and Epsom Salts. It was he who, after her mother died, came to visit Dora at school every month, rolling up in the Daimler, utterly astonished to be told girls were not allowed visitors outside of exeats or exceptional circumstances. 'But m'dear girl!' he'd expostulate to the headmistress. 'Driven all the way from Somerset! Merely want a cup of tea with my darling Dora! Be on m'way after that, promise!' And his kind brown eyes resting on hers as if he couldn't quite believe she was there, his warm hands clasping hers, his hands fumbling for the ribbon-tied box of teacakes and fondant fancies he always brought. And always a good present, too – a book, a slingshot, a horse pick, a jolly decent brooch for her sixteenth.

But her father had also been certain Charles was a good thing, and therefore, with sadness, Dora knew he could not be trusted. She screwed up her list, dropping it into the ashtray and pouring a small quantity of tea onto it. She had no use for it now. She shut the little notebook and slid it into her cape again, then simply sat, quietly contemplating.

The tea was cold now. The fondant fancy, though, was still delicious, and Dora wolfed the rest of it down. She drew *The Guilty Fiancé* out of the paper bag and opened it, marvelling at the thrill of a new book again.

'Want some more hot water, dearie?' The Nippy appeared at her elbow, preparing to whisk her teapot away. She was the embodiment of her name – small, bustling, neat, with black hair that shone so much it was almost blue. She had beautiful arched eyebrows, careful eyeliner, and her nails were bitten almost to nothing

'Just the bill, if you don't mind.'

'I don't mind.' She produced a slim pencil from her lace pinny pocket. 'Anything else I can get you?'

A sudden impulse made Dora put her hand on her arm. 'Yes. Do you know any nice boarding houses?' She stopped. 'That sounds rather odd. You know what I mean.'

The Nippy's eyes widened slightly. 'Well, perhaps I do. For you?'

'Yes, for me. I don't want to live in an opium den or a house of ill repute. And I'd like it to be central.'

'Oh I see. Wasn't sure what you meant. There's a nice place on the Marylebone Road. Susan lives there. Lots of actresses and so forth there, too. I mean, *proper* actresses,' she added. 'I say!' she called, in a low voice. 'Susan, come here a minute.'

Susan came over briskly, turning her tray on the side and sliding it under her arm, then straightening her cap. 'Morning, Miss,' she said, in a not entirely friendly tone.

'Morning,' said Dora. 'I say, your friend here—' She gestured to the first waitress.

'Minnie,' the Nippy answered.

'Minnie, thank you. Minnie was telling me you live in a nice boarding house. I wish you'd let me know if it'd be suitable for me. I'm looking for somewhere to board for a few weeks.'

'Oh!' Susan smiled, and looked more friendly. She reminded Dora of someone. She had a gap between her front teeth, curly light brown shingled hair, and nice eyes.

'It's the Three Corners Club, Miss, and it's ever so nice. Opposite Madame Tussauds. Awfully popular, I'm only in there because a Nippy here left to get married and gave up her bed. She wishes she'd stayed there now stead of getting married. Anyway, I like it there, even if Miss Pym's a bit of a tartar, got to be careful to keep on the right side of *her*.'

'Who's Miss Pym?'

'Well, she's not a landlady. I'm not really sure what she is, but her title's the Superintendent. Does good works. They say she was a spy in the war. Some people say she's a Russian princess. I'm not sure. But her heart's in the right place. Been ever so nice to me. The food's cheap and warm and the furniture's decent, and Miss, I've been in some places you wouldn't wish on your worst enemy.'

'It sounds absolutely wonderful,' said Dora. 'Is it safe? You know, I mean—' She faltered.

'Safe as houses, they lock the door at night and Miss Pym does it herself and if she's not on the desk there's an awfully nice watchman, Douglas. He can't be bribed, either, more than his job's worth. Which makes everything much simpler, you know, and if you're having a bit o' trouble –' Susan rolled her eyes, theatrically – 'Douglas steps out and belts them one. Nice dancer at the Windmill followed home by ever such a fishy chap, younger son of a duke would you believe, peeved 'cos she wouldn't have a drink with him – forces his way through the revolving door – whole group of us in the lobby – old Dougie shouts "Stand back, young ladies!" and lamps him. He broke his nose! And do you know, Miss Pym must have had a word, because it never come to court. He even wrote a letter of apology.' Susan sniffed. Minnie folded her arms.

'He was a right one. Lord Andrew Pettifogger. Awful chap.'

'His old man's mad,' said Susan, reasonably. 'Duke of Champflowers. To be fair to the poor chap. Has a pet spider he keeps in a wooden box in his pocket. Calls it Derek.'

Dora shook her head. 'His name sounds familiar,' she said, remembering the lists in *The Times* of attendees at grand balls which Kitty Nairne used to read avidly, longing for a handsome prince, whilst Laney Warburg, being an American and proud of it, stood behind her, aided by Natty Lansdowne, pointing out ever more ridiculous names. 'The Master of the Rolls . . . the Duke of Otterburn . . . the Mistress of the Wardrobe . . . Lord Cosmo Witherington.'

She felt desolate for a moment, wondering what these remaining dear friends, scattered to the four winds, were doing, and telling herself again she must contact Natty. Tommy was in Jaipur and Laney was continuing her studies in New York; Kitty, of course, was another of the dead girls she knew: she would never again hug a pillow to her chest pretending it was a handsome prince, tears of laughter streaming down her face, never practise waltzing with Laney, going over the footsteps so she was flawless and could capture the affection of the husband who would impregnate her with such ruthless efficiency that she died.

What will become of us, of this generation? Dora found herself thinking, a wave of sadness sweeping over her. She shivered violently, and pulled her cape around her frame, patting her notebook. Susan watched her, concerned.

'Listen, it's a lovely place, but there's rarely a spot available and it's first come first served, you see.'

'Oh.'

'Yes, that's the trouble. But why don't you come over and have a look, this evening if you want?'

Dora, slightly taken aback, nodded. 'Thank you. When do you get off?'

'Six tonight, so I should be at home from seven o'clock, Miss. What's the name?'

'Dora Wildwood.'

She nodded. 'I'll tell Miss Pym to expect you. I'm Susan, Miss. Susan Fox.'

'Susan Fox.' And perhaps because she seemed so familiar, something made Dora say: 'Fox. Do you know a Stephen Fox?'

Susan's face froze. Her jaw set in a mulish expression. 'Do I?' she said. 'He's my brother. Useless waste of space he is. Does he owe you money?'

'Oh no,' muttered Minnie, polishing her tray and beginning to back away. 'Not the brother. Don't mention the brother.'

Dora said: 'How extraordinary. I think I saw you yesterday, having an argument with him. No, he doesn't owe me money.'

'Hm. Well he gets everywhere. How do you know him?'

'We're involved in a case, I'm sorry to say.'

'Not the murder in the library, round the corner? You the young lady who found the body?'

'I am.'

'Well I never.' She folded her arms, her expression grim. 'I know you can't tell me anything about it. So you can remind him from me what I came to the station to tell him yesterday, his mother would like a visit when he's not too busy saving the world. Funny how being that important means you don't see your mum, and after all she's done for you.'

'I will,' said Dora meekly. 'Tell me something,' she added. 'Why's his middle name Mavis?'

'How do you know that? Never mind. Well, it's our dad, see? He was a wrong'un, our dad. Bent as a nine-bob note, thought the world owed him a living. Always sucking up to someone else in the hopes they'd give him a free ride somewhere. Grew up on a grand estate he did, dad was a groom. Well, our dad befriended the lord of the manor, hoped to be adopted by him 'cos he had no children. Well, when Stephen was born he wrote to him to say he'd called his firstborn son Mavis, after his son. Got a letter back –' here Susan paused, to stuff a napkin against her mouth, and quell her rising amusement – 'saying that was his daughter's name. His son was called Arthur, or George, you know the sort – of – thing. Mavis was his daughter —' Here Susan clutched Minnie, unable to contain her hysteria. 'Oh, that's cheered me right up. Haven't thought of that in ever so long.'

'Susan! Minnie!' A man sidled up to them, smooth as a seal in a black suit and gold brocade waistcoat. 'I'm sorry, madam. Are these girls bothering you? Our Nippies are very professional, apt to be a tad too much so sometimes, and I'm afraid, Miss, they like to think everyone wants a chat . . .' He clicked his fingers as Susan, who was standing up now, her face flushed with laughter, patted her face. Minnie nudged her, as if to say, *be serious*. 'Back to work!'

'It was I who was talking to them, not the other way round.' Dora stood up with an agreeable smile at the girls, leaving her money on top of the bill. 'I must be off too. Thank you so much. Susan, I'll see you later,' she said, under her breath, on the way out.

Susan nodded. 'Thanks, Miss,' she said, and they were away again, the two of them, nipping around the hushed, carpeted room, the scent of lilies and Earl Grey tea hanging delicately in the air.

Dora walked back down Piccadilly, ostensibly looking for a bus stop. In reality she wanted to shake off the memories of the previous day, of running, terrified, along the wide street, Charles hot on her heels. On impulse, she swerved off the street and into Fortnum's, whose duck-egg-blue canopy and red-bricked façade, festooned with Jubilee decorations, she had noted the previous day.

She wandered in a daze through the heavy double doors: it was like entering another world. Sticks of twisted barley sugar and bonbons in glass jars, and macarons piled high in pastel towers, and vast, ornate china jars of tea lining the far walls: Assam, Lapsang, Countess Grey.

Strange to think of it, but beyond the local post office in the village near school she could not recall going into a shop on her own, with her own money, to purchase whatever she liked.

'One must not think of this as one's local shop,' she told herself firmly, staring longingly at a potted stilton and a tin of biscuits.

But nevertheless, suddenly she felt the situation required marking. She had a wallet, and in it the money she had withdrawn from her account, and she was here, in her trousers and her cape, with her notebook. She had gone to London. She was here.

Clasping a box of peppermint creams in her gloved hands, she took them to the wood-panelled service area, where a young woman wrapped the beautiful blue box in ribbon, and handed them to her with a smile. 'Enjoy them, Miss,' she said, and Dora replied:

'Oh, I absolutely will. Thank you so much.'

She clutched them under her arm as she hopped on the number 38 bus going up through Shaftesbury Avenue and Bloomsbury.

She sat on the top deck, right at the back, staring out at the bustling, fascinating vista of the city, the maids in the windows of a grand hotel dusting, the ladies in heels tripping along the street together, one in a floor-length mink coat, the man sitting outside the Palace Theatre, his trouser legs neatly folded up under his legless torso, cap out on the ground: *Help a brave Veteran*, the sign said. The rotund policemen strolling past the lounging men waiting outside the Salvation Army who stood with pale faces, caps under arms, the boys playing truant from school, the grand gentlemen in top hat and tails greeting each other on the steps of a gentlemen's club. Somewhere in these streets was a murderer, the person who knew how Sir Edwin had died. Dora watched it all, popping peppermint creams into her mouth with regularity as if they could fill the hole, stop her noticing everything: every one a life, every one carrying a secret.

12

Miss Pym supposes

'We've nothing at the present time,' said Miss Pym, peering over her glasses at Dora from behind the desk. 'But if you care to call back later in the month, perhaps something may have become available, though it is very much first come, first served.' She took off her glasses and laid them carefully on the counter, then polished the cameo brooch at her throat with a fine lace hand-kerchief. Dora watched, mesmerised. 'Miss Wildwood: I should warn you, this is a hostelry for professional women only. I assume you *have* a job.'

'Oh yes,' Dora said brightly, holding Miss Pym's gaze and crossing her fingers behind her back. 'That is to say,' she said, shaking her head, 'I am about to start a job.'

'That,' said Miss Pym, 'is not quite the same thing.'

Dora drummed her fingers on the desk. 'I came to London in a hurry,' she said, in a quiet voice. 'I needed to get away.'

'I see.'

'I won't take the place for very long, Miss Pym. It's until I'm settled.'

'Yes, I understand.' Miss Pym did not extend sympathy. 'Take heart, Miss Wildwood. I shall add you to the list.' She clicked her tongue. 'Might I ask for two referees, in the meantime?'

'Of course. Mr Michael Dryden,' said Dora, boldly. 'Acting Chief Librarian at the London Library. And Venetia Strallen, the novelist. She is at 44, Mecklenburgh Square.'

Miss Pym's eyes narrowed, but she took out a large ledger, tightly ruled, filled with cramped lines of handwriting, and wrote this down. Dora looked around her as she did. She had jumped off the bus at the top of Tottenham Court Road and walked up

Marylebone Road on a whim, clutching her Ward, Lock & Co. London guide book.

She had one of her senses – the good kind – as she approached the boarding house. The hall of the Three Corners was panelled in warm wood. It was quiet, after the roar of traffic outside. She could smell beeswax polish, and cigarettes. Someone upstairs playing jazz on a gramophone, and she could hear very faint tap dancing.

'I have to ask them first,' she added. 'I only met them both yesterday. You must think I am a most unsatisfactory person,' she said. 'But I am trying not to be.'

Miss Pym shut the book with a snap. 'Sometimes –' she blinked heavily – 'girls can be rather foolish, you know. It's my life's work, expanding the horizons of our young breed. Explaining to them that we must fight for our own advancement.' She took off her glasses. 'But yet, so many of them are utterly resistant to it.'

'That must be vexing,' said Dora. 'I suppose the thing about being young is either one feels no obligation to fight for advancement whatsoever or one feels it all the time.'

Miss Pym looked slightly taken aback. 'Well yes. I was in the latter category. Now as I say, we have no spaces at the moment, but—'

'Henry! Henry, put me *down*, darling! Oh!' came a high, breathy voice, screeching with joy. 'Henry! You are *awful*! People will *see*! Oh, such happiness, darling! Here we – no, Henry, you *mustn't*!' the voice finished, on a note of ecstasy. 'Oh! Really? Henry! *Henry!*'

Into the lobby appeared a dishevelled blonde girl, held aloft like a dumbbell by a small – extremely small in fact – dark man with thick arms and a small moustache. He was staggering under the weight of his prize possession, his face slowly turning redder and redder, and he was grinning widely, whether with joy or in a rictus of concentration it was hard to tell.

'Primose!' he uttered. 'Primrose Iolanthe Wilson! Will. You!' He stopped, his face turning purple now, as his cargo writhed ecstatically in his arms. 'Marry. Me!'

'Oh Henry! Yes, *yes*! A thousand times, yes!' Primrose called, turning over like a fish, and causing Henry to fall to the floor, bouncing slightly and giving out a howl of agony as his new fiancée landed heavily on top of him, whereupon she planted his face with many kisses.

'Run away. With me now. Before father arrives!' said Henry faintly, struggling for breath. 'Come on boat. Train! I say. Let's go to – oh, anywhere! Salzburg?'

'I'd utterly adore that,' said Primrose, staring at him intensely and holding his head between her hands. 'Oh Henry. Yes please.'

'Do you need,' Henry said, sitting up. 'To fetch your things, my best beloved?'

'Absolutely not, darling! Let's go now.' Slightly ruining the air of spontaneity, she added, 'I left a packed suitcase behind the desk, just in case you did ask me, you see. I'm all ready!'

'Oh you are marvellous. My mother will simply adore you, Primrose.' They fell upon each other again, with much moaning and kissing.

Dora and Miss Pym watched this touching scene together, in silence. 'Miss Pym,' said Dora, after a while. 'May I ask you something?'

'Of course. In just one moment. Miss Wilson,' Miss Pym called across the lobby, and the girl turned. 'Do excuse me. I strongly advise you not to travel to Salzburg.'

'You can't tell me what to do any more, Miss Pym!' said Primrose Wilson, tearing herself away from the lips of her intended. 'I've put up with your petty rules and prejudices against pretty girls for long enough!'

'It is indeed none of my business what you do, Miss Wilson, but when you refuse to settle your bill for weeks at a time, borrow several pairs of nylons and don't give them back and use up all the hot water you must expect repercussions. I advise you not to got to Austria because—'

'I don't care what you say!' Primrose Wilson said, standing up indignantly. 'Let's go, Henry! I'm leaving and I'm never coming back!'

'One moment, my sweet,' Henry called, and pulled her against the wall, where they carried on embracing.

'At any moment Austria might be overrun by Nazis,' Miss Pym said clearly. 'It's coming, sooner or later. Your grandmother was a Sassoon. They will know this, Primrose.' Dora saw Primrose's face freeze a little with uncertainty, before she turned back to her Henry. 'You will be interned or worse; most likely you will never escape.'

'Don't be a stick-in-the-mud.'

'It's my reason for living, Primrose. Why don't you go some-where else? Chichester. Whitby? Peterborough. The latter has a remarkable cathedral.' But they paid her no attention and, after a moment, Miss Pym turned back to Dora, her face a mask. 'Miss Wildwood, you wanted to ask me something?'

'I assume this means a place has become available,' said Dora, as the happy couple murmured softly to each other, both sobbing and clutching each other's faces. 'Is that correct?'

'Quite correct, Miss Wildwood. It's a pound a week, including breakfast and hot water,' said Miss Pym, with faint weariness in her voice. 'Normally we advertise as well, but I've had a spate of extremely silly girls. You,' she said, shutting the book sharply, 'are not a silly girl. Miss Wilson, would you and your guest be so good as to move outside? You are cluttering the hallway and inconven-iencing Miss Wildwood. If you please.'

Primrose, pushing her bouncing curls out of her face, turned a flushed, happy smile on Dora, clinging onto her fiancé's arm. 'All the best, Miss Pym,' the little man said gruffly. 'All the best. This should cover it.' He laid a five-pound note down on the counter, and slicked his hair to one side. 'So,' he said casually. 'You think Austria's a bad idea, then.'

'Yes,' said Miss Pym calmly. 'Go to America, if you want to get away from here.'

'Hitler is a friend to England,' said Henry stubbornly. 'Those who are against him are against innovation and growth and modernity. We must fight the old imperial forces. You don't under-stand, madam.'

'I understand all too well, young man,' said Miss Pym. 'I wish I didn't.'

'Come on, Henry,' said Primrose. She waggled her fingers at the two women. 'Goodbye! Tell Susan where I've gone, will you! She'll want to know. I'll send a postcard!'

'Good luck,' said Miss Pym, as the door banged behind them, and there was peace and quiet again, the scent of beeswax, someone singing, some faint laughter, and the clip-clop of hooves from the road. Dora watched her rearrange her features, back to the mask-like semblance of calm.

'If it's convenient, I shall move in tomorrow,' said Dora. She put two pound notes down on the counter. 'Here's some more money for you. A red-letter day.'

'Indeed,' said Miss Pym drily. She held out her hand and, slightly to Dora's surprise, enfolded it in her own. 'Well, Miss Wildwood. We were rather distracted, but I make you one promise, the same promise I make to all my girls whilst they stay here.' She glanced out of the revolving doors to where Primrose Iolanthe Wilson and her Henry stood, momentarily separated, waiting for a taxicab. 'I promise you that, within these three corners and these four walls, you will be safe. Welcome.'

13

A supper party

'A *boarding house*?'

'Dear Dreda, it's perfectly respectable. It's for young professional women.'

Lady Dreda put down her scone. She wiped some jam from her fingers, her dark eyes dilated with horror. 'Dora, you must have lost your mind, my dear girl! You can't move into a *boarding house*. They're funnels for the white slave trade, apart from anything else . . .' She trailed off. 'FUNNELS.'

'I don't think the white slave trade is quite the threat people make it out to be.' Dora held out a box of peppermint creams. 'Here! Have the last of these. I bought them today. They're absolutely delicious—'

'How can you say that!' cried Lady Dreda, wildly misconstruing her. 'Honestly, Dora. They're rife with fleas, and slatterns, and – and oh – oh! horrible, damp rooms, and predators. Unsavoury types who prey on young women and oh, Dora dear! You're a Wildwood! Two days ago you were engaged to Charles Silk-Butters, about to become one of the great ladies of Somerset. You can't simply throw that all over,' said Dreda, clasping her hands together and fixing Dora with an imploring stare, 'and become a – a –' she cast around, feverishly plucking up two peppermint creams, and throwing them into her mouth – 'oh, some caddish type's *bibelot!*' she finished, mumbling.

'What on earth is a bibelot?'

'It's a plaything, a useless trinket,' said an amused voice from the other end of the book-lined room. 'Dreda darling, as ever, you're hopelessly overreacting.' Venetia Strallen lit a cigarette and came towards them, her silk jacket swinging about her, her face framed by its soft tangle of ash-blond hair, the circles under her eyes the only faint sign of her distress. 'I'm sure Dora knows what's best for her. Where is this place?'

'The Three Corners, Marylebone.'

'Ah!' Venetia clapped her hands. 'Of course. Do you know, Mummy and Daddy wanted me to stay there when I moved to London, can you imagine, but I checked into an hotel. Awfully naughty but –' she shrugged, simply – 'not very Me. But you'll love it there, Dora, much more your sort of place. Dreda darling, Three C is fine, and if she's anything like Elizabeth, it's pointless trying to stop her.'

Gosh, she is *marvellous*, Dora thought. Lady Dreda had lured Venetia from her flat in Mecklenburgh Square by telephoning and promising her a light supper of chicken salad, blackcurrant sorbet, and sympathetic company. 'I've told her,' she said to Dora when Dora arrived back, rather dishevelled, 'I've said to her, "Venetia darling, you are amongst *friends*. Who want to take care of you. Let us take care of you." The vultures, you see,' she had added darkly. 'They're already circling.'

When Venetia arrived, staggeringly beautiful in black, her pale face and ash hair luminous in the evening lamplight, she had fallen upon Dreda, who held her for a few moments, merely saying into her hair, 'So sorry, my dear. But it's all over. It's all over.'

*　　*　　*

They had had supper, Dora biding her time before breaking the news of her impending departure, assuming other matters would of course take precedence, but no mention was made of Sir Edwin's death.

Now, after dinner and upstairs by the fire in the drawing room, Venetia's face, pale and drawn, and delicate, broke into a small smile as her eyes rested on Dora. 'Dora's a wise child. She doesn't want to leech. It's so tiring, having to be grateful all the time, Dora, isn't it?'

'You understand,' said Dora. 'I'll stay on for a couple of days, Dreda darling,' she said, turning to Lady Dreda, who had sunk into her chair and was sipping a small glass of sloe gin.

'Well,' said Lady Dreda gloomily. 'You will do what you want, of course.'

'We could paint the town red. Let me take you out to supper, to say thank you. What do you say? Tomorrow?'

'Us? Out? Tomorrow?' Lady Dreda said. 'I haven't anything to wear.'

'Dreda, be spontaneous for once,' said Venetia Strallen. 'Darling, you never go anywhere!'

'Oh, foot. I went to Lord's, last summer. That was jolly good.'

'That's not the same thing, darling.' She turned to Dora. 'When we were at school, Dora, her father came to take her and a friend out in a *car*, in a *car* – most of us had never seen a car before and your mother and I hung out of the window begging to be picked to go with her – but she said no, she simply wouldn't go, it was too chilly out.' Her eyes sparkled. 'Me, who never had a mouldy visitor the whole time I was there! My ghastly old parents who dumped me there and forgot about me.'

'Well, darling, they were in India helping lepers,' said Dreda. 'They couldn't very well hop on a train to see you at the weekend. And your father did catch typhoid from one of them, remember.'

Venetia shivered. 'Oh D. Don't remind me.'

'And your mother was trapped out there for three years because the Army refused to pay for her passage home.'

'She's always so literal,' said Venetia, smiling. 'That's why we're friends, Dora. She adores being blunt—'

'It's called telling the truth—'

'Ignore her, Dora darling – and I love making things up. The utter cruelty of her. She's had a beautiful Schiaparelli jumpsuit made, Dora, it's divine. She even went to Paris for the fitting, but she won't wear it anywhere. Imagine.'

'Now Venetia. I don't like going out when it's getting dark. You know that. I'm very happy at home with a good book and a good drink and my wireless, listening to Mrs Bundle in the kitchen pottering about and Maria's sewing machine above me and the lamplighters clambering around outside in the night air. I don't want to go out,' said Lady Dreda firmly, and Dora thought to herself how very nice that seemed, and how lucky Lady Dreda was. 'The jumpsuit is being mended by my talented Maria. She can adjust anything, she is marvellous.'

'What about the Worth coral silk number?'

'Oh! I'm not wearing *that* again. Last time I wore it to the Embassy Club for that jolly dinner –' she paused, and Dora realised it must have been a night with Sir Edwin, and that this was best skated over – 'that old hag Lady Violet Tabor was in exactly the same frock.'

'Tabor,' Dora said. 'Why, a Lady Violet was in the library yesterday, wasn't she, Miss Strallen – in the Hall, just before—' She broke off.

'Yes,' said Lady Dreda, carrying on as if Dora had not spoken. 'And she ignored me and then, as I was leaving, she glanced at me *though she knew perfectly well it was she who looked like a trussed-up walrus in the thing and not I* – you *know* my shoulders are far better than hers – and she said, "dear, dear".' She paused, licking her lips anxiously. 'Awful woman.'

'How too ghastly,' said Venetia, putting her silver head on one side, sympathetically. 'Just because she's had some success with that dreadful biography of Princess Louise – I must say I didn't care for it at all. And do you remember how vile she was about the poor Duchess of York at that dinner for those wretched three-legged Highland Terriers? Goodness, why be so cruel? It's hardly as if that woman will ever amount to anything, poor dear – but Edwin always said—' She faltered, and a quite extraordinary look crossed her face – as if she were remembering having forgotten. 'Oh—' She bit her lip. Her face was quite white. 'Do excuse me.'

'Of course, dear Venetia.' Lady Dreda sat back in her chair, her face taut with misery at her friend's grief. Dora watched Venetia

Strallen's slender fingers clamp themselves over her lovely mouth; the glint of the sapphires and diamonds on her finger; she heard Venetia's muffled sob as she staggered to her feet, stumbling once, and left the room. As the door closed behind her, Lady Dreda leaned forwards.

'*Don't* mention Sir Edwin, Dora dear.'

'I didn't!'

'You as good as did,' said Dreda, rather unfairly. 'I tell you, she can't bear to hear his name. Terrified she'll lose control. She might cry. Absolutely worst thing.'

'Right,' Dora said. 'Is crying the absolutely worst thing?'

'Dora, you know it is. My mother was the same when Daddy got caught in the sandstorm with that shaman. Never spoke his name again. Couldn't bear to.' She added, musingly, 'They say it's the fastest way to get over them.'

'How curious some people are,' said Dora. 'I want to talk about Mother all the time, but absolutely no one wants to listen.'

Lady Dreda's smile grew fixed. 'Well, the mystery of your dear mother—' She sat up and started shuffling her piles of *Illustrated London News* and the *Journal of Cocker Spaniel Breeders* around on the embroidered ottoman, very awkwardly. 'She died doing what she loved, and that's the most one can say about *that*.'

'Don't you think it's rather strange, though?' Dora said. She was sitting on the pouffe next to her, and leaned over to stop a pile of magazines sliding onto the carpet. 'People say that all the time, but she didn't really love killing butterflies. She loved spotting them. She loved being out in the fresh air, peering into hedgerows, but she never killed them. That's what everyone gets wrong. She didn't – and I don't understand it.' She wiped her eyes. 'I don't understand why she went to Switzerland in the first place. I don't understand why she left.'

'Oh dear Dora. She left because of your father. To try to take up interests again – yes, interests, Dora, which she had let go when she was married and—' She grasped Dora's heart-shaped face in her hand, and in a low voice, pinching away a tear, she said: 'You mustn't cry, my dear. She saw all that you are, she knew the girl you were and the woman you would become. Elizabeth would never have left you without wanting to come back. You must believe that. Nor would she have left without being certain you could take on the world by yourself.'

The two women stared at each other, and Dora was afraid of the intensity of Lady Dreda's stare. A log fell from the grate onto the stone, crackling loudly and breaking the heavy silence. Sparks flew into the air and onto the carpet. Dreda leaned forward and firmly slapped them out with a magazine as Dora sat back on her heels.

'Do *you* know what happened then? She stayed with you the night before she left. Did she say anything unusual? Do you know how she died?'

Dreda shook her head. 'I only know what you know, darling. The chalet was empty . . . the door was open . . . the jar with the specimens was smashed on the floor . . . they found her at the bottom of the mountain, neck broken, so it would have been very quick, Dora. And they said she'd arrived with a fellow amateur lepidopterist and they had quarrelled and she was travelling alone. You know all this, my dear. But still, I don't think we'll ever truly know what happened.'

'I have to know,' said Dora, standing up and pacing. 'It's why I came here. To ask you about it, to talk to her old friends. It's—' She was about to say it was a stroke of luck she'd made the acquaintance of Venetia, another dear friend of her mother's, so soon after her arrival, but reflected that the circumstances of this meeting were not exactly joyful, and pressed on: 'It's why I want to be an investigator.' She turned to the door, to make sure Venetia couldn't hear. 'Only "investigator" sounds so silly. But someone who stands up for the dead. Tries to discover what happened to them. A detective.' She thought of Lily Jubby, how no one had taken any notice – men got angry, girls were murdered.

'Language please, Dora.' Her godmother poured herself another drink. 'I understand you don't want to marry Charles, but I can't believe you're cut out for life in London. How, please Miss, will you live in this boarding house? You've never cooked a meal for yourself, never cleaned a bathroom, and you have *no* idea what the Tube is like.'

Dora cleared her throat. 'I may be very unworldly but I know how to fend for myself, you know. I've cooked most of the meals at Wildwood since I left school. I can poach a turbot, Dreda darling, I have a poaching tin. Albert found it at a house sale, ours was crushed in a door by Carine in one of her rages. Isn't that jolly? I can identify a death cap, which makes me an awfully useful person to pick mushrooms with. The larder is simply bursting with chutneys and jams and so forth, I do so enjoy it. And Muzz used to make me do the housework to save Mrs Lah Lah. Her sciatica was so dreadfully bad. I can scrub a kitchen range till you can see your face in it. Well . . . sort of,' she said, her face falling at the memory of an afternoon scrubbing till her knuckles bled . . . 'you know, they're made of rather dull cast iron and scrubbing them is something of a waste of time. And since I've been in London I've taken five buses. The nine, two thirty-eights, a fourteen and a twenty-three. And today I took the Tube. The Bakerloo line.'

Not for the first time, Lady Dreda sighed at the eccentricity of her dear friend Elizabeth's approach to child-rearing. She did not consider it hypocritical that she enjoyed a life of independence and leisure because she had both inherited and married money made by men, and it had been many years now since the night she had stayed up sobbing to greet the dawn, because her father would not let her make further enquiries into studying law at Queen Mary's College in London. Like so many women before her, she had convinced herself she was glad she'd forgotten what it was like to want to be truly free. She said gently:

'I expect your father in town any day now, my dear, to take you back.'

'Mother would have wanted me to go on. I know she would . . .' Dora unclenched her fists, knotted in her lap. 'I *found* him, Dreda. It was simply ghastly.' She swallowed. 'And I can't give up on it until I understand.'

'Until you understand what?'

'Who hated him so much they wanted to kill him. Because everyone hated him. It's extraordinary. Everyone who knew him save his own sister. Yet Venetia loved him. She was going to marry him. I just don't understand it.' Dora shook her head.

'Why, isn't it obvious?' Dreda took out a handkerchief and delicately patted her mouth. 'Dora dear. How naïve you are. He was wealthy beyond even her wildest dreams. She was going to give up writing, give up racketing around the country looking for plots. She was going to be able to live in Mount Street being a lady of leisure. May in Venice, summers in Ireland, winter on the Riviera. I'm sure,' said Dreda, 'some women would put up with a lot for that. They'd even put up with someone like Sir Edwin.'

Dora said under her breath: 'But she is so beautiful. And clever—'

'Exactly,' said the practical Dreda, her voice softening. 'I think, my dear, being beautiful is sometimes something of a bore. Men want to own you, y'see, and women don't like you. And they don't like it when you're clever. Oh no! I think she –' she clicked her fingers – 'she saw a way out. And I don't think she realised what she was getting herself into. The first thing was that she was going to stop writing the books.'

'Didn't she want to work?'

Lady Dreda glanced at the door. 'Of course not! She was exhausted. She'd had her success, she kept saying it was time for Dorothy and Agatha to have their turn but I'm not sure she really meant it— Ah.' Her voice dropped. 'That's her now, dearest, that scent of hers is almost overpowering.' She carried on talking, smoothly modulating her tone to a chirpier conversational sound. 'Well! Here you are, my dear, and that's that.' Venetia nodded, closed her eyes, as if to say: *thank you for not mentioning it.* 'I'm just saying to Dora, Venetia my love, it seems she must go, but she's welcome back here at my little *castello in la città* at any time. Any time at all.'

'You're awfully brave, dear Dora. What will you do?' said Venetia, smoothing down her skirt. 'A girl must earn a living, after all.' She sighed. 'She must.'

'I'm going to be a detective,' said Dora promptly, ignoring Dreda's frantic arm gestures. Venetia laughed, wildly.

'You funny thing. You're not serious.' Her lovely face broke into an incredulous smile. 'Dora, dear God. Who – how do you go about setting up on your own in business like that? I must say, it's terribly brave.'

'I want to be like you,' said Dora boldly. 'You've written such wonderful books and given so much pleasure to people, really all round the world. You bought a mink coat with your own money and a flat and, oh, everything you need. You're free!'

Venetia pressed her slim fingers to her mouth. 'My dear, I'm anything but free. You have no idea. You – *you* are free, now. More than you realise.' She gave a twisted little smile. 'Oh Dora, you remind me of your mother, so very much. Dreda, don't you agree, darling?'

Dreda simply nodded, her elbows propped up on her knees. 'Yes, it catches me sometimes. Darling Elizabeth.'

'As if she'd knocked on the door and come straight in, chattering about a book or a bird's nest,' said Venetia happily.

Dora smiled, as if it didn't hurt to hear this, and there was an awkward silence when there came a sudden, loud knock on the door, and the three of them jumped. Dreda gave a strangled yelp. 'Oh dear me. Who *can* that be at this late hour?'

'If it's Charles, do tell Maria, don't let him in,' Dora said.

'Dearest, she's been told not to. Do not fret,' said Lady Dreda calmly.

Maria was at the door. There were low, intent voices, as though she was remonstrating with someone. 'Late . . . imposition . . . unfortunate.'

'What is it?' cried Venetia. 'Oh, who is it?' She was uncommonly agitated; her tangle of blonde hair shining around her head, her large eyes without expression, plucking frantically at the antimacassar next to her.

'Dear Venetia, it'll be someone who's come to the wrong address,' said Dreda, putting out her hand to soothe her. 'Ah, Maria. How can I help you?'

Maria was standing at the door, furiously adjusting her cap.

'Madam, a Detective Inspector Fox is here, and he says it's urgent, and he needs to see you.'

'Goodness me,' said Venetia, standing up. 'What can he want?'

'Would you like a drink, Detective Inspector?' Dreda roused herself and stood up, walking over to the sideboard where the sherry decanter was kept.

'A little late for me, Lady Dreda, but thank you.' Fox stood in the doorway, and nodded at Dora. Dora saw him look back at Maria, almost as if he was making a point. *I told you they'd want to see me.* And then he gave Maria a swift smile, and Dora saw her blush, and knew she'd noticed his forearms too.

Fox coughed. 'Good evening, Miss Wildwood.'

'Inspector Fox.' Dora nodded. 'Did you want Miss Strallen?'

Venetia Strallen turned to him, her face ashen. He said, quite gruffly: 'I'm afraid so. Miss Strallen, I wanted to ask you a few questions.'

Lady Dreda held out her arm. 'It's awfully late.'

Venetia Strallen stopped her. 'It's fine, Dreda darling. My guard dog is most punctilious, Detective Inspector. I understood you called round earlier today. I'm awfully sorry to have missed you.'

Mr Fox said, 'That's quite all right.' He saw Dora's questioning expression and added, somewhat woodenly: 'I followed up a few enquiries and we established Miss Strallen was one of the last people to see Sir Edwin alive before he returned to the library yesterday.'

'He dropped round with a small gift. To urge me on to the final finish, you know. He always gave me such encouragement,' said Venetia. 'I've been having such a tricky time with the new novel, you know; Michael Steyn – that's my publisher, a darling man but such a taskmaster – he – and the public of course – wants a new one every year and I find it harder and harder. I was in a pickle and Edwin – he brought round a hamper from Harrods and we sat on the floor together and ate it. The mess afterwards . . . you should have seen it! All my favourite things, cucumber sandwiches, ginger cake, tinned peaches – he was so very thoughtful . . .' She knitted her fingers together.

'Was he quite well when you left? Your neighbour, Miss Grantham, a very observant lady, thankfully, said – ' Stephen Fox flipped a notebook open – 'she said you hurried after him. She said he was walking fast and you had to run down the stairs to catch up with him and that he slammed the car door and didn't appear to be speaking to you. She said you were in tears.'

Venetia Strallen stopped. She nodded. 'It's true. He was very short-tempered and he was rather – cross about something going on at the library. Sometimes he needed calming down – I thought it was my job, you see, my job to do that.'

Dear God, Dora thought. What a miserable existence.

'And then we left together – I was going in to collect a book, I have Carruthers on Tuesdays, he drives me about, you know, so I gave Edwin a lift into town – he kissed me goodbye, in a much better humour, and went into the library and I carried on before I remembered I'd left my notes there the day before, which is when I saw you, Dora. And I can't stop thinking—' Her voice broke. 'If I'd simply gone into his office and given him another kiss, I'd have prevented it all – he wouldn't have eaten the Turkish delight, he wouldn't have gone to the Stacks, he wouldn't have – have been murdered . . .' She buried her face in her hands.

'Turkish delight?' said Dora.

'Mr Dryden told me,' said Venetia. 'I assume the toxicology report isn't in yet. I assume too, as the fiancée, I must be seen as the chief suspect—'

'Venetia!' said Lady Dreda, scandalised. 'My dear girl!'

'I want to be honest,' Venetia Strallen said. Two spots of red burned on her pale cheeks. 'I want this business settled, as quickly as possible – my poor darling. As if having a short temper was a just motive for murder . . . And now – oh gosh – what now, Inspector? In the mysteries I write, the handsome detective doesn't simply turn up late at night to have a drink.' Detective Inspector Fox looked rather pleased. 'He only ever arrives when there is news. Bad news.'

'I'm sorry to say there's been a break-in at your flat,' said Fox.

'Oh dear God, what next?' said Lady Dreda, and Venetia Strallen cried out at the same time: '*No!*'

'I haven't seen the damage yet. Sergeant Crispin is there already. My car is outside. We'd like you to accompany us there, Miss Strallen,' Fox said, very gently.

'She shouldn't have to go. I'll go,' said Dreda determinedly, climbing off the sofa.

'Thank you, Lady Dreda, but it has to be Miss Strallen.'

'Of course,' said Venetia, standing up. 'Don't worry, my dear.'

'We did find some items of interest pertaining to this case in the hallway of the flats, Miss Strallen.' Fox swallowed, as if trying to establish whether he should divulge this information or not.

'What?' cried Dora.

He nodded at Venetia Strallen, who was gasping for breath. 'Two screwed-up pages from a book, Miss.'

'I know which one,' said Dora slowly. '*The Killing Jar*, by Cora Carson.'

'Yes, Miss Wildwood,' said Fox, nodding. Lady Dreda stared at her goddaughter.

'It was . . . the one with Edwin when he died,' Venetia said, speaking very slowly. 'Where did you find them, again?'

'On the landing outside your flat, Miss Strallen. Scrunched up so tightly it's a wonder the young lady who found them recognised them.'

'Almost left for you to find,' said Lady Dreda. 'How awful. How beastly.' Her handsome dark face was flushed with anger. 'Why – what do they *want*, Venetia?'

'Did anyone see anyone arrive, or leave?' asked Dora.

'They exited via the fire escape. I'm sorry ma'am. I'd be grateful if you'd come with me.'

'Of course,' Venetia said. She stood up, placing one shaking hand on her friend's shoulder. 'Awfully sorry, Dreda old girl. Thank you for a delightful evening. We will dine again without interruption another time.'

'I'll come with you,' said Dora, responding to a glance from her godmother. 'You don't mind, do you, Detective Inspector?'

Without waiting for an answer, she hurried out of the door and down the stairs.

14

Make me a willow cabin at your gate

Mecklenburgh Square was only a couple of minutes' drive in Fox's Wolseley. The night was ice-cold, the clear sky studded with stars. Dora thought about the owls calling in the beeches behind Wildwood House, how bright Jupiter was at this time of year, the stars a glittering shower of pinpricks in a black velvet sky, how some mornings the first breath you took outside hurt.

Venetia sat next to Dora, her pale face illuminated by car lights. 'Hurry,' she murmured, under her breath. 'Why don't they hurry?' She seemed hardly aware Dora was there.

'The young miss you mentioned.' Dora leaned forwards. 'Was this the upstairs neighbour? The one who found the torn pages? Was she the one who raised the alarm?' she asked Fox, from the back seat.

He had been concentrating on driving, mouth set, his face grim in the shadows, beard black. He had a sickle-shaped scar on his temple; Dora wondered how he'd got it. She thought of his bright, determined sister, Susan, the way she'd carried two trays with silver teapots filled with boiling water, delicate cakes that must not be crushed, and set them down so gracefully, noting who poured, what cakes were eaten, how she was a noticer, someone who saw what needed to be seen.

Fox did not answer immediately, then turned right into Guilford Street. 'Esmé Johnson, Miss, the novelist. She raised the alarm.'

'What?' Venetia Strallen exclaimed, suddenly alert. She gripped the seat and pushed Dora aside. 'What on earth was *she* doing in my flat? Honestly, how *could*—'

Detective Inspector Fox said casually: 'Miss Johnson claims you invited her round for a drink. To discuss something important.'

'I did no such thing,' said Venetia. Then she paused, and pushed the flat of her palm upwards from her forehead slowly. 'Or did I – I can't remember. Before—' She looked up. Her expression was desolate, like a small child. 'I keep forgetting things.'

'You've had a shock, Miss Strallen.' Detective Inspector Fox stopped the car outside a white stucco terrace lined with black railings. He opened Venetia Strallen's door and said kindly, 'It's quite usual to forget things after something like this. Sergeant Crispin will fill us in. He took the call at the station. He's up there now.'

He handed Venetia out gently, giving a half-bow, then made to shut the door. 'Oh, I nearly forgot about you. I'm most dreadfully sorry,' he said, peering in at Dora.

The previous Christmas her stepmother Carine had given her a very ugly hat which Dora had thought the worst present possible but then she had unwrapped her second present, which turned out to be a folding ruler. 'I don't understand this present, forgive me,' she'd said.

'Me not either. But it, it remind me of you,' Carine had said with a shrug as Dora unfolded the wooden rule, mystified. 'You 'ave to learn to fold them up right.'

As she unfolded her long, skinny legs from the cramped car Dora was reminded of this, and for the first time thought Carine might be correct about something. She hurried after Fox and Venetia.

*　　*　　*

Mecklenburgh Square was quiet, save for a lone dog barking in an open window. Detective Inspector Fox nodded to the policeman on the door of the building at the corner of the square.

'Evening, Crispin,' he said.

'Sir. Miss Strallen.' The stolid policeman hesitated. 'And – evening, Miss—'

'This is Miss Wildwood. Family friend, found the body yesterday in the Mountjoy case.' Fox did not change pace or tone as he said: 'She's our eyes and ears on the ground in the library.'

'All right,' said Sergeant Crispin, pushing his helmet up above his forehead with one finger on the brim, mouth downturned in nodding acceptance. 'Evening, Miss.' He sneezed, and flashed Dora a quick smile; she nodded briefly, trying to look like she was used to tagging along in police investigations, pronouncing on rigor mortis, bullet entry, alibis, etc.

'Ah! Good evening, Sergeant,' she said, adopting what she hoped was a low, clipped, professional tone, which unfortunately came out as a low, angry, wolf-like growl, slightly Russian. '*Gudevenig Sargunttt.*'

Sergeant Crispin looked surprised. He glanced at Mr Fox. 'Right then. Would you like to come this way, chief? Ladies?'

'I'm afraid, Dora. Will you stay close to me?' Venetia Strallen whispered, and she threaded her slender arm through Dora's. Dora patted her hand.

As she climbed the wide stairs she found herself stopping for a split second, almost to catch her breath. If she'd have been told yesterday morning, as she shivered on the milk train into London that barely thirty-six hours later she'd be in her favourite author's flat helping the police with a murder enquiry she'd have pinched herself to see if she'd lost consciousness, like the time at school that Tommy had dropped the side of a pommel horse right onto the back of Dora's head during gym and for three days afterwards she had thought she was Perkin Warbeck. (She still, in fact, found any mention of him extremely moving, and though never able to say this to anyone else, as they'd think she was utterly crackers, she did wonder at times if the whole incident had awakened some past life memory, that perhaps she had been a Tudor washerwoman at Hampton Court. This was not the first time she had wondered if it was she, Dora, alone, who felt the boundary between the past and the present was sometimes thinner than tissue paper, that she sometimes, without meaning to, was able to poke her finger through a tiny tear in time, then her nose, peering into the past, able to feel and smell and see things that no one else could. But as I say, she did not say this to anyone else.)

'This way, please.' Venetia indicated the first-floor landing to Dora and Fox. 'My little place is just here – thank you so much, Inspector. Thank you, Sergeant Crispin. Can you tell me what happened?'

Sergeant Crispin cleared his throat. 'Yes ma'am. Esmé Johnson, ma'am, she said she arrived at six p.m. as she said you'd requested and rang the doorbell, but there was no answer. After five minutes the lady on the floor above, Miss er –' he looked at his notebook – 'Grantham, she was leaving, so Miss Johnson explained she was here to see Miss Strallen and gained access to the building itself, and went up to your flat, Miss Strallen. Haaahhaacchhrump. Excuse me. Someone was in the flat. She could hear them. She said she heard banging, and things being knocked over.' They were at the door now. 'Miss Strallen – I'm afraid it's a terrible mess. Mind how you go, now.'

'Yes,' said Venetia grimly. 'It would be.'

'There's one other thing,' said Sergeant Crispin, as they reached the front door. 'Didn't like to mention it before.'

'What? Oh – oh my God,' said Venetia Strallen.

The door swung open, wide, banging on something behind it. There was a scuffling noise, and a terrible smell; Dora put her hand to her nose. She knew that smell.

'Oh dear God,' said Venetia. 'What on earth *is* that?'

Dora peered over her shoulder, and the three of them followed the sergeant into the room. Venetia screamed.

'My God,' she said. 'Why? Who would do this?'

It was an elegant room, high ceilings, long windows, walls painted a cool, dark forest green, heavy rugs on the floor, an ornate gold mirror above the mantelpiece.

All around the room were lewd slogans, painted on with some kind of distemper that stood out, dirty cream against the dark walls. 'I don't even know what that one *means*,' Dora said, pointing her finger. 'And that one is spelled wrong. It's Evil

Murderer with an e, not Murdurer with a u. Well, it is, how silly,' she added, as she saw Fox grind his teeth.

'Here,' he said, suddenly looking across the room. 'What's this?'

On the mantelpiece was a creamy ivory skull. It was the length of Dora's hand, slim and long. There were little pointed teeth, still attached to the jaw, gleaming pearlescent in the dim light. On a thick, watermarked sheet of writing-paper someone had written, in perfect copperplate:

It should have been you

The paper was clamped in place, pierced by the sharp pointed teeth. It fluttered in the breeze from the open window.

'I don't know what animal that is,' Fox said. 'Do you, Miss Strallen?

'Get it out of here,' said Venetia, shuddering. 'Please – oh please do.'

Dora glanced at Detective Inspector Fox and to her amazement found he was looking at her, rather blankly. 'Well, Inspector, it's a fox,' she said, staring down at it.

'Are you sure?'

Dora nodded. 'I'm good at skulls. The villagers used to line them up around the maypole, to ward off evil spirits.'

Detective Inspector Fox was rather white. 'How do you know it's not, say, a badger?'

'Oh you can tell it's not a badger. The bone is too delicate. Look at the teeth. They can really tear you to bits. I knew a child – well,' Dora said, collecting herself, as she saw Venetia shoot a glance at her, half appraising, half curious. 'We don't need to hear that story now. But that's its scent you can smell, and that's a fox skull. I'm sorry, Venetia.'

Venetia Strallen swallowed, with a shuddering sigh. 'My letters from Sir Edwin – his gifts to me – I must just make sure they're all right. Do excuse me a moment, won't you?'

She vanished into the next room. Dora heard her letting out a sob as she did.

Detective Inspector Fox turned to Dora.

'Earlier I said your help would be appreciated, Miss Wildwood.'

'You did.'

'So, in this situation, what would you advise? Do you think this is a coincidence?'

'The fox skull? No. Someone wants to warn you off. Actually when one thinks about it, it's rather like the villagers on May Day, placing the skulls around the maypole. It's shock value.'

'Is it?' said Fox, quite fascinated.

'Don't you think it is? The question,' said Dora, 'is why they see you as a threat. Or why this was done. Whoever left this there was alarmed. By you? Perhaps.' She glanced into the doorway, touching the detective lightly on the arm. 'Ah – forgive me. We should make sure Venetia – Miss Strallen – is all right.'

A cry came from the bedroom and she flinched, hurrying into the next room, leaving Fox staring at the skull. Venetia Strallen was standing by her dressing table, holding a dripping mass of something in her hands.

'Look,' Venetia said slowly. 'Gone. Edwin's letters to me – they're all gone.'

White roses lay scattered around the room. She held up a sodden flat sheaf of papers tied with dark ribbon, ink running down over her fingers, onto the carpet.

'They stuffed them in here,' she said, gesturing to the low, wide-necked glass vase on her dressing table, gesturing to the roses that had been displaced. 'He wrote to me . . . every day.' She gave a great, shuddering sigh. 'Every day, Dora, a letter would arrive, telling me he loved me, that he would take care of me, what fun we'd have together. We were going to Venice, you know, after we married. He'd write to me telling me how it would be different . . . what it'd be like . . . And now they're all gone. Nothing left.'

Dora stepped forwards, and held up the corner of the wet slap of paper.

'*Orsino's mistress, and his fancy's queen.*' As she read aloud, the corner she was holding broke away, the paper dissolving into mulch in Venetia's hands.

'Gone,' said Venetia. 'Look, I'll lay it carefully – there – near the fire. Perhaps some of the letters can be saved.'

'What's the line from?' said Dora curiously. 'I know it – I'm sure.'

'*Twelfth Night*,' said Venetia. 'He called me Olivia, after the countess. It's my middle name, you know, and that's what he used to call me. *Make me a willow cabin at your gate.* One of his letters started like that. And they're gone. They're gone—' She gave a juddering sob.

'Yes,' said Dora, worried. 'Oh, I wish I'd retained more at school. I don't remember a word of it. I'm so stupid. Remind me of the quote again.'

Slightly surprised, Venetia quoted: '*But when in other habits you are seen, Orsino's mistress and his fancy's queen.*' She laid the pulpy mass of letters down, very carefully. '*But let concealment, like a worm i' th' bud, feed on her damask cheek,*' she said, almost to herself.

'They're typewritten,' Dora said.

'Yes; Sir Edwin had a problem with his hands. The Boer War. Some tendon was sliced and he couldn't hold a pen. He could type with two fingers, though.' She shook her head, silver hair falling in her eyes, and Dora saw tears, dropping onto her silk dress. 'She could have left me the letters.'

'She?'

Venetia looked up. 'Oh, you know who I mean. Esmé Johnson. That bitch. She's like a giraffe, always looming over everything.'

'Why do people keep bringing giraffes into this,' said Dora hotly.

'Why not? You know it's her. Who else can it be? Who else?'

'Venetia – really, I would be very careful—'

'Careful!' Venetia said, slamming her hand down on the table. 'I am careful! You have no idea how careful I have to be! No idea at—'

'Everything all right in there?' Fox called from the sitting room. 'Are we safe?'

'Yes, yes,' Dora called back. 'Perfectly. Venetia,' she said quietly. 'You must tell me, and then I can help you.'

Venetia Strallen nodded. 'I haven't told you everything,' she said. Dora could see a muscle, twitching at her temple. 'Why I've been so scared. Because it's so fantastical, really. Someone tried to kill me. Last month. Sir Edwin knew.'

'Really?'

'Oh, yes. He was onto them. Yesterday he told me he'd had them followed and it was obvious who it was . . . You see it wasn't just him . . . and me . . . there have been other incidents. Other members of the literary set, you know . . . A young girl died this August . . . Poor thing . . .'

She leaned closer to Dora. Outside, the dog was howling louder than ever. 'That's why they did away with him. That's why they've come here tonight, I'm sure of it.' She tugged at Dora's elbow. 'You must believe me. They wanted to finish what they started.'

'Oh Venetia,' said Dora. 'How utterly terrifying. Do tell . . . Oh!' She jumped. Stephen Fox was in the doorway.

'Sorry to startle you, Miss Wildwood. This murder attempt you believe took place . . . Could you tell us what happened, Miss Strallen?'

He took out his notebook, ostentatiously, again. Dora noticed it this time. 'Oh!' she exclaimed. 'You *do* have a notebook!'

'I've always had one,' said Fox, she thought unconvincingly. He turned to the second page, and licked his pencil.

'Yes,' said Dora, her eyes grave. 'I'm sure.'

Venetia, glancing almost fearfully at Fox, swallowed. 'Well, you see, I – I was walking through Brydges Place,' she said. 'After a rather . . . *difficult* lunch with my publisher, let's say.' She gritted her teeth. 'Do you know Brydges Place, Dora?'

'No.'

'It's behind the Coliseum; it's the narrowest street in London. I love it,' she said, a smile lifting her lovely eyes for a moment. 'I love those hidden corners, those mysteries. All the stories that haven't been told. Two people couldn't fit past each other. You quite expect Sherlock Holmes to step out of the shadows. Anyway, it was a nasty rainy day, very grey. I heard footsteps behind me, getting faster, and closer. Breathing – I could hear breathing – and a voice. It was –' she hesitated – 'it was cold, like a raincloud, that's all I can say about it.'

'A man or a woman?' Dora said.

Venetia shook her head. 'I'm not sure. Whoever they were, they said: "It's your turn next" and swung at me with a cosh. Well, I screamed, and I don't think they were expecting it, and then I turned, very quickly – catch them off guard, that's the key, and I jabbed my fingers into his eyes. Well, *she* – I mean they, *they* screamed then, and fell to the floor, and then got to their feet again and ran away – but I ran before they could get me.'

'Where did you go?'

'The Jackpot,' said Venetia Strallen simply.

'The *Jackpot*?' Detective Inspector Fox said, in tones of surprise.

'What's the Jackpot?' Dora asked.

'The most notorious drinking den in London,' said Detective Inspector Fox grimly. 'Not a place for a nice lady.'

'I'm not a nice lady,' said Venetia, smiling. 'But I have friends there,' she said with a smile. 'From researching my books, you know.'

'It seems as though you knew how to handle your attacker,' said Detective Inspector Fox, after a pause.

'Martial arts,' said Venetia Strallen simply. 'I wrote about the opium trade in *Lady, Be Good!* Took some lessons with ever such a nice chap in Chinatown.' She looked up at Stephen Fox. 'You seem shocked, Inspector.'

'It's . . .' Detective Inspector Fox paused, and softly bit his knuckles. 'No, not at all, only – Miss Strallen, why on earth didn't you tell us this?'

Venetia Strallen looked from him to Dora, her face blank, her eyes dead. 'Because,' she said in a monotone, 'my experience is, when you are a woman over a certain age, absolutely no one wants to hear you complain. Even if it's about attempted murder.'

'What about your publisher?' Stephen Fox flipped back the pages of his notebook. 'Mr Michael Steyn.'

Venetia shrugged. 'What about him?'

'What was the difficult conversation with your publisher about?'

She shrugged. 'Opposing views. I think he should promote my books more than he does. He's only interested in the new. You must know I mean Esmé Johnson. Oh, that woman. She gets everywhere, like ringworm. Inspector, my head aches so dreadfully I can barely see. Would you mind very much if we concluded the interview tomorrow?' She turned to Dora. 'My dear, I don't want to stay here tonight. Would you ring for a cab? We can go back to Dreda's.'

'Of course,' said Dora, and she went downstairs. In the doorway she found Sergeant Crispin, standing guard.

'Bit of a mess in there, you're right,' she said. 'Just taking Miss Strallen back to my godmother's. She's not feeling up to further questioning.'

'*Halloo your name to the reverberate hills, and make the babbling gossip of the air cry out: Olivia!*' said the sergeant, somewhat to Dora's surprise. 'I a-heard you quoting it there, upstairs,' he added.

'That's beautiful,' said Dora.

'My dad was a one for Shakespeare, you see.'

'We only did Lamb's Tales at school, not the actual plays,' said Dora, and Sergeant Crispin regarded her with pity. 'Did he worship her? Orsino, I mean?'

'Oh yes,' said the sergeant. 'But –' he screwed up his mouth, put his head on one side – 'how do you say it? False, like. Not real love. Like it was convenient for him to be in love with her, and who cares what she thinks. Not like the real thing – you know the real thing when it comes along.'

'I don't,' said Dora. 'But you put it beautifully.'

'Well, you do, Miss. I knew the moment I saw my Elsie, you see. Twenty-five years, and I rub my eyes sometimes at how quick it's gone, what a lucky fellow I am. Yes, I do.'

Dora smiled. She said: 'Oh I see. Thank you very much.'

'Right you are,' said the sergeant, nodding, as if he'd just directed her to the nearest bus stop. 'Well, good night, Miss. And here – mind how you go,' he said. He held something up. 'Ain't safe out there tonight. Look what I found, in the bushes.'

Between his fingers he held up a small, pearl-handled gun. It glinted in the darkness.

Dora cleared her throat. 'Good golly,' she said, and she peered at it. 'That's mine. Well, at least, I had it but it vanished. Pretty thing, isn't it?'

Sergeant Crispin peered at her. His face was grave. 'Is it, Miss? What was you a-using it for, if you don't mind my asking?'

'I used it to threaten my fiancé, but I haven't seen it since. That was yesterday. How – how funny to find it here.'

'I wouldn't say it was funny,' said Sergeant Crispin grimly. 'Hanging off a branch it was. Like someone threw it there. Someone in a hurry.'

15

In which Dora receives two books

Breakfast at the Three Corners was a relaxed affair. Light from high windows poured onto the golden stone floor and onto the warm wooden tables at which girls sat on long benches, chewing toast, sipping coffee and tea, hands wrapped round mugs, in the warmth of the sharply cold autumn mornings.

At one end, reading *The Times* with a puckered forehead, was Miss Pym, her short grey bob as always perfectly straight, her wide fawn wool trousers and white shirt always perfectly pressed, her notebook at her side, ready for the day ahead. Sometimes she would cut an article out and pin it to the noticeboard, something of interest for the girls – a free exhibition perhaps, or a note about a sale at Debenhams on silk stockings, or a new lending library opening nearby. The noticeboard itself was a treasure trove of useful information. 'Found – one gold earring (probably not gold). See Miss Pym.'

'Wanted: young woman to act as co-respondent in divorce case. Please ask Lily,' to which had been added a note by Miss Pym: '*NO GIRL to participate in this. See Miss Pym.*'

Dora tried to wait until the rush was over so the girls who had to get to offices and shops had the chance to eat first. Her job at the London Library had a start time of ten a.m., which was most pleasing. One morning, a few days after she'd moved in to the Three Corners, Dora was reading a letter that had arrived with a parcel from her father.

Dear Dora

Here is the book you requested. Take care of it please. No I haven't read it. I use it to prop open the window, let fresh air in, you know how important fresh air is, and I like looking at the colour plates, reminds me of your mother. I send it care of this women's flop house at which you apparently now reside being still ENTIRELY UNABLE to fathom what would make a child of mine abandon herself utterly to pleasure, and drag the Wildwood name through the <u>GUTTER.</u>

I am still in Paris. I sense a weakening of Carine's resolve and have hopes that she might be persuaded to come back to Wildwood before too long. I would like it if my sole offspring were there to greet us, also to make sure the bramble has not fully taken over. You say Albert has not been able to get into the house; you say the bramble has proliferated inside and somehow fastened the front door. Why does he need to get into the house? What have you asked him to do? I don't like that boy walking in and out as he pleases. No Dora, the bramble is not alive and trying to curse us. Stop listening to his nonsense.

As for the fungus in the gatehouse, has he eaten it? It may prove to be delicious. I hope to be back for Christmas. Carine sends you her sincere regards. I have bought a new tie, it has horseshoes all over it, it is quite delightful. My best, your loving father WILDWOOD

That morning, Miss Pym had nodded and said, 'Good morrow, Miss Wildwood,' with something approaching a smile, and handed her the letter and parcel from her father.

'Good *morrow*,' Dora had replied, shaken fully awake at the sight of her father's handwriting.

After Dora had sat down, Susan, always one to notice things, and quick to take people off, had leapt on this.

'Good *morrow*, Dora,' she'd said, and the other girls had rubbed their sides with hilarity. 'Good *morrow*. Oh I say, old chap. Good *morrow*.'

Dora, well schooled in the ways of girl cliques, had laughed good-naturedly. 'Good *morrow*, Susan,' and given a circular twirl with her hand. 'Do let me know if you want to borrow my cold cream for that rash, by the way, darling. I hate to think of it spreading further.' Susan had sunk back into her seat, blushing fiery red as the other girls edged away, and Dora gave her a glance. The glance said: I like you very much Susan, but don't try to take me on.

As she was leaving breakfast Susan had approached Dora. 'What ho, Dora, sorry about before,' she'd said. 'Minnie and I are going to go out for a bit of a wah-wah this evening. Bite to eat at Quag's, spot of dancing at the Café de Paris. A couple of chaps we know are shouting us – Neil Bluman, utterly dreamy –' here her eyes almost turned heart-shaped, like Mickey Mouse upon seeing Minnie – 'and his brother Jim who's always around as our spare chap, we call him Spare Jim, and there's a *third* brother, Dora, he's called Terence. They've oodles of money, father had a stall in Chapel Street Market twenty years ago, now he has twelve shops up and down the country. Imagine, Neil went to Le Touquet last year. On a plane. For the *day*.'

'You're so vulgar, Susan,' said Minnie. 'But it's true, darling Dora. Do say you'll come. It'll be a real wah-wah, like Susan says.'

Dora hesitated for a moment.

'See,' said Susan, nudging Minnie. 'I told you she wouldn't come. I told you she'd be chicken.'

'I was wondering what to wear,' Dora said. 'My godmother has said she'll lend me evening clothes. She has a midnight-blue velvet sheath dress and a mink stole.'

'Sounds awfully staid, Dora darling. You're not going to tea with Queen Mary. You're out for the night in the fleshpots of Soho with Prince Eddie and his crowd.' She gave a wink.

'She also has a silvery sequinned top and trousers, sort of an all-in-one affair,' said Dora, musing. 'She says it's called a jumpsuit.'

'Oh Dora. So you'll come?' Dora nodded, smiling. 'You'll look like a film star,' said Susan, pleased. 'Won't she, Minnie?'

'I should say. Your Stephen was right.'

'What did your Stephen say?' said Dora, taken aback.

'Oh.' Susan rolled her eyes. 'He said you reminded him of Myrna Loy. And we all know he's sweet on Myrna Loy. I told him not to go soft on you, it'd only lead to trouble.' Dora gave a rather loud snort of a laugh, like a machine gun.

'Ha! Well, I don't know what there is of that, I do – I must say!' she said, incoherently.

Susan stared at her. 'Oh dear,' she said. 'Oh dear oh dear. Listen, darling. Wear the silver thing, it sounds wonderful.'

'Thank you.' Dora pushed the letter and the book away. 'But that's not really the issue. The issue is whether I should go at all –' The others looked blank. 'Well, the business with the body in the library—'

'It's not *your* dead body, is it? Come off it, Dora. You need a good time. Take your mind off all of it.' Susan clapped Dora smartly on the shoulders. 'The Bluman boys are terrific fun. Meet us back here this evening.'

'Sevenish?'

'Sevenish . . . !' Susan and Minnie laughed uproariously, laughed till tears ran down Minnie's cheeks and Susan had to be slapped on the back because she was having a coughing fit. 'You all right, darling? Dear me, country girls. Ten, Dora. Be ready at ten p.m.'

The breakfast room was almost empty. Dora drank some more coffee, savouring the warm sunshine in the quiet room. She knew she ought to write back to her father by return, but that could wait a little while.

'More post,' Miss Pym said, materialising by her side. 'I overlooked it, I do apologise. Another parcel for you.' She handed Dora a brown-paper package, and Dora fumbled with the string, pulling it off hurriedly. 'How kind, someone's sent you a present.'

'It's not a present. It's not kind, either,' said Dora. She looked up at Miss Pym, eyes dancing. 'It's from the most egomaniacal person I think I've ever met. I haven't met many authors, but this one really does give them a bad name.' She held up a copy of *Death on a Train*, and quickly scanned the card that accompanied it.

Dear Dora, this literary baby, not yet birthed into the wider
world, but still safe in his mother's warm ~~gut stomach~~ *insides*
comes with vast love and affection and hopes that we meet again
soon – my apologies for not sending this book straight away – I
have been utterly laid LOW by recent events – do forgive your
new friend Esmé and I hope you are not to desperate for a new
instalment of Barnard Castle – he does so love meeting new
readers – he is a funny old chap and I do so love writing him – I
do so hope we meet again soon – when time allows, for I have to
write, to tell the stories that present themselves to me!
   Bisouxes!
   Esmé Johnson

'Someone needs an editor,' said Miss Pym, reading over her shoulder. Dora let the book fall onto the table. 'I can't quite face it this second. Murder mysteries – to think I used to love reading them.' She gave a sigh, and rubbed her eyes.

'You look rather pensive,' said Miss Pym, and she began piling up discarded cereal bowls and coffee cups.

'I am rather.'

'Can I help?' Miss Pym vanished inside the kitchen for a few seconds then the door swung back out and she emerged, empty-handed. 'I've always been jolly good at listening.'

'Oh, it's this case. I can't seem to make any headway on it. Something's stopping me. And it sounds dreadfully vain but I've always been so good at working things out, until now. I really thought – oh well.'

Miss Pym cocked her head, interested. 'What case are you talking about, Miss Wildwood?'

'The murder of Sir Edwin Mountjoy, in the London Library. It was the day I arrived in town. I found him, you see.' She saw Miss Pym's eyes widen, and went on hurriedly, 'And I'm starting to wonder if I've missed something jolly obvious. If there is a pattern, you see. Because something doesn't make sense.' She gave Miss Pym a frank smile. 'Something other than murder, of course.'

'What's that?' Miss Pym said, fiddling with the bright jade beads around her neck.

Dora glanced at her, watching as she clicked each bead along its string with her slim fingers. 'I keep thinking about him. His eyes, really. I keep seeing his eyes, his face pressed down against the floor. His hands clenched by his sides. He wasn't scared, Miss Pym. He was *furious*. He wasn't expecting to die; he despised the person who killed him, thought they were nothing, utterly worthless . . . So when they poisoned him . . . when they did this to him . . . I think he was terrifically angry because they were *there*, and *he could see them*. It's the way the Stacks are designed, you see . . . through the gaps in the floors, one can be several floors below and look up and spy on something or someone in Science and Nature, for example . . . That's the beauty of libraries, you see - everything is laid out perfectly sensibly. There is a pattern. A is for, oh, I don't know, Albert. B is for Butterflies. C is for . . . C is for Cora. And D is for . . .'

She broke off.

'D is for Dora,' Miss Pym put in, helpfully.

'D is for Death,' said Dora. She shivered, and stood up. 'Why doesn't it sit quite right to me? What am I not seeing?' She was quite still, her face frozen, before the telephone on the wall rang loudly, and she gave a little start.

Miss Pym stood up to answer it. 'Yes?' she nodded, fingers running over the jade necklace. She ran her free right hand through her short waving hair, her fine profile casting a shadow against the cream wall, and Dora thought again how terrific she was, a games mistress everyone had a crush on. 'Yes. Yes, Mr Fox.' She handed the telephone to Dora. 'It's Stephen Fox. He has a message for you.'

'Who? Oh – thank you,' said Dora, coming to her senses. 'Good morning, Mr Fox – ah, I see. Yes. Thank you. But—' She was silent for a moment, and then her expression changed. 'But do you realise what this means? No? Dear God. No, I can be there in ten minutes. Please, hurry. And Fox? Make sure no one touches anything in that office. Especially not the sweet drawer. Did you—Drat, the man's gone.'

She put the phone down.

'You're awfully pale. Has a goose walked over your grave?'

'Over someone's,' Dora said, and she pulled on her cape. She shoved the two books into her satchel, and jammed on her beret. 'I have to go, Miss Pym,' she said. 'How could I not have seen it?'

'Seen what?'

'The pathologist has delivered his final report. It confirms that Sir Edwin was murdered with arsenic. There was only Turkish delight in Sir Edwin's stomach, laced with enough arsenic to kill a Scout pack, and in addition there is evidence of poisoning from several days before. That's why he didn't have lunch. He'd been feeling rotten for days – I wondered why a man like him had so little food in his stomach.' She raised her hand in farewell. 'He'd been eating the damn Turkish delight in his office. And that afternoon he must have stuffed his face with it. Something made him so furious he had to. Forget the book – I've been looking for the wrong memories, the wrong images.'

'What's the rush?'

'Something someone said yesterday to me as I was leaving the library—'

'What?'

'Thank you,' said Dora. 'He said "thank you for making my Tuesday sweeter". I didn't know what he meant.' She opened the door. 'Oh dear—'

'Be careful, Dora,' said Miss Pym – but to thin air, for Dora was already out on the street and hailing a black cab.

16

Why it should be forbidden to eat in a library

Michael Dryden, Esq., Acting Chief Librarian of the London Library, sat in the Chief Librarian's red leather chair, gazing down at the gold tooling on the Chief Librarian's desk. It was this desk, they said, which was stained with Tennyson's tears, which fell as he wrote *In Memoriam*, his sobs audible as far away as Nubian History on the fifth floor. It was this desk at which the Chief Librarian had listened to E.M. Forster outlining his plans to save the library when membership had fallen away almost to nothing. It was this desk behind which every librarian since the Great War had sat to lead one of the great institutions of British public life, and that person was now . . . he. Him? His . . . ? His head throbbed.

He stared at the box of Turkish delight, the pistachio-studded cubes dusted with icing sugar glowing a beautiful rose-pink, nestled invitingly in the beautiful duck-egg-blue tissue paper in its distinctive blue and gold box.

> *Dear Mr Dryden,* (the note with it said)
> *Hope this makes your Tuesday sweeter. A reminder to take care.*
> *We know too much and are in danger. These are delicious, simply*
> *my favourites. Yours, Dora Wildwood*

He would not admit he was a little hurt it was Turkish delight; it was pathetic to mind that she had forgotten her promise to send him peppermint creams. Saliva pooled in his mouth; he could resist no longer. He thought about plunging his hand inside, shovelling one dusky pink cube into his mouth, the musky rose-flavoured sweetness melting on his tongue. His stomach ached, and he clutched it, pain sluicing him. It felt like someone was stabbing him with ten, twenty different needles; and the panic he felt at the pain was almost as bad as the pain itself.

Michael Dryden was in a bad way.

Since he was a young boy and overlooked for the junior football team in Woolwich, Mr Dryden, Acting Chief Librarian of the London Library, had been a worrier. And the sign that he was worrying was stomach pains.

His older brother Wilfred was first in everything. A right one, people used to say of Wilfred – but not Michael. 'Michael's the brains,' their mum used to say, yanking him away from under a pile of small boys pummelling his thin body, marching him home, knees knocking together, face and legs covered in dirt, sobbing quietly. When no one was looking she'd rub the mud off his face with her thumb, caressing his cheek, and when someone appeared she'd cuff him round the ear. 'Think I'm soft, do you? Get off.' But when they were gone she'd ruffle his hair, drop a secret kiss on his head. She believed in him. 'He'll turn out right, little Michael. Just you wait and see.'

Bill Dryden, his father, had laughed at this. 'That boy? I wouldn't fancy his chances against one of Rosie's paper dolls, let alone a proper lad.' And Michael, obscurely, was happy to hear someone else understood, knew what Michael knew: his second son was a weakling, an idiot, and a laughing stock.

'You wait and see,' Clare Dryden would say, and that was all she'd say, not wanting to rouse her husband's quick temper.

And Mr Dryden's mother was right, even if she never lived to see her theory borne out. His big brother Wilfred had grown into a bully and a sadist, torturing cats, dogs, and girls, even smacking his mum round the face with the back of his hand once after she scolded him for being rude to her, though he'd never dare lay a finger on their father. He understood the hierarchy. His father was stronger than him.

Michael had intervened though, and punched his brother – the only time he'd landed a punch on him. He'd got a smashed nose in the process, but Wilfred had been momentarily confused by his mother hitting him with a tray and hadn't noticed eighteen-year-old Michael, squaring up, landing him one. It had felt awfully good. The bad luck of it was one of the neighbours had called a passing bobby in and Michael Dryden had found himself hauled up in front of Lambeth Magistrates' Court, paying a fine, ordered to spend two weeks in jail and with a criminal record to boot.

Two days after his thirtieth birthday Wilfred had been blasted to nothing at Passchendaele, no trace of him ever found in the mud. Michael wondered sometimes if Wilfred's last few seconds on earth made sense to him too, wondered if Wilfred had accepted that this was a part of war, as his head was torn from his body, his guts bursting out through his skin, his bones splintering in the air like shattered glass.

Their dad had never got over it. But it was the making of Michael, and his mother. Michael, who had been passed over for conscription because of his appalling eyesight and asthma, passed his school exams and went to work in Lambeth Library, working long hours, almost drunk with happiness on the smell of books, the different publishers' colophons and their addresses, the touch of cloth under his careful fingers, learning how to care for ancient volumes which had stood on the shelves for decades and doubtless would for decades to come, the comforting order of the library, A-B-C-D, the peace. The *sound* of books.

He had a plan, for the first time. He left home in the dark to save the bus fare and walk, eking out his sandwiches so as to pay his parents what rent he could as well as put money aside each week, and bit by bit he worked his way up, first as assistant librarian at Lambeth, then chief librarian, with use of an office. He saved and saved and spent the money on one good suit, on pocket handkerchiefs from the Army and Navy, and acquired a taste for Lapsang Souchong tea. He read *The Times* every day, learning about everything from Abyssinia and Arthur Balfour to Virginia

Woolf and the Weimar Republic. These were not affectations, but explorations, working out what he liked, what he wanted to be.

A few days after his own thirtieth birthday, he had applied for the role of junior librarian at the London Library and been offered the post.

The subscription library founded by Tennyson himself and Carlyle, a tall, slender building standing sleek and welcoming in the corner of St James's, the most exclusive, discreet district of London between Buckingham Palace and Savile Row, fringed with the gentlemen's clubs and outfitters: it was to him the embodiment of heaven on earth, and he did not care if it was sacrilegious to say so. And here he was walking up the steps of the institution where his particular hero Siegfried Sassoon had been a member (Sassoon hadn't been too weak to fight, not like him) praying his collar studs would stay in, his shoes were polished, that it wasn't obvious how second-rate, how unclean a person he was.

To walk up those same steps every morning, to have the responsibility of polishing the famous owl that stood in the window of the fourth floor, to restack the steel stacks with books that had been lent and returned by some of the greatest minds of the day . . . to breathe in and smell the air, warm with paper and ink, to greet the ladies and gentlemen who passed him on the stairs and were sometimes kind enough to nod or acknowledge him in some way. Once, he had stumbled, and one of them, a lady novelist from a most distinguished family, had even said: 'Careful there, Mr Dryden!'

Him! Michael Dryden, of Peckham. Whose teacher had said, with confidence: you'll never amount to anything. And he'd always thought it was such a funny thing to say to a child – so final. He would look back and wonder how he had found the nerve. Perhaps his mother's whispered words had been enough. 'He'll turn out all right, little Michael. Just you wait and see.' Every evening he would solemnly pick up his briefcase, step out onto St James's Square again, pausing to breathe in the fresh air, then walk the few minutes to Piccadilly Circus, descending into the bowels of the underground then emerging at Kilburn, where the air was fresher still, and the bus home. He did not miss South London. He had shaken its dust from his feet. He was a bold explorer now, migrating from Peckham to Cricklewood – with Janice, whom he'd met at a dance hall, who had a shingled bob and a gap between her teeth, who loved gardening and Douglas Fairbanks and who could balance the household accounts in seconds. And they had a wind-up gramophone and there were dances, and picnics on the Heath and meetings in halls about workers' rights and women's suffrage and a Tube that carried you into town and everything, everything was steady, and calm, and his stomach almost never pained him.

And then the old librarian, Sir Jolyon Forbes, had retired, and Sir Edwin Mountjoy had joined. And Michael Dryden had to remind himself what it was like to be unhappy again. Mountjoy had gone through the staff one by one, winkling out the bad things, the secrets. That nice boy Ben's family scandal, what it was Mr Dryden never knew but it kept Ben terrified and compliant. The threat of dismissal from the library for being from somewhere else and having different-coloured skin: he let it dangle over Zewditu Amani, though she had lived here for years, was brighter than him by far, and though she and Michael had spent hours discussing the books they'd read, competing with each other to find the most obscure title in the library. And of course, Sir Edwin had dug around in the library files and discovered Michael's criminal record – the shame of it, which no one in his current life apart from kind old Sir Jolyon had known, not even his wife. And if he wanted he could have dismissed him.

'Watch your step with me that's all, Dryden, you hear me? Watch your step.'

Smiling that shark-like fat smile – he didn't know how a smile could be fat but it could when Mountjoy smiled at you. As though he saw him for what he really was, as his teacher and Wilfred saw him – a misfit, an awkward oddball. No one important, not really!

* * *

Michael Dryden gazed at the note from Miss Wildwood, staring past it as the snakes coiled around his stomach, the pain now so bad he could barely see. He stared at the cube of Turkish delight in his hand, wondering how it had come to this. One of the things he'd despised about Sir Edwin was how gross he was, food over his mouth and tie, how he spat tea out when he talked to you.

But he, Dryden, had found he could not stop eating sweet things since Sir Edwin's death. Several times had asked Miss Bunce, his secretary, to pop out and buy cream cakes from Fortnum's, selection boxes from Charbonnel et Walker in the Burlington Arcade . . . He would ask her to bring them into Sir Edwin's office – now his office – where she would set them down on the mahogany desk with the leather top and gold tooling and retreat, where he would open the box, lifting out each cake or chocolate one by one, cramming them into his mouth, like a guilty child. Miss Bunce never asked where the cakes went, and he never brought it up. Never told the truth: 'I do apologise that there were no cakes today. I ate them all in my office, Miss Bunce. Help me.'

He knew something was wrong, he'd read books about analysis. He was afraid – terrified more like it, but he didn't understand why. He knew too, that in behaving like this, in failing to step up to the mark, he was confirming what those he most despised always accused him of. Weakness, ineptitude; secretive, trying behaviour. His father, then Wilfred, then Edwin Mountjoy. His fingers hovered in front of his drooling mouth, tongue peeking out to taste the dusty icing sugar; the scent of rosewater and honey filling his nostrils . . . he opened his mouth:

'*PUT THAT DOWN!*' he heard someone shout, as suddenly the door flew open, with a bang. The Turkish delight jumped out of his fingers, landing on Tennyson's tearstained tooled leather with a thud.

'Oh dear, I'm so sorry!' Dora Wildwood burst into the room. She dumped her satchel onto the chair and shut the door – again, with too much force, so the walls and shelves shook. He could see Miss Bunce as the door closed on the outside world, adjusting her glasses and frowning in mild dismay. Michael Dryden jumped up, brushing the icing sugar from his once-immaculate flannel trousers. He gave Dora a broad smile, and dropped the rose-coloured cube back in the box.

'Miss Wildwood,' he said, his voice tight with pain. 'What a very great pleasure it is to see you,' he said. 'You're early for work today. Usually you don't turn up until about ten thirty.' He leaned on the desk for support.

'That's unfair, it's always by ten,' said Dora, and she gave him a strange smile. 'But please listen to me. Mr Dryden, 'I must insist you must put that down. *Now*,' she said, in a tone of voice which froze the marrow in his bones. 'Thank you so much.' She shut the lid of the box, and said: 'We'll leave it there for the police.' She nodded. Mr Dryden slid the box away from him, his hand cold. Dora, still wearing her gloves, took it and placed it on the shelf. 'Turkish delight is really horrible, Mr Dryden. I promised to send you peppermint creams, didn't I?'

Michael Dryden stared at the box, then at her. 'You didn't send these to me?'

'No fear. Can't stand the stuff. It tastes like – oh, I don't know. Axle grease covered in icing sugar. Beastly.' She smiled down at him, the picture of health, her rosy red cheeks fresh with sharp autumn air, hair blown from the outside wind. 'Dear Mr Dryden, you look awfully pale, if you don't mind me saying. Are you quite well?'

He handed her the note silently. Dora read it.

'They got me wrong,' she said. 'They don't know me as well as they think they do. And they're lazy. Or inexperienced. This worked before as a means of killing someone, so they used it again.'

'They?' Mr Dryden swallowed. 'What's in the Turkish delight?'

'Arsenic,' she said. 'The icing sugar was laced with it. You didn't eat any, did you?'

'I had one, yesterday.' Dora clicked her tongue. 'Can't have had much in it, though I was rotten all night.' He clutched his stomach. 'I thought it was my old bilious complaint. My diet, so restrictive, you know. I smoke a pipe, to loosen the lungs and aid digestion, but still, I do suffer.'

But he slowly stood more upright. He had ingested poison – and he had survived.

Dora cleared her throat and lowered her voice. 'I say. Would you – come with me? To the Stacks? While we wait for the police? I'm sure it's nothing. But I realised something rather important last night, before Mr Fox telephoned about the Turkish delight . . .'

'What's that?'

'Someone apparently tried to murder Venetia Strallen, a few weeks before Sir Edwin was killed. A few days ago someone went to Venetia Strallen's flat, and caused havoc, destroying her letters from Sir Edwin, daubing messages on the walls, creating a mess. I think they were trying to distract us. On the way here I asked myself: distract us from what? We must be onto something if they think we need distracting. And it's so innocuous, I almost missed it.' She had crossed her thin arms and he realised her face was pale. He stood up, and opened the door. 'Come with me. We'll go there now.'

*   *   *

Through the library they walked, through the Issue Hall where Mikey Clark was flirting with a pretty young man with a cowlick and a three-piece suit on the front desk, and Zewditu Amani was stamping books whilst reading *Dusty Answer,* which was propped up on a bookstand next to her. Next to her, Ben Stark was writing in a ledger. Michael Dryden saw him raise his eyes as they passed, saw the look that crossed his face when he saw Dora, the faint tightening of his jaw as he watched her calmly walking through the space, eyes fixed on the door to the back stacks, somewhere else. He nodded. He liked Ben. He often felt sorry for him, knowing what lay ahead for him, though most would think him a lucky devil.

'Good morning, Miss Wildwood,' Ben said, but Dora did not hear him; her mind was elsewhere, and Ben Stark flinched, as though he had been slapped. Mr Dryden watched Stark's eyes follow her, and knew Stark saw what he, Dryden, saw in her too: that she was good, which was different from being nice, or jolly, or decorative.

Outside his office a telephone rang and Miss Bunce, his secretary, answered it, in a low voice.

'Who was that?' Dryden called, breaking the silence of the Issue Hall. It felt transgressive, raising his voice like that. He enjoyed it.

Miss Bunce stared at him in surprise. 'Detective Inspector Fox is on his way over,' she said.

'Miss Bunce,' Dora said, walking back to her desk. 'Sorry to duplicate questions Mr Fox might have asked you already – would you mind telling me, how was Sir Edwin when he returned from lunch, just before the murder took place?'

Miss Bunce stood up at her desk, brushing down her tweed skirt. She was about fifty, neatly dressed, her hair piled haphazardly on her head, a large, Charles Rennie Mackintosh-style pewter brooch at her throat. She put her head on one side, considering the question.

'Well, the inspector didn't ask me that, Miss Wildwood, and I didn't tell him, and I wondered if I should,' she said eventually, turning slightly pink. 'Because it's been worrying me ever so much, you know. Sir Edwin wasn't well.'

'Really?'

'No. He had a dreadful stomach ache, and I wanted to call Miss Strallen, but she was writing that day and he made me promise not to disturb her, not to worry her. But you see I *knew* he wasn't well. I think I should have stopped him going into the Stacks. I should have called a doctor . . . But he was tricky to help, you know. We'd had words the previous week . . . he'd told me I should be let go for a few . . . *errors* that had happened, and I – I didn't want to make him angry – so I watched him walk off and I knew . . .' She produced a small linen square and blew her nose.

'I knew he wasn't right and I didn't do anything. I've felt so dreadful about it all.'

'Oh Miss Bunce,' said Dora crisply, fishing about in her pockets and producing another handkerchief. 'You absolutely shouldn't.'

Miss Bunce took the handkerchief and sobbed even more loudly, all restraint gone. 'I as good as killed him!'

'That is simply not true. Now then, Miss Bunce,' Mr Dryden said kindly. 'You mustn't fret. You're not to be let go; I wouldn't dream of it. I need you far more than you need me!'

She turned her tearstained face to him. 'Oh Mr Dryden, thank you ever so much,' she said. 'You're ever so kind.'

He winked at her. 'It is nothing less than the truth. Who else would I entrust with the key to the secret cabinet containing Shakespeare's letters to the Dark Lady herself, hm? Hm?'

'That's very true,' Miss Bunce said, winking back. 'Shh now, Mr Dryden!'

'Well I never,' said Dora, pretending to find this hilarious. 'Another mystery solved!'

Miss Bunce gave a small, hysterical laugh, and sat down, pocketing both handkerchiefs and threading some paper into the typewriter. She smiled up at Mr Dryden, as if he were extraordinary, as if he'd just shown her the lost city of Atlantis.

Calmness, and a sense of order, suddenly prevailed. Michael Dryden told himself how lucky he was, how much he loved this place. He watched as Mikey leapt away from chatting up the young man, and out of his desk, smoothly inserting himself between an old lady and the door which she was unable to open, helping her down the steps onto the square: gently, without being instrusive. He watched the old lady, in a mustard-coloured jacket, standing outside in the square, waving her stick at him in gratitude. He saw Ben Stark, his tall frame bent over the New Titles shelf, searching for a particular title he thought might be enjoyed by a young poet whose stammer was so great he spent all day in the library, hiding out amongst the books. He saw Ben's face as he turned back, bearing the slim volume, talking lightly, nodding patiently as the young man struggled to thank him. These are good people, book people, Mr Dryden told himself. He felt certain he was walking towards something bad, he knew it, and he wanted to prolong this small, sweet feeling of calm, of pleasure in life, of musty books and gentle eccentricity, of acceptance of anyone and everyone, of love of learning. A world to which Sir Edwin Mountjoy had been utterly unsuited.

'Now, let us go,' he said to Dora, opening the door at the back of the Issue Hall, which led out into the back stacks. They climbed the stairs, standing at the edge of the metal grilles, looking up.

Dora stepped forwards, going up the stairs first. There were no lights on on the floor above them; they were walking into darkness. The metal shell clanged and echoed, their feet the only sound. It was quiet otherwise.

'Third aisle along. Here.'

She led the way, pulling the light switch. A small bulb crackled and flickered, casting shadows across the floor. They were in the middle aisle of the first floor of Science and Nature.

'What did you want to show me, Miss Wildwood? Another novel? Oh dear.'

'Not a novel. No, not this one.' Dora blinked. Steeling herself, she moved towards the middle row. She leaned forwards, her shaking fingers scanning the shelves.

'I think he had to come to this spot, the afternoon he died. And the murderer knew it. They knew he was looking for a particular book, one that the murderer had defaced. And they knew he mustn't find that book but they were too late. And this book *wasn't like the other books that had been mutilated*. Do you see?' Her throbbing voice grew louder into the silence of the library. Someone, far away on an upper floor, hissed:

'Please! Shhhhhh!'

It was such a comforting sound, she wanted to laugh.

'What was—' Mr Dryden cleared his throat. 'What was the book?'

Dora's slender fingers reached into the dark, grasping at nothing. Between Carey and Casey was an empty space. '*The Killing Jar,* by Cora Carson. It's a rather obscure book about killing methods of butterflies in the Swiss Alps and Swiss lepidoptery in general. It so happens for reasons that will become clear that my father has a copy, which I received from him this morning. The author lives in Switzerland, and sent it to him when it was published, a year or so after my mother's death. She thought it would be of interest to him, and to me. I couldn't read it—' She looked stricken. 'And my father didn't read it. He used it to prop the bathroom window open and look at the colour plates of the butterflies. My mother was a keen butterfly hunter – she was, in fact, in Switzerland on just such a trip when she died.' Mr Dryden's eyebrows raised themselves into inverted wings. 'Yes, it's a little strange, isn't it?' said Dora, trying to keep her voice steady. 'The title page was on the floor, after I found the body. The shell of it was found, you remember, on the shelf, but the middle missing and replaced with Esmé Johnson's latest novel. A few pages were screwed up and abandoned outside Venetia Strallen's apartment. I had a feeling I recognised the book. But first, not realising my father has our copy, I asked my friend Albert to find it and send it to me. It has taken him a while to get into the house. A large bramble has taken root over the autumn – my father and I having not been at home for several months – and it has grown rapidly inside Wildwood House. It began under the floorboards.' Dora paused. 'I should have really paid it more attention. But I didn't, which is most dispiriting.'

'Dear Miss Wildwood! But what has that to do with this?'

'I wonder,' said Dora, staring at the space on the shelves. 'Many things take root without us noticing. The trick is to learn when to pluck them out and when to accept and live with them. This book,' she said, taking her father's copy out of her satchel. 'The murderer had removed it and defaced it,' said Dora, 'presumably because they didn't want anyone to know what was in the book.'

'Why? What was in the book?'

But Dora shook her head. 'I will read it and let you know.' Her heart was thumping so loudly she was sure he must be able to hear it. 'But it's rather odd. I can't quite make it out. Do you understand?' And she gazed at the shelves again, the signs on each end. 'D is for Death,' she said, extremely quietly.

'No, my dear,' said Mr Dryden. 'I understand none of it.'

'Dora will,' said a voice behind them. Dora turned, with a start. There was Ben Stark, waiting at the edge of the row of shelves.

'Miss Wildwood,' he said. 'Forgive me. I didn't want to disturb you – only that—'

'Ah! Mr Stark!' said Mr Dryden, looking from one to the other. 'Miss Wildwood – dear girl, here is the very man, you see. The very man. A fine young man, Mr Stark.' He beamed at him, and rubbed his hands, apparently fully restored. 'A fine young man. Why don't you two strike up a friendship, what? Haha!'

'Thank you, sir,' said Ben Stark, who was rather red. 'Too – ah kind. I came to check you were both all right. Some of the bulbs have blown in this part of the library.' She saw his face in the dark, a pulse beating against his temple, his fine hands holding a torch. 'It's rather dark and since the mur— the unfortunate events, I wanted to make sure Miss Wildwood wasn't—'

'Mr Stark, perhaps you could tell us if you've read the book we were discussing, *The Killing Jar* by Cora Carson?' said Dora.

Her tone was polite, as always with Ben Stark. Since their first meeting, a strange constraint had fallen between them, as if both knew something about the other person, too much, perhaps. They had awkward professional conversations – 'Thank you Miss Wildwood, but that is a quarto book and as such should be shelved down there, with the other outsized titles.'

'Thank you, Mr Stark.'

'Mr Stark, could you advise me as to the location of *Time and Tide*?'

'In the basement, two stacks along from *Country Life*, one along from *Punch*.'

'Thank you, Mr Stark.'

She felt it was unfair of Mr Dryden to have noticed this constraint.

'No, Miss Wildwood, I regret to say I hadn't read it before it was removed.'

'Zewditu – Miss Amani and I have been searching through as many books as we can and the fact remains, it is still the only one of the mutilated books we've unearthed that isn't a murder mystery,' she managed to say with some composure.

Ben Stark said: 'Now I come to think of it, in the months before the murder it was either out on loan – I assumed that was the case, anyway – or simply not on the shelf.'

'I think Scotland Yard will want to know that.'

'I can tell them,' said Ben. 'If you think it's of use.'

Michael Dryden nodded. 'I'm sure they'll want to know.'

'Don't worry,' said Dora. 'I'll pass it on.'

'You will?' said Ben Stark.

'I am helping the police with the case as a sort of . . . job.'

'You are?' Ben Stark said. 'Is this a job? In addition to the job you barely perform here?' He folded his arms too, partly hugging himself and a smile crept across his thin face. 'Fascinating.'

'That's my other job, yes,' said Dora with dignity. 'But I'm not doing that at the moment. I act with the authority of Scotland Yard,' she added, wondering if this sounded as unlikely to him as it did to her.

'You are employed – by Scotland Yard?' Ben Stark said. He cleared his throat politely. 'To work on this – case? The most high-profile murder case in London?'

'Not *employed* exactly but – yes, that's right,' said Dora blithely. 'Detective Inspector Fox wants my help.'

They stared at each other across the Stacks, she with both hands on her hips, he with a hand propped under his chin, examining her with cool detachment, in that way she found so irritating.

'I see exactly,' Ben Stark said eventually. 'You're one of those . . . yes, one of those shelf-stacking girl detectives I'm always hearing about, trained up by Scotland Yard to trip over, insert oneself at the scene of the crime, then use one's position from within to hunt down dangerous criminals. I think I read about them. What's your next case, overthrowing Mussolini?' he continued, drily. 'Revolutionary gardener, disguising yourself as an expert in Chinese cherry trees in the Roman Botanical Gardens?'

'Cherry trees are Japanese,' said Dora, crisply. 'I should have thought you of all people would know that, given Mr Dryden has such faith in your knowledge of science and nature.'

'Books about,' he said. 'Not real life. Hopeless at real life, Dora. I wait to see with interest what else you can do. A magician-cum-publican undercover in Soho?'

'I will have you know I know a publican who moonlights as a magician,' said Dora. 'Ian Magellican. He runs the Blind Cow in Norton Muchelchamp. He can make three boiled eggs disappear, I've seen it. So – there, there you go. You must feel extremely foolish.'

'Ian Magelli – ' Ben Stark took a step backwards, and leaned against the Stacks, staring at her. 'Dora – I – honestly, Dora.'

Dora gave a small shout of laughter which echoed around them. 'Oh, you are impossible. You know how silly it sounds. I do too. Don't you trust me?'

'Actually,' he said, 'I do.'

'Well, I'm glad. It's really none of your business, I regret to say.' She frowned as she saw the light in his eyes. 'It isn't.'

'But Dora,' he said quietly. 'It *is* my business. I wish I could explain how – but I can't.'

'Why not?' she said, aware Mr Dryden was listening, but that this was suddenly a conversation between the two of them.

'Because it's not my story. Not really. Perhaps – one day.'

She was silent, not sure what he meant, unable to read him. He cleared his throat. 'I hate to sound mysterious,' he said. 'It's ridiculous. Miss Wildwood, let me know when you have read the book. And thank you.' And with that, he turned, and left.

*　　*　　*

'Is he always this opaque?' Dora said aloud, after the door had closed behind Ben Stark. Her cheeks, Dryden saw, were red with heat; she pressed her hands to them.

Mr Dryden sighed. 'I wouldn't know, my dear Miss Wildwood. He has a difficult time of it with his people. They want him to go into the family business, toe the line, marry the girl they want, all of that. He won't, and it is a very unhappy situation. Very unhappy. Poor chap.'

'But that's dreadful,' said Dora. 'Oh dear, parents. What's the family business? Butcher? Baker? Peppermint creams maker? One can always hope, Mr Dryden.'

'One of those,' said Michael Dryden vaguely. 'Yes, one of those. Awfully clever chap, he read botany and geology at Oxford you know, he was a cricket blue, not that he ever talks about it. He was stamped all over by Mountjoy – one of many, I'm sorry to say – ahh . . . forgive me.' The pain returned again, briefly and he clutched his side in agony. 'But it's much better now. So much better. Thank you, Miss Wildwood.'

'Well,' Dora said severely, 'that is why you should really have more notices up saying "no eating and drinking in the library". It encourages most unhealthy habits. My mother, when she went to Switzerland to trap the butterflies, that final trip, took some Kendal Mint Cake with her, and it was the only time I never knew her—' She stopped. 'Dear me. No.'

'What is it, Miss Wildwood?'

Dora held up one finger as if to silence him. 'A moment, please. Oh no. Oh . . . it can't be.'

'Come and have a cup of tea,' said Mr Dryden. The events of the past hour had left him exhausted but he felt lighter, calmer than he had at any point since Sir Edwin's death. He stared at this remarkable young woman, bobbing her way back down the stairs, humming lightly to herself. 'Miss Wildwood—'

'Call me Dora, dear Mr Dryden.'

'Dora, you're a marvel. I very much hope that your detective shelf-stacking portmanteau career is the success you deserve. I have no doubt it will be.'

'We must try,' she said with a faint laugh in her voice, but when she spoke again her tone chilled him to the bone. 'Though I don't think we quite yet see it, dear Mr Dryden, I'm sorry to say we are both in grave danger. And I am starting to understand how.'

17

Out out

'No one goes out dancing until after eleven, Dora,' they'd said.

It was 10.20 p.m. – yes, twenty minutes past ten *at night* – and very cold. As Dora sat in the reception area of the Three Corners, wiggling her toes, she wondered if it would be rude to simply go back up to her cosy little cubicle and fall, exhausted, between the sheets.

After several hours standing and stacking books in the darkest corners of the library, struggling back on the bus with all the other shop girls and waitresses and workers, then queuing for the bath, it was pleasant to sit for a while, utterly still, slumped onto a worn leather banquette, with nothing to do except think. It was warm, and quiet, the only sound Miss Pym turning the page of her book. The smell of beeswax polish, and perfume – an anonymous centralised scent fug provided by every resident and her particular scent – hung lightly in the air. The lights glowed orange-gold. Someone, somewhere upstairs, was playing a gramophone.

Dora let her mind wander, observing the day from a distance. She had started to see that she did not ever want to live without the library in her life. She loved going there every day. The old chestnut seller on the corner of the square, who grinned and said: 'Morning, Slacks!' every time she passed by in her wide-legged trousers. (Maria had made her two new pairs, in midnight-navy brushed cotton lined with black silk, and dark brown and mustard tweed. She had sewn her name on the inside – *By Maria*, in raspberry-pink copperplate embroidery.) The apple Zewditu cut up and shared with her every mid-morning, golden and sweet. Ben – it was always Ben they saddled with these tasks – that very afternoon, having to explain to Lord Someone on the telephone that Mikey could not personally leave the library now to get on a train and deliver a cache of books to Aberdeenshire, with many regrets. His outraged expression when he'd replaced the phone. 'These old-guard types, expecting us to skivvy for them,' he'd said, his face grim. 'Up the workers!'

Her mind drifted back to the dramatic start in Mr Dryden's office, the box of Turkish Delight, the episode in the Stacks with Ben, the mystery that surrounded him. *'I hate to sound mysterious,'* he had said.

'I don't know what I like best,' Mikey had confided in Dora, eating a slice of Zewditu's fruitcake as they'd sat in the square together in the weak sunshine, watching Ben as he strode past them, headed towards Lower Regent Street. His tall frame was straight, tense, his face a mask. 'Ben Stark when he's angry or Ben Stark when he's trying to hide how posh he really is.'

Dora watched Ben raise his hat to someone as he stepped off the kerb to let them past. Then he disappeared out of sight.

Things like that about him – his easy, kind manners, his outrage, his sense of fun – kept her watching him. She had realised, since starting to work at the library, that she was always looking for him. She did not understand why, and it bothered her. There were questions, like why all the defaced books were murder mysteries, bar *The Killing Jar*; or why someone wanted to harm Venetia Strallen; or why she had accepted Sir Edwin's proposal when he had so obviously been a difficult, cruel man; or the question of the second poisoned box of Turkish delight, that were starting to make sense. But Ben Stark did not make sense to her. Something about him was unreal, and yet – when she came and leaned on the counter and asked him for advice about whether a book on water sources should be shelved in Public Services or Rivers, she found she could talk to him about almost anything.

'He's a good person,' Zewditu had said to them both that lunchtime. 'Leave him alone, he has much to worry about.'

'They're all the same, that lot. The nobs. He tries to hide it, you'll see. He'll be first ordering us to lick his boots when he's in charge.' Mikey sniffed.

Zewditu shrugged. 'My country is overrun by fascists,' she said. 'It is not the ones you know whom you should fear. It is the ones who come promising a solution to problems you did not know you had, Mikey.'

'Trust no one, that's my motto,' Mikey had said, leaning over and swiping the last piece of her cake.

*   *   *

The revolving doors turned, blowing in leaves and fresh night air, and a girl who lived on the floor below Dora fell inside, laughing and brushing down her velvet evening coat, pulling her cloche hat from her head, shaking out her bright curls. 'Oh dear! I didn't see you there, dear!' she said, sliding a finger behind each heel and removing her shoes. 'So awfully cold tonight!' She hiccuped; her eyes met Dora's: bright, sparkling, cheeks flushed.

'Have you had fun?' Dora enquired, feeling rather like an old stork in a fable, looking disapprovingly down her long nose at the young and vibrant damselflies dancing on the pond before her.

'*Hic!* Excuse me. It was *such* fun!' The girl picked up her key from an unsmiling Miss Pym, who was reading *The Stars Look Down* and eating an apple. 'We had champagne – so much champagne! Whole place was awash with it! Do excuse – must go up – about to fall over! Night, Piss Mym! Night, you!'

Dora had been 'out' out once before, when she, Natty, Tommy and Laney had broken out of Babington House School for Girls. It had been a disappointing evening for Tommy and Laney, who wanted to experience glamorous London nightlife and both being from abroad (Rajasthan and New York respectively) believed that England and London were essentially one and the same place. They did not understand, really, that London was over two hundred miles away. And Natalie 'Natty' Lansdowne wanted to go because she always wanted to escape, no matter what she was doing.

These three had entrusted Dora with the finer details of the expedition and thus found themselves, to their total disgust, walking through the Valley Gardens in Harrogate to admire the dahlias, then sitting down to a slap-up tea at Bettys. Dora was very happy, knocking her T-bar shoes together, wolfing down plate after plate of scones. Natty gazed out of the window. But Laney and Tommy were appalled. They found scones disgusting, and said so.

'They taste sour, Dora.'

'They're supposed to. You put cream and jam on them. And look – do try a fondant fancy. They're absolutely delicious.'

'Have you ever eaten pomegranates?' said Tommy warmly. 'Pomegranate seeds are delicious. We have a tree at home in Jaipur overhanging a pond and when there's a full moon I swim there and pluck a whole fruit off, then break it apart and pick out the seeds and gaze up at the stars and the old rose-coloured stone of the palace. That's delicious, Dora darling. Whatever this is . . .' she brushed the crumbs of the scone between her slender brown fingers 'is not.'

'Perhaps you'd prefer their cinnamon toast – I say, could we have some more tea?'

Tommy had actually stood up. 'Excuse me,' she'd said to a passing waitress. 'Do you think you could find someone to drive me back to my school? I've been captured by a mad woman and forced to drink tea and eat this sour cake and it is most disgusting. I wanted to go dancing. I'd like to go back now.'

'Oh please no,' Natty had pleaded. 'We don't need to go back just yet.'

'We do,' Laney had added. 'Come to New York with me, Natty and Tommy, and I'll take you for a malted shake and dancing at the Apple Mingo Club. This has been very sad,' and the four of them had waited outside the large glass windows whilst the kindly staff at Bettys found someone to drive them back to school, and

Lady Natty stood with her arms folded, because she never wanted to go back to school, she wanted to escape her life altogether. But the other three laughed about it on the way home and that night in the dorm. Everything was still rather funny, then.

*   *   *

Dora remembered this evening as she waited for Susan and Minnie, in the famous Schiaparelli jumpsuit mended and brought over by Maria that afternoon. She liked Maria, and wanted to be friends with her, but didn't know how to ask – and didn't want to put Maria in a difficult position. It was not done to ask a busy young woman who has crossed town to bring you an exquisite outfit your godmother is lending you before she returns home to scrub a sink and change the sheets: 'I still haven't seen *The 39 Steps*. Do you want to see *The 39 Steps*? Also, I like you, do you like me?'

Instead, when Maria had arrived, she had held out her hand. 'How do you do? Thank you so much for bringing it over.'

Maria had taken off her scarf and hat, and shaken out her coat carefully, looking around her. 'What a cheerful place this is.'

'It's lovely here,' Dora had said. 'You know, I think you should move in one day. Ask Dreda to help set you up in business.'

'Oh!' Maria had said, flushing with embarrassment. 'Miss Dora, that wouldn't – I couldn't.'

'Yes,' said Dora. 'You could, you know.' She reached forwards, to take the box tied with ribbon. She set it down on the bench and pulled apart the bow. The two young women leaned over, and Maria gently parted the layers of tissue paper. They stared down.

'Oh my,' said Dora. 'That is beautiful.'

Maria had sighed. 'Isn't it? Isn't it just?' They had looked at each other and smiled, and Maria had said: 'I'm awfully sorry, I have to get back for Mrs Bundle, Miss Dora.'

'I hope I'll see you soon. Thank you for this. I think you should make your own jumpsuit, one day.'

'I'd like that,' said Maria. 'I thought of one in oak-green silk.'

'Beautiful. And claret. With a secret pocket. One always wants a pocket.'

'Oh, of course,' said Maria, and she smiled and nodded.

'You're awfully good to Lady Dreda, you know. Thank you.'

Maria shrugged. 'She's awfully good to me. We're all right, her and me and Mrs B. And – and you of course.'

And she'd smiled again and waved goodbye. 'See you soon.'

'*Dora*! We're here!' A voice recalled her to the present and Dora jumped, and smiled. As she saw them, pushing each other through the doors, Minnie with a jewelled headband in an ivy-green silk gown, Susan in a beautiful black crêpe cap-sleeved dress cut on the bias threaded through with gold, falling into the lobby together, their faces flushed, she felt excitement flood her body. Something that had been coiled tight unfurled inside her.

'Come on, Dora,' they cried. 'Neil and Spare Jim are waiting. Ever such a nice fella, Jim, you'll like him. He's taking us to dinner first.'

Dora turned round to gather her purse and velvet coat. She stood up, smiling. Minnie and Susan were silent. Then Susan gasped.

'Blimey. Why didn't you tell us you scrubbed up?'

'Oh my, Dora, you look just lovely,' said Minnie, her mouth open. 'That – it's like – something out of a film.' She stared at the silver jumpsuit, whose richly textured appearance, the sequins like rippling water, reminded Dora of the glittering shield bugs that sat on the yarrow in summer.

'Thank you awfully,' she said now. 'It's my godmother's, and she loves clothes, but she never goes out. I'm glad it's finally coming out with us.'

Minnie touched her hair. 'I always thought it was a shame you're so tall, but look at you, you're a queen.'

'Good Lord, please don't,' said Dora.

'And those diamond hairclips – well, they're beautiful.'

'They were my mother's.'

'That material,' said Susan, stroking it. 'It's divine. She's right, you look like a queen.' She put her arm through Dora's. 'You make nothing of yourself, normally, that's all.'

'And why should she?' put in Miss Pym, from her reception booth, clearly unable to contain herself any longer. She threw her apple core neatly into the waste-paper basket. 'Women must be judged on more than their looks if we are to achieve true emancipation.'

Susan and Minnie rolled their eyes. 'Couldn't agree more, Miss Pym,' said Dora, quite briskly. 'But it is fun. Susan, the cut of that dress is perfection. I saw Margaret Lockwood in something very similar in the *London Illustrated News* last week. And Minnie, you look divine, I love it when you wear that ivy green, it's delicious.'

'It's my favourite colour,' said Minnie, pleased. 'I'd have everything green if I could.'

Dora drew on her white velvet evening jacket. Without thinking, she said, 'Your mother liked it too, didn't she?' Minnie stared at her.

'How did you know that? She won a bolt of green silk at the factory raffle when I was five. Made me a new dress every year with it she did. When I grew out of them, I'd cut them up for hairbands and bags and suchlike.' She waggled the evening bag on her wrist, looking at Dora rather curiously.

'I thought it was something like that,' Dora said, hurrying past the moment.

'How did you—' Minnie said again.

'Oh, something you said once. Shall we go?'

Miss Pym said: 'Have a lovely evening, girls. Don't forget the key when you're back.'

'She won't,' said Susan, nodding her head at Dora. 'She's got eyes in the back of her head, that one.'

'Good night, Miss Pym,' said Dora, and they pushed themselves through the revolving door slightly giggling and fell onto the pavement, where a gentleman in white tie and tails was waiting. 'How do you do,' Dora said to him.

'How do you do, Miss Wildwood,' he said politely. 'I'm Jim Bluman, this is my brother Neil – I say, it's damned jolly to have you along with us tonight – Terence is going to meet us at Quaglino's. He's been detained at the office—'

'Dora,' said a loud voice, and a figure appeared from the shadows around the corner from the building. 'Dora – I say.' As he came towards her the light from the gas lamp above fell across his thin face, and to Dora's horror she saw it was Charles Silk-Butters, in a cape, of all things. He reached out for her hand – she moved away, behind the two girls.

'I say,' said Jim easily. 'Does she know you?'

'Now look here, you mind your own business,' said Charles, and with a vicious side-kick he levelled Jim, who lay sprawling on the ground.

'Here,' said Neil, who was the mirror image of Spare Jim, only several inches taller. 'That's not on. That's not on at all.' He took off his jacket, but Charles pushed him from behind, so hard that Neil bounced against the side wall of the Three Corners, hit his head, and sank to the ground. Minnie screamed.

'Neil!' said Susan, dropping to his side. She stroked his cheek, almost tenderly. 'Oh dear God. Neil, can you see me?'

'Not sure,' said Neil. 'Give me a kiss, Sue old girl.'

'Leave off. Oh, go on then. Oh no. Jim, wake up, do, there's a dear. Jim! Neil! Oh *Lord*.' She stood up, and said furiously to Charles Silk-Butters. 'Cor, you are the bleeding *end*. We don't have enough men tonight as it is. We never do, and now you've biffed one of them in the head. I could murder you.'

'Ow,' groaned Jim, curling up into a ball.

'What do you want?' said Dora, turning to Charles.

'For you to come with me, Dora,' he said, his voice too loud. 'For you to stop this nonsense. The forces around London are dreadful, I had to buy a new collar and studs yesterday as well as all my meals and I tell you, I can't keep it up.' Minnie gave a snort. 'I'm starting to think I'm wasting my time.'

'You're *starting* to think that.' Dora put her hands on her hips.

She saw the fine black hairs on the back of his thin white hands. His nose, with the pink, flaring nostrils. His eyes, sunken into the skull. His signet ring, his tattered old silk cape, his cigarette case, gleaming gold in his hand – these trappings of wealth and privilege, like the orb and sceptre, and yet he looked like a penny novelette villain.

She said wearily, 'Charles, I've told you already, I'm not coming back. I don't know why you've stayed to hear this again.'

Charles's eyes narrowed. 'I've stayed because someone was kind enough to advise me to stay. To arrange accommodation for me.'

'Who on *earth* would do that?'

He gave a thin, pleased little laugh. 'Shan't say. I can stay there as long as I want. Get in the car, Dora. It's time to go home.' He reached out for her.

'You leave her alone,' said Susan. She stepped forwards, and pushed him away. Charles stopped, absolutely astonished. His head moved backwards, his chin merging with his neck, and he flicked her on the forehead. 'That all you got?' Susan said, laughing. He kicked out at her, his face red with rage. 'Oi, you stop that now,' she shouted. 'Minnie, get him! Not like that, you bleeding idiot! Like this!' Dora saw Susan pull back her fist, drive it forwards with such force that as it landed on his cheek. Charles staggered back, like a character in a cartoon. Minnie hit him, hard, around the head with her handbag. On the ground, the two Bluman boys were still struggling to get up.

Charles wheeled around, like a bowlegged sailor, eventually taking shelter in the shadow of the building. 'I'll come back tomorrow, and the day after, and the day after that,' he said calmly, gingerly wiping his face.

'Would you mind moving along, sir, otherwise I shall be obliged to call the police,' said a clear voice, and Dora heard a cracking sound, and looked towards the revolving door of the Three Corners to find Miss Pym standing there, holding a large brown whip in her hand, the tip of which she curled slowly across the floor.

'Good God,' Charles said feverishly. 'Who's this damned virago?'

In answer, Miss Pym raised the whip and very gracefully flicked her arm out. Like a reel of thread the tip wound itself around Charles Silk-Butters' midriff, curling round until he was encased like a cocoon. Miss Pym calmly pulled him towards her. He kicked out furiously, and she yanked him so that he staggered, almost pulling her to the ground.

'I am Miss Pym, and your language, let me tell you, is not becoming of a gentleman. I have a policeman on his way, should you care to remain. I'm sure he'd gladly take the details of a man caught loitering outside a ladies' boarding house with malicious intent.' She nodded at him, her expression outwardly neutral, but Dora knew, very simply, she was made of rage. 'You ask who I am, what I'm playing at. Well, I spent a year living with the circus where I picked up a number of useful tricks. But you may care to know I have also been in prison numerous times. I know what they do to nice boys like you. I tell you again, be on your way, sir.'

Charles opened his mouth, then closed it. Miss Pym unravelled the whip, and it fell away from him, like a ribbon sliding off a present. Charles jumped, then scuttled sideways, like a black crab. 'I say—' he called, but did not say more.

Dora watched him vanish into the night, and looked down. Where Charles had grabbed at her outfit the sequins were crushed, some torn clean off.

'Miss Wildwood, I am on the reception desk until midnight should Mr Silk-Butters appear again,' said Miss Pym. She swept a speck of dust off her jacket and looked up at them with a grim smile, twisting the whip around and around until it was neatly coiled again. 'Ladies, please be careful, and oh – go off then, enjoy yourselves.' She turned, and went inside.

'What a woman,' Spare Jim, Susan's escort, had slowly climbed to his feet again and was rubbing his jaw. He was staring at Miss Pym's retreating form. 'What. A woman.'

'Who,' said Minnie, panting, 'was that?' She adjusted the pleated folds of the bow at the front of her dress.

'He was my fiancé,' said Dora, brushing ineffectually at the crushed sequins on her jumpsuit. Someone had spent hours sewing them on, their efforts ruined, and this somehow made her more furious than anything. '*Was* being the operative word, you understand.'

'Lovely way he has with him, eh?' Susan patted her arm.

'He's a mummy's boy who should have been told to sharpen up his ideas. They're never told they're wrong, you know. They're so cruel to the daughters, not the sons. Tell the girls they need changing, tell them they'll be out of house and home and that they're too loud too clever too tall too – much. Not the boys.' Dora said. Her anger seemed to be growing inside her, unfurling its wings.

'He's utterly evil, poor darling Dora,' said Minnie, tucking her arm through Dora's.

'He's not evil. He's very, very stupid. He believes radiowaves create magnetic waves that are controlling us all,' Dora said. 'He made me bury my wireless in the churchyard after we were engaged.' She hauled Neil to his feet and he dusted himself off. 'Susan Fox, where did you learn to hit someone like that?'

'My brother the policeman,' said Susan. 'Took me aside when I was thirteen and showed me how to land a good one. Got me out of trouble a few times. There isn't a man I can't floor. Watch out, Neil, darling,' she said.

'I say,' said Neil happily, rubbing his chin and still looking rather dazed.

'I had a fella who used to hit me, and I ran away,' said Minnie unexpectedly. 'Miss Pym saved my life, offering me this place here. Sent him off with a flea in his ear the one time he turned up, too.'

'She's a real lady,' said Dora.

'She is. Are you all right, Dora?' said Minnie.

'Yes,' said Dora. 'He is my biggest mistake. But one learns, you know.' She turned around. 'Oh dear, oh no! Poor Neil's down again.' She sank to the floor next to Neil, who was rubbing his backside and shoulder and moaning.

'Marvellous indeed,' said Neil, somewhat shakily clambering to his feet with the help of his brother. 'Awfully sorry I was *hors de combat* there, Minnie darling—'

'No idea what that means,' said Minnie companionably, 'but let's get in the car and go dancing. As Dora says, everything's fine now.'

Dora nodded, her mind whirring. Charles knew where she was now. Someone was paying for him to stay on. The same someone who wanted her out of the way.

18

One must keep dancing

Even in a slightly unconventional household like Dora's with a chaotic father and a vague mother, things were done properly; the blood memory of correct behaviour was not so easy to shake off. One could not go to church without gloves. One did not play with boys after the age of six. One must write bread-and-butter letters, and get used to pins being stuck into one for party dresses whilst boys went to prep and boarding school and played sports and stayed away from the estates they would one day manage.

One grew up noticing what went on in the village, the fact that the man sent to prison for poaching was only trying to feed his family because there was no work. Or the part of the river where the otters built their dens, where the kingfishers were. One remembered Mrs Lah Lah's sciatica and did not ask for breakfast in bed or order ridiculously complicated meals. One did not say 'notepaper' or 'toilet' or 'serviette'. And it was fine, nay welcomed, to visit an ailing tenant, but it was not fine to sit on tombstones with the local farmer's son making up spells and comparing sizes of different body parts (which is what Dora, aged ten, had once been caught doing with Albert).

Through the course of that glittering, long evening that unfurled like a banner and fluttered in Dora's mind for years afterwards, it slowly dawned on her that to be truly relaxed and enjoy oneself, *really* truly, was quite different from what people meant by 'having fun'. It turned out that Spare Jim and Neil and then, when they were joined by the missing brother, Terence, were hilarious: self-deprecating, and jolly, that stories about what happened at synagogue or Mrs Bluman's gefilte fish recipe that went wrong were funny even if you didn't know the places or people involved, that Minnie had a way of telling a joke with her face and eyes that made Dora howl with laughter, and as for Susan, Dora understood more clearly than ever how much she – and perhaps, her brother, too – wanted to take control to remove the burden of it from others.

In short: she discovered she liked laughing from the tops of buses, and delicious, secretive London, its grey forbidding buildings with hidden entrances into basements where men and women glittered like fiery comets in the night; at Quaglino's, that she liked the huge curving staircase, the cavernous room in pale pastels, the clink of heavy crystal glasses, the taste of champagne, snails, proper French frites, quail eggs, and chicken Kiev, and more champagne, and the heady, beautiful, woozy scent of lilies in vases and women's perfume, and the sight of other woman in dresses sewn over with stars, and sequins, and carefully curled glossy hair, and silk like flowing water, and the attendants in the cloakroom who held out a towel to you and the silver bathroom fittings, the patterned carpet, the gaiety and laughter, how all of it, *all of it*, was fun, and bright, and shining, and so loud you could not hear the sound of Charles's feet on the creaking stairs, the clink of the same old crockery handed down through the Wildwoods, the same old carols sung at Advent, the constant drumming patter of autumn rain.

Spare Jim and Neil were not just decent types, politely addressing the waiter and the doorman. They were also practical, they knew the right buses, they were interested in world affairs – 'we blooming well have to be,' Jim said to Dora. 'We're from a long line of pessimists, you see, the ones who left in time,' and only long afterwards, when two of the brothers were dead, did Dora understand what he had meant. Susan and Minnie knew far more about labour laws, the fight for workers' rights, the struggle for universal suffrage, than she'd ever learned at her exclusive ladies' seminary. Her mind, and her eyes, were opening slowly, the pinpricks that she'd noticed since arriving in London: the poverty, the cracks through which respectable people fell, the struggle to even exist when you were poor and in a vast city, trying to get by.

And then there was music – such lovely music. First, while they ate their meal, a gang called the Rhythm Sisters, who sang 'If I were the only Girl in the World', 'Isn't it Romantic?', 'My Heart Stood Still' and 'You're the Top'. And then Ambrose and his Orchestra, a swing band who played 'Lover', 'Begin the Beguine', and Dora's favourite, 'Little Girl Blue'. She had heard 'Little Girl Blue' the night after Charles had proposed to her, their first official engagement as affianced couple, at a coming-out dance for Bryony Fulcher, her schoolfriend who lived in Clampett Bottom. Certainly no one else had paid any attention as the band played, but she had, Charles's mother's engagement ring – a giant, ugly garnet – weighing down her slender hand, looking all wrong, all, all wrong there.

Sit there and count your little fingers
Unlucky Little Girl Blue

She watched as Ambrose and his Orchestra played it now, the leader a slightly awkward, tall Englishman with a drooping face, shining eyes, body attuned to the rhythm, and the singer, a marvellous girl in a black silk teagown, puffed sleeves, sparkling diamonds in her ears, whose voice caressed the sad, sad words, as if it were just her there in that restaurant, singing to herself. Dora listened, eyes shining, hands clasped under her chin.

'Isn't it wonderful?' she was saying, as Susan and Minnie clasped her hands, moving her away from the band.

'As the song goes,' said Susan, patting her hand. ''S wonderful. But we're off to the best place in London. Quag's is super but Dora . . . it's nothing compared to the Café de Paris. Nothing bad ever happens at the Café de Paris: I say, do look lively. It's one a.m. Everyone should be there by now.'

*　　*　　*

Everyone who was anyone went to the Café de Paris. It was the place to be seen, a place for young and old, but mainly young. You had to be beautifully dressed, to have money to spend on champagne, but it was not like the restaurant at the Berkeley Hotel or the ballroom at the Dorchester or the Travellers Club, where one had to be a member of the right set, preferably the daughter or son of a lord.

One could hear the drumming beat as they walked along Piccadilly: something primal, it thudded in your chest, and Dora thought again of her first day in London, how fast she had run along Piccadilly, and tightened her grip on Spare Jim's arm. How far from home she had come, and how very fortunate she was to be here.

'The Notables are on tonight, and they're awfully good. Denis Mainwaring,' said Neil, as they entered the lobby. He tightened his white tie, and brushed his shoulders of the last vestiges of his encounter with Charles Silk-Butters. 'Jolly good trumpeter. Been to New York, he has. Played on Broadway. Hot damn, mama! Oh, two please, yes, thanks awfully,' he said, handing his cape and top hat to the cloakroom attendant, and carefully lifting Dora's white velvet jacket from her shoulders. 'Quite a crowd in tonight, as a result.' He lowered his voice. 'And, Miss Wildwood, they *say* Bertie will be in later.'

'No,' said Minnie. 'And what about *her*? Mrs S?'

'All of them, the whole shower.'

'Who are you talking about?' demanded Dora, as they descended the stairs.

'The Prince of Wales, and Mrs Simpson,' said Susan, looking around to make sure they weren't being overheard. 'What a mess it all is. Here Neil, give me a hand, would you?'

'Oh! Susan! I think it's awfully romantic,' said Minnie. 'He's so handsome.'

'It's certainly not that,' said Susan, sounding rather like Miss Pym. She shook out her skirt, and briskly checked the seams of her stockings. 'It will not end well – my brother spoke to another officer last week who told him some extremely alarming information. About the pair of them.'

'Oh, your brother,' said Dora, reckless with champagne. 'What does he know?'

Susan rolled her eyes. 'Nothing, I expect, and he wouldn't tell me this himself, I got it out of Mum. He's a Nazi, Minnie, your handsome Prince.'

'No he's not,' said Minnie, laughing.

She nodded. 'He jolly well is. He supports Hitler. Thinks he's done Germany no end of good.'

Minnie pushed her friend's arm. 'Well really, hasn't he, though?'

Susan stared at Minnie, as if seeing her for the first time. 'I don't think you know what you're talking about,' she said soberly, and she clutched Neil's arm more tightly. 'It's – oh!'

They had reached the bottom of the stairs. The doors flung open, and they were inside.

The scent of perfume and cigarettes was stronger than ever, the atmosphere different to Quaglino's: more uninhibited, looser, the sense of being in on something. The underground location meant every sound was amplified, playing in your heart and lungs, shaking you up, bringing you in.

It was a huge, dark room, with a wide staircase down to a polished wooden dance floor, barely visible beneath a mass of heaving bodies. Lining the walls were booths and tables, and men and women standing, sitting, laughing. One woman, in a multicoloured sequinned dress, spread her arms wide, showing a glittering waterfall of rainbow colours, like a butterfly. Her group cheered. The atmosphere was like nothing else – a perfect, hot, intense, exciting cocoon, you felt it as you walked in, the music, the heat and heavy scent of perfume and cigarettes undercut by sweat assailing your senses. Everyone was beautiful, everything was stylish, every line in the place from the curve of the staircase to the shape of the bar was elegant.

Dora narrowed her eyes, then she felt Susan's hand slip into hers.

'It's something, isn't it?'

Dora nodded. She could feel the champagne lighting up her body, a cool breeze ruffling her hair, her arms. She was smiling, and knew, in that moment, that she was beautiful. She felt a huge sadness, a longing for something or someone, that she could not quite name.

No one else would understand it, but this was the moment she had waited for. The nights dreaming, the days dreading, the loneliness, the sense of life flying past, stills on a movie reel.

'Oh please, let's dance, shall we?'

'Champagne!' Terence called. 'I'll get this booth, girls, you go orf and enjoy yourselves.'

They were playing 'The Continental'. 'Miss Wildwood, would you care to dance?' said Spare Jim. Dora nodded, eyes sparkling, and they danced into the throng.

'I say, you're a jolly decent dancer, Miss Wildwood.'

'Oh do call me Dora, won't you? Thank you, so are you.'

'I've got two . . . Dora. Do forgive.'

The music swelled, and the crowd roared.

'Two what? I beg your pardon?'

'Left feet,' Spare Jim bellowed at her, laughing, and holding her closer in his arms. 'Left –' he waggled one foot – 'feet. I say Dora, you are tremendous fun.'

'Tremendous – what? Oh!' she said, laughing, as the music subsided again and her voice echoed in the sudden quiet. She looked over his shoulder. 'My goodness. That's them. Look.'

A little group stood at the apex of the grand staircase: an extremely tall man with a long, long face, moving some people out of the way then, as if they were in a circus, the reveal of a short man in immaculate tails, a woman in black next to him.

She was sinewy, like a monkey, her jaw large, her eyes dark and unreadable. He was fair, and handsome, but his eyes were huge and vacant and he looked to Dora like a boy in his Sunday best, not a grown man. There were three others, the tall man, a woman in shining slate sequins and another woman in fuschia pink, who kept whispering in the Prince of Wales's ear, and laughing loudly. They were all laughing at something, and then Mrs Simpson reached out and touched the Prince of Wales's arm, just a split second, and he turned and gazed at her, fully mesmerised.

Dora could not quite believe she was seeing it. And how disappointing they were – he so small, so insubstantial, she so oddly repellent, her skin shining, her mouth clamped tightly shut, no mystique about her at all.

Dora carried on dancing, more frantically than before, the music swelling once again. Perspiration slid down her body, but she did not care – no one else seemed to. She could not believe it of herself, that she was there – it was the centre of the world, and she was there – she who two weeks ago had been calling out for chickens with a tin can and shaking grain over a muddy yard . . . She was free, in charge of her destiny, she was Rosalind, Jane Eyre, Dorothea Brooke, Lucy Honeychurch, Irene Forsyte. She spun around, and around, exhilaration taking hold of her, and then the music stopped, and she and Spare Jim applauded wildly, and then she felt a hand on her arm, clutching at her, and she turned, abruptly.

'Dora! Darling! I thought it must be you!' a voice said. A very slim, dark-haired girl with blue eyes was clasping her hands, kissing her, smiling. 'My goodness, how absolutely topping. You look beautiful, how lucky to be a tall girl! We thought you'd died of old age in the countryside or something.'

Another girl patted her shoulder. 'It's Giraffe!' she said, in far less friendly tones. 'Look at you. Trousers! Oh and that funny coat you've got on!'

'Natty! Laura. My goodness,' Dora said, gripping their hands and embracing each of them in turn. 'But I wrote to you! I thought you must be out of town.'

Lady Natalie and Lady Laura Lansdowne were the daughters of the earl her father had been so keen to hob-nob with; Natty had been her special friend, the one who nursed her through illness and stroked her hair when she missed her mother. She was clever, and kind, and interesting, and knew everything about the natural world, from woodlice to bumblebees, and had at one time wanted to be a doctor when she left school. And, as with the trip to Bettys, leaving school, leaving her own life was what she most desperately wanted to do, though why she was so desperate about it Dora was never quite sure; even she could not fathom it; she only knew her friend was unhappy. Dora had written to her after she'd come to London, but had no reply. And here she was, in front of her. The Café de Paris was magic indeed.

'Sit here,' commanded Natalie, ushering Dora into her booth. 'You don't mind, do you?' she said, smiling politely at Spare Jim, who understood he was not needed for the moment, gave a polite bow, and ambled off. 'Tell me everything.'

'Yes, everything.' Laura spread her skirt carefully about her.

'Go away, Laura,' said Lady Natalie, sharply, elbowing her sister off the edge of the booth seat. 'I want to talk to Dora alone.' Laura stood up and stalked off, furious. 'Where's Laney?'

'She's in New York.'

'Oh, poor thing.' Natty scrabbled for her cigarette holder, her skinny fingers clattering on the table, on the ashtray. 'Sorry. I'm dreadfully clumsy. Have you heard from Tommy?'

'Yes, last month. She's getting married next year. I do so awfully want to go.'

'Married? Oh, but me too!' said Natalie, holding up her hand. 'There, you can come to my wedding instead and you won't have to go to mouldy old India . . .'

'Oh darling! What wonderful news,' said Dora, wondering why Natalie's hand was shaking, why she was so thin, her eyes gaunt, darting round the room. 'Tell me all about it!'

'Of course, but first you'll have to tell me where you've been.'

'Me?'

'Yes, Dora. You utterly vanished, all the girls wondered what had happened to you.' She coughed, watching the band. The music was low. 'Because you were *Dora*. Always thought you'd – I don't know, darling – *do* something, start a movement, start a fire, start a baby before everyone else.' She took a long, long drag on her cigarette, jittery fingers pointing to Dora.

'I had to come home for Father. I was engaged, briefly – but that's all off.'

'Really?'

'Yes. Old family friend. I – couldn't go through with it. So I rather left him in the lurch and came to London.'

Lady Natalie Lansdowne stared at her. She licked her lips and said: 'I don't want to be married either. Oh darling, it's awful, isn't it?'

Dora remembered the nights Natty had stroked her hair, some of the things she'd said when she thought Dora was asleep. 'Well,' she said, 'I don't mind men, if they're presentable and well behaved and like books. Just not that man.'

'I can't stand the idea of any of it. I tried to top myself over the summer, darling.' Natty stubbed her cigarette out into the ash-tray, grinding it away.

Dora felt sick. She looked at Natty, whose bulging eyes were bloodshot in the glittering blue-silver lights of the dance floor. 'I didn't realise things had been so bloody. How rotten. What can I do?' she said.

'You can't do anything, darling, it's happened. Just talk to me. I shake less when I'm busy. I can't seem to help it, these pills they have me on. It doesn't matter, now Diana's gone I don't very much care what happens.'

Diana. Dora screwed up her eyes, trying to remember. 'Diana? Wasn't she your best friend, Natty darling?' Natalie nodded. 'What happened to her?'

Lady Natalie pressed her fingers to her mouth. She shook her head, as if trying to prevent the words, the sounds she wanted to make, from escaping. They stared at each other.

Very gently, Dora put her hand on her arm. She was terrified the music would swell again, that she wouldn't hear what Natty said. 'Natty – what happened?'

'Natty! Darling!' Someone from the Lansdownes' group, a bovine young man whose tails were slightly too large for him, lunged between the two of them, a Nebuchadnezzar of champagne in his pink fist. 'Up to mischief with some other filly, eh? Who's this?'

'Shut up, Andrew, you ass,' said Natalie, and she pushed him away with a sharp shove so that he staggered and retreated, eventually swallowed up by the carousel of the dance floor.

Dora swallowed, and turned back to her. 'Natty darling, you don't seem well. What's happened? Who – why are you—'

Natalie gave an enormous grin. 'Darling Dora, let's not talk about it any more. I can't, they're watching, that ghastly oaf Pettifogger is one of Daddy's spies and he'll be back in a minute. And I won't, because even though I don't care, they're dangerous, and I don't want you getting into trouble. So tell me, who was your fiancé? And however did you manage to run away?'

As best she could, over the incongruous strains of 'Yes! We Have No Bananas' Dora told Natalie what had happened with Charles, how she had felt it was time to leave Wildwood House at break of day, how she was working at the library. She left out the part about finding a dead body. She could see Susan and Minnie and the men, waving at her from the other side of the room, Susan raising her eyebrows. *You all right?* She waved back. *I'm fine.*

Laura Lansdowne danced up to the booth, and stood looking over them. 'Your fiancé is looking for you, Lady Nats darling.'

'Stop calling me Lady Nats,' said Natalie dully.

'They called her that in the funny farm they sent her to in the autumn,' said Laura. She turned back to Dora, hooded eyes, watching for her reaction. 'I miss school awfully, don't you? I know *Lady Nats* does. Do you remember lights out night? When Natty was found in the san with Audrey Manners and—'

'That's enough, Lolly,' said Natty repressively. 'Shut up. Audrey was showing me her new torch. That was all.' She gave a small, artificial laugh. 'Just do shut up.'

'Natty darling,' said Dora, as Laura danced away again. 'I want to hear about your fiancé. Who is he? Tell me all about it.'

'Well, I was a deb last year, you know,' Natty said, in a falsely bright and amusing tone. 'Oh, look, they're playing again. I do love this song. There's Lady Orla Craigavon, you know, so beautiful, there's her brother Donal . . .' She waved at them, slightly too enthusiastically, as Dora watched curiously. 'Now, where's Rutherford gorn? He's my fiancé, darling, you must meet him, Dora. *You'd* like him.' Her voice was too high; it hovered above the soft music.

'Did you enjoy it?' Dora said. 'Being a deb?'

Natty stopped scanning the room. In a normal voice, she said, 'Actually, bits of it were rather nice. And the sense that one is doing what one's people want, you know—'

'I should think the dresses and everything like that makes it rather fun doesn't it?'

Natty drank some more champagne. She said carefully: 'I was with Diana, so it was wonderful, seeing her every day. We simply loved being together, you know. But the rest of it wasn't fun. It's the same people over and over, the same conversations, same girls, same boys, same chicken mousse to eat and ices and champagne – you dress up to be presented to the Queen and you sit in a car for three hours on the Mall, waiting for them to let you into the Palace, and the photographers swarm all over the car and you have to sit there and smile. And people wait till the queue forms and then they stroll out to the line of cars and push each other aside to gawp at you through the window, peering in at you and staring, and you can't go anywhere. Just have to sit there and wait for the queue to move forwards.' She paused, as a song ended, and there was applause, and then when she spoke again the words tumbled out, faster and faster. 'It's like a nightmare, actually. "She looks like a fish." I kept hearing them saying that about the girl in the car in front, whoever she was. Standing there, darling, staring right in at her. "Look at her, fish eyes and that funny pout." Poor thing. As if she couldn't hear, as if she was a statue just to be looked at, not a girl with feelings. Of course the boys just walk in. Because no one needs to examine the boys.' She gave a bitter, high laugh. The band had not started playing again yet, and several couples turned around. 'Sometimes I just wanted a glass of milk, Dora, that's all – the same waltzes and these earnest, earnest boys who are so careful not to tread on your toes and often you want to scream – do you remember running up to Tor Point and scream-ing into the wind so loudly we were hoarse for days afterwards?'

'I do,' said Dora. 'I wish I could do it now.'

'Me too,' said Lady Natalie. She blinked, her heavy black lashes fluttering on her cheeks. 'I hate this. I don't want any of it. I want a job, and a life of my own. But that's in the past now! It's my job to marry so Daddy doesn't have to worry about me. And after this summer . . . there was no point in any of it.'

'What happened this summer, Natalie darling?'

She took a deep juddering breath. 'I tried running away, but they found me, you see. I went to a dance without Mummy, with a friend's mother, and didn't go home, and I hid out in Embank-ment Gardens and someone gave me half a crown for dancing for them, and someone else gave me a top hat and I went to a party –' she rubbed her eyes – 'I can't really remember. I'm not sure what I thought I'd do . . . I hadn't planned it out. You have to plan it out, don't you, darling?'

'You do.'

'They found me on Embankment and I was swinging from a lamppost—' she stopped, looking at Dora. 'People usually laugh here. They think it's funny. Or that I'm dreadfully silly.'

'I don't think it's funny, or that you're silly,' said Dora. 'What happened next?'

'I slipped and fell into the river and the policeman, oh he was so cross. He was such a dour man. Had a beard, can you imagine, darling? He kept saying "Now see here, Miss"' as if that'd make me fly up out of the river back to him. But I didn't care. I remember thinking well, Diana's dead . . . I might as well drown . . . they dragged me out somewhere by Blackfriars and I was ill. I got into enormous trouble and they sent me to a san, a sort of dreadful place in Surrey with a matron who kept stripping me naked and giving me cold showers.' She looked up at Dora with a trace of her former impishness. 'One might have quite enjoyed it, but not like that. And they've got me on these pills . . . ever since then I haven't been quite right, darling, I can't stop shaking you see. And it's the funniest thing, I can't ever seem to get warm.' She took another drink, her mouth baring in a rictus Dora found distressing.

'Natty darling. How horrible. Why, though? Why did you run away?'

'Diana was gone. And I didn't want to live any more.' She pulled at the silken collar of her dress. 'There.'

'Gone where?'

Natalie pulled her closer. Dora could smell her stale breath, her heavy perfume. 'She died,' Natalie said, very quietly. 'She was killed. But I'm not allowed to talk about it. I'm not allowed to tell anyone.'

Dora leaned back, gently gripping her friend's thin upper arms. 'She was – she what?' She wondered if she'd misheard.

'She was murdered, darling.' Dora's eyes widened. Natty pressed her hands onto her friend's shaking fingers. 'You think I'm making it up. Someone – anyway, someone – shot her, and she died.' She leaned forwards. 'We loved each other,' she said, her voice hoarse, and hot in Dora's ear. 'We were going to go off and live together, Dorset somewhere. I was waiting for her . . . I saw it, darling. They killed her. She fell to the ground. *Whoomp. . . .*' Natty stopped, and drained another glass of champagne. 'They were after her. Our families . . . It's the only reason. She was going to work and I was going to find a job – she loved books, you see.'

'Books?' Dora swallowed.

'Yes, she was something in an office and she loved books.' Natty was too drunk now to form the words properly. 'She had to deal with authors. Oh, some of them were terribly difficult! Some of the things she'd tell me. But she adored it, Dora, she really did.'

'What kind of an office?' Dora said. 'She didn't work in a library, did she?'

'No, darling, nothing so boring as a library. Hah! That's what I say to Rutherford!' She moved her mouth slowly, as if surprising herself. 'He gets awfully cross with me when I do . . . No, it was Bedford Square, where all the publishers are. *You* know. But I'm telling you one moment she – she was alive, then she was dead . . .'

What have they done to her? Dora found herself thinking. What pills is she on, how is she being kept in this state?

'I had to come out of there, I had to,' Natty said, pulling threads of silken blue from the fringe in her evening dress. 'They locked you in your room at night . . . they cut your fingernails so short so you didn't scratch anything, so short the stubs bleed and you can't use your hands for anything—' Her voice broke. 'For anything at all.'

The noise from the frenzied band was swelling. Natty looked up and about, and slowly worked a bright smile across her face, like someone turning a crank. 'He's coming this way. He's seen you.'

'Who?'

'Rutherford. My fiancé. And he's not so bad even though I can't tell him any of it—' She leaned forwards. 'We both know what we have to do . . . Here he is! Ben darling, this is my old schoolfriend, Dora Wildwood. Dora, this is Ben. Earl of Rutherford, you know. The Westmorland Rutherfords.'

Dora looked up and saw Ben Stark in front of her, his hand outstretched. She was so astonished she took it, without speaking. 'Hello, Dora,' he said.

He was not wearing glasses, and a woollen waistcoat, and a badly fitting tweed jacket with patches on it. He was in dazzling white tie and sleek black tails that sat perfectly on his tall, slim frame. His hair, which was usually sticking up on end or falling in his face, was combed back. His black shoes shone so brightly they glinted in the darkness.

He held her hand for a moment longer, and she felt the slight pressure of his fingers on hers. 'You look lovely,' he said quietly.

'Ben,' Dora said, recovering herself. 'What – hello.'

Lady Natalie did not notice this awkwardness. She slipped her arm through her friend's. 'Ben's bookish, like you. He's got a job in a terribly dull library, but he'll give it up when we take on the estate. Fearfully exciting, isn't it?' Her small, skeletal fingers scrabbled at Ben's arm. He put his larger hand over hers, calming, soothing. Dora watched, how he folded his fingers around hers, quelling the fidgeting, and how she glanced up at him in desperate gratitude. 'Ben's not one for shooting but he'll have to learn, and my father says he'll teach him. He said he didn't like it, but Daddy said he didn't have a father to teach him and he'd like it soon enough, didn't he? Daddy is rather a monster.'

'Shooting.' Dora stared at Ben, who nodded again.

'Darling,' Natty said, 'I must go and find Laura, she's vanished again and I'm worried she's up to no good. We can't afford a repeat of last time with the waiter.' She swallowed, her eyes moving around like black beads, rattling in her too-large skull. 'Be kind and talk to Dora, will you? I want you to love her, she's one of my dearest friends.' She stood up slowly, the threads of the dress shimmering around her, and kissed Dora on the cheek. Her cheekbone clanged against Dora. 'Dora darling, I'll say good-bye, in case you dance off. You must come and stay when we're married. Isn't it jolly, what all us old girls are up to? All round the world, wives and mothers for the Empire. Good – goodbye, darling.'

And she was gone.

'I didn't,' said Ben Stark, into the silence that ensued. The band had paused, the brass shaking out their instruments, the leader mopping his brow, the audience exhausted.

'Didn't what?'

'I didn't like the shooting,' said Ben. He ran his fingertips along a silver cigarette case on the table, his attention focused on it. 'I don't care for her father. He has huge red ears. None of them read books. They laugh at Natalie all the time. They're vile to her. They laughed at me for reading Dickens. I mean it's not exactly Plato, is it? What's wrong with reading a bit of Dickens? But they said I was a bookworm.' He blinked, and smiled. 'I think they meant it as an insult. God. Excuse me. Do – excuse me, Miss Wildwood.'

'Dora,' she said. 'You must call me Dora now. Really.'

'Dora,' he said. The applause, a wall of sound, seemed to ebb away as the song ended. In the background was the awkward clink of glasses, of gay chatter, of people moving chairs round and slamming doors. Prosaic, almost daytime sounds. Someone in the band cleared his throat. A young man in the crowd shouted:

'What's the hold-up? Waiting for Hutch?'

There was laughter. The Royal party, ensconced in a corner table, smiled, and Dora saw the Prince of Wales clapping uncertainly. He had very short, stubby fingers. She turned away, and saw Natalie, weaving her way across the dance floor, shawl wrapped tightly around her skeletal shoulders. Dora watched her disappear into the ladies' cloakroom, followed by another, grim-faced woman behind her.

She turned back, to find Ben's eyes on her.

'I didn't—' she began, but she wasn't sure how to go on.

'I know,' he said. 'Believe me, I know how it looks.' The band started playing the opening chords of another song and Dora gave a small gasp: a soft, wistful, charmingly rhythmic version of 'Little Girl Blue'.

He offered her his arm. 'You like this song, don't you?'

'How do you know that?' She was acutely aware of him, all of a sudden; the rasping heavy cloth of his evening jacket; his fingers, resting lightly on the back of her rib cage; his eyes, locked onto hers, grey, warm and all-seeing.

'You hum it when you're shelving the books. Don't you realise?'

'No,' she said, staring at the floor in confusion.

'I hear you,' he said. 'All the time. Sometimes I hear it when you're not there. Would you have this dance with me?'

His arm around her waist, they danced into the centre of the crowd, as the band played on, and the singer held out her hands, a thrilling throb in her voice as she sang. Just one piano, one soft, brush of the drums, and the faintest ribbon of a clarinet.

Sit there and count your little fingers
Unlucky Little Girl Blue

Ben was saying something, conversationally, into her hair. 'Look, you'll wonder why I hadn't mentioned—'

'I haven't wondered anything, honestly,' said Dora. She leaned back in his arms and stared at him, thinking again how utterly the evening dress changed him. He was someone else in it. 'I don't know you well enough for it to be any of my business. But you should know Natty was a dear friend of mine at school.' She hesitated, as he swung her around a corner, and their grip on each other tightened, thrillingly, his hand on her back, his fingers tightening around hers. 'She doesn't seem very well.'

'She isn't. She is addicted to something, but I can't find out what. Benzedrine or cocaine, I suspect, perhaps Medinal. She takes sleeping pills as well. She is very ill, but her family won't admit it. She won't admit it. I don't know what to do.'

'She's marrying you to get away from them, even though she doesn't love you.'

He smiled down at her. 'Did you know Mikey's scared of you,' he said. 'He thinks you have special powers. He thinks you should be at the Palladium three nights a week, performing feats of perception, and he's probably right, you'd make a killing.' And they danced on, in the silence right at the heart of the noise, the heat, and the music. 'If I can get her away from them . . . give her some space . . . somewhere calm . . . perhaps I can help her. This child-hood friend of hers, you see . . . She won't talk to me about her – it's only what I've picked up here and there. I don't even know her name. Something happened over the summer. Not sure what, exactly . . . but her family kept it out of the papers; Lansdowne contacted Lord Beaverbrook and threatened to cancel the lease on the print works. If she stays with them she'll die. I'm pretty certain of that.'

'Why do you have to marry her?' said Dora. He dipped her, and they spun around together, whirling faster and faster . . .

'Because of the reasons I've just given you, Dora.'

'No,' she said, in his ear, louder than ever as they danced close to the band. 'That's to help *her*. If you don't love her, why are you doing this? You can marry who you want, surely.'

'I had an older brother.' Ben clutched her tightly, his breath on her ear. 'He died in a car accident, a couple of years ago. I was supposed to be the spare; now I'm the heir. I have to . . . ensure the line . . . I have to keep up the house, it's in a dreadful state . . . there are people relying on me, livelihoods, the whole vil-lage, really. So what I need doesn't really matter.' He shrugged. 'It really can't matter . . .'

'It does matter, it matters awfully,' said Dora, her voice thick, but he didn't seem to hear her. 'You matter,' she said, louder than ever. 'So does Natty. Both of you do.'

He shook his head. His eye fell on the Prince of Wales. 'I don't feel sorry for myself. I feel sorry for George, my brother. He would have been the perfect Lord Rutherford. Everyone adored him. He loved shooting, too.'

'And Natty?'

'She was earmarked for him,' he said, tightly. 'Has been since birth, our families are old friends. I've known her all my life. The father is a monster, so's the mother, and the sister is a fair way to being a combination of them both. Natalie has to get away from them. I wouldn't let her down for anything. I can't.'

'Yes.'

They had danced to the other end of the floor, in front of the band. Dora thought of the shuffling waltzes, the awkward, toe-stubbing foxtrots, the agony of dancing with men who couldn't, didn't want to dance, and what it was like when you were with someone who did. She found she could not quite look at him, and glanced over his shoulder, nodding at Susan and Minnie. Susan was dancing with Neil, her eyes sparkling. Minnie was tapping her foot on the sidelines, smiling at them both.

'Your friends are wondering who this stranger you're dancing with is, Dora,' Ben said in her ear, and swung her into the centre again, so they were surrounded by other bodies, as the song reached its climax, the soft, insistent rhythm of the bridge.

'I am, too,' she said, really without thinking. She felt his breath, hot against her neck.

'No,' he said. 'I know you and you know me,' and they drew themselves into the centre of the dancefloor, out of sight. Very lightly, his lips brushed against her skin. She glanced at him quickly, and his eyes met hers, and he pressed a finger onto her neck, as if imprinting himself on her.

She leaned back to look up at him and felt his arm tightening its hold on her. They stared at each other, unsmiling, not breaking a step. Her face burned; he breathed as though he had been running. Dora felt as if she were stepping off the edge of a cliff, letting herself go, with nothing to break her fall.

So it has happened, she felt herself think, her head spinning.

'I don't know what to say,' she said. 'Except that I wish you both every happiness. She's a lovely girl.'

'She is,' Ben said.

They were still in the middle of the dance floor, hemmed in on all sides by couples. She could hear him, perfectly clearly, his breath warm on her neck, and she longed to pull his head down, to feel his lips on her skin, to bring him into her.

Don't do it, she wanted to say – and she had to bite her lip to stop it. 'Ben—' she began, with no clear idea of what to say.

'It'll be all right when she's better,' he said, in a small voice. 'When I've helped her. But oh, she doesn't read. She doesn't like making strange jokes. She's not enthusiastic about things, Dora. Butterflies, and strange country customs, and London, and book-shops. And I don't know her.'

'Yes,' Dora said, in a small voice. Her fingers pressed into the soft cloth of his dinner jacket, the firm spine beneath.

'You see from the first moment, I knew I knew you, Dora,' he said, his voice hoarse, and close in her ear. 'Does that make sense?'

'Yes,' Dora said again, shaking her head. She put her fingertips on his chest, on the white starched cotton, to feel his heart under-neath. 'Of course it does.'

He nodded, and straightened his back.

She was afraid to look at him, afraid to face the force of the feeling. She could feel his heart, thumping, his hand tightening around her waist, as though the two of them were in the whirl-pool, being sucked down into the depths.

Sit there and count your little fingers
Unlucky Little Girl Blue

'What will we do?" she said, eventually, as the final chorus started up.

'Now? Keep on dancing, until the music stops,' Ben said. 'Just keep dancing with me, Dora, just a little longer, while we can.' He took her hand from his chest, his fingers tightened around hers again and his thumb, encased in her hand, moved against her palm.

And so that is what they did.

19

Death in Damask

Dear Dora

Thank you for yours. So you've been at the Paris Café, well you'll have to tell me all about it. I should love to see such a place one day.

I tried to get back in the house but the bramble seems to have grown into most of the drawing room and the hall and now up the stairs. It's very dark in there. I think someone needs to break in and have a proper look. Do you want me to use the hatchet? Perhaps write and ask your father for permission first, he doesn't like me much and smashing down the door with a hatchet won't improve relations will it.

You're right I did read an Esmé Johnson last year. It was good but not as good as Venetia Strallen. Very similar though. I think someone might have told her it's not done to steal from someone else. You said you were going to go and see her publishers. Ask them why they can't get her to think of her own stories? It can't be that hard can it, to my mind, certainly not as hard as plough-ing a field or picking the last of those damn potatoes out the ground every year or being up all hours to birth the lambs.

All the swifts have gone now and the last of the sparrows took off yesterday. I have seen the squirrels go to the oak tree down in the Wildwood with their nuts; rumour has it that ten of them chickens over at Harwood Hall have been killed ready for hanging for Christmas. They can't find anyone to look after them since you've up and gone and Charles SB hasn't come back yet being as how he's put it about that someone asked him to stay on as a favour to them and persuade you to change your mind about him. I think he's saving his fat face myself from coming back and whole village laughing at him till Doomsday.

Seen two small Coppers which is remarkable this late in the year.

It's been a mild autumn but now November's here Dora things are changing. I was sorry not to see you with me All Hallow's Eve. There were the usual disturbances and I saw the old faces as ever, my old Ma popped by to wish me all the best but the Green Man didn't trouble me and you know that's been bad before.

All the honey has gone in and I'm enjoying some as I write this to you. Here's the evidence.

Anyway Dora this is just to say I do miss you ever so much. If you need me to do anything you just send word. Any word, I'll know. I'll know course I will.

ALBERT T. JUBBY

P.S. Let me know about the hatchet.

P.P.S. Wanted to mention we had someone round here asking about your mother and her going to Switzerland. Funny fellow. Suit too tight for him. Said he was police. Said it a few times like he was something special. I told him to sling his hook. Don't think he liked it much. He had a beard.

'Mr Steyn will see you in a minute, Miss Wildwood,' said the elegant young man behind the curved desk in the dark reception. 'He's dealing with an Important Matter. Would you like a cup of coffee? Glass of sherry?'

It was ten o'clock in the morning. 'Thank you so much,' said Dora. She smiled at him and shook her head. 'But no sherry for me.'

'Oh.' The young man put his head on one side. 'Are you *sure*?'

'Quite sure.'

The young man sat back down at his typewriter, sighed, and with extremely exaggerated hand movements proceeded to start typing, so loudly and elaborately banging the keys that Dora was sure he must just be doing it for effect. She'd never really been in an office before, apart from her father's solicitor's office in Bath, and that was quite different: a quiet, hot room in a Georgian building. This, though it was a Georgian building too, was a hive of activity, a dark wood-panelled corridor lined with covers and bookshelves, a strong smell of cigars and heavy perfume, and three secretaries in a row, clacketing away in the far corner, at the back of the building. A lift, next to where Dora sat, thudded as the doors sprang open every ninety seconds or so, making her jump. Occasionally a door into some kind of inner sanctum would open, and Dora would glimpse a group of men in suits, roaring with laughter around a table. Publishing books was obviously an extremely jolly business.

A man with round purple glasses and a glorious peacock-blue and green silk waistcoat bustled in, slammed a sheaf of paper down and bustled out again. 'Tell *'ER*,' he bellowed, spit flying, as he banged open the doorway to stand on the threshold, 'I'm not jolly well changing it again so she can go boil 'er *'EAD*.'

'Rawston Cummings,' said the young man, after the door had banged shut behind him.

'That does sound painful,' Dora said.

'Rawston Cummings,' the young man repeated. He peered round the giant typewriter. 'Head of design. Very temperamental. *She's* asked for changes to the cover. And Mr Steyn will do anything she wants being as how she's the Queen Bee. Till . . .' He lowered his voice. 'Well . . . the Worm Turns. You know. Because the worm *always* turns, in the end.'

'Who are you talking about?' Dora asked, bewildered. But the young man shook his blond, silvery hair.

'More than my life's worth to say,' he muttered, and turned back to his exaggerated typing.

'Thank you,' said Dora vaguely. She could feel her stomach was about to rumble, and shifted on her seat. She had slept very badly again, then overslept and missed breakfast at the Three Corners, and she was hungry.

Albert's letter had unsettled her, with its talk of the damn bramble completing its invasion of Wildwood House, like something from *The War of the Worlds*, Charles Silk-Butters still in town, Stephen Fox poking around in her and her mother's affairs, but also because she missed Albert. But it was more than that – it was talk of the changing seasons, which were not so visible in London, and All Hallows' Eve which she had missed, and creatures abroad in the night, in the hedgerows, in the sky. She loved autumn, the soft dying light gilding the ochre trees in the winding roads and lanes towards Wildwood House, the drifts of fallen leaves in the graveyard near her mother's grave, the scent of wood smoke, the last light evenings before the darkness came. Here, the talk was not of spirits abroad, crab-apple jelly and wood storage but the General Election, Mrs Simpson, and velvet collars on winter coats.

She was no closer to solving the mystery of who had killed Sir Edwin Mountjoy. She was afraid, coming back to the Three Corners sometimes, that Charles would buttonhole her again, though she told herself firmly Charles was a joke, a character in a film who slipped over a lot, at whom the audience knew to laugh.

But most of all she was sad, because she was in love. This sadness consumed her, it was not the fizzy dramatic addictive feeling of when one first falls in love and longs for the other person night and day, though she did long for Ben, edging carefully round corners for a glimpse of him if she heard his voice whilst she was stacking shelves in an out-of-the-way section. It was not the love she had hoped to find, it was a longing, like the pains she had had as a young child when her legs woke her up at night. 'They're growing, darling,' her mother would tell her, smoothing her hair. 'They're making you nice and tall so you can conquer the world.'

Increasingly Dora was realising her mother had been wrong, and that, plus the aching loneliness of loving someone you could never have, left her feeling sorrowful. She did not wash her hair, or brush down her cape. She chewed the skin around her nails, and said no, gracelessly, when Zewditu Amani asked her if she would like to come with her to a Sunday Concert featuring

Women Composers at Conway Hall followed by a sandwich and discussion of current events with some other no doubt excellent young women. She snapped at Minnie when she poked her head around Dora's cubicle to ask if she could borrow some hair slides, she did not seek out Susan, knowing Susan would notice, and she did not write back to Albert.

And at the library, reshelving the books, she looked covertly for Ben but avoided him where she could and when she couldn't was politely distant and he, in turn, was to her. The surprise of it was almost as painful as the reality of it.

'I'll be in late tomorrow,' she'd called out to the Issue Desk as she was leaving the previous day. 'Have to visit Venetia Strallen and Esmé Johnson's publishers.'

'Good night,' Ben had called, then looked up, realised it was Dora, and stared at her. He held her in his gaze for several heart-stopping seconds, touched his hand to his cheek then looked down again, and all Dora could think of, as she let the door bang behind her and emerged into the sharp chill of a November evening, was how extraordinary that once she had known the feel of his lips on her neck, of being in his arms, his firm hold, his quizzical smile, and she wanted, then and there, in the chair in the publisher's waiting room, to slide down to the floor in a puddle of tears. And thus, dear reader, it was ever so.

*   *   *

'Forgive me for keeping you waiting!' said Michael Steyn, spreading his arms wide and gesturing for her to sit down. 'Do give me one moment.' He lifted up and dropped various pieces of paper, with a helpless air. 'Now where was it . . .'

Dora gazed round the office, which she saw at once had long ago been a Georgian lady's bedroom: duck-egg-blue panels with gilded plaster cornicing, against which shelves stuffed with books leaned, sometimes rather haphazardly on the uneven floorboards. She wondered if Mr Steyn had spotted the fragment of paper sticking out from one of the architraves, with a tiny scrap of copperplate scribbled across it – love letters, stuffed into a hiding place.

Every spare surface was entirely covered with either books or papers – manuscripts stacked in towers on top of the shelves and chairs and the wide windowsills, wire trays with sheaves of letters, both typed and handwritten. On Michael Steyn's desk was a telephone, and a photograph of Mr Steyn with Venetia Strallen, both in fancy dress, he as a lion, she as a Tudor Queen, and a typewriter – but all of these were almost entirely submerged in paper, too. The blotter was dark navy, the victim of the upturned bottle of ink on the floor, she supposed.

'I do hope I'm not disturbing you,' said Dora. She found it hard to concentrate and wondered whether it was the mess. She couldn't stop thinking about the Georgian former inhabitant. Had she sat in bed drinking hot chocolate and scribbling secret billets-doux to a lover? Had she been scared, had she given birth in this room? Something had happened in here. Her radar twitched in certain places and this was one: she folded her hands in her lap, calming her thoughts.

'Not at all.' Mr Steyn slapped his hands on some papers then gave a cry. 'Hah! There it is!' He brushed the papers away and produced a fountain pen. 'Let me just sign this.' He scribbled on a sheaf of documents. 'There. SIGNED!' he said, so loudly Dora jumped. 'Just initialling it – now this is ready to be posted! My dear, forgive me. Busy day, that is all. A few unhappy birds chattering this morning but I think, *think* all is well for now. Jolly dee. Authors, my dear Miss Wildwood – but I shall say no more.' He mimed buttoning his mouth shut and placing the button, apparently detachable as well as invisible, into his waistcoat pocket, then mopped his brow, and pointed to the plate of biscuits. 'Dauntry! Dauntry love, come in and fetch Miss Wildwood a coffee. Would you like a coffee, my dear?'

The young man appeared in the doorway, and gave her a friendly smile. 'This is Dauntry Forbes,' said Michael Steyn, smiling with apparent pleasure at his assistant. 'He's been with me since –' he faltered slightly – 'it was August, wasn't it?'

She saw Dauntry Forbes frown, very slightly. 'Yes, August, Mr Steyn.'

'He was living off his wits before I employed him, weren't you, Dauntry?'

'Picked me up at the Moon and Sixpence, more like,' said Dauntry, nodding at his boss with a faint grin. 'Tries to hide it but it's true. She don't want a coffee, Mr Steyn. I've asked her.'

'Oh! How marvellous of you. Just the usual for me, dear,' said Michael Steyn. He turned to Dora. 'At exactly eleven a.m. every day I have a cup of very strong coffee with a little tot of something in it.' He gave her a beaming smile. 'If I've a lunch with an author who's going to shout at me, you see. Just to see me through. Takes the edge off the shouting. Dreadful thing, shouting. Can't stand it.'

'He hates giving bad news,' Dauntry Forbes said fondly, looking at his boss. 'He's a pussycat.'

'Oh that's not true! I'm a panther when I need to be. Rarrrh!' Mr Steyn curled his fingers and gave a small growl, which came out sounding rather like something between a cough and a belch. He looked at Dora, and mopped his face with a large, brightly coloured handkerchief. 'My dear, you said when you telephoned that you wanted to discuss Esmé Johnson and Venetia Strallen, and I have of course had a visit from that nice Sergeant Fox.'

'He's actually Detective Inspector Fox.'

'Really?' Michael Steyn seemed taken aback. 'I liked him, don't you? Lovely—'

'Anyway,' Dora said, gently breaking in. 'I did want to ask you about Miss Johnson and Miss Strallen. You see I had the distinct feeling there was more than mere professional rivalry between Venetia and Esmé, from something Miss Strallen said.'

'Oh dear. Oh . . . dear.' Mr Steyn's face clouded over, but it was gone in an instant. 'Do you know the story of Solomon and the baby? Well, when it comes to rivalries between authors I'm afraid sometimes I feel I am Solomon, having to decide which half of the baby to keep after I've chopped it in two! Have a Chocolate Oliver, dear girl.'

Dora bit into a biscuit gratefully, as the door opened and Dauntry re-entered, bearing a tiny enamel cup. 'Thank you, Dauntry,' Mr Steyn cried with great relief, and mopped his brow again. 'Just here, please, dear.' He wrinkled his nose. 'Is it my special batch?'

'Just how you like it,' Dauntry Forbes said.

'Oh good. Levantine beans, you know. Rose Macaulay brought me back some, poor dear Rose, always on about that extraordinary novel of the Levant she means to write . . . Dauntry makes it the Turkish way, so much sugar you can stand your spoon up in it, then Goslings rum, most satisfactory. I am a creature of habit. Look at this. Venetia brought me a lovely set of cups to celebrate *Murder at the Ritz*, for it's all set at teatime, you know. Such pretty things. . .' He held the pearlescent blue cup up to the light. It gleamed, and he smiled. 'Thank you. No visitors or calls, Dauntry, and leave the door ajar, please, as it is so stuffy in here today, is that clear?' Michael Steyn said. 'Now, where was I?'

'Esmé Johnson and Venetia Strallen, Mr Steyn,' said Dora patiently.

'Oh . . . Oh yes.' And he glanced uneasily towards the door. 'I should say it began when Esmé Johnson stopped working for Venetia and started to write her own novels. They met at the London Library, you see, and I think Venetia took to Esmé – Esmé was a huge fan of Venetia's books, and was clever enough to let her know, most effusively! Trust me, they can't hear it enough times! Hah! Anyway,' he said, suddenly serious, 'I daresay Esmé didn't forewarn Venetia she was writing a book though I don't see why she should have, every two-bit secretary's writing a novel these days. Dauntry's is called *My Fair Lad* and I must say it's really awfully good. The Book Club are on standby to take a huge quantity when he's finished it, such fine author photographs, you quite understand. Oh! Where was I? Yes, I did not appreciate Venetia wasn't happy when we snapped Esmé up. But she's jolly good,

I must say, quite the thing of the moment, fast cars, European travel, athletic blond men and madcap heiresses, all of that. You could feature in one, if you wanted, Miss Wildwood! Hah! What was I – oh, yes. Well, we published the first, *Ding Dong Death,* and it was a sensation, my dear. I thought Venetia would be delighted for Esmé, after all she was her protégé. And for a while at least she must have been putting a brave face on it. But oh no.' He lowered his voice, flattened his palms on the cluttered desk and leaned forwards. 'She read the proofs of *The Guilty Fiancé.*' His small round eyes were huge. 'Came bursting into the office one morning. Six months ago, it was. Said Esmé Johnson had lifted a plot off her and copied half the characters, all *sorts* of terrible things. She looked quite mad, actually. Lipstick on wrong, hair a mess – oh, dreadful.' He shuddered at the memory. 'Such a beautiful woman, but when she's angry . . . Not nice. Not nice at all.'

Dora brushed the last of the biscuit crumbs away. 'How dreadful' she said drily. 'But the accusations of plagiarism . . . are they true?'

'Ah!' Michael Steyn swivelled round in his large mahogany chair, jumped up and took a book down from the shelves. 'I know where they all are, you see!' He handed over a copy of *The Guilty Fiancé.* 'Wonderful book. A tour de force.' He rubbed his cheeks with pleasure. 'You must take a copy, my dear. Here. The critic of the *Daily Punch* said he hadn't read a book since *Mock Turtle* that he'd enjoyed so much. Readers love her. She's now, she's fresh, she's tomboyish, she's got *something*, and of course, she's played tennis with the Prince of Wales, and that, my dear, gives her an edge over Venetia Strallen, much as one wouldn't *dream* of reminding her of it.' He lowered his voice still further, crouching over the desk, so that the light from the emptiness of Bedford Square bounced off his gleaming pate: 'One does have to be careful with the lady novelists, you see,' he said. 'They're very sensitive. About everything.'

'But surely Miss Strallen has done extremely well for Morpeth, Neild & Steyn?'

Mr Steyn's smile became more fixed than ever.

'Oh yes, yes, very well, very well indeed,' he exclaimed, nodding furiously. 'Oh my yes! We've published all of her books, you know, there was a period when she *was* Morpeth, Neild & Steyn . . .' He was quiet again for a moment. 'Of course, she'd rather be lying in bed eating marzipans, by her own admission! But we set her up with a desk here—'

'Here? In the office?'

'Oh yes. She likes the rhythm of the day, you know. Coming in here, working in her own little office, going out to dinner afterwards. Awfully lonely business, writing. Hard work, too, once you're on the treadmill of it.'

'Really?' Dora thought of Albert. 'It's not – working down a coalmine though, is it?'

Mr Steyn clutched his heart, as if she had wounded him. 'My dear girl! What a reductive argument. Are you saying if something isn't as dreadful as working down a coalmine then it can't also be hard, in its own way? That one's job can't be difficult, even if it's writing a sermon or arranging bouquets of flowers or singing on the stage at Covent Garden? These are all very hard, in their way, and so is writing, for without beauty, and art, and religion, what are we? We're nothing, my dear, we're machines, robots out of a science-fiction novel, nothing more, and producing art is not easy.'

It was Dora's turn to press her hands to her burning cheeks, ashamed.

'Tricky thing, success. And Venetia knows it. She had a fine old time of it, *To Catch a Killer*, that was her first book, she was young and devilish pretty, girl about town, everyone's favourite. The newspapers loved her, terrific time of it we had, and then *Murder at the Ritz* . . . this is fifteen years ago now. Of course, she wasn't as young as all *that*, but old Venetia . . . damned good at fudging things, you see . . .

'She'd had a strange childhood you know, only child of elderly parents who sacrificed everything for her, sent off to school very young, then they both died so she was quite on her own. She told me once she had no one to stay with in the holidays. So she always wrote, a way of keeping herself company.'

'That's terribly sad.'

'Oh, but most truly successful novelists have had dreadful childhoods,' Michael Steyn said happily. 'Makes for the most terrific material.'

'Anyway my dear, for a period all was well. Venetia was correcting page proofs, signing foreign deals, sailing to New York every time her book came out there, giving talks at every Women's Institute and Working Men's Club in the land, autographing copies at any bookshop that would have her, answering fan mail – one year, 1930 I think it was, she had a thousand letters, answered every one of 'em, and on top of that, Miss Wildwood, she was writing a book a year.' He shook his head. 'Quite remarkable. But she always said, character is formed in the shadow of the valleys, so remember that when you're at the summit.'

'That's very good,' Dora said slowly. 'My mother used to say the same.'

'She has a way with words, Venetia. Nothing like Esmé – Esmé's a sensationalist, she works her socks off, she's got *It* – whatever *It* is, and she'll be bigger than any of them one day, mark my words, but she's not the writer our dear Miss Strallen is. And she doesn't care about the writing. But Venetia does,' he said, staring into the middle distance. 'She cares most dreadfully. *Death in Damask*, you know, something of a flop – oh, it nearly killed her.'

'I heard two girls talking about it in Hatchards,' said Dora. 'They were awfully rude about it. I felt for her, and she wasn't even there.'

'Well, that's it. You understand. Very few people do. I don't, really, and I've been an editor for twenty years.' Mr Steyn smiled, and held out his hands, as if admitting guilt. You and I can have no comprehension at all of what it's like when someone's nasty about your novel. Venetia told me once it's not like a wound, because a wound heals. She said it's like a dull vice gripping your skull, crushing you with misery, flooding your senses with all the worst things you think about yourself all day, every day. The business with *Death in Damask* really shook her up. I thought for a while she'd give up writing altogether.' He nodded, his expression grave. 'And then she went away for the summer and came back and started writing again. Venetia has iron in her, I tell you. She knuckled down and wrote and wrote. Something changed her that summer. Whether it was time away or time to reflect, she came back and a month later she met Sir Edwin and a year after that they were engaged and my dear, she was so happy. It was as if she was Cinderella and he was Prince Charming. He gave her her spirit back, her belief. It's why *Lady, Be Good!* is such a fine book. Dare I say it, it's her best yet – the twist! My dear!'

'Oh, I know,' said Dora. 'The silver tray riddled with bullets! But they weren't bullets, they were Braille markings!'

'The heiress with the pet hare and the hair lip!' Michael Steyn interrupted her, his face red with joy. 'And of course—'

'*Edgar Dunnett's mother's porridge spurtle!*' they chorused together. Mr Steyn clutched the desk and laughed, looking around, almost wildly. 'Oh that's good. Very good.'

He stood up abruptly, went to the window, and looked out, then sat back down again. 'Yes, she needs the wind at her back. Pressure, you know. When she delivers the goods: oh, my dear, there's no one, *no one* to touch her. Dear Venetia. Esmé knows it, she knew it, they all do. Even a relative dud like *Death in Damask* is still worth ten of the others. And one knew, of course, the great tragedy was, once she married Sir Edwin there'd be no more books.'

'Yes, she said that. But I wasn't sure if she meant it, really. You think so? None?'

'Dear me no. He was a very traditional man, Sir Edwin, he did not want a wife who worked.'

'That seems dreadfully wrong,' said Dora. 'Did you believe her when she said she was happy?'

Mr Steyn shrugged. 'I did believe her, yes. She would have been entertaining very interesting people, London society, he and his sister were very well connected, moved in the best circles you know. Richenda Mountjoy is a close friend of Her Majesty, I am given to understand. And my dear, you know I think the charm of writing was starting to pall.'

'I can't imagine how,' said Dora. 'It must be tremendously jolly, scribbling away at a book and then seeing it in a bookshop or in a newspaper and having one's fans ask for one's autograph. I thought Venetia was wonderful at it.'

'She was. She is. They adore her.' He leaned forwards. 'But you talk to any of the lady novelists, and all they do is complain, I'm afraid. You don't pay them enough. You don't give them the right jacket. They don't want to be seen as crime, they want to be seen as social drama. They want Vivien Leigh to star in their films. They won't go to Foyles and pose for a reporter. Or go into the East End and ladle soup for some blasted orphans. They want you to write to the *Times* to complain their reviewer said the book was sluggish, which it jolly well was because they wouldn't change the fifty-page set-piece in a parallel universe that has nothing to do with the plot even though you asked them *so* carefully. They don't want to be Penguins: terribly vulgar, the paperback. Then they *do* want to be Penguins: marvellous invention, the paperback.' He rolled his eyes, most enthusiastically. 'Honestly, often I wonder if they're more trouble than they're worth. Good for them to know there's always someone coming up behind them.' He looked at Dora hopefully. 'You don't write, do you, m'dear?'

'Me? Good grief no. I'm more in the detection line. Mr Steyn, correct me if I'm wrong, this is rather awkward, but from what I understand that would have been a blow to your business, if Miss Strallen had given up writing, wouldn't it?'

'What? Oh, terrible,' Michael Steyn said gloomily. 'She was a big seller for us – here, you're not suggesting *I* bumped Sir Edwin off, are you? Saving my cash cow?'

Dora hastened to assure him that was not what she meant.

'I should hope not. I'm not one for underhand dealings anyway but that would be beyond the pale. No, no.' A thought struck him, and he brightened up. 'Hah! Perhaps I'll have a word with Penguin, too. She might let me sell to them now. Depends how desperate she is. Dreadful spendthrift, our little Venetia, and how she'll get by now he's dead heaven knows.'

'Wasn't she making money from the books, Mr Steyn?'

'Of course, of course, we paid her very well, very well indeed. No doubt about that, we've always been very fair, and twenty per cent of home sales, her agent practically broke my arm over the royalties. Venetia's always broke! She has such expensive tastes!'

Dora looked around the book-lined office, out into Bedford Square, the autumnal plane trees flame-coloured against the silver-grey stone, a hunched street-sweeper following a straight line amongst the cobbles, a woman scurrying past him across the square, cutting the line in two. 'But Mr Steyn,' she said, struggling to understand in the welter of information circling her. 'Did she – do you believe Venetia Strallen when she says Esmé Johnson stole her plots?'

'My dear! Stealing – it's such a *strong* word.' Michael Steyn's eyebrows rose so high they almost vanished into his hair. He waggled them up and down. It was like seeing dancing insects, the furry little black caterpillars that became striped tiger moths.

'Esmé has been very prolific in a short space of time,' he said eventually. 'There have been whispers . . .' He hesitated. 'But then . . . Who's to say? Certainly not me. A good editor defends their authors . . .' he said with a small smile. 'To the death. And I have faced death down for them. For her.'

Dora leaned forwards. 'I'm sorry. I'm not clear what you mean.'

'Surely not.' Michael Steyn looked down at the small cup before him, and stirred the coffee gently with a matching small blue enamel-coated spoon, and she saw not the round smiling face, but the haggard bags under the dark eyes, a slight tightness about the small pursed mouth. The room was cold, the light from the square dull, and suddenly white. Dora stared at Michael Steyn.

She knew, as their eyes met, that he was hiding something, that he was utterly afraid . . . that he had been, long before she walked in.

'You must understand, I'm not unlike Venetia, or Esmé, trying to conceal my humble origins. My father was a grocer, you know. I grew up without books. And everyone has them now. There's a library on every street corner. These authors of ours, they make people so happy. What does it matter how they do it? Really?'

He tapped the spoon three times, lightly against the china. It gave a soft bell-like ring, strangely hypnotic.

'What is it, Mr Steyn?' Dora said quickly.

He laid the spoon back down on the messy desk, shook his head, smiled at her.

'You're scared of something, I know. Do tell me.' She tried to keep her voice steady, like gentling a nervous horse. 'Mr Steyn . . .'

Slowly, Michael Steyn took a large gulp of coffee. He swallowed.

'It's too late for me,' he said, smiling at her, his bald head gleaming softly. 'It should have been me back then, not poor Diana. Poor darling girl. I should have understood. Of course it's you. It's you, you've spooked them.'

'I don't know – what you mean. I'm so sorry.' Dora's throat was tight. 'Mr Steyn, who's Diana? What are you talking about?'

'They killed Diana—' Michael Steyn said, his voice a ghastly, tight croak. He clutched at his throat, fat fingers gripping the pulsing, thick neck, whose veins stood out, bright blue against his pale skin. 'Find her friend. Her little sad friend. She told her all about it. The killing jar – she told her the truth about it . . .' He blinked.

Dora didn't understand what was happening. . . The book-lined walls seemed to be closing in on them. She could see his bald head, gleaming now with perspiration. His face was red. He tugged at his collar. 'Of course . . . always knew it . . .'

'Knew what, Mr Steyn?' Her hands fumbled across the cluttered desk, reaching for a smeared crystal tumbler filled with water. 'Drink this – Mr Steyn, have some water – help! Mr Forbes! Get help!'

Michael Steyn had frozen, his face a liverish purple, and he muttered:

'Oh, my dear, there's no point. No point. It's my turn now.'

He fell forwards, his lips landing onto the leather-trimmed ink blotter with a squelching sound, his large body jerking. Spittle frothed at his lips. He reached, with one agonising movement, for the small enamel coffee cup, head fixed on the desk, and laboriously knocked the rest of it over. The brown liquid soaked into the ink-stained blotter, and started fizzing, eating away at the gold tooling, the green dye, the leather underneath. His right eye, fixed on Dora, unblinking, stared at her, then simply froze.

For a moment Dora was unable to move. And then she leapt up, calling for help, and it was as though everything was in slow motion – her waistcoat, sliding to the floor. Her hand on the door, Dauntry Forbes's expression, a lock of his silver-blond hair falling in his face as he jumped up, mouth hanging loose. For a while all Dora could hear was his voice, screaming, over and over again, patting Mr Steyn's lifeless face, his heavy hands.

It wasn't until she heard the police siren, a few minutes later, as she sat out in the reception area again, a blanket around her shoulders, shaking almost without restraint, that she realised she had been present for two murders, she who would not use her mother's own killing jar to kill butterflies.

20

Silly young women

'It doesn't look particularly good for you, you must admit that,' said Fox. He glanced at Dora, walking silently beside him, a large blanket wrapped around her shoulders. 'I have to ask you some questions, Miss Wildwood. Are you listening?'

Dora nodded, absently. They were on the Embankment. It had rained solidly for the past two days and now winter was creeping towards them, his icy fingers waiting to snatch at her, at the name-less hundreds hurrying around her. Dora stared out at the river, rushing past higher than ever, pulling the blanket, which she had borrowed from the publishers, around her.

At home in Somerset she had a thick coat, walking boots, tweed skirt, thick woollen jumpers. Every November the River Chance flowed fast and high, flooding the fields down the hill from Wildwood House, and then the frost set in. But in London the seasons hid themselves from you and Dora had been caught unawares, and was insubstantial in silk, cardigans and her cape, not her oiled woollen coat. She was not ready for winter.

Fox said: 'Firstly, the gun. We found a gun in the bushes, outside Miss Strallen's flat, and you recognised it.' She did not answer, and he said roughly, 'Dora – Miss Wildwood – are you listening?'

'Yes. Yes, of course I am.'

'Can you explain that?'

Dora pulled herself together. 'Not why it was in the bushes outside Venetia's flat, no.'

'Why did you have a gun?'

'Someone who lives with Lady Dreda gave it to me by mistake. It wasn't hers either.'

'Did you ask them about it? Lady Dreda, or the maid – Maria, is it? I assume that's who you're talking about. Didn't you think it was important?'

'I asked them, but I knew it wasn't anything to do with them,' said Dora. 'If it had been, do you think my godmother would have given it to her maid to dispose of? And if it had been Maria's gun – why or how she'd have a gun in the first place I have no idea – would she really have taken it to Paddington station to meet her employer's goddaughter off a train and then mixed it up with some sandwiches? Hardly. She'd have hidden it away, thrown it out somewhere. Women are used to doing things in secret, keeping ourselves private, practising little rituals others don't know about. She wouldn't have blithely handed it over to me and not known about it.' Fox opened his mouth to say something, but Dora cut flatly across him: 'And it doesn't work to say it could have been a double bluff, either. No one double bluffs by giving a total stranger a gun, Detective Inspector.'

'Nevertheless,' said Fox, recovering himself, 'you didn't say you'd been given a gun. You didn't say you'd subsequently thrown the gun away—'

'I lost it,' said Dora. 'I think it fell out of my pocket whilst I was sitting on the steps of the London Library. So something else picked it up. I had it for thirty minutes, and then I didn't. Which is not the same thing at all.'

'Why didn't you mention it, then?' He saw her hesitate. 'You don't seem to understand, Miss Wildwood, the gravity of your situation.'

'I was afraid,' she said simply.

'Of what?'

'Of my ex-fiancé. Of being forced to submit to other people.' Dora stopped and looked up at him, rearranging the blanket around her shoulders. 'I was glad to find that gun in my pocket, even if the method by which I came by it was rather odd. I have been someone else's problem all my life, you see. I was tired of it.

And with all due respect, my having a gun has little relevance to a case where two people have been poisoned.'

'It was found outside Venetia Strallen's flat, Miss Wildwood. Someone threw it away. Around the same time someone went into her flat and created chaos. Someone desperate.'

'Do you think I killed him? Michael Steyn? It would have been awfully easy for me to slip the poison into the coffee. Less easy for me to poison Sir Edwin Mountjoy, I wasn't inside the library when he ate the Turkish delight. But I'm sure you can find some loophole that means I was.'

'I know you didn't kill Michael Steyn,' said Fox briefly. 'Your fingerprints aren't on the coffee cup.'

'The poison was in the coffee before it was served to him,' she said. 'I should imagine via the water or the beans. Thus it's perfectly possible for me to have added it beforehand.' Dora held up a finger. 'But in any case, alas for me, the door was open. Mr Steyn asked specifically for it to be left ajar.' She caught his expression. 'You look pleased with yourself, Detective Inspector. I wonder why.'

Fox bounced on his feet. 'That was a code. It meant, keep a watch out.'

'How do you know?'

'Because Dauntry Forbes was working for us,' said Fox grimly. 'He's a junior detective. He was able to hear all of your conversation. We planted him in the office, at Mr Steyn's request. Mr Steyn was worried about his safety, with good reason. Someone tried to kill him in the summer.'

'Who?' Dora asked, astonished. 'Why didn't you tell me?'

He looked at her and gave a short laugh. 'Miss Wildwood, you're saying I should disclose confidential details of a case to you, simply for your delectation?'

Dora narrowed her eyes. 'It was you who asked me to go and see Steyn.'

Fox shrugged. 'You suggested it. You suggested talking to Miss Strallen, and Mr Dryden, and drawing up the list of books you keep saying will reveal something though it hasn't, so far as I can tell—' She started to speak, but he cut across her. 'You seem to be under something of a misapprehension about the working methods of the Yard, Miss Wildwood.'

Dora stared at him in disbelief. 'I thought we had an agreement, however vague, that I would involve myself—' She stopped, realising how ridiculous this sounded. 'You asked for my help.'

He gave a small, angry-sounding chuckle. 'I worried that I had given a false impression at the time of our initial conversation. Now I see that I did. I said it would be useful for you to be at the library. Nothing more. I apologise. The facts remain, and we are no closer to a solution, and another person is dead.'

'Detective Inspector Fox, you confound me.' Dora closed her eyes. Her cheeks were burning.

Fox scratched at his beard. He said: 'This is murder, Miss Wildwood. Not a committee meeting for your village's annual summer party.'

Dora's eyes flew open. 'Don't be patronising. We don't have a village summer party. We celebrate the Summer and Winter Solstices with a pageant, if you must know, then we crown a goat with hops or holly, depending on the time of year.'

'Ah,' he said, angrily cracking his knuckles. 'You take the sense out of everything.'

'"*Better be without sense than misapply it as you do*,"' Dora said, sharply.

'What's that supposed to mean?' His eyes darkened.

'*Emma*. You'll find Jane Austen usually says it best, Detective Inspector, though I think if you met her you'd deliberately misunderstand her rather than reveal your own weakness, as you do with so much else. Anyway – what were you saying?'

'To be frank, Miss Wildwood, it is clear to us the crimes are linked and part of a wider campaign against various figures within in the book trade. So far the only deaths are Sir Edwin and Mr Steyn, but that's not to say others haven't almost succumbed. Someone tried to poison Mr Dryden, as you know. A printer in

Essex lost a finger when a paper-cutting machine fell on him out of hours. And, of course – as you know – there have been several attempts on Miss Strallen's life.'

Dora walked on briskly for a moment, chin sunk onto her chest. 'What book was he printing?'

'I'm sorry?'

'The man at the printers. The one who lost his finger.' She clicked her fingers, almost in impatience.

'Amos Longfellow, his name. He was supervising the printing of one of Venetia Strallen's novels. You see, a picture emerges, if you apply proper methods—'

She shushed him, impatiently. 'You haven't mentioned someone. The secretary.'

'I'm sorry?'

'The secretary before Dauntry Forbes? What happened at the publishers this summer?'

Detective Inspector Fox shook his head. 'That is a private matter, unconnected with the case. Besides, it's not for the faint-hearted.'

'I am not faint-hearted,' Dora said.

He sighed. 'The Honourable Diana W., I shall call her, had been secretary to Mr Steyn since February of this year. She was an extremely able young woman with ambitions of becoming an editor.'

A name, swimming up towards her, like Natty, swooping up through the murky depths of the river, choosing to live. 'Diana,' Dora said. 'The Hon. Diana Waters, you mean?'

'I thought you might be acquainted with her,' Fox said, in a neutral tone.

'Actually I wasn't,' said Dora. She had been shivering since the murder, and now she felt her fingertips tingle; as though sense were returning to her body. She understood – in part, but she understood. *Oh Natty. My sweet friend.* 'But I know someone who was. And I should have seen it.'

Fox went on. 'One evening, Diana left the office with an important letter for the post which Mr Steyn had just signed. She walked past the garden square. She was seen to stop, as if someone was calling her. There was a small sound, nothing loud. She collapsed to the ground. She had been shot, and died instantly.' He stopped. 'The bullet went into her eye.'

'Dear God.' Dora covered her mouth with her hands. 'And did no one link it to Venetia Strallen and Amos Longfellow?'

'They were then seen as isolated incidents. Miss Waters' private life was complicated, shall we say. Her family was concerned over her friendship with another – I will say no more.' The tips of his ears had turned red. 'There was reason enough in the family to want this hushed up where possible and so it was not given the attention it deserved, kept out of the papers, and so forth. A piece of good luck for the murderer.'

'Yes, indeed,' said Dora. 'I still can hardly—' And then she looked at him again.

'I should have seen it too,' he said, in clipped tones. 'And I blame myself for it. Both of us, you see, did not let ourselves come to the correct conclusion.'

'If Diana had been a boy, she'd have inherited most of Suffolk, you know. She'd have been able to buy her own publishing company. She'd have had all the freedom she wanted.'

'Yes, and if I'd been one of Lord Waters' cronies, or more like Sir Edwin, you see – but when you aren't born the right way you don't have the right school tie, and then you don't have the right conversations, shall we say.' Fox nodded, with a smile. 'That's why I make an ass of myself, so often, as you've been kind enough to point out. I want to stand out. So they don't get at me for the other business. The business of being not like them.'

'I'm sorry.' Dora looked at him, and they both shrugged, knowing there was little they could do about it. 'So what happened after that?'

'After that?' Fox blinked, recalling himself to the narrative. 'The next day, Steyn left the manuscript of Venetia Strallen's new book on the table, packaged up ready to go off to the printers. While he was at lunch it was torn open. They wrote *Someone will punish you* over all of it. And other – ahem.' Detective Inspector Fox coughed. 'Some unsavoury words, besides that. Accusations of a most hysterical kind.'

'Like what?'

'Quotes from Shakespeare, *Twelfth Night*, things about butterflies, furious scrawling – whoever wrote it broke a nib on their fountain pen. In effect, accusing Venetia Strallen of being a woman of—' Detective Inspector Fox stopped.

'Are you blushing?'

'I most certainly am not. It's a little delicate, that's all.'

'You are blushing. How darling. Don't worry. You're saying they were accusing her of being a prostitute.'

'Miss Wildwood—'

'I have a great aunt,' said Dora. 'My father's side. Remarkable woman. Flamstead Wildwood. Runs a shelter in Bermondsey for fallen women. She says it's nonsense to say they're fallen. She calls a spade a spade, Detective Inspector. What a mess it all is,' she said. 'And an innocent girl murdered. You let the family press-gang you into silence,' she said, 'and so someone got away with murder. Two more murders, in fact.'

'We were pursuing our enquiries, but these were centred around the likelihood that the Honourable Diana Waters was murdered by someone from her lifestyle who had a grudge against her. A bohemian sort, one of those drug addicts that congregates around Brenda Dean Paul and her filthy lot in Chelsea . . . most unsavoury.' He stopped. 'We embarked on a line of enquiry that did not prove to be correct. We weren't to know, you know.'

'No, you're only Scotland Yard, after all,' Dora said scornfully. Fox smoothed his hair down. 'What was the letter he was signing at the time?'

'Who?'

'Michael Steyn signed a letter Diana Waters was about to post when she was killed. What was it?'

Mr Fox looked at his fingernails. 'I don't know, do I?'

'You didn't ask at the time?'

'It seemed of paramount importance to investigate the surrounding areas for miscreants, foreigners, anyone who might
cause trouble – by the time we'd completed our searches the
offices had been thoroughly searched and tidied up.'

'So the two people who were present when Mr Steyn was signing
a letter are now dead, and the letter itself is unidentified.' Dora
rummaged in her cape pocket. 'And why does it make me think of
something? Something . . . I can't remember.' She took off the blanket, folded it over and handed it to Fox. 'I said I might go home. I
think I will, in fact. It makes sense. I shouldn't have come at all.'

Detective Inspector Fox looked taken aback. 'What?'

'If you don't need me, that is. And you say you don't. I won't
ever try and go to a party to which I'm not invited, that's my
motto, you know. I understood you wanted my help; that is not
the case. I shall return to Somerset tomorrow.'

'Why, may I ask? I mean,' said Fox, recovering himself. He took
out his pocket watch, and looked at it, seemingly unconcerned.
'Just so we have our stories straight.'

'That poor dear man – Mr Steyn – I can't forget his eyes.' She
swallowed. 'I watched him die. I thought seeing a dead body was
bad enough but watching someone die is quite different.'

'I know,' he said.

'You do?'

'Yes. Miss Wildwood, Scotland Yard is extremely busy. We've
got workers marching in from all round the country, stoking civil
unrest, some young idiots from Oxford thinking they can climb
Eros, Mosley and his crew stirring up trouble in the East End, not
to mention this affair we're now being asked to prepare for.'

'What affair?'

'War,' he said solemnly. 'It's coming, you'll see. And you'll forgive me, but I've no use for yet another posh girl who thinks the
world revolves around her. Besides,' he said with a short laugh,
'you're dangerous. Every time you're left alone with a man he
dies.' Dora's dark eyes, which had been fixed on the churning
water, flew open.

'How dare you. How *dare* you get angry with me just because you can't crack the case. Honestly, Mr Fox, you're the limit. I drop clue after clue into your lap, I act the fool so you can nose around asking questions and in return you behave in this appalling fashion.'

'Appalling,' he mimicked.

She stared at him. 'Why are you so furious? It's a perfectly simple case, if you can only put your mind to it.'

'Furious?' He rocked back on his feet. 'Because . . . you're a baby. You think the world is made up of fiancés and silk dresses and nice godmothers willing to help you. You glide off the train wanting to be a detective and a plum case falls into your lap. You swan into the Three Corners and bag the next available room bumping off the people on the waiting list—'

'Miss Pym gave it to me because—'

'Because you sound right!' he shouted, and a bird flew out of a tree, and a little boy playing in Embankment Gardens dropped his stick. 'You're the kind of girl the Three Corners wants. You'll always get by because you look the part and my sister won't because she looks like what she is – a poor East End girl who's gone without her whole life, who used to pass out on the way back from school 'cause she'd not eaten all day until I started sending money back to them. You don't see what's around you. It's a dreamworld to you.'

'A dreamworld! You think *I'm* the one living in a dreamworld.' Dora stared at him, her cheeks burning with anger, and shame. She shook her head slowly. 'You coward. Blaming me for your case going wrong. Do you know what I ran away from? Do you know how scared I've been? How there aren't any women like me, because we're not allowed to do – oh, *anything*? I saved up for the train fare for months, putting money by, a bit here and there, because I had nothing except fine silks and a stupid ring no one else wants. I couldn't earn money. I'm supposed to be decorative. And have children.' She spat the words out, her mouth twisted, her expression ugly. 'Susan earns a good wage. She'll run something one day, I wish she ran something now! She doesn't need you any more, and you don't feel useful, and you're so *very* angry about it. God dammit!' Dora swore, and clamped her hand across her mouth. 'You're a bully, they all are, but you're worse. You could be so clever, so skilled, but your self-importance blinds you.' He stared as if she'd slapped him but she pulled away. 'I've said too much. And to think I liked you, Stephen Mavis Fox. You utter idiot.'

Fox was rigid, his face pale. He glanced up at the towers of Scotland Yard, lights burning in the dusk. 'Look, Miss Wildwood. I shouldn't have gone that far.'

'The way you talked about Natalie Lansdowne. You saved her life. But she's a silly upper-class girl and you couldn't make it more obvious you despised her. You didn't stop to ask why she was so miserable she wanted to die. What had happened to her. If you had, all of this might have been prevented.' She pulled her cape around her. 'And the worst part of all is, I was going to tell you today.'

'Tell me what?'

'Who the murderer is, of course.'

'You know?' Stephen Fox took a step back, staggering slightly as he came off the kerb. 'Don't be ridiculous. You can't possibly know.'

'Of course I do,' she said. She gave a small smile. 'I see things no one else sees. I notice things no one else notices. And I have to cover it up. Cover myself up, appear different. I've been doing it all my life.'

Fox fumbled in his pocket for his notebook. He said hoarsely: 'Who is it, then?'

Dora shrugged. 'It doesn't matter, not now. They will only target one more person now.'

'How do you know? How do you know *that*?'

'I told you. I see things.'

'Like what? Tell me what you've seen?'

'Various things. My gun found outside Venetia's flat.'

'It's not yours.'

'I know it's not mine, you utter ass. The disappearance of Lady Natalie Lansdowne.'

Fox looked bewildered. 'What does that have to do with it?'

'She has everything to do with it, as you'd know if you'd troubled to look. She is the key to the whole business. What else . . . Oh, yes. The plot of *The Parsonage Affair* – most instructive—'

'I don't have time to read books, Miss Wildwood. I have an investigation to lead.'

'You should, you'd be surprised what you find in them.'

Detective Inspector Fox laughed, with something like relief. 'Miss Wildwood, you've lost your mind.'

She smiled up at him grimly, her eyes burning with fury.

'Do you know what my mother used to say?' He shook his head. '"Trust your first instinct." She was right about that, but it was too late. They killed her anyway.'

'Your mother was killed?'

Dora said, her voice soft: 'They said it was suicide, or an accident. *Suicide!* The nonsense people tell themselves rather than face the truth. And do you know what she said to me before she left? She told me to find Venetia Strallen.'

'Why?'

'She said I had to keep her safe. Those were her exact words. And I thought she was crazy – she'd been crazy, those last few weeks since she'd left my father and gone off to Switzerland . . . But she telephoned, especially, from Montreux to tell me, the day before she died. She was right. Someone should have kept Venetia safe. Sir Edwin understood that. He saw she had to be protected . . . that someone would stop at nothing to – to ruin her career.

'Don't you see? Everyone around her has been targeted, and the danger grows greater every day. A printer, her fiancé, her publisher, his secretary . . . you mark my words, a terrible accident will befall Venetia Strallen by the end of the week unless you keep her safe. Now. That's my last word to you on the subject. The rest, I'm sure, you can find out yourself. Thank you for –' she spread a hand out – 'well, pretending to take me seriously, for a while, anyway. Goodbye, Inspector.'

She strode towards Embankment Gardens, and turned up a narrow lane between the twin cream edifices of the giant new Shell Mex House and the Savoy, and then, suddenly, as he began to run after her, she was gone. Immediately afterwards, of course, he realised he shouldn't have let her go. But by then, it was too late.

21

The dangers of Harley Street

'But you've only just got here, Miss Wildwood. It seems a shame to go back so soon.'

'Nevertheless, I must. Thank you, Miss Pym.'

'There's two weeks' notice. I hope that is clear.'

'Very clear.' Dora took a look at her Three Corners laundry bag, embroidered with the symbol of three interlocked Cs. She folded it, smoothing it over with her hand, and slid it across the reception desk. 'I am so sad to be going. I will forever be in your debt.'

'How so?'

'You took me in,' said Dora, her voice wobbling. 'And you have done the same for thousands of other young women who needed a new start. A refuge. A room of their own.'

'Well, it's hundreds of young women,' said Miss Pym drily. 'And most of them left the place in a terrible mess and I often wish I hadn't bothered. But I take your point. Where are you going?'

'Oh,' said Dora vaguely, 'a man about a dog. He wasn't real either. Goodbye, Miss Pym. By the way, what's your first name? I should so like to know.'

Miss Pym flushed. 'My name? It's Cleone.'

'Cleone. How beautiful,' said Dora.

'It's Greek. It means,' said Miss Pym, proudly, '"Glorious".'

'Your parents named you well. Was your father – or mother – a classicist?'

'No,' said Cleone Pym briskly. 'My father was a locksmith from Newcastle who wanted to better himself and who spent every spare minute in the library going over *The Times*, and reading books about the ancient world. Obsessed with Greece, he was. Life's ambition to go there. He was called Robert Pym, Miss Wildwood. Bob. He believed in education for women and he adored Homer. But I'm not related to anyone interesting. No one you'd find interesting anyway.'

'I'm sure I would,' said Dora. 'And if you don't mind my saying so, it sounds to me as if your father *was* a classicist.'

Miss Pym was slightly pink. 'Goodbye, Miss Wildwood. A reminder about the two weeks' notice, that you are welcome to stay until then. Do take care of yourself, won't you? The Three Corners is always here if you need it. Come back any time.'

'That's – oh, that's very nice to know. Thank you so much.'

Dora stepped out of the Three Corners and onto the pavement. It was two weeks since she'd arrived in London. A cruel wind sliced the hats off hurrying commuters on the Marylebone Road. She shivered, chilled to her bones, wrapping her tweed cape around her, and walked down Harley Street. A thick, smog-like haze hung in the air. She had removed most of her possessions to Lady Dreda's the previous, awful day, when she had realised what she had to do. One more night at her godmother's, her last night in London.

Dreda would be waiting for her, in the cosy drawing room with the crackling fire, the piles of buttered anchovy toast and Madeira cake and Assam tea, and the thought of it warmed her even as she shivered in the cold. The thought, too, of what she must accomplish daunted her, but it had to be so. The inquest on Sir Edwin Mountjoy opened next week. His funeral was tomorrow.

As she walked down the wide boulevard-like Harley Street she gazed as ever with interest at the young women, the elegant wives and mistresses, and the grand dowagers emerging from grand white buildings and scurrying into waiting cars, the secretive doctors' plaques on doors that did not advertise their business.

Nearing Portman Square, a door to a particularly grand-looking nursing home opened and a girl came running down the steps, a collection of gawky arms and legs, stumbling slightly at the last, and almost running into Dora. Down the way, a car sat waiting for her. Dora caught her, and righted her.

'Natty? My goodness, darling, is that you? I've telephoned you often, they've said you're out every time or can't come to the phone. I've been awfully worried about you.'

'Dora!' said Natty. 'However are you? I was meaning to drop you a note after the Café de Paris – but Ben said you were very busy and I didn't want to disturb you. I wasn't sure if he wanted to keep me away from you or didn't want you to have to cope with me – I'm not sure of anything!'

She looked dreadful, her golden hair tangled and matted flat with some substance, her face pale, but it was her eyes that were most distressing, bulging in her horribly thin face, the skull slightly too large, as if the life were draining out of her, the skeleton all that remained. Her wrists were like spindly sticks. She clutched at Dora, and it felt like a cold wind's touch. But Dora held her, steadily. She kissed her cheek, and gently clasped Natty's elbows.

'Are they helping you in there?' she said softly. 'Why do you go there?'

'To make it better. Mother says so. They give me an injection – it perks me up. And I'm nice to Ben, and can face things. And forget what I saw.'

'What you saw?'

Natty shook her head violently. 'I won't say.' She began to shake.

'Darling, Ben wouldn't want you to do that, not for him,' said Dora. 'He's a good man. You must tell him.'

But Natty shook her head. 'I can't,' she said. 'The wedding is in a month's time. He mustn't know.'

'I think he does know, darling.' Dora smoothed her hair. Natty's fingers twitched and she plucked at her brows; the eyebrows were almost gone, only one or two sparse hairs left on her eyelashes. Dora's fingers itched to slap the shaking hands away. 'I know him. Ben is a decent, kind man, Natty. He loves you—'

'He doesn't love me. And I don't love him.'

'I mean he cares awfully about you,' Dora said. 'Don't you see that?'

Natty scrunched her hands together, clenching them into a double fist. She laughed, shaking her head. 'Oh gosh. Dora, you're perfectly potty sometimes, you know. He cares about *you*, darling,' she said with a ghastly, shaking laugh. 'Do you know, he talks about you all the time. It's a *coup de foudre*, for him, anyway. I know. I've seen it before. I *had* it, before . . .'

'I—' Dora began, but then she was silent.

Natty blinked several times, then rearranged her warm fur jacket. 'They think I'm a lost cause . . . so they talk in front of me, and I notice things other people don't . . . it's awfully funny really, how much I see. And darling Ben: I think it'd be easier, almost, if he openly despised me. Instead it's worse, because we're painfully grateful to each other. I'm glad he knows you, by the way – I wish—' She coughed hoarsely, her body racked with convulsions. 'Forgive me, darling.' She gave Dora a ghastly smile. 'Oh, we'll make each other miserable . . . I can't – bear the idea of being with him. When I think about Diana . . . What it was like with her . . . Her hands, Dora.' Her sunken eyes searched Dora's, her face crumpling with misery. 'Do you know what it felt like . . . slipping into the water? As if I was free again.'

'Natty,' Dora said, utterly miserable. 'I wish it wasn't like this for you. It doesn't have to be, you know.'

'It does. That's it.' Her attention was caught by a bull-necked man emerging from a Daimler on the other side of the street. 'That's Lugg, our chauffeur, you know. He spies on me. Hi! Wait a minute, Lugg; I'll be there directly,' she called, and he nodded, leaning against the car, watching them.

'You can change things,' said Dora. 'I did. It'll be frightfully hard but you can. There's an awfully good line in *The Valley of Death*. The heroine escapes the clutches of the dreadful solicitor and clambers up the hill to safety and when she thinks she can't go any further, do you know what Edgar Dunnett says to her?

"Keep going, my dear. You didn't come this far just to come this far."' Natty was staring at her. 'I always think that's awfully good,' Dora finished. 'Don't you?'

'*You didn't come this far just to come this far.*' Natalie laughed again. 'Oh, yes. It is good.'

'See. Venetia Strallen is usually right. Now darling, if you can go into a nursing home for a bit, get off that dreadful stuff, whatever it is. And— Darling, why are you laughing?'

Natty gave another short laugh. 'Venetia Strallen didn't write it, you know. But it is an awfully good line.'

'What do you mean? It's from *The Valley of Death*. I remember reading it, it was the year after my mother died, I must have read it four times, you know.'

'Well, I can't really say.' Natty glanced up at the street, at a car driving up from Portman Square. 'But Diana always said when she worked with Mr Steyn most of her paperwork was to do with Venetia. Keeping her out of trouble.' She was looking up and down the street. 'I ought to go now, Dora.'

Dora stared at her, bewildered. 'Was Esmé Johnson one of the people Michael Steyn was paying off on behalf of Venetia?' She said quickly. But Natty's attention was fixed away from them.

'That car's going awfully fast, isn't it?'

Dora's mouth was dry. 'Natty darling. Was Esmé blackmailing Venetia? She was, wasn't she? Is that what Diana told you?'

Natty nodded. And Dora saw now too that the car was barrelling towards them, down the road at great speed, tyres screeching, burning, as if being pursued by someone or something. 'Thousands, they were paying her. She'd just put in another demand, and that is what they were authorising. She's a snake, Dora, a talentless snake – the worst kind of writer, she's a leech – oh Dora!'

The car was not on the road. It had mounted the pavement and was heading for them. Very slowly, as if in slow motion, Dora saw it was not being pursued – it was in pursuit, and they were the quarry. 'I say!' said Natty, suddenly snapping out of her lethargy. 'God dammit! Dora, move out of the way, for God's sake! *Move!*'

*　　*　　*

Dora heard a loud thud – a scream – a hand reached out, yanking her away so hard she staggered back, and all the time someone was shouting her name, so loudly everyone else was turning to look, yelling, screaming really – over and over – the most awful, vile words she had ever heard and then something hit her and she was falling, backwards, onto the pavement, banging her head as she landed and then – and then there was nothing.

*　　*　　*

As a child, Dora Wildwood had always hugged herself to sleep; when she was too tired, or frightened, or alone, or the night her father got word of her mother's death, somewhere on a mountain in Switzerland. She had got into bed and hugged herself, arms wrapped tightly around her slim frame and so it was that she was found when the police arrived, scant minutes later, her life-less form across the pavement, scorched black tyre marks on the ancient paving stones and the smell of burnt rubber, and Natalie Lansdowne stroking her hair, sobbing, clutching Dora's heavy, too heavy hand in hers.

22

The Switcheroo

The following day was the funeral of Sir Edwin Mountjoy, Chief Librarian of the London Library. Despite the unfortunate circumstances of his death it was, of course, a grand affair, as befitting a man of his stature. The funeral procession began from his home in Berkeley Square, taking in Piccadilly, where crowds of curious onlookers – some cognisant of the identity of the deceased in the vast black hearse drawn by eight horses, some not – lined the road, before turning down past Fortnum & Mason and along the gentlemen's outfitters, perfumeries and old public houses of Jermyn Street, heading into St James's Square where it circled the old private gardens once, slowly, so that staff members of the London Library not important enough to be invited to the funeral could line up outside the tall thin building in the north-west corner to pay their respects, which they did, nodding very slightly in the howling, darkening wind. The hearse proceeded back up to Wren's glorious St James's Piccadilly, where the great and good of London literary society were gathered.

A minor incident occured as the coffin was unloaded and carried into the church, the pallbearers staggering slightly – Sir Edwin had not been a slight man. One of the pallbearers, righting himself, was jostled by a common woman in the crowd outside the church, the *Express* reported.

Someone low-born, of no consequence, but whose actions, attempting to press bunches of heather upon the mourners, screeching and crying upon such a solemn day, did not endear her to the crowd, a few members of whom bustled her into the church porch without further ado.

The *London Illustrated News* reported that Venetia Strallen, the chief mourner, walking behind the coffin next to Sir Edwin's spinster sister Richenda, collapsed on the way into the church and had to be supported by Mr Michael Dryden, Acting Chief Librarian.

Miss Strallen, greatly distressed, was on her way into the funeral when words were spoken between her and the novelist Esmé Johnson, words which this publication considers most regrettable and will not be repeating. Miss Johnson shouted and declared Miss Strallen to be a crook and a thief, and was asked to leave the ceremony, which she did. Miss Strallen – whose dignity throughout proceedings was remarked upon by almost all – was shown into the second porch of St James's, which gives out onto the back entrance on Jermyn Street. She was given a few moments to recover, being overcome with grief, whilst the coffin and pallbearers proceeded on their way down the aisle. Eventually, having taken some water and heard some words of comfort from the Right Reverend Hubert Boniface, Bishop of Kensington, she emerged, heavy veil in place, stopping only to complain loudly about the dreadful common gypsy who, having been herded into the porch, had approached and harrassed the already besieged fair fiancée of the deceased on this most painful day as she gathered herself in the porch. All present greatly admired her pluck. Measures were taken to eject the gypsy woman, but it seems the ne'er-do-well had already vanished from the back porch onto Jermyn Street. Thus the service was able to proceed, Miss Strallen most nobly keeping her composure throughout, though many noted Miss Richenda Mountjoy was sadly discomfited during the final hymn 'Christian, Dost Thou See Them?' at one point exiting her seat to point at Miss Strallen during the second verse: 'Christian, dost thou feel them / How they work within / Striving, tempting, luring / Goading into sin?' However,

*it was not remarked upon beyond noting, Miss Mountjoy's antip-
athy towards her brother's fiancée being well documented.*

Afterwards, people would ask why they hadn't seen it coming.
Why a woman whose life had been in danger multiple times in
the past few months had not had some police protection. For
when they came to leave the church, and the pallbearers appeared,
and the hearse waited patiently on Piccadilly, and the mourners
prepared to depart to the Travellers Club where a few light refresh-
ments would be served, something most remarkable happened.
Miss Richenda Mountjoy, who had vocally opposed her brother's
engagement to Miss Strallen, leaned over as they left the church
together, and with no warning seized Venetia Strallen's shoulders,
pinning her arms tightly to her side.

Mr Dryden, Miss Amani, and Mr Forbes clutched at Miss
Mountjoy. Dauntry Forbes was able to hold her firmly, but it
turned out it was not her whom they should be holding.

'I've had enough,' Miss Richenda Mountjoy shouted, her bellow-
ing voice, echoing around and over the ancient stones, out toards the
waiting crowd. 'You're a dreadful woman, not nearly good enough
for my brother. He told me you cheated, Miss Strallen. He knew all
about *The Killing Jar.* He said your true colours were there for all to
see and, madam – now we shall see them!'

With one white-gloved hand she yanked the veil from her
brother's fiancée's face – and gave a scream.

The woman staring back at her was not Venetia Strallen. She
was nothing like Venetia Strallen. She was, in fact, the gypsy who
had disrupted proceedings, only of course she was not. She was
an actress, Jane Wilkinson, and she had been paid a handsome
sum only the day before to play her part. Venetia Strallen had
been tied up, bundled into a van and left in the darkest depths of
the London Library – they had taken her in via the back entrance
on Mason's Yard whilst all the staff were still gathered outside at
the front of the building for the funeral. She had been dumped in
the Parliamentary Records section, on the sixth floor, where no

one had ventured for months and it was, they said, a wonder she was alive.

*   *   *

Detective Inspector Stephen Fox received word of this turn of events at the bedside of Dora Wildwood, in the University College Hospital. He stood listening to the particulars from Sergeant Crispin in the dark, cold room on the third floor. He turned from him as he finished, looking at the lifeless form of the girl in the bed beside him.

'They say there's very little point anyway, sir. Her father has been informed. He said –' Sergeant Crispin sniffed – 'that he'd travel immediately back from France, once his horse race was finished.'

'Leave me with her for one minute,' Detective Inspector Fox said sharply. 'Just leave me alone.'

When Sergeant Crispin had departed, puffing his way back downstairs with some difficulty – 'I ain't never seen him like this, not even over that girl in the Hippodrome revue, Lily what's-her-name –' Stephen Fox turned back to the still form, his face as pale as the girl in the bed's.

'She warned me,' he said softly, watching her black lashes, fluttering slightly on her white cheeks. 'She said it was dangerous. But she was wrong. It was her turn.' He stared at her face. 'Damn you, Dora. Couldn't you have got out of this one? To explain to me what the – the hell it's all about?'

Dora opened her eyes. 'Well really, that's not fair. I can't do everything,' she said, rather croakily, and Stephen Fox jumped so violently and so suddenly he knocked a glass of water off the side table. 'Do be careful,' she added.

Detective Fox stared down at her, his beard seeming to bristle, and then he began to laugh, gently at first, rubbing his sides, his cheeks, then more loudly, so it rang out in the small room. Dora watched him, blinking, and then raised one hand, and he stopped abruptly.

'Sorry,' he said, mopping his eyes, and the sheets, with his handkerchief. 'You are extraordinary. Any of that – any of it true? The storming off? The vows about going home?'

'All of it,' said Dora. She scratched at the bandage wrapped around her head. 'But I did wonder if someone would try to get rid of me at some point, so I wasn't entirely surprised to see that car come barrelling at me, and when I woke earlier this morning I was able to make a few telephone calls. What's happened,' she said, blinking slowly and raising herself gingerly up in bed, 'whilst I've been out? Gosh, I do feel strange. Everything is – oh, it's spinning. Quite fun actually.'

'You were unconscious for almost two days, Miss Wildwood, I think you're minimising the gravity of the situation.'

'Only a day in fact,' she said. 'I woke up last night you know and had a nice rest in bed rereading *The Railway Children* which a gloriously kind nurse found for me in the nurse's station library. I'm ready now. Ouch.' She touched her bandaged head. 'This, however, is rather inconvenient. It starts to bleed again every so often. It's most unpleasant, you know, sitting there with blood running down one's face.'

Fox reached over for the bell. 'I'll call for Sister. She'll want to have a look at you – ow. Stop it.'

'Don't,' said Dora, grabbing at his arm.

'Here!' he said, playfully, but she tightened her grip.

'I said don't.' Her eyes were huge in her pale face, and she scratched at the bandage round her head. 'Listen to me for once, will you? I've been trying to tell you for ever so long now and you won't actually listen. If Venetia's to be kept safe, no one must know I'm recovered. They must think I'm dead, or as good as – let me finish,' she said, as he tried to speak. 'They want me out of the way, and they will act accordingly if they think that.'

'But Venetia's not safe,' he said. 'Someone trussed her up at the funeral and left her in the London Library this morning.'

Dora's eyes grew even larger. 'Right,' she said, chewing her lip. 'Of course. Yes, of course they did.'

'She is very upset. She has checked into the Langham and acquired a bodyguard. She says she has lost all faith in Scotland Yard—'

'Now, why would she say that, I wonder,' Dora murmured.

'Miss Wildwood, I was really here to interview you about what happened yesterday,' Detective Inspector Fox said, struggling, as ever with Dora, to keep control of the conversation. He flipped open his slim notebook, and licked his pencil. 'Can you remember the moments leading up to the accident?'

'Well, it wasn't an accident, was it?' said Dora. 'They were driving right at me. And I could see them very clearly—'

'You saw who it was?'

'Oh yes. But I wasn't surprised.'

'Who was it? Was it Esmé Johnson?'

'Esmé?' Dora shook her head in amusement. 'No, it was Charles Silk-Butters, my erstwhile fiancé. And I do think anyone would agree he's gone too far this time.'

'Oh,' said Detective Inspector Fox. 'Silk-Butters, eh?'

'Which leaves us in an interesting position,' said Dora, sitting up straighter. 'You believed the murderer tried to kill me, and that they have in some way attempted to do away with Venetia Strallen too. But Charles was nothing to do with the murder of Sir Edwin – apart from the fact he doesn't know him and has no motive, he had an alibi for the time of the murder. The mystery is not him.' She started to climb out of bed, but Detective Inspector Fox pushed her back, gently but firmly. They stared at each other, surprised.

'I apologise,' he murmured. 'I shouldn't – but – you're damned provoking, you know. Dora, I—'

He put his hands out towards her.

'No,' she said, shaking her head. 'Don't.'

She pressed her hands to her cheeks. Both of them stayed perfectly still. Suddenly there was a knock at the door and a rattling of the handle.

'Sister wants me to check on the patient, Detective,' came a concerned voice. 'Could you open the door please?'

256

Fox gestured to Dora to lie back on the bed again and close her eyes, which she did. He opened the door. 'I apologise. It's not locked,' he said. 'Just stiff.'

A nurse with heavy brows and a facemask tucked behind her headdress poked her head around. 'I wanted to make sure—' She glanced at Dora. 'Still asleep, is she? Poor little thing.'

'She is.'

'I'll take her pulse.' She came in, smoothing down her snowy-white laundered skirt, and looked down at Dora, who lay apparently unconscious in the bed. 'A little fast,' she said, after a minute. 'Could you go and get Sister for me, sir?' she asked, her face reddening. 'I'm a little worried – I don't want to leave her.'

'Of course,' said Detective Inspector Fox. He leaned out of the door, looking down the long pistachio-green corridor, the parquet floors. 'Ah – where would I find her?'

'At the station along at the end there,' said the nurse. She had a slight accent that he could not place. 'Go along, would you? We mustn't waste time.'

Fox hesitated, then he went out into the corridor, and walked up to the nurses' station, where a tall, rather forbidding-looking older woman sat, drinking a cup of tea. 'Sister?'

She looked up. 'Yes?'

He said, as though reciting a lesson: 'One of your nurses sent me. She said you ought to come and have a look at Miss Wildwood – in room three six seven – she said she's still unconscious and her pulse is rather fast.'

'Miss Wildwood?' Her face was blank. 'But I was in there only ten minutes ago, and we were chatting. I made her a cup of tea. I told the others not to disturb her – Detective – where are you going?'

For Detective Inspector Fox had turned and was running as fast as he could back down the corridor, towards Dora's room, cursing loudly. 'You stupid bloody *idiot*,' he was shouting, as he reached the door and rattled the handle, to no avail. 'You idiot – of course you shouldn't have left – of course – Sister! Open this door! Ah,

Crispin, you're here. Go around to the front of the hospital if you please. Immediately. Watch for anyone leaving, via the door or a window. Be discreet. Don't frighten the horses.'

Sergeant Crispin did not react, but simply nodded. 'Yes, sir,' he said, turning smartly on his heel, and he left. 'Sister – what's your name?'

'Sister Pargeter.'

'Someone impersonating a nurse has gained entry to Miss Wildwood's room and is now refusing to let me in. Do you have a spare key?' She nodded. 'Would you fetch it, please?'

'Yes, of course.' She hurried back down the corridor.

Fox, feeling like the biggest idiot on earth, rattled the door again. He could hear muffled shrieking, and the sound of someone moving around the room, heavily. 'Let me in, dammit,' he called through the keyhole. 'This is Scotland Yard. I demand you—'

He fell through the door, which gave way suddenly. He landed on the threshold.

The room was empty.

The window was open, and the net curtains billowed in the breeze. Detective Inspector Fox ran to the window, looked out. He could see Sergeant Crispin, on the street below.

He looked up, and shook his head. Nothing here.

'She was going to get out that way,' said a voice behind him, and Detective Inspector Fox turned round, and stared. 'But I managed to stop her.'

The door swung gently shut and revealed Dora, standing in a white hospital gown, barefoot, like an avenging angel. But she was not alone. Next to her, a figure wrapped in white sheets, like a mummy, a figure whose face was entirely concealed, a figure who had round their waist, preventing them from throwing off the sheets like a straitjacket . . . a sparkling diamante belt. They were being held firmly by a hospital porter, a man Fox did not recognise.

'She copies everything Venetia Strallen has. I too coveted that belt,' Dora said, conversationally. She nodded at the stranger, a handsome, fair man as tall as Fox, who struggled to contain the writhing, shrieking figure he was gripping. 'This is my best friend Albert, Mr Fox. Albert Jubby, this is Detective Inspector Fox.'

'Afternoon,' said Albert Jubby, dipping his head slightly. 'Pleasure.'

'Mine too—' Fox began. He moved towards Dora, catching the faint scent of her that always haunted him – lily of the valley, mixed with spice and fresh air, leaves, and grass. 'He's a porter here?'

'No, of course not. He's from Combe Curry. Deepdale Farm is next door to ours. The Jubbys have farmed the land there for centuries. Albert owns a scythe they actually used to behead a cohort of Roundheads who attacked the village.' She turned to Albert. 'That's right, isn't it? I wired him last night when I came round.'

'I sliced the top of my finger off showing it to you, don't you remember?'

'Course I remember,' said Dora, rather crossly. 'I had to pick it up.'

'I can show you, sir,' Albert began, making to unravel himself from his grip on the apprehended culprit, but Fox interrupted:

'No, that won't be necessary, Mr Jubby. Hold them, would you please. Tightly.'

'What is all this commotion? Miss Wildwood, you should be in bed, unless you want me to call the doctor out again—' Sister Pargeter appeared in the doorway as Stephen Fox slowly untied the diamante belt. 'And who are all these visitors? Who are you?' she said to Albert Jubby. 'I've never seen you before.'

'I'm Albert Jubby,' said the young man, glancing at Sister. 'Hope you don't mind me mentioning it, but did anyone ever tell you you look just like Googie Withers?'

Sister Pargeter blushed. 'I say,' she said. 'Get on.'

'You know who's here, don't you?' Dora said to Stephen Fox, ignoring Albert. 'You must have worked it out by now.'

He nodded, his fingers fumbling on the belt. 'I think so . . . but I'm just not sure. It seems so incredible.'

'Real life usually is,' she said, as he threw off the sheets and flinched at the figure, who snapped at him, teeth bared, spittle flying in all directions.

'Oh, but I love your books!' said Sister Pargeter, clasping her hands together. 'What a thrill!'

Dora said nothing, but flattened herself against the wall, palms pressed flat to the peeling paint, and watched. She was rather pale.

'Esmé Johnson,' said Detective Inspector Fox. 'I arrest you on suspicion of the murders of the Honourable Diana Waters, Sir Edwin Mountjoy and Michael Steyn, as well as the attempted murders of Venetia Strallen, Michael Dryden and, of course, Miss Dora Wildwood—'

He turned to Dora, who had protested. 'No, Miss Wildwood. For once, just be quiet, would you. And sit down. For God's sake, rest.'

'I agree,' said Sister Pargeter. 'Someone will be in trouble if you get ill again, and that's a nasty injury you've had there. And as for you,' she said, turning to Esmé Johnson, who was struggling in her bedclothed straitjacket, as Detective Inspector Fox clapped the handcuffs onto her, 'I'm most surprised, Miss Johnson. I was so looking forward to the new book, too. How disappointing.'

'There won't be a new one,' said Esmé Johnson, struggling against Albert Jubby, her eyes bright with tears. 'You idiotic woman. There won't be a new one. I can see how it looks. It's not me. It's damn well not me, not in the way you think, but you won't believe me; I tried for so long to give you what you wanted, you readers. Always complaining. Always wanting more. It's never enough.' She peered at them, her round, babyish face red, her careful curls in disarray. 'I was in here to make sure you were safe – you won't believe me

Dora gave a short laugh. Oh dear, she found herself thinking. I'm going to have to Say Things. She cleared her throat.

'You've forgotten the other crime,' she said. 'The one that led to all of this in the first place. The real reason these dreadful events took place.'

'Blackmail,' said Detective Inspector Fox, pointing a shaking hand at Esmé Johnson. 'Esmé Johnson,' said Detective Inspector Fox. 'You do not have to say anything if you do not wish to do so, but anything you do say may be used against you—'

'The evidence is all there,' Esmé Johnson said, and she started to laugh hysterically. 'Read the books. It's in every single one of them.' She turned to Dora. 'You know dear, I thought you were brighter than this.' Sergeant Crispin and Albert Jubby had her by the upper arms. Esmé Johnson gave Dora a small, vicious smile, all her little white teeth on display. 'I thought you, *of all people*, would want to work out who the murderer is.'

Dora was very pale, but she said stoutly: 'Well, I can't be right about everything, can I?' Esmé Johnson merely laughed.

'This is ridiculous. I should not be accused like this.' She yanked hard against Albert and Crispin; they tightened their hold on her. 'Good Lord. I've worked hard my entire career to reach the top. Why on earth do you think I'd jeopardise it? Do you know what it takes to get to where I have? Why do you think I risked everything to come here, to warn her?'

'Warn her? You were trying to kill her!' said Fox hotly.

'Dora Wildwood, look to yourself, my girl.' Esmé Johnson stared at Dora, green eyes huge in her round face.

'Take her to the station,' Fox said, anxious not to prolong this. He turned to Dora, who had started to speak. 'No, Miss Wildwood. I must insist you remain in bed. This is in the hands of Scotland Yard.' Dora sank onto the bed, almost with relief, as Sergeant Crispin bustled Miss Johnson, laughing wildly, out. Fox, with satisfaction, stood in the doorway. He was breathing heavily. 'At last. I shall call in on you tomorrow, Miss Wildwood. I hope you continue to recover. But for now, it is done. '

'It's never done,' said Dora blankly. 'But for now, this is enough.'

23

Detective Inspector Fox concludes the chase

Dear Albert

I will be returning to Combe Curry in the next few days but have some business still to complete in London. Could you break into Wildwood House again and hack away at the bramble with the hatchet, if necessary? I am absolutely well again but can't quite face not being able to get back into the house and I do so loathe overdone symbolism. Thank you.

Thank you, too, for coming to my rescue last Wednesday. Dear Albert I was so very glad to see you. It is awfully lonely in London, though I do love it here, but one doesn't realise until one is presented with an old friend how terribly important they are. I hope your journey back was without incident and that the drat- ted wolves have not returned to the village in your absence.

Yes you are right, Charles Silk-Butters is arrested and charged with dangerous driving. He claims never to have met Esmé Johnson, and that she never offered to pay him to inveigle me out of the way but he is in general an unreliable witness as you know. (The magnets, not to mention that pet snail of his he was always saying could recognise him.)

After you have wrestled with the bramble would you do me another favour, Albert dear? Could you nudge Bryony Fulcher Charles's way should you be chatting to her at the next meet? They are alike as two peas in a pod, even down to the mous- tache; I kick myself I didn't notice it before, as it would have solved all my problems. She is horse-mad, strong as an ox, keeps chickens, believes in Mysticism, has teeth virtually at a horizon- tal angle, childhood friend of Baba Metcalfe and if I may be so indelicate is absolutely indiscriminate in matters of the boudoir; in fact she once told me she'd never met a man who could keep up with her either there or on the hunting field. I very much hope he will go to prison; when he is released he can marry her; they should deal very well together.

Dear Albert I do love winter at Wildwood as you know and I ache to be there. Please set aside the sticks as usual for our Midwinter rituals. You asked what is to be done about the giant fungus and the fact that it may well soon have grown to a point where it blows the windows out of the gatehouse. I have written to father to point out it is his responsibility to deal with when he returns, which it looks increasingly likely he will not for some time, being detained waiting for Carine who is currently in a château outside Angers, taking a health cure for an anxious spleen which consists of the administration of raw liver upon the naked body three times a day by an expert in this field, her childhood friend, a count called Giscard d'Andouillette. Father says the château has some exquisite tapestries and he has made friends with a milkmaid in the village. I do not pretend to understand any of this, but for the moment it seems Wildwood House is empty and I will return there and stay some time (only not in the gatehouse).

The trial is set for January and as you say it will be better when it is all over.

I am quite well, only shaken up. I feel very foolish for having been so wrong. There is something I cannot help turning over in my mind, and it is the final piece of the puzzle. I feel my mother very close to me these last few days, as if she is behind me, as she was when I used to write my silly stories in the drawing room, or when I was climbing a tree and about to fall down. She used to hover, unobtrusively. She let me make my mistakes, but she was always there, to help me to try again.

I think she is trying to help me now. As she set off for that final walk in the Alps, with her knapsack on and her sturdy boots and her butterfly net, she did not expect to make a mistake. She did not expect to die. I feel her near me, just as I did immediately after she was killed. It is central to the mystery of her, and me and it is that we all want to be free, and some people will do any-thing to stop us being free Albert. I have worked it out, at last, but I find I shrink from the truth, for it is awful.

Thus I'm certain I must see the business through to the end. But this entire interlude makes me even more sure being a detective is <u>not</u> for me and if I mention it to you again upon my return, you have my permission to tell me to go and boil my head.

Thank you again, dear Albert, and I will write soon.

Your Dora x

She was finishing this letter when someone tapped her on the shoulder. 'Come on, Dora,' said Susan. 'Sorry to shock you. It's only that you walk so slowly these days, we ought to go.'

'Charming.'

Susan grinned. 'I don't want you to have to hurry to the cin-ema, you still being a bit under the weather.'

'I'm extremely well now, thank you. A week in bed has refreshed me enormously,' said Dora. 'Everyone should do it, from time to time.' She stirred her hot chocolate.

'Well, Robert Donat don't wait for anyone. Minnie! You ready? Put on that cape of yours, Dora, and let's get – oh,' she said, her voice changing. 'Look who the cat's dragged in. What do you want?'

'Hello, sis.'

Detective Inspector Fox strode into the warm, quiet dining room. He looked around, uncertainly.

Dora had not seen him since the day in the hospital. 'Detective Inspector Stephen Mavis Fox,' she said, partly to hide the discom-bobulation his presence caused her. 'How do you do.'

He folded his arms and looked down at her. 'I'm fine, thank you. You're rather pale. I hope you're not overdoing it.' He kissed his sister. 'Mum says when are you coming to see her?'

'I'll be over Sunday when I've finished at the café,' said Susan. 'Make sure she's got some nice grub on the table for me. I'm not having scrag end again.'

'She's getting eel pie from Manze's in. No scrag end for the prodigal daughter.'

She nudged him, and laughed. 'Only 'cause I knew how to fix the drains, Steve. Unlike my brother.'

'Oh . . . belt up,' said Stephen Fox, his face a picture.

'He can still do no wrong though,' said Susan, but she was smiling at her brother. 'Whenever he turns up it's like Captain Scott's returned from the Antarctic. Lays out the new china. Does all his washing. She even puts a little sweet on his pillow at night, just like in the Ritz.'

'How do you know what they do in the bedrooms at the Ritz?' asked Minnie, innocently.

'That's enough of that,' said Susan, slapping her friend's wrist. 'Off with you.'

'So,' said Dora, trying not to laugh. – 'Mr Fox, has Esmé Johnson appeared at the magistrates' court yet?'

'No. It's tomorrow. Charles Silk-Butters has, and has been arraigned and sent down. Miss Johnson refuses to leave her cell at Holloway. I don't know why. The publishers tell me they can't print copies of her books fast enough. She's never been so successful. I thought she was the type to milk it for all she can.'

'I went to visit her last week. I asked her not to,' Dora said. She put down her cup.

Fox gaped at her. 'Why would you do that, Miss Wildwood?'

'Ah, well. Something in my mother's favourite book,' said Dora. '*Wuthering Heights*, have you read it?'

He shook his head impatiently.

'Well, you should. It explains everything about passion, and madness and the way women are moulded into a person they frequently have no desire to be. My mother used to quote from it a lot,' said Dora. '"*I wish I were out of doors! I wish I were a girl again, half savage and hardy, and free; and laughing at injuries, not maddening under them! Why am I so changed?*"'

'Ooh, I like that,' said Susan.

Fox said, 'That's all very nice. But what's *Wuthering Heights* got to do with anything?'

'Everything,' said Dora. 'Everything.' She added quietly: 'Sometimes one has to be locked up to understand freedom. I have been thinking an awful lot, in my hospital bed, and back here.' She stood up. 'In fact, I have some unfinished business on the case which I should like to conclude before I return to the countryside and it would be lovely to see you, Mr Dryden, and Miss Strallen, and – oh, various others, to let them know the results of this thinking.'

'You go on, girl,' said Susan admiringly.

'Oh.' Detective Inspector Fox clicked his fingers. 'Well. Dora – Miss Wildwood, perhaps you would attend a meeting at the London library with me? The Acting Chief Librarian would like us to set down the sequence of recent events to the library's board of Trustees. There are several concerns about the direction the library is taking. Someone has suggested rescinding membership to authors of detective novels. You might want to help me—' He blinked, twisting his cap over in his hand. 'I wondered if you could—' He cleared his throat.

'You still don't know how she did it, do you?' said Susan callously. 'You need Dora to explain it to you. Oh, that's rich.' She gave a throaty chuckle. 'Minnie, listen to him. He told Dora she wasn't good enough to be his police pal. And now he's having to come to her – hah! Oh, stop, I'm laughing too much. Cap in hand he is! To beg her to help him. Cap in hand!' She leaned against the wall, struggling for breath and guffawing. Her brother ignored her.

Dora stared at him. 'You do have a nerve, you know,' she said eventually. 'But yes. I will come, even if it means missing the cinema. I've been thinking it all over, you know. Really rather shocking, some of the things I've realised. Thank you for asking me.'

'I'm most grateful,' said Fox.

'I shall see you,' said Dora, reaching for her hat, 'at five p.m. today.'

'No, you won't, because they've asked us for tomorrow at ten,' said Fox, with satisfaction. He flicked his pipe out of his pocket and put it in his mouth.

'I shall see you,' Dora called after him, with some semblance of dignity, 'At ten a.m. tomorrow. Good day, sir.'

'Come on, Dora. Spare Jim's shouting us White Ladies at the Ritz beforehand,' said Susan. 'And now we can go dancing afterwards too. Do hurry up.'

'Yes,' said Dora, putting on her beret and gathering up her gloves. 'Let's hurry. I want to enjoy myself. I've been inside too long, chewing the cud.'

'Disgusting,' said Minnie, who had a pathological fear of cows and would not drink milk. 'It doesn't make sense.'

'It does,' said Dora. 'But they have four stomachs. It starts as grass and it ends up as creamy milk. That's a small miracle. It starts off as one thing and becomes something quite separate. Like caterpillars and butterflies . . .' She stopped. 'Yes. Of course. How foolish of me.'

'What, Dora? Hurry up.'

Dora turned back and scribbled something in her notebook. 'The final piece of the puzzle,' she said. Her eyes were huge; she stared into space. 'How extraordinary.' Minnie and Susan, used to her by now, waited a moment. 'Giraffes, you know, have four compartments in one stomach, not the same thing at all. Oh dear,' she said sadly. 'I wanted to see a giraffe whilst I was in London, and I think I never will.'

'There's time,' said Susan kindly. 'It's Minnie's birthday next week. We could all go then. You're welcome with us any time, Dora.'

'Perhaps,' said Dora. 'You're very kind.'

'Don't say that,' said Susan hastily. 'Shh. Right. You got your gloves on? Finally! We can go.'

Since the Ritz has never been known to make a bad White Lady, and no one has ever not thoroughly enjoyed *The 39 Steps*, an extremely jolly time was had by all.

24

Dora Wildwood untangles the last knot

'Ladies and gentlemen, thank you for coming today,' said Detective Inspector Fox, scanning the thronged Members Room. 'We have asked you here to clear up matters surrounding the various attacks upon the London literary set, if I may so term them—' He cleared his throat lightly, obviously expecting a murmur of assent of some kind but none was forthcoming, and he stumbled over his next words. 'Well so – and forthwith, I should like to ask Miss Dora Wildwood, who has been – ah – essential – to this investigation – to explain the sequence of events.' He sat down, wiping his brow. He thought to himself that he had never perspired until this case. Until he'd met *her*.

'Thank you,' said Dora, standing up. She walked to the large windows that looked out over St James's Square and turned to face them all. It was a beautiful late autumn day. A fire burned cheerily in the grate.

She was not nervous. She told herself this was the last task she had and then she'd go home, back to Wildwood, back to a quiet life.

They were all there: the board of the library and massed ranks of members, Gertrude Jephson, pen poised, Lady Violet Tabor and, next to her, a face like thunder, Richenda Mountjoy. Mikey Clark from the front desk, Zewditu Amani, kind Miss Bunce, and dear Mr Dryden, who seemed to have expanded a little since she last saw him, rather as if he was only now breathing out for the first time. He nodded at her, smiling. *I know you can do this,* he seemed to be saying. She reached for a glass of water, on a table at the end of the second row, and someone touched her arm; she looked round to see Lord Rochford, about whom people only ever said one thing: that he was very well connected. He smiled at Dora in a friendly manner, pressed her arm, and slid something into her pocket.

'A letter for you. Read it later. Good luck, Miss Wildwood,' he said, and she nodded, rather puzzled. Her fingers reached for the note but then she saw that on the row behind him was Ben Stark. He only glanced up, very briefly, his eyes meeting hers.

'Hello, Dora,' he said. 'I'm glad to see you up and about. It sounds rotten.'

'It was. I wanted—'

He simply said: 'Yes. I know. Darling girl. I'm glad you're alive.'

It filled her with strength, warmth, her eyes instantly brimming with tears of joy, the sheer pleasure of simply being able to stand so near to him, so close she could touch him. But she drained the glass of water and did not reply. She did not think she could bear to see those calm grey eyes meeting hers, the understanding in them, the world they held. His crooked, funny smile, his voice as he said things that amused him – oh, she hardly knew him and yet she entirely knew him, bone deep. That was all.

'Good luck, Dora,' someone said from the front row, and she turned to see Venetia Strallen at the end of the row, leaning forwards, and Lady Dreda Uglow next to her. Venetia's beauty, as ever, was breathtaking – it seemed to Dora all the more so because of the lines around her eyes, the faint shadows under them, the ash-blond hair with its tint of silver-grey. Next to her Lady Dreda's face was creased into a multitude of painful expressions, apparently all at the same time. Lady Dreda did not like leaving the house.

Dora stared at Venetia. 'Gosh. I don't know,' she said suddenly. 'I don't know where to start.'

Venetia leaned forwards. In her low, thrilling voice she said: 'Yes, you do, darling. Tell us how you saw it and we can all start to move on from this ghastly business.'

Dora nodded, chewing one nail. 'Yes,' she said, certainty flooding her. 'Thank you, Venetia. You're right.'

*   *   *

'I should like to thank you all for coming,' she said, her voice filling with confidence. 'Detective Inspector Fox has asked me to lay in front of you various facts concerning the murders of four people: the Honourable Diana Waters, shot through the eye with a bullet last August at Morpeth, Neild & Steyn Publishers, in Bedford Square; Sir Edwin Mountjoy, poisoned with arsenic in the London Library three weeks ago, 22nd October 1935, and Mr Michael Steyn, poisoned with cyanide, again at Morpeth, Neild & Steyn Publishers two weeks later, 4th November 1935. Also, the assault resulting in the amputation of a finger upon Mr Amos Longfellow, a printer, at a printing works in Essex in September, Mr Michael Dryden, via poisoning again, and myself, by running me down with a car, to which there was one witness, Lady Natalie Lansdowne. In addition, there is the unsolved and mysterious death of my own mother, Elizabeth Wildwood, in Switzerland, whilst on a butterfly-hunting trip, four years prior to this but I did not, for some time yet, see that this was relevant.'

She paused. The effect on the assembled company of this speech was remarkable. It was obvious that most of them had had no idea they were dealing with more than one murder, and the sum total of the crimes, listed then, was shocking.

'This is terrible,' said Mikey Clark, chewing his fist. 'Here, Dora! What on earth—'

'Shh,' said Zewditu repressively. 'Let her speak.'

'She's all right,' said Ben Stark. 'Dora knows what she's doing.'

If Dora heard any of this she did not react, but went on. 'I like to write things down, and have done since I was a child. It helps me to feel calm, to make sense of things. Often, do you know, simply writing a little list is most soothing.' She opened her notebook, in which she had kept copious lists since her arrival in London. 'Several points struck me the day after I arrived and found Sir Edwin's body in the library. I should like to read them out to you, if I may.

'The first, and most singular point to strike me, was that no one liked Sir Edwin Mountjoy, his sister aside.' She ignored Richenda Mountjoy's furious, icy expression. 'He was not a good man and it is germane to the mystery of his death, as at that point I could – and I think anyone could – identify five or six people who had reason to want him dead. And that this seemed to be the point at which the mystery had begun.

'But it had not. In addition, before his death, someone had been removing books from the library, cutting them out of their binding, filleting out the pages they wanted, then returning the empty shells of those books to the shelves. There were two notable facts. The novels were old, and had not sold many copies. Their authors languished in obscurity – only two were alive and only one of those, Mr E.L. Palmer, troubled the library with the tales of woe over his titles that were mysteriously being defaced. He was dismissed by Mountjoy as a crank; I did not understand why until later. With the help of Miss Amani, I was able to compile a list of every one of the books that had been defaced in this way in the library. She tracked them down, some of them fifty years old or more, scouring booksellers and libraries across the city. She read the ones she could find. She wrote a list summarising them which I have here too.' Dora waved the paper. 'Do you know what's interesting about this piece of paper? The plot of every single one of these books bar one has been lifted straight and used in another, more recent, novel.'

A rustle of interest blew across the room, as a dry log crackled in the grate, sending out sparks. 'What does that mean, Dora?' Venetia Strallen said, her hands clasped. 'Who was using the books?'

'A good question, Miss Strallen.' Dora cleared her throat. Detective Inspector Fox watched her warily. He knew Dora Wildwood by now, too well. He knew she was getting too comfortable up there. He was certain a story about some primitive aspect of life in Combe Curry was about to rear its ugly head. He'd been there a couple of weeks ago, poking around, to meet that local druid she kept talking about. Find out a bit more about where she'd come from. What her mother was like. Whether this fiancé was real or not. And no one would tell him anything. He hadn't even been able to see inside Wildwood House. Literally, because a thorny bush of some description was pressing up against the windows. From the inside. 'And you don't even want to see what's in the gatehouse,' Albert Jubby had told him, darkly. Fox had returned to London as soon as he could.

'In fact,' Dora went on, waving her finger, 'Sir Edwin's murder was the latest in a series of crimes committed by a desperate person – a person intent on concealing their first crime – a minor crime it would seem in comparison – the crime of plagiarism.

'But ladies and gentlemen –' Dora looked up at the massed ranks of the great and good, hanging on her every word, at Richenda Mountjoy's outraged scowl, at Venetia next to her, leaning forwards, her dark eyes huge in her pale face – 'the trouble with plagiarism is it is not just a crime in itself, it is a crime that damages the soul. It is taking the work of one person and passing it off as your own. It is like the greenfly on the roses every summer, sucking the very sap out of the flower, its essence, the reason for its success, its scent, its beauty. That is what the plagiarist does. And Esmé Johnson, whom most of you will know was the protégé of Venetia Strallen, knew all about plagiarism.

'On a page in my notebook I drew a triangle. *Stealing books – stealing livelihood – stealing lives.*' She held it up. 'I came to see that the person who had been cutting out these pages from the books was desperate – so desperate that they would do anything to protect themselves. Yet there was one book which tripped them up. It was the damaged book that Sir Edwin discovered, the afternoon of his murder. *The Killing Jar*, by Cora Carson – not a work of fiction, but an examination of killing practices of butterflies in the valley near Montreux, in Switzerland. Coincidentally, I thought, it was where my mother died. It is a dry, academic work. A warning? A sign? A clue? I think the intention there was never to plagiarise it. But to prevent anyone else reading it. Why? What was in it? With long-forgotten detective novels of the late Victorian and Edwardian era no one was particularly concerned. Such novels are ten-a-penny, they say. It is the lot of the novelist to be so disregarded. But this was a beautiful book, with ten colour plates, presented to the library by its author. And someone wanted it removed.

'Sir Edwin found it, mutilated and torn into pieces on the floor. He already knew that someone was stealing books and defacing them, but not to what purpose. But when he found *The Killing Jar* mutilated and in its place inserted *The Guilty Fiancé*, a work in which Miss Johnson hints, yet again, at a relationship between an odious man and a glamorous lady novelist, he was able, I think, to put two and two together.'

She paused. 'Who knows why the murderer saw fit to put that book there in its place. But in doing so they showed their true colours and they made their first mistake.

'He marched to the Stacks, with the book in his hand, to see if there were other books so defaced. But he had already eaten arsenic, you see. The arsenic sent to him by a friend in a box of Turkish delight from Fortnum & Mason. He had not felt well when he arrived back from lunch with Venetia Strallen. She said they had a picnic and ate everything, but there was no Turkish delight in the picnic and the autopsy later revealed his stomach was almost empty.

'Miss Bunce, Sir Edwin's secretary, said she did not stop him wandering off into the Stacks because she, along with so many others, was afraid of him. And there he met his death. In fact, he had been poisoned with arsenic. He had been stuffing his face with Turkish delight all week. He had not felt well for days, but kept eating the sweetmeats. He was greedy man. Everyone knew that.'

Richenda Mountjoy gave a small, barking sob. Gertrude Jephson, next to Miss Bunce, patted her arm in a comforting manner. 'Dreadful man,' she said, in a too-loud whisper.

'We come to the third point, the attempts to silence those who got in the way, beginning with the threat on Mr Dryden's life. Someone sent him a box of Turkish delight, smothered in arsenic mixed into the icing sugar. It was, in fact, the same kind of box of Turkish delight Sir Edwin had fatally consumed. Why was the murderer afraid of Mr Dryden? Because they thought he knew more than he did, in particular that *The Killing Jar* was the book that Sir Edwin had discovered defaced. *But he did not know this.* In addition, I myself was subject to an attack by an angry ex-fiancé – I believed, at the time, that this was a dreadful case of sour grapes, but only afterwards did I see that Charles Silk-Butters, my ex-intended, had been set up by someone else, someone who wanted to get rid of me and who had put him up in an hotel, and told him he should not leave town without me otherwise the stain on his name would be too great. Yes, this person was an arch manipulator, but they were also making mistakes. The two boxes of Turkish delight, sent to two men – it showed they were desperate, running out of ideas.'

Dora paused here, and lifted her eyes to the door, opening almost silently, to the tiny figure creeping into the back of the large room, unseen by the majority. 'The irony of all this is the murderer plagiarised several novels, but their narrative there was most powerful. By convincing this desperate, bullying man of my guilt they nearly succeeded in pulling off the perfect murder – getting someone else to do the crime for them. It almost worked. It almost led to my death.'

'The fourth point concerns the murder of the Honourable Diana Waters—' But she was interrupted.

'Dora,' said Venetia Strallen, clearing her throat. 'Aren't you going to mention the attacks on me? They were obviously by the same person – Esmé is very strong, as you know—'

'No, I'm not,' said Dora. 'For the reason that those attacks didn't happen, as you know.'

Venetia's head turned to one side, if she had been slapped. 'What are you talking about?'

'Thank you, Miss Strallen. I will come to them in a minute.

'The events at Morpeth, Neild & Steyn are the most heinous, to my mind, of the whole affair. An innocent girl was found dead on the street outside, and it was seen as the work of someone linked with drugs, the seamy underbelly of London's gangsters, the cocaine-addled bohemian wastrels in Bloomsbury and Chelsea – yes, this line was pushed from the start without anyone really supposing that it was to do with the deceased's line of work.' Dora avoided Detective Inspector Fox's eye. 'There was undoubtedly a failure to investigate further. Diana Waters was Mr Steyn's assistant, remember, drawing up most confidential documents and letters, helping Mr Steyn in his work. She had seen so much, and she knew where the bodies were buried – forgive the pun, but it applies in this case, both literally and literarily.' Dora allowed herself a small smile here and saw Ben Stark rolling his eyes, a smile playing across his face as if to say: *now is not the time, Dora.*

'The Honourable Diana Waters was a young society beauty who had, to her parents' consternation, refused to conform in several ways. She insisted on earning a living: taking a job at a publishing house, getting the bus into Bloomsbury every day, consorting with artists and other types, instead of going to finishing school, meeting other debutantes in Harrods and going for ballgown fittings in Belgravia. The other ways in which she did not conform need not concern us now.' Dora cleared her throat, and went on. 'She incurred the wrath of Esmé Johnson early on in her tenure at the publishers, for reasons unspecified, and Esmé wanted her gone. Diana's great friend and – and – her confidante – Lady Natalie Lansdowne is here today and is willing to testify in court as to various occurrences in the months Diana worked for Mr Steyn.' Stephen Fox turned, scanning the room for this new witness, who was sitting by herself in the back row, tiny, slight, in black, but utterly composed.

'During that time three separate claims of plagiarism were filed; responsibility for dealing with and processing these claims rested with Diana Waters. It was an important task but one which Miss Waters was able to fulfil. She was a capable young woman. One summer's evening, having asked Mr Steyn to sign the final letter settling payment to the blackmailer, Diana Waters left Bedford Square.

'She had asked for the day off the following day and was bound for Brighton on an evening train. Her friend Lady Natalie, who was waiting for her, watched as she fell backwards, collapsing to the ground. Only later did the police think to search the garden of the square. It is large, luxuriantly green – and it was discovered that, exactly opposite where Diana Waters had been standing when she was attacked there was a trampled section of bush and grass, where clearly the murderer was waiting for her, and where they fired the gun that killed her at close quarters. A small pistol, with a mother-of-pearl handle, small enough to fit in a pocket. Diana Waters had turned to face the murderer, and was shot through the eyeball.'

There were gasps, and moans, from the audience. 'Miss Wildwood—' Stephen Fox cleared his throat as if to interrupt, but Dora cast him a compelling glance and he shrank back against the fireplace, dodging out of the way when the flames licked at his backside.

'Diana Waters was twenty-two.' Dora cleared her throat, her eyes drifting to the back of the room. 'She did not deserve to die, but she knew too much about the practices of those who had secrets to conceal. Michael Steyn, the publisher, had enabled those practices, turned a blind eye to them for too long, but soon he, too, became a liability: nervous, on the verge of revealing too much, and so he, too, had to be murdered – a tragic event at which I was, unhappily, present. And I started to see that this was not revenge, or jealousy, or hatred, or madness. It was simpler than that. It was that an author had to keep her place at the top.'

Dora shifted her weight, glancing up to make sure Detective Inspector Fox and Sergeant Crispin were in place, at the back of the room. 'Three years ago Esmé Johnson, an ambitious young woman who desired above all things money and fame, started to work for Venetia Strallen as her secretary and researcher. Almost immediately it became obvious to all that Miss Strallen, whilst talented, was under immense pressure. She had come back from a private trip to Switzerland, where she was gathering material for her new novel, depleted and depressed. She had once been the toast of literary London – she was beautiful, witty, clever, and the novels were so very good – weren't they, Miss Strallen?'

'I really don't understand what you're talking about, darling Dora,' said Venetia Strallen, blinking. The glittering diamond on her left hand revolved between her fingers. 'I don't much care for the insinuations, either, so do please explain yourself.'

'Very well,' said Dora. 'I will. You're a good writer, but in common with many writers you're something of an egotist, and you stopped wanting to work so terribly hard. And it *is* hard work, strangely enough. I think being a successful author became a double-edged sword – you had to grind away producing more words for so long that I think it became a burden, not a pleasure. And you started running out of ideas.'

Dora paused. She looked at Venetia Strallen, who was very still.

'Esmé wanted fame at any cost. She was a pharmacist's daughter from Beckenham, thrilled to be working with a lady novelist at the summit of her profession, one who could ease her passage into the world of literary London, show her the ropes. But Venetia Strallen was not interested in helping anyone up. She had got there herself by hard graft – the two of them are more alike than they'd cared to admit – her father was a doctor who, to her disgust, went out to India with her mother to help lepers. My godmother remembers her pain at what she saw as this abandonment by them at a young age. She had won a scholarship to a girls' boarding school where she met the right sort of friends, and she possessed a beauty that secured her admirers and gifts which she shrewdly used at every opportunity—' Lady Dreda, next to her friend, slowly turned towards her, but Venetia did not meet her questioning stare. 'Most of all she knew how to write, and she knew how to present herself. She had worked so very hard, for fifteen years. She didn't want anyone – *anyone* – to get in her way; she had dealt with those who did, so far. She had recovered from the events in Switzerland. She had to stay on top, give more and more every year. Others were snapping at her heels. The pressure was too much for her. And there was Esmé, this ghastly little upstart, bobbing about talking about how she wanted to write, how she was going to be a success.

'Venetia had dealt with rivals before, seen them off. But Esmé was different. Esmé was persistent, like fungus in gatehouses, or fiancés who don't understand the word no. And so when Esmé Johnson – who is quite safe at this very minute in Holloway gaol – discovered, quite by chance, that Venetia Strallen was staying late in the London Library, prowling the Fiction shelves for works of detective or mystery fiction, and then – yes, cutting out and copying the plots herself for her own books – she had the information she needed. She never revealed herself to Venetia Strallen – that would have been too obvious. She sent threatening letters asking for money to her, care of the publishers. She wasn't interested in the money, though of course it helped. She was interested in destroying the woman who had refused to help her and needed, as she saw it, taking down a peg or two. Of course, she denies all this. I think she'd rather be hanged for murder than admit she's a common blackmailer.

'But she left Venetia Strallen caught in a trap, for three years or more, and like a trapped animal she struggled, lashing out, trying to take down or contain the person responsible. And after a while, I am afraid, when she saw there was no way out, she turned again to murder. For she had killed before, anyone who had got in her way. I am certain Venetia knew it was Esmé who was blackmailing her. But she did not need to kill Esmé Johnson. She could use the blackmailing against her – they were locked in a dance of death together, the one as bad as the other, the plagiarist and the blackmailer. But there were others, in danger of discovering how she maintained her position at the top. And they had to go.'

Silence gripped the room. Lady Dreda turned to her best friend again. 'Venetia darling,' she said, and Dora could hear the effort she took to keep her tone light. 'Really, how exhausting. It can't be true, can it?'

'Be very careful,' said Venetia Strallen, standing up, and point-ing at Dora. 'My friends are here. You can't make accusations like that. You! An eccentric little beanpole, tied to your mother's apron strings, who barely left home till you were shunted off to boarding school, for you to have the *nerve* . . . !'

'I am my mother's daughter, Miss Strallen, and that is precisely what gives me the nerve, as you very well know,' said Dora calmly. 'Do sit down, please.

'For a while Miss Strallen contrived to attract Sir Edwin's attentions – not difficult, given her beauty, and success, and his corpulence, and loneliness – and thus was given a reason to be at the library; she was given status, the chance to stop writing and do nothing, and for a while it seemed that would work out very well, thank you. I think she started to see this would be her way out. To stop having to have ideas! To stop being hunched over the typewriter! But Venetia herself, in *The Valley of Death*, wrote the words *Keep going. You didn't come this far just to come this far*, and I think she realised after a while that they applied to her. To want to give up is one thing. To be constrained, and kept captive, like a beautiful butterfly, fluttering on display –' here Dora looked directly at Venetia, for the first time – 'unable to be free – when one has worked all one's life to be independent, to live well. I do have sympathy with you for that.'

'Slander,' murmured Richenda Mountjoy, leaning back in her chair, eyes shut. 'Dreadful slander.'

'It's not much fun, knowing the rest of your life will be with this man, is it? That your property is his, your life is, effectively, in his hands. And then Sir Edwin discovered it was she who was defacing library books – possibly he caught her one night, when they were both at the Library – and when he confronted her about it, she was unable to disguise her scorn, her derision, her belief he was a laugh-ing stock. The joke of a man like him, who knew nothing about books, heading up a library, who could not see how lucky he was, lucky to have ensnared her, lucky to be where he was. Venetia Stral-len has always believed she was slightly better than everyone else.

'I think there was a dreadful row one lunchtime at her flat in Mecklenburgh Square – perhaps contrived, perhaps not – and by the time Sir Edwin came back into the library he was furious. And this is how I think events unfolded. He sits down at his desk, full of venomous rage at this woman who has ensnared him, so he sees it. He pulls out the central drawer, his hidden stash of sweetmeats, and starts eating Turkish delight. The results of the autopsy show there was hardly any food, but arsenic in his stomach from the days before. He has not felt well for a while. Perhaps he has found evidence in Venetia's flat, perhaps she has revealed too much to him – we will never know. But he is humiliated, cornered, and angry. He has, of course, been poisoned, with the same Turkish delight which Mr Dryden was sent a few days later. Venetia prides herself on doing her own research, and she knows her business when it comes to poison. Sir Edwin shouts at the staff, in the Issue Hall, then storms up to the Science and Nature section in high dudgeon, holding the hardback shell of the latest book Venetia has ruined – why? We shall see presently – and that is where the poison overcomes him, his heart gives out, and he is found minutes later, by me.'

'This is absolutely ridiculous,' said Venetia Strallen. Her fine nostrils flared, in contemptuous humour.

Dora ignored her. 'We come to the other murders and attempted murders. The attempts are easy to deal with – Venetia Strallen staged both attempts on her life herself – the alleyway incident did not happen beyond her scraping her own arm against the wall, and the events in her flat where graffiti and threatening messages were left everywhere was a dramatic if sloppy attempt to disguise any incriminating evidence. Venetia had not had a chance to tidy up since the disastrous picnic where she and Sir Edwin had their final war of words. She had no choice but to vandalise her own flat before absenting herself before the police called round, then going out to supper with her friend Lady Dreda Uglow. It was she who soaked the letters from Sir Edwin in water, she who faked her devastation at their loss but of course she who knew they could not be kept, showing as they did the deterioration in their relationship, from adoration on his side to contempt and fury.

'Esmé Johnson, of course, suspected all this and had gone round to Mecklenburgh Square, perhaps to extract evidence. Had the police entered with her as Esmé Johnson wished they would have found, of course, the shells of the books, not all of them – she disposed of them eventually, after she had used the ideas therein – but the one she was most anxious to keep from others: *The Killing Jar*, by Cora Carson.

'Now this is the book I have mentioned several times before and which I have read, having my own copy which was sent to my father by the author, some time after my mother's death. It mentions in passing, and without naming names, the story of a talented amateur lepidopterist, who had gone missing and was found dead, but the details were very vague. It is a story not mentioned anywhere else, but known to Professor Carson because she was staying in the same hut at the same time . . .' Dora waved a letter in the air. 'I wrote to her, and she was able to fill me in on the details of that trip, of two old friends who went away together on holiday to Switzerland, of how one of them uncovered the secrets the other was trying to keep, how the first woman begged her friend to turn herself back from this path, of how angry the friend was. . .' Dora paused, gathering herself together, and cleared her throat. 'Professor Carson had left the hut and moved on the day before that last fatal argument but later she recalled it, and wondered if she had unwittingly overlooked someone's murder. She gave me the details quite freely, when I asked for them. She had included it in the book as an example of why the keen butterfly hunter keeps chasing butterflies, even at great personal risk. But . . . we must leave that trail. For now. For now . . .'

Fox glanced around him. The audience was still, frozen in time, willing her on. He saw, with curiosity, the agony written on the face of Ben Stark. How he sat forwards, lightly in his seat, his lanky, easy frame alert, eyes never leaving her, ready to jump up, to rush to the front if she needed him.

Well well, Fox thought to himself, and he was obscurely angry. That's how the wind sits, then.

'Venetia Strallen murdered her friend because she stopped being on Her Side. People have to be on Miss Strallen's side. Mr Dryden, who had formerly been on her side, was in danger once she saw he might discover it was she who had been defacing the books.

'I had no idea,' said Mr Dryden, shaking his head, his eyes filled with tears. 'None at all. I feel very stupid.'

'Dear Mr Dryden, it is your good nature that makes you so exceptional a candidate for the job of Chief Librarian, and it will,' said Dora briskly, 'be an outrage if it is not given to you. Do not trouble yourself. Me? she wanted to bump off, because she knew I'd seen the book on the floor, before she'd had a chance to put it back on the shelf, pages filleted and all. I am Elizabeth Wildwood's daughter, one of her oldest friends, and she was terrified I would start to remember, would start to ask who the friend who was on holiday with my mother was – my mother never told us she was going with Venetia, of course, she wanted to tackle her in private, in the Alps, away from everyone else. That trust was what killed her. Even their other old friend, Lady Dreda Uglow, had no idea Venetia had been in Switzerland when my mother fell to her death. Venetia must have worried I would wonder. But I didn't. I didn't realise, of course, that my closeness to my mother blinded me to the truth for rather too long.

'Venetia was waiting in a remote part of the library, Parliamentary Records. It is where she later hid herself. After she had watched Sir Edwin die, two floors below, she waited again until I found the body then nipped back to remove the book, just to be on the safe side. Happily I remembered what the book was.' Dora tapped her forehead. She caught Stephen Fox looking at her, surpressing a smile. 'And then I started investigating, and she really didn't like it. It was she who had bumped into, and then charmed my erstwhile fiancé, Charles Silk-Butters, into staying on in London, and paid for him to stay at the Langham. She touched on his vanity, told him that I should be "brought to heel". But sadly for her he could not accomplish this.

'The deaths of Diana Waters and Michael Steyn were especially cruel. Diana, as I've said, had her life in front of her, and was utterly unconnected with Miss Strallen's web of deceit, but such was her paranoia, her all-consuming lust to vanquish Miss Johnson that she could not let her live whilst there was a chance Diana could spill the beans about what she'd done. And Michael Steyn – dear, anxious, jolly, disorganised Michael – he who took her to Sheekey's for lunch and flattered her and wrote letters to booksellers telling them how marvellous her latest was, even when it wasn't, who said no to Penguin so the demand grew even greater, who never challenged her over her plagiarism and helped her more than he should, dear Michael, who'd been with her from the beginning, even he had to go. He knew he had helped create the monster. And he knew too much.

'The cyanide was fast-acting. He immediately understood he was being poisoned. You had visited him that morning, before Dauntry Forbes was in – you had your suspicions about him – and whilst you were waiting you contrived to poison the ground beans. He used a special blend, which everyone knew. Michael Steyn was a good man. He'd escaped a pogrom in Odessa as a child. His parents came to England with nothing at all; he had taught himself to read English. And you took all that away, as you did for poor Diana. All those lives, lost. Those books, stolen. For what? For your ego.'

Venetia clapped, very slowly. 'Darling,' she said, her glittering eyes wider than ever, her humorous smile fixed. 'This is gripping indeed, worthy of an Esmé Johnson – it's a little too sensationalist for me you understand. But sadly, you've no proof.'

'I must say,' said a sonorous voice from the second row. 'Miss Strallen is correct. There is no proof at all. A dear lady is being defamed in the most damaging terms.'

'Thank you, Lord Rochford,' said Venetia, turning slightly towards him. 'Some sense, at last.'

'I say let the girl finish,' said Gertrude Jephson, rising slightly from her chair, and patting at her coil of hair. 'She's almost done, and my instinct is that we should listen to her. But still: where's the proof, Miss Wildwood? Eh?'

Dora didn't flinch. 'Miss Amani?' she said. 'Would you give me the list, please?'

'Of course,' said Zewditu Amani. She stood up, smoothing down her blue-and-green silk skirt, and moved to the front of the room, smiling at the assembled group, most of whom had their arms folded by now. They did not want to believe. They wanted this to be a farrago of nonsense. It was . . . easier that way.

'Here,' said Zewditu, 'is a list of Venetia Strallen books, and next to it the books that have been damaged and their similarities to Miss Strallen's books. It's really quite striking.'

'A few details, here and there,' said Venetia, laughing. 'It's hardly indicative – there are five plots, you know, dear girl, maybe you should read more English novels . . .'

'Oh I have,' said Miss Amani brightly. 'I've read pretty much every book in the Fiction section, you know. I came to London from Ethiopia with my father, who worked in the High Commission, and I have lived here since I was five. English people aren't as friendly as I'd have hoped, not to start with. And I did not have Bertie then.'

'Bertie is her dachshund,' put in Dora, helpfully.

'So I read a lot. Every section of the library, from A to Z. Apples to zoos, you know. Books, you see,' she said, quietly, 'books keep you company when there is no one else. Here, let me read the opening lines of Paul Frederick's *The Parsonage Affair*, first published in 1902:

> *The smoking car lay on its side, wheels gently turning in the ditch.*
> *'Oh dear!' said George Dubois. 'Ten miles from Edgbaston*
> *and the engine has overheated! What shall we do, my dear?'*
> *His wife, a long-suffering brunette named Evangeline, folded*
> *her hands and smiled at him. 'Nothing else for it, my dear.*
> *Have to throw ourselves on the mercy of the local parson. I say!*
> *There's the rectory, now.'*

'And Venetia Strallen's *Whisky, Soda and Arsenic*:

> *The car lay on its side, wheels gently turning in the ditch.*
> *'Oh blast!' said Tommy Duval. 'Ten miles from the Oval and*
> *the axle has given out! What shall we do, my dear?'*
> *His wife, a long-suffering blonde, snapped her compact case*
> *shut and smiled at him. 'I'm gasping for a drink. Nothing else for*
> *it, m'dear. Have to throw ourselves on the mercy of the local par-*
> *son. I say! There's the rectory, now.'*

Zewditu Amani closed both books and took out the piece of paper again. 'It wouldn't matter, because they're both good books, but I did some sleuthing myself, and Paul Fredericks died in poverty a couple of years ago, aged eighty-two. He had no idea an updated version of his novel would be the Book Club choice and sell over a hundred thousand copies in one year alone.'

'Doesn't seem very fair,' said Dora, to Venetia Strallen. 'Does it.'

'Maybe, but it's not proof I murdered anyone,' said Venetia Strallen. She folded her arms, her mouth set. She was deathly calm.

'Oh, but we have proof of that, too,' said Dora. 'Because someone here today saw you murder Diana Waters, hiding in the bushes in Bedford Square then casually strolling away. She saw you, because she was hiding too, because she did not want to be spotted. She saw you call out to Diana, saw her turn towards you. She saw you shoot her in the face. She has lived with that ever since, in silence, and she is now strong enough to testify against you in court—'

And then Lady Natalie Lansdowne stood up. 'Yes,' she said, softly, gripping tightly onto the back of the chair in front. 'I am.'

At the sound of her voice, Ben Stark stood up, immediately walking around the assembled throng, and went to her, holding her hand. 'Natalie,' Dora heard him murmur. 'Why didn't you tell me?'

He put his arm around her, very gently, and they sat down together, she gripping his hand.

Dora blinked hard, turning back to Venetia Strallen.

She was very white, and her face was pinched, its great, transfixing beauty suddenly repellent. Dora saw the guileless sparkling blue eyes, how full of hate they were, how yellow her teeth, how careful, how beautiful but repellent every bit of her really was.

'Well, jolly well done, Dora,' she said. 'It's extraordinary really, that you've pulled this farrago off. It won't hold up, but jolly good luck trying.'

'What about this?' Detective Inspector Fox said, holding up a piece of paper. 'Natalie Lansdowne removed this from Diana Waters' body. It's the letter she was taking to keep safe at home at his urging. It is to Michael Steyn. It threatens him with murder. I'd be interested to have the handwriting analysed.' He read out:

> *I have said before that I will do what needs to be done to main-tain the status quo, Michael. Be in no doubt that this is still true. I will destroy you if you try to expose me.*

'That,' said Dora, 'the testimony of the shop girl who recognised you as Venetia Strallen, even though you were wearing a beret and a muffler and speaking in a French accent, and who remembers selling you a box of Turkish delight, then another a week later, the fact your thumb print is on the gun which you hid under a floorboard in a panic at Dreda's, the fingerprints of yours all over the books in the Butterfly sub-section of Science & Nature – as well as the witness to a murder, is a compelling case, you must admit.'

'Damn you,' said Venetia Strallen, bolting from her chair, but Dora clutched at her fiercely, wrapping her arms round her and squeezing her tight.

'Let me go, you little bitch,' Venetia Strallen hissed. She managed to free one arm, and waved it about, and Dora saw with horror the sinews, the dense, ropy musculature of her upper arms and realised how strong she was. She stared into her sparkling blue eyes, and saw with fascination and horror they were completely blank, nothing behind them at all.

'Venetia Strallen,' Fox intoned. 'I arrest you on suspicion of . . .'

Dora did not hear the rest; a cloud had descended over her, sucking the sunlight and energy she had stored, and she sat down, abruptly, on the chair, head in her hands. Venetia Strallen started to protest, and then suddenly she hissed, a long, low, heavy exhalation, her eyes like slits, her teeth bared, like a cornered animal, and her shoulders drooped, as Stephen Fox clapped the handcuffs on her.

'Well Dora. This is a nightmare,' said Lady Dreda Uglow, turning towards her goddaughter, looking pale. 'What on earth have you wrought, my dear girl?' Dora looked up, hands still covering her face. 'I'm very, very proud of you. 'I don't know how – I don't understand *any* of it. But my God, dear girl, your mother would be so very proud too. I wish . . .' She trailed off.

'Thank you, dear Dreda,' Dora said. She watched, without expression, as Ben Stark and Natalie Lansdowne left the room, his arm firmly around her, neither of them turning back.

'You did marvellously,' said Michael Dryden, coming up to her. He patted her arm fondly. 'Honestly, when I think that two weeks ago . . . You've saved us, Dora, saved me in so many ways.'

'It was nothing,' said Dora, untruthfully. She swallowed. 'Oh goodness, it is all so awful, isn't it.'

'My dear,' said Lady Dreda. 'Can I ask you what you believe happened in Switzerland?'

'Switzerland,' said Dora, as if returning from far away, and she cleared her throat, looking at them both, aware that Venetia was listening to her, as Fox put the handcuffs on her and read her her rights. 'I won't be able to prove it, but I think Venetia Strallen killed my mother out in the mountains north of Montreux. Venetia went at the last minute, you see. I did not know she'd been there. No one did, apart from Michael Steyn. My mother had always said Venetia needed taking care of. She used to talk about her as if she was deserving of special treatment. So dangerous, you know. Poor Muzz. I suspect she asked her along, to try to talk to her: I think my mother started to see what she was up to – she was like me, you see, she could just see things, I can't explain it. I think Muzz tried to bring her back from the brink and they rowed, and Venetia saw Elizabeth was more dangerous to her alive than dead and the way – the way to do it was to push her to her death.' Dora paused.

'There were a few points about my mother's death that didn't make sense to me,' she said lightly. 'I was seventeen at the time. It rather started me off, thinking, puzzling, trying to understand. I always wondered why the butterfly net wasn't broken.

The line was that she had been hunting, had slipped and fallen. But Venetia must have taken it off her before she pushed her. Or perhaps she was holding it for my mother as she used the killing jar. I won't ever know. They found her, at the bottom of the ravine; she was lying in a small stream, quite happily really, there were spring flowers everywhere. She loved spring. And it was easy for Venetia to return to England, to carry on with life.' She turned to Venetia, standing, shoulders sloped, the glitter on her jacket, her hands, dulled in the cloudy light from the big windows. 'To lose the irritation of my mother telling her she was doing the wrong thing.

'So she could go on, writing. Signing autographs. Making money. After all, she'd worked so very hard for it, hadn't she? I think the final straw for her was *The Guilty Fiancé*, Esmé Johnson's thinly-veiled account of my mother's murder, which I have read and bears little relation to the events, and was nothing more than Esmé making suppositions – correct ones – in order to rattle Venetia's cage. The irony,' she added, 'that Esmé Johnson was really very like her, is lost on both of them. And that reminds me,' she said to Fox. 'She can be released now, can't she?'.

'I'll have her out tomorrow,' he said. 'Don't worry. She told me she's got an idea for a marvellous new book set in Holloway.'

Venetia Strallen gave a cry of anguish.

'How could you, Venetia?' Lady Dreda said to her friend. 'All that talent, the joy of the job – how could you, darling?' Next to her, Maria stared at her, her eyes burning with anger. 'And how could you have hidden the gun in my house? After you'd killed that poor girl!'

'I had to hide it somewhere. I had to get rid of it. I knew there was a loose floorboard in that room from the time I'd stayed there. What else was I supposed to do? Keep it? It was fun, really, tricking you. Scrabbling around on my knees, lifting that board up with my fingernails, hoping that maid who has ideas above her station wouldn't catch me, but I almost hoped she would, then I'd drag her into it and blame her for something . . .' She stared at

Maria. 'I never liked you, you know. Creeping up to Dreda, with your drawings and your clothes and your *wanting to get on* . . . oh it's all so tedious . . .'

Standing next to Detective Inspector Fox, handcuffed, Venetia was a deflated person, air draining out of her, as if she were flaking away, insubstantial, nothing to her. Her face seemed grey, the animation that gave her so much of her beauty gone. 'It's over. No more of it all,' she said, her voice halting as if she were literally running out of energy. 'More titles, more intrigue. More words, always more words. The publishers, the fans, the booksellers, always wanting *more*. Sign this, charm that person, send a free book here, write that person a letter, more words, more words . . . Address this audience, wear these pearls, go to that dinner party . . . more words, always, always more words until you've none left . . . Trying to stay on top of it all, always, one step ahead . . . And then . . . him.' She gave a shudder. '*Him* . . . He always wanted more, and it was never enough.' She gave a wild, high laugh. 'And now I don't have to ever again. I don't have to have any damned ideas, ever again. Ever again. I'm sorry about Elizabeth.' She turned to Dora, baring her little yellow teeth, as if she might bite her. 'But she was like you – she saw too much and she thought the world was full of goodness. She was utterly wrong.' And then she pulled her jacket collar around her, and shook her hair, standing upright, as if to face an audience. Behind her, Detective Inspector Fox slid his arm through hers, ready to escort her out of the library for the final time, and Venetia Strallen smiled her beautiful, intoxicating smile and turned to Dora. 'Well, I expect you're happy now, aren't you?'

'On the contrary,' Dora Wildwood said. 'I am very unhappy.'

*　　*　　*

And she turned and walked out of the warm, wood-panelled room, out into the clear, golden November day, carrying the little suitcase she had brought with her three weeks ago when she'd arrived. She walked through Green Park, through the piles of leaves sifted into brown, crisp drifts, past Buckingham Palace and Marble Arch, and the Serpentine, where two lone swimmers were splashing about in the autumnal cold. She walked over the bridge, watching the lovers holding hands, the Daimlers purring down Park Lane, the newspapermen selling the latest edition of the *Evening News*.

When she reached the other side of the park, and the white stucco mansions of Bayswater, she walked through quiet garden squares and falling leaves until she reached Paddington station. The whole walk had taken her under an hour.

'Well, it was an adventure,' she said to herself. The train pulled out of the station, and she stared through the soot-flecked window, feeling quite flat. She popped the last of the peppermint creams in her mouth, letting it melt slowly. 'But in the end I didn't even see a giraffe.'

It was not until she was almost home, passing through Crumpton Mangy that she found the note. It was neatly folded and dropped inside a capacious pocket of her cape; she had forgotten all about it.

> *Dear Miss Wildwood*
>   *I dare not approach you during this morning's meeting but am extremely desirous of your help. Knowing how exceptional your work on this dreadful business has been, I wondered if I might treat you to tea one day, perhaps at the Ritz?*

'Dash it,' said Dora, half standing up so that the nervous young man opposite her, who had asked if he might close the window for he was afraid of flying soot smuts, gave a strangled yelp of alarm. 'I say! Someone wants to take me to the Ritz. For tea.'

'How m-marvellous,' said the young man, hand at his throat, eyes bulging with fear. 'Good for – for you.'

Dora smiled at him, sat back down and carried on reading.

It is a most confidential and delicate matter. A year ago a Brownie Pack and Girl Guiding Company was established at Buckingham Palace, for the young princesses and their friends, to teach them about friendship, duty and service. I am very sorry to say that last week, their Brown Owl was murdered. We have reason to believe she was in possession of secrets about HM Queen Mary that, if discovered, could be extremely damaging to Crown, and country.

If you think you can be of any help in this matter, I should be most grateful.

Please burn this letter.

Yours truly,

Lord Rochford

Equerry to Her Majesty Queen Mary

Dora tore the letter into small pieces. She stood up again, opening the window, throwing the squares out into the fresh air, like confetti. She watched them fly away, then reached up to take her case down. She did not see the large clod of soot fly in and hit her unsuspecting fellow passenger gently in the face, like soft, black snow. She thought of her mother, of her favourite Madeira cake, of butterflies, and of freedom.

'Excuse me,' she said to the guard, further down the carriage. 'I have to get off the train!'

'We're not at Combe Curry yet, my dear,' he said.

'No, I know,' Dora said, in a tone that sounded like weariness but was, in fact, masking intense joy. 'I'm needed in town again to solve a murder. And even better, someone's taking me for tea.'

Acknowledgements

I started writing the story of Dora Wildwood to cheer myself up with no idea of it ever being published. It was merely the story I told myself in the autumn evenings, on trains, sitting in bed on Sunday mornings with a cup of coffee. It was whatever the writing equivalent of a comfort blanket is. Slowly, joyfully, the character and her story emerged, and I had the time of my life doing it. I have always wanted to write detective fiction and, since I was a child, I have voraciously read every classic crime novel there is. However like most writers I am cripplingly insecure, and it was not until the wonderful Carolyn Mays, then at Hodder, suggested I might consider writing the next in the series of Lord Peter Wimsey detective novels that I ever thought of myself as a person who writes crime. The plan came to nothing, but my first thanks is therefore to Carolyn for thinking 30s detection was something I could do, and for giving me some belief in myself.

My second and very large thanks is to Jo Dickinson, then and now at Hodder, for taking Dora on and embracing her, and for the brilliant, determined, kind way she has lead me through this process. It has been a total privilege to finally work with her and I know how fortunate I am. Thank you for everything Jo.

Huge thanks to everyone at Hodder and Stoughton, in particular Alice Morley, Alara Delfosse, Sarah Clay, Kate Norman, Claudette Morris, Lewis Csizmazia and of course to Oli Malcolm, Katie Espiner, Rebecca Folland and everyone at Hachette, with a special thank you to David Shelley.

And thank you to the people I am lucky to work with at Curtis Brown – Grace Robinson, Emma Walker, Emma Jamison, Samuel Loader, Hannah Young, Matthew Gray and of course Ligeia

Acknowledgements

Marsh, my West Country soul sister. But most of all, thanks to Stephanie Thwaites, my agent, who gave me a compass both literally and figuratively. You are a good deed in a dark world and I'm more grateful to you than you can possibly know. (And you give agents a good name, so watch out.)

Thanks finally to everyone who cheered me on over the past couple of years in ways big and small: all the SWANs but especially Ronnie Henry, and Cally Taylor and Sue Mongredien for lunch, the Loki lady novelists Carey, Casey and Manning, Tasmina Perry, Shona Beats, Katie Dougan Hyde, Penny Clayton and Gemma Knight, with special thanks to James Coleman.

I have loved libraries all my life. *D is for Death* is a love letter to careful cataloguing and the great work of librarians up and down the country. I would like to say an especial thanks to everyone at The London Library, my favourite place in the whole world, my office and home away from home.

I wrote Dora to explain feeling like a giraffe a lot of my life, like someone who is too loud and tall and doesn't quite fit in. As I grow older I realise a lot of women feel like giraffes, but they're told they ought to be nice shiny ponies. Dora's definitely a giraffe. Here's to giraffes!